GARDEN OF WRATH

GARDEN

OF

WRATH

Shane Wesley Shelton

Believing Magic Books

This is a work of fiction. Names, characters, places, and incidents are either products of the author's imagination or, if real, are used fictitiously.

Copyright © 2014 by Shane W. Shelton

First U.S. edition 2014

ISBN 978-1-941570-23-4

Printed by Amazon CreateSpace

Artwork for all covers in the Believing Magic series purchased on Shutterstock.com

Grammatical and line editing for all books in the Believing Magic Series by:
Karen Robinson – Freelance copy editor and proofreader
Bachelors, English & Masters, English | Texas A&M University, Doctorate, English | Perdue University, Faculty Fellow | Ivy Tech Community College teaching English and Composition

Second Editing and Final Read Through Proofing for all books in the BM series:
Sherri McDougald – English major at University of North Florida
Artist: acrylics, ink, pencil/charcoal, and glass etching
Contact for any work requests at: sherrir30@yahoo.com

Interior book design and ebook conversion by:
Jimmy Sevilleno – professional interior book designer and ebook conversion specialist

Cover artwork tweaked and adjusted and prepped for print by:
Jeesun Hwang – Graphic artist and designer

Believing Magic Books
13 Kingfish Avenue
Ponte Vedra Beach, Florida 32082
visit us at **www.believingmagic.com**

Contents

Meridith & Ambrosia

The Wicket Street Knitting Circle

IT WAS SATURDAY, thirty minutes after 8 a.m. in a patch of privately owned woods just outside London.

Meridith was as poor as a stray dog and lived in a closet-sized flat, while Ambrosia was an heiress and independently wealthy. The two old women carefully navigated the well-worn trail, occasionally reaching out to one another for support on the slight ups and downs, ever mindful of the gnarled and twisted roots at their feet. The chill in the morning air made their stiff joints complain, and the two women returned the favor and complained about their joints.

Over the years Ambrosia had given way to plumpness in her legs and bottom as some women were want to do, while Meridith still had a sticklike frame from top to bottom, with no bottom at all, but for whatever reason Meridith had begun to bend at the back while Ambrosia remained straight and true. Meridith's theory was that it was all a matter of ballast. She affirmed that if she had a keel as weighty as Ambrosia's she'd still be straight and true as a mast. Ambrosia complained about the waddling gait her oversized derriere forced upon her.

They argued about the imbalance of the whole situation each month they came to the Glade, as Ambrosia's ample keel became heavier and Meridith's mast more bent. Balance in nature, in the way things were and the way things were meant to be was important to them. Always had been. Always would be.

The women emerged from the wood and stood at the edge of the Glade, surveying the crowd of over a hundred other women who were already there, voices chattering away. The Wicket Street Knitting Circle was an innocent enough sounding name for this coven of London witches, and the name had served them well for over seventy-three years. Stately silver-haired matrons, young and innocent-eyed girls barely past their naming at twelve years of age, and every age in between gathered in the Glade. The Knitting Circle was a kindly group of Wiccans, wise women, sages, spiritualists, and pagans, not a malevolent brood of dark hags who gathered around cauldrons cooking up mischief, but strangely enough, that was exactly what they were planning. Cooking up mischief and brewing it in a cauldron.

"Fie! What's all this then!?" muttered Meridith crossly, surprised at the size of the gathering already here. By dark it would probably be a crowd unlike any they'd ever seen before.

"Rubbish and toads!" Ambrosia stood stock still and pointed a gloved hand, quivering with indignation. "Is that a portable telly!? Some idiot has brought a telly! In-t-the Glade! Look there!"

"These young girls have no respect at all," muttered Meridith, just as incensed as she watched the crowd of women who'd gathered around the television. "It's all going to hell I tell ya."

"In a hand basket!" agreed Ambrosia primly as they pressed onward.

"If we're gonna have a telly, why'd we even bother trompin' way out here?" Meridith said almost wearily as they reached the edges of the gathering. "If this ain't a sacred place we shoulda just met at the Starbucks. Then we could-a drank some vile American coffee as we talked about this damned American problem!"

"What we'll be doin' tonight wouldn't go over well in a coffee shop, Meridith," said Meridith's youngest daughter as she walked out of the crowd toward the two women. Robin was in her mid-thirties with three children of her own, the youngest of which walked beside her, holding her hand.

"Ganna!" cried Cricket as she ran to her grandmother.

Meridith bent her stooped frame and hugged the child greedily, whispering to her and telling her she missed her dearly and that she loved her. She held her tongue for the pleasure of the child, but Ambrosia did not.

"See here, miss! Nothing's been decided yet! Don't be speaking like we've decided because we haven't. We've got no business getting involved in this, Robin!" Ambrosia said firmly.

"We have to get involved, Am. The Black Witch can't be killed with guns and bombs; only magic can kill her."

"So you plan to use dark magic to kill this poor girl then." Ambrosia gave her a disappointed shake of the head. "I thought we taught you better than that."

Robin refused to let her good mood be blunted. "Aunty Am, don't get all worked up," she urged with a smile. "There will be covens all over the world doing the same thing we're doing here. This is going to be huge! Thousands of covens and pagans and everything else, all casting spells, while at the same time all the church people are praying and praying." Robin was animated and excited, and she wasn't the only one in such a state. The whole glade was bubbling with happy, purposeful energy.

"Even the Pope has called Saturday a day to fast and pray for righteous judgment on the wicked. The Muslims and the Evangelicals are doing the same. Everyone's working together, Aunty Am."

"And if everyone started jumping off cliffs or playing in traffic, you'd do it too then?" Ambrosia puffed up and put her hands on her shelf-like hips, but Robin ignored her and just hugged the irritable old nag.

She didn't hold a grudge against Aunt Ambrosia, just her mother. Ambrosia had helped her get through nursing school. Her firm hand had also kept her from getting into real trouble when she wouldn't listen to her mother anymore. When things were tight, Aunty Am had kept her lights on more than once. She owed her tons.

"You should see the new video they're showing of the Black Witch in Paris. It shows her horns and her tail and a magic portal that they used to get from Amen Hale to Paris! You just have to see it, Am!" She took Ambrosia's arm, walking the other woman toward the television as she talked. Meridith walked with them, talking quietly with Cricket, but she kept an ear to what the two were saying.

"They have interviews with people who saw her yesterday at a wedding. They say that she actually thinks she's a god now! The wedding went bust and the groom walked out on the bride in a horrid blow up, and then the poor bride ended up killing herself, she was so distraught! But of course," Robin rolled her eyes, "the Black Witch just raised her up from the dead."

"Oh my!" Ambrosia crooned, caught up in the story. "Well, no matter how well you plan them, weddings are touchy things."

Robin moved on to the more sinister stuff. "Peggie and Yanna burned a DVD last night that shows an interview someone did for the American news. Someone who left Amen Hale yesterday. They talk about the human sacrifice they did on the lawn the night before, where the Red Witch raised some other girl from the dead by killing some soldiers that they captured. You've got to see this guy talk about what it's like living in there! It's ghastly!" And she sounded delighted that it was as she towed her aunt along.

"This witch hasn't harmed anyone who hasn't first spit in her face," Ambrosia said, shaking her head as she let herself be hauled toward the set. "I watch the news and I go online too, Robin. She warned everyone, fair and square, right up front, to leave her be. And then they went and blew her up! I'd say the girl has good reason to kill them. And are we not all gods and goddesses in our own way?"

"Oh please!" Robin scoffed. "She's a demon, Am. She's got horns on her bloomin' head! And a tail! We have to fight fire with fire. Magic with magic. We need to kill her. She's evil. Her whole coven is evil!"

"And you know all this yourself do you, girl?" Her mother spoke quietly beside her, unable to stop herself from speaking her mind. "You haven't seen her heart, Robin. You're just followin' the crowd and that's never good. If the devil were to come, I doubt he'd be wearin' horns and a tail so we'd all look at him, point a finger and say, 'There be the Devil.'"

Robin just scowled at her.

"You should see what she looks like on the telly, Ganna," Cricket said, looking up at her grandmother. "She looks scary."

"What is the threefold law, Cricket?" Ambrosia asked the young girl crisply.

"What magic and energy we send out comes back threefold." Cricket answered right away, then added more, "Which is why we're not supposed to do dark spells on other people because the darkness will come back three times worse than what we sent out into the world."

"True, sweetling," Ambrosia said. "And what do you think about casting a black curse at the Black Witch and her coven?"

"But she's evil, Aunty Am. We should fight against evil." The little girl answered with some of her mother's condescending, overly patient tone. Robin, watching the exchange, gave her daughter a smile of approval.

Meridith nodded with her own smile of approval for Cricket and risked speaking to the girl in front of her mother. "Aye, child, you're right, we should be fighting evil. But we should fight it with good, not more evil. If all of us witches were to beg the goddess and god for their favor and blessing upon this poor girl and her coven, and all the churches praying were to ask their gods to help this girl be good, don't you think that would work better than calling up more evil? Better than reaching for Black Magic? Better than becoming murderers ourselves?"

"Yeah, right!" barked Robin viciously. "You didn't have any problem reaching for your belt when I got out of line, Mom! Why didn't you just 'wish me well!' and try to be encouraging instead of beating me bloody!?"

"That's not fair, Robin!" Ambrosia snapped, giving her a hard glare, and then turned to the child to give her a dose of medicine before her mother took her away. "You've had your naming, Cricket. You're a witch, be ye twelve or a hundred and twelve, and you'll answer for yourself for what you do tonight, not your mother. You think on that if you intend to spit in Mab's Cauldron and add your curse to the rest."

Robin grabbed her daughter's hand. "That's enough from both of you! Stop trying to scare her." She stalked off, back into the gathering, pulling Cricket along.

"You're a witch now, Cricket!" called Meridith. "Trust your own feelings on what to do, child!"

After waiting an appropriate moment to get some distance, Ambrosia asked Meridith a question.

"So, what do you think?"

"I think you got a fat ass and I got a hunched back."

"About the curse you old hag!" Ambrosia snapped, upset herself at Robin's behavior, Cricket's safety, and by what was happening in the Glade. And she didn't like to be reminded that she had a fat ass! She knew it was there! "Meridith, you've not given me a straight answer yet! I know you've an idea on it. Now I'll have it."

Meridith sighed wearily, feeling her age and the ache in her heart as she told Ambrosia her say.

"This girl's been through what life does to a body, ups and downs and all that, and she's taken her lumps along the way for sure, but she's not laid a hand to any in this glade. It won't matter a wit to most of these fools though. And it won't matter to the churchmen and women praying for her death today."

"If she's innocent, do you think the curse and the prayers will hurt her?" Ambrosia asked.

"Of course they will. But it won't end tonight even if I wish it would." Meridith sounded disappointed in herself as she added, "And I hate to say it, but I do wish it."

"Why would ya wish for such a thing, girl?" Ambrosia asked, truly surprised.

"What happens after this is done, Am?" Meridith asked. "Once the blood spills and dries on the ground, what then? What do you think will grow from the ground we soak with red? What do you think will happen when the Black Witch sees someone she loves die? Someone she can't bring back from the dead no matter what magic she tries. What will happen when the dark spells stir the bowels of hell like eggs whipped in a blender? I'm afraid, Am. I'm afraid of what will spill out of this girl after the whole world spits in her face. If she dies, hopefully she'll take it with her."

"Well, what do you mean to do?" Ambrosia asked breathlessly, surprised at the dark, determined look on Meridith's face. "You don't mean to curse her along with the rest, do you? Not after what you said to the child. What was all that talk of blessing and fighting evil with good then?"

Meridith wiped at a tear that rolled down her wrinkled cheek. "I'm just a broke back, old woman who wants to hold her last grandchild some before she's too grown up to hold. That's what I want to do. But we don't always get what we want now, do we?" Her voice was bitter and angry. She pined for Cricket horribly. Meridith took the handkerchief that Ambrosia offered her and blew.

"I haven't decided myself on what I'll do, and that's the truth." Meridith finished her say, then blew her nose again.

Ambrosia took Meridith by the arm. "Well, come on then, you old crow."

"Where to?" Meridith asked, raising her bushy brows and righting herself as much as she could, trying to regain some of her lost dignity.

"To have a look at that damned telly!" Ambrosia declared as she waddled through the crowd. "If I'm to spit in Mab's Cauldron I'd like to see who I'm spitting at."

Brent Meecham Treadway

A New Day

Brent broke from the dark canopy of massive oaks, crunching sleeping lilies under foot as he dashed across the flower-filled expanse of open space that stretched from the tree line to the wall. He turned and squatted in the shadow of the wall, resting on the balls of his feet as he scanned the night for any signs of pursuit. He hid there in the shadows and waited. He'd evaded notice from those within Amen Hale, but those without saw absolutely everything, and he was counting on that. He was sure that all he needed to do now was wait.

Temptation had fallen right at Brent's feet twenty minutes ago, and he'd acted on it. "A" had inevitably led to "B," just as one potato chip led to an empty bag or one murder to a shooting spree. A single moment of panicked weakness brought the other actions. He had left the royal bedchamber with Princess Emma's jeweled belt tucked into his black, leather jacket. No one had noticed.

In the wake of what had happened to Princess Rain, the place was upside down with panic, weeping, and confusion. He remembered what he'd done, but it all had a dreamlike quality about it. Even now, Brent felt as if he were standing outside of his own body watching as someone else did these things. The blaring voice in his head that had screamed "NO! You don't want to do this! Put it back!" was silent now.

He hid in the shadow of the wall hunkered down among the knee-high lilies. He kept reaching out to the nearby stalks, plucking and forcing open the tightly closed pods that were slick with pre-dawn dew. The knifelike ache of betrayal in his heart had dulled to a bearable sting, and his churning guts had calmed. The muscles in his arms and legs seemed to be regaining their strength as well. Less rubbery and uncoordinated. Brent squatted there with his strangely silent mind and his numb, unfeeling heart, as his nervous hands sought out sleeping lilies to kill.

It was the 6th of August, early Saturday morning, 4:33 A.M.. Four days had given the government time to take root and grow comfortable with the order of things. Twelve thirty-foot tall towers had grown like massive metal trees, each erected a safe distance from the wall and evenly spaced around the property. Cameras mounted atop these towers added to the images captured by aerial drones, both of which completed the overhead view of the satellites in orbit.

All video feed and intel now flowed through secure channels to teams of analysts who examined absolutely everything. They knew the laundry ladies and gardeners by name. Each man, woman, and child within the compound had a detailed file updated every time they stepped foot outside or were spotted though the windows so their movements could be charted and tracked.

Analysts had watched the unusual panic and activity over the past few hours. There was much conjecture and guesswork about what was going on, but the guessing was about to end. They were about to get some answers and perhaps a great deal more. The night shift of coffee spiked, overworked men and women crowded the video screens and watched as a rope ladder was thrown down to Brent Meecham Treadway, age twenty-four, born and raised in Savannah, Georgia. Former employment: cellular sales at a mall kiosk. Entrance date to Amen Hale: early Thursday morning. Designated "Place of Service" within the Kingdom: Security.

However, it appeared that Brent's only concern at the moment was his own security. They watched as he grabbed the ladder, looked left and right, and paused. Surveillance room D-20 was usually a quiet, tense room filled with whispered words, intense pressure, and a rigid atmosphere. At that moment, however, it sounded more like game night at a sports bar as over-caffeinated, wired up analysts sang out loudly or hissed through clenched teeth.

"Get up that rope, you *son of a bitch*!"

"Go! Go! Go! Go!"

"Come on!"

"Do it! Doooo IT!"

"Get the hell out of there!"

"Climb you little shit! Climb!"

"NOOO!"

They wailed as he broke and ran. Coffee spilled and curses flew as they watched a treasure trove of answers plunge back into the woods. The commandos atop the wall didn't jump down to pursue, although they wanted to. The orders were crystal clear and came directly from the President. No U.S. soldier was to set foot inside Amen Hale under any circumstance without his *verified* consent.

The cameras followed Brent's movements back through the woods, and they watched as he walked back toward the Manor House, no longer skulking or hiding in shadows but walking in the light, up the path, through the doors. As it turned out, it was a momentary setback. Twenty minutes later a group of thirteen snuck out to a different part of the wall and were assisted over the side and out of Amen Hale. They had the answers that they wanted, but they did not have Brent Meecham Treadway.

Alfred Freeman

A Morning Run

ALFRED OPENED HIS door to find Sandabal standing there smiling at him. He was one of the talkative guards, which was good, even if all he talked about was his wife and sports. Neither subject interested Albert, but from time to time something useful slipped out as he jabbered away. Yesterday Alfred had asked to go for a pre-dawn run and Sandabal was here to escort him out to the practice yard where he was sure a few unhappy soldiers in sweats were waiting to join him on his run. Alfred quickly picked up on Sandabal's odd behavior. He was acting strange. Edgy.

Alfred wasn't too surprised. All the politely crafted lies ran dry yesterday when he and the other teens from the drug study finally realized that they were basically in a prison. A comfortable and accommodating prison, but one that gave them no privacy at all, no access to their parents or the outside world at all, and they were constantly at the mercy of doctors who poked and prodded and pestered. One way or another, it was still a prison, and Alfred hated it.

He stuck his head out into the hall and looked left and right, taking in the presence of the two soldiers who held guns at the ready. Both soldiers were "on," despite the early hour. Their eyes were alert. They stood tensed, ready for action. The guns weren't pointed at him—yet—but the safeties were off. And "big" didn't begin to describe these men; they were huge. Fighting men. Two walls of muscled flesh.

Alfred looked back to Sandabal. "So that's how it is now." It wasn't really a question.

"Sorry, Alfred. They were worried how you'd react after yesterday," Sandabal said, acting weirder by the second. "Things will go back to normal once they see you're not going to go crazy and go for a gun and start shooting everyone."

"Normal." Alfred gave him a look that said the rest.

"So, you gonna go run some or are you gonna try some shit?" Sandabal said rudely, almost taunting.

Alfred sighed. He turned and walked back into his room, leaving the door open without giving Sandabal an answer. He dropped onto his bed and stretched out.

Sandabal watched from the doorway. He hadn't shut the door and gone away. Alfred knew he was waiting for something and he had a pretty good idea what that was, but he had no intention of giving it to him.

"I want to see a lawyer," Alfred said as he stared up at the ceiling. "Unless I don't have the right to a lawyer. Even the Gitmo detainees get a lawyer."

"I'll get you a lawyer right now," Sandabal said. Alfred turned his head to face the man and watched as he reached up and turned his cap around on his head. "All right, son, now tell me what the problem is," he said in a mocking tone.

Alfred laughed. It was a good laugh, like he really thought it was funny.

Sandabal fumed.

"Are they gonna to give you a pay cut if you can't bait me into going for your gun?" Alfred asked. "I want a lawyer, sir. I want to talk to my parents. I'm a U.S. citizen and I have rights."

"You really are just a gutless pussy, aren't you." Sandabal spat as he took a few steps into the room, not giving up. A last press to get the reaction he wanted and a jab to soothe his own embarrassment.

"Stand down," came a voice over the intercom system. Followed a second later by, "Get out, Sandabal."

Sandabal froze. Cursed under his breath, turned, and started toward the door. He heard the bed squeak and had time to spin half way around before Alfred's kick connected right in his hip. He took flight, crashing into the wall out in the hall. Sirens started going off as Alfred followed, stepping out into the hall, smiling and at ease.

Sandabal was writhing on the ground, sucking wind and grasping his hip. Alfred looked left and right, relaxed and unbothered by the two huge soldiers that had their empty guns trained on him. Beyond them, at both ends of the hall soldiers were spilling out and stacking up, going to knees and taking up positions. He noticed that those distant men were armed with bean bag shotguns, a weapon they might actually use.

"Either of you two know Sandabal's wife?" Alfred asked the two big men over the blare of the siren.

Both men shook their heads no while still keeping up the charade, holding the empty weapons trained on him and staying about ten feet back. The groups at each end of the hall did not advance but stayed where they were, watching and containing. Alfred's room was in the middle of the hall, sixty-five feet from both groups, which was beyond the effective range for a bean bag shotgun, though if they all went off at once it would make for one hell of a game of dodge ball.

Alfred wasn't worried about them. He casually pointed a finger down at the man on the ground who had both hands holding his hip. "You've got a broken pelvis, Sandabal. Looks like a bad break too." Alfred shook his head in mock sympathy. "That kind of break will take a couple of months to heal. Your lady might get lonely. A woman as hot and bothered as yours." Alfred gave Sandabal a wicked grin. "You told me all about her. I'm sure you've told everyone. She's a wildcat, right? She wants it every night—and every morning."

"You did this on purpose!" Sandabal spat, gritting his teeth in pain.

Alfred laughed, "Of course I did. You may be my lawyer," he reached down and picked up Sandabal's hat from the floor where it had fallen and stuck it on his head backwards, "But I'm your wife's psychiatrist, and she's been complaining about your little dick for months. After six or seven weeks without she'll be calling Pizza Hut just to—"

"You fuckin' shit!" Sandabal went for the hidden gun on his leg. The gun that actually had bullets. The gun he wasn't supposed to be carrying.

Alfred played his part, looking scared as he raised his hands and backed up toward one of the huge soldiers while Sandabal fumbled at his pants, trying to get at the weapon. Alfred ducked behind the huge soldier just as Sandabal cleared it from the holster. A shot was fired. The man he hid behind jerked and cursed. Alfred held the man as a human shield and waited for another round, but it looked as if Sandabal was either smart enough to wait or finally coming to his senses.

There was lots of shouting, none of which could be heard over the noise of the blaring siren. The big soldier he was holding upright was gut shot, which meant he hadn't been vested up. Both of these big men had come with no body armor and empty weapons, thinking it was going to be hand to hand combat.

Alfred backed down the hall, holding the wounded man in front of him until he reached another door and opened it. Sandabal started squeezing off more rounds now that he saw that Alfred was making his way to safety, but the poor guy Alfred held caught the bullets as Alfred leaped into the room and slammed the door shut behind him, leaving the now very dead soldier to drop in the hall unseen and unheard, like a tree falling in the woods.

Shikith was poised in a catlike crouch as if she intended to dodge bullets. Alfred was a bloody mess.

"What'd you do, Alfred?" she yelled over the blaring siren. The horrible noise finally ended. Alfred shook his head and put his hands up in a helpless gesture.

"Shikith, I did not start this! All I wanted to do was go for a morning run. When they came to get me they gave me shit, so I went and laid back down in my bed, but the guard came into my room and got nasty. He even called me a pussy, trying to get me to fight." He looked at the camera in the corner of the room. "Tell her.," he ordered. When there was no response, Alfred picked up an empty soda can and threw it at the camera.

Of course, he hit it.

"Tell the girl what happened!" he ordered. "And tell the truth."

The intercom came to life. "One of our guards got out of hand and started insulting Alfred. Alfred kicked him out of his room. A very hard kick," the voice added, sounding annoyed, "and then he insulted the guard until he went nuts and started shooting. It wasn't entirely Alfred's fault, Shikith. Will that do, Alfred?"

Alfred shook his head no. "Tell her the whole truth. You gave the guard orders to come into my room and pick a fight and I didn't rise to the bait. You wanted me to go for his gun. Tell her the TRUTH!" Alfred yelled, angry. "You tried to set me up!"

Alfred heard the doorknob turn and moved in a flash to the back side of the door. Shikith dropped to the ground. Alfred watched as the barrel of a bean-bag shotgun poked through the cracked open door. He waited until just the right moment before snatching the weapon away while at the same time the "voice" on the intercom was warning the men in the hall that he was lurking behind the door.

Too late.

Alfred shouldered the door shut as soon as he had the gun, dropped to the floor, pressed the bulbous bean-bag loaded barrel to the flat of the door at floor level and fired.

BANG!

He was rewarded with an eight by ten inch hole which opened up at the bottom of the door and a clear view of about eight men, all wallowing on the ground, grabbing at their feet and legs. He'd "spilled" the beans. The impact with the wooden door had ripped the bean bag open, creating a nice spread of non-lethal plastic bead buckshot, along with a more deadly spray of wooden door splinters. It was like bowling, the pins were down. He frowned though; two guys were still limping around so it wasn't a strike.

Shikith had been busy. She had a dresser that she was shouldering his way. Alfred ran to her and took over, pushing the dresser in front of the door, blocking the door and shutting off the view from the hole at the bottom.

Alfred looked up at the camera again. "Are you done?"

He threw another soda can, dinging the camera from halfway across the room. "Are you done?" he asked again, already searching for another projectile.

"Yes, Alfred. We're done," came the flat monotone voice.

"Good!" Alfred shouted. Angry but still composed.

"Are we both good now, Alfred?"

"Tell everyone to stay in the hallway. Have a doctor come to stitch me up. I took one in the leg."

"You're shot?" A little emotion from the voice. Alfred couldn't tell if it was concern or satisfaction.

"Grazed," Alfred corrected. "Just a few stitches."

"The doctor is out in the hall right now, tending to the wounded. Do you want to go out to him or have him come in to you?"

Alfred looked at himself. He had blood from the guy Sandabal shot up all over him. He felt the sudden need for a shower and maybe a toilet to throw up in. He'd never actually seen someone shot before, let alone killed.

"Going out in the hall would be stupid. As your test proved, you're the one who's stupid. And I'm fresh out of restraint. I'm gonna go take a shower and get cleaned up. That'll give your stupid guards a chance to get their act together. Leading into this room with a weapon after someone just tried to fill me with lead was beyond stupid! What did he expect me to do, put my hands up and trust him not to shoot me? I'm a bit low on trust right now."

Alfred waited. When there was no reply he threw one of Shikith's shoes at the camera which hit hard enough to knock it off kilter.

"Sorry, Alfred. Yes, it was foolish. I heard you," the voice replied mechanically. "We will not enter the room. The doctor will be waiting for you in the hall."

Alfred picked up the now empty shotgun, strode into the bathroom, and got busy busting cameras, tearing the room apart in his search. Shikith stepped in behind him and made herself as small as she could in the corner, watching him go crazy with the butt of the weapon. He smashed the mirror and then crushed the camera that she always thought was behind it but never knew for sure. Marcia had lied about that too. She'd told them that there were no cameras in the bathrooms.

Alfred went into the shower and busted out a tile with the butt of the gun (like he already knew where to look) and pulled out another camera. He went around the small room, knocking holes in walls and bashing anything that might possibly contain a camera until the place was a wreck. He scanned the outside room again, pulled the door shut, then rushed to the toilet and threw up.

Shikith searched through all the stuff under the sink and all over the floor and found some gauze and band aids then sat down on the debris-strewn tile floor awkwardly. The cast on her arm made everything awkward. The weight of it made her clumsy for the first time in her life. She rested her back against the tub as she waited for Alfred to finish. The toilet flushed and Alfred stepped over her legs and went to the sink, turned on the water, and rinsed his mouth.

"Are you okay, Alfred?" she asked.

"I guess."

"What happened?"

"I was going to go on a morning run, like I said. When they came to walk me to the yard, the guard had two soldiers with him. They hoped I'd be pissed and go for their guns. When I didn't, the guard called me a pussy, trying to piss me off. I still didn't go for a gun, but I kicked him in the butt and knocked him out of my room. Then he went for his gun and tried to shoot me. I hid behind some other guy and jumped into your room."

Alfred felt down to his leg and grimaced. He started to pull the sweats up from the ankle but they weren't that loose and the graze was higher up, above the knee.

Shikith had already gotten herself up off the floor. She sat on the edge of the tub and waved Alfred over, her hand holding the gauze.

"Just take'em off, Alfred, and come here."

Alfred hesitated uncertainly. Shikith was a nice girl. Tall, athletic, and well muscled. She'd been sleeping when all the shooting had started. Her shoulder length hair was wild and rigid, sticking out this way and that. She was pretty. He'd been nice to her, and polite, but hadn't let things go too far. He'd been keeping his distance on purpose because he thought he might make a break for it some time soon and he didn't want to feel responsible for someone else. She would slow him down.

The sweat pants came off and he walked over to her. The tail of his t-shirt covered most of Alfred's groin and white underwear as Shikith splashed some rubbing alcohol onto a wash rag to dab at the three-inch red gash. Alfred couldn't help but notice that she kept glancing to his groin, and though he tried to keep his mind at ease and on other things, certain physiological reactions started to happen. His body reacted to her touch. The attention of her eyes. Her obvious desire, mixed with all the adrenaline coursing through his veins, was a chemical cocktail that challenged his iron will and constant vigilance. Blood moved to other places. Soon his underwear was quite lopsided.

"Sorry," he said.

"If you're gonna get in the shower, Alfred, I should wait on the gauze or it'll just get wet," she said, ignoring his apology.

Alfred nodded. Watching where her hands went. How she moved. But some incessant voice in the back of his head warned him not to get distracted. He needed to stay alert. Someone might come.

She reached into the tub and pulled out some of the bigger shards of tile from where he'd bashed at the walls with the butt of the shotgun. She tossed out the shower head that he'd knocked off, searching for cameras, then she stood and turned on the water. It shot out of the nub of a pipe with enough pressure to still be a decent shower.

Alfred stood there, as still as a statue and watched as she pulled a plastic sleeve over her arm with a cast then unbuttoned her shirt awkwardly with one hand. She put another plastic cap on her head to protect her hair then pulled her shorts and underwear off and stepped into the shower.

Once she was standing in the tub/shower, Alfred reached down and grabbed his sweats off the floor and pulled them back on. He grabbed the alcohol and a couple of other useful items and wrapped them up in a towel before opening the door without a word to Shikith who stood naked in the shower, watching him as the water rained down on her. Alfred was sure he heard her crying as he shut the bathroom door.

Cornelius and Believer

Judging Brent

GUARDS ROUSED THE King, although they knew he'd probably only slept for an hour at most. Things needed attention, but no one dared trouble the Queen or any of the Princesses for any reason, which left the menfolk to handle the ugly business of running a kingdom and dealing with problems.

Dressed and ready for his day, Cornelius, accompanied by Believer, exited the royal bedchamber to find one of their own security men kneeling on the carpet in the middle of the living room. Other grim-faced guards stood around him as if he were a prisoner. A black duffle bag lay at Brent's feet. Cornelius and Believer both recognized the young man. He looked calm as he knelt there, head up as he watched them walk toward him.

"Bring a chair, and blessed be, is that coffee I smell?"

One of the guards brought a chair for the King of Amen Hale, who sat and made himself comfortable and thanked the servant who'd been thoughtful enough to prepare a cup of fresh coffee, exactly how he liked it.

"Tell me the story, Brent. And start at the beginning," Cornelius began, his voice calm and fatherly.

"Yes, my King," Brent began.

"Am I still your king, Brent?" Cornelius asked.

Brent didn't blink or cry, and his voice was steady and sure as he answered, "Yes. Even if you cast me out, you will still be my King. Even if you give me to Princess Bethany as a sacrifice, you will be my King."

"What did you do?" Cornelius asked.

"When Princess Rain died and all the panic started, and Princess Mary got ahold of the scissors, Queen Cathryn commanded us to remove anything the princesses might use to hurt themselves within their grief. She was worried about Princess Emma's belt."

He reached down to the bag and pulled out the jeweled ruby belt, each red ruby the size of a domino. He laid the belt on the floor and continued his confession. "Once I had the belt in my jacket there was so much confusion and so many people coming and going, it was easy to slip away. I went to the garage and took the supply of petty cash the men on outside missions use." He extracted two bundles of cash from the bag and laid them on the floor beside the ruby belt. "I went to the wall and waited. After three or four minutes, the soldiers threw down a rope ladder for me to climb."

"What did they do when you changed your mind?" Cornelius asked, then took a sip of his coffee.

"I ran away. The soldiers didn't follow or enter Amen Hale, though they called to me from the wall."

"Do you even know why you did what you did?" Cornelius asked. "Obviously, you didn't truly want to do what you did or you would have crawled up that ladder. What made you do it?"

Brent bowed his head and answered as he stared at the belt and money. "I've thought on it, my King. The Queen was screaming, everyone was yelling and crying, the Black Lion was gone, and the Princesses were all going mad." He paused, remembering the moment. "Everything was falling apart. And I had the belt in my hand." He glared down at the ruby belt. "It glittered as it caught the light," he said softly. "And then it was in my jacket. And then I was walking away from all the yelling and shouting."

Cornelius had heard enough. "Enough. I forgive you, but now comes the unpleasant part, I'm afraid." He handed his coffee cup to a waiting servant then stood and stared down at the young man as he pronounced his judgment. "First, go to the Cathedral Hall and write what you have done in the Book of Shadows. Tell your account of all of it, as you saw it and felt it. After that, go to Lucius and tell him what you have done and tell him that I have forgiven you. Let him assign you to whatever he feels he can trust you with, but if he can no longer use you then report to Byron. If Byron feels there is no place of service he can trust you with, return to me, and more drastic measures will be taken."

"My King?" Brent asked.

"Yes?"

"Before I go, may I see her?" he asked, eyes pleading as he looked toward the bedroom where she now slept.

Cornelius walked Brent to the bedroom door that opened before them as they approached. Dan held the door and watched as Brent Meecham Treadway stepped near and looked inside. He watched for a moment and then backed out of the room with a smile on his face. After Brent departed, one of the other security officers gave their King a brief status report. A Korean man named Kipum Park.

"Your Majesty, we've had many people leave Amen Hale this night."

"Any other guards?" Cornelius asked.

"Two, my King. Oconell and Pendegrass with his entire family. We don't have an exact count, but we believe that thirty or more fled while they thought Princess Rain was dead. We think some few others may still be hiding in the woods or preparing to flee."

Cornelius sighed. "Let them go, but make sure they do not coerce anyone to leave against their will, that includes wives or children of an age to know their own mind. And keep an eye on the valuables that aren't tied down and the antique silverware in the kitchen."

The guard grimaced. "Sorry. Chef Andre's reported it pilfered, Sir."

Believer's red eyes gleamed bright as he started to laugh, his deep rumble making the other men turn to look at him. "They will flee Amen Hale with a bag of sand," he said. "In their greed they have forgotten the curse upon metal that surrounds the wall."

The rest of the room shared in the moment of mirth before starting the labors of a new day in Amen Hale and seeing what else had grown legs and walked off in the night.

Cornelius and Believer

Meeting Cassadan

CASSADAN STOOD ON a coffee table within the circle of two delicate arms belonging to a young girl of ten or eleven years. The smiling child held a fan of cards for him to study. There were five other players kneeling around the table, all younger boys and girls, teenagers and pre-teens, playing cards with the tiny being. Five black clad security men stood around the table but there were so many others gathered around it was hard to spot them in the press of spectators. Forty or fifty people had gathered around the table watching the card game and watching their incredibly small celebrity visitor.

One of the servants noticed Cornelius and Believer striding purposefully into the Entry Hall and called out, "The King comes! The King comes!"

At the cry everyone turned around and went to their knees, some looking toward their King but most staring down at the ground uncertainly, not sure if they should look or not. Things were that way in Amen Hale. Very few people knew how to react, so most everyone overreacted. The teenagers jumped like frightened mice, quickly laying their cards face down or casting them aside completely in their haste to kneel and make some room as Cornelius and Believer stepped up to the table.

Cassadan, at an inch and three quarters tall, bowed at the waist and held the bow. He was dressed in fetching, sky blue pants and an excellently tailored black top with white, lace ruffles at the cuffs. His exquisite, white boots were almost knee high and shoulder-length, silver hair framed a youthful face that held a happy, casual smile. He looked to be little more than a teenager himself if you were to judge by his face alone, but his actual age was impossible to guess.

One of the senior guards named Reese did the introduction. "My King, I present Cassadan, Attendant of Queen Taunwee, The Twilight Star."

Cornelius gave Cassadan a respectful nod of greeting. "Welcome, Cassadan. If you are ready, I believe it is time we spoke."

"As you will, King Cornelius." A surprisingly "big" and normal sounding voice came from the miniscule man in his fine and fashioned attire.

"Reese, escort our guest to the Green Room. I will be in directly."

Cornelius watched as a pair of insect-like wings unfolded from Cassadan's back. He fluttered up and gracefully landed on Reese's shoulder as if he were already used to that perch. Once the two were away, Cornelius turned his attention to the kneeling folk about the table. He eyed the teens with a stern look. "Have you children just risen from bed or have you stayed up all night?"

The teens cringed, and some nodded their guilty, silent confession. As Cornelius surveyed the rest of the crowd he noticed more than one set of bleary, red rimmed eyes among the adults which he could tell was caused by crying; the lack of sleep just added to what was already there. His stern expression softened.

"Please, my Lord, how is she? And how is our Queen?" asked one woman who couldn't hold her concern a moment longer. At her words the others looked up, anxious to hear.

"Be at peace," Cornelius soothed. "Believer and I just left them and both are well. Rain sleeps with her head lying in her mother's lap with her sisters all around her in bed. Now rise and be at ease."

The group did as they were bid, gladdened by the good report and talking quietly among themselves, but one young girl remained kneeling while the others began to go about their business. She caught Cornelius's eye. Her eyes were squeezed shut and she smiled as she prayed. It was a sight that Cornelius himself was still getting used to seeing, but one he was sure he'd see much more of in the days to come.

Cornelius and Believer entered the Green Room and went to the two chairs in front of the large oak desk where Cassadan sat, legs crossed comfortably, unbothered by the supple and flexible, white boots he wore. The small man seemed totally at ease in the largeness of his surroundings.

"Do you like to play cards, Cassadan?" Cornelius asked once they were seated.

"No. But the children were crying, and the game helped both the children and their parents calmly pass the time," he answered simply and sincerely, his speech clean of titles or platitudes.

Cornelius nodded, raising his eyebrows at the empathy Cassadan's words implied and still somewhat surprised at hearing a normal-sized voice coming from so small a package. Believer's mighty scowl he'd worn upon entering flattened out, bent even by the basic goodness of Cassadan's response.

"I wish our peoples could have met under better circumstances," Cornelius said. "I understand that Queen Taunwee has agreed to forgive my daughter's accidental trespass?"

"She has," Cassadan confirmed. "She knows what happened was an accident. My Queen's words were, 'What's done is done.' It was a tragedy, but she bears no ill will toward the young goddess or toward Amen Hale."

Cornelius took note that he referred to Rain as a goddess. "I understand you have a list of items to be provided as reparations." The account side of Cornelius had itched to know more of this particular detail when Dan had mentioned it. Reese handed him a sheet of paper, filled from top to bottom with writing. Cassadan spoke as Cornelius scanned the page.

"Taunwee suggested the gifts as a way for the goddess to feel she was helping those whom she has harmed. It was meant only as a help for your daughter, King Cornelius, and not to be a burden."

Cornelius was reassured as he scanned down the page. The list contained simple things. Salt. Fine cloth in various colors. Tanned leather. Mostly raw materials and nothing sinister at all. It almost seemed too simple. Not enough by far.

"It will be a comfort to Rain," Cornelius agreed. "She likes things that are tangible. Something that she can see." He handed the list of items back to Reese. "Queen Taunwee is as wise as she is forgiving. Cathryn is sure that her warning made the difference in saving our daughter last night." Cornelius's face fell and showed his weariness as he added, "It was a very close thing. It has been a difficult night for all of us."

"King Cornelius, what happened to the goddess?" Cassadan asked. "I was told many things by your people, but there was much confusion. Might I be told what actually occurred so I can give my Queen an accurate account upon my return?"

"Father, may I speak to Cassadan before we share more?" Believer asked.

Cornelius introduced Believer to his guest. "Cassadan, this is my son, Believer, the Prince of Clouds. He is Rain's husband."

The tiny face showed confusion as to the familial association as he stood and bowed to Believer.

"It would be a pleasure to speak with the Prince of Clouds." He walked across the desk, getting closer to Believer, as if he wanted a closer look at something that, comparatively speaking, was the size of a mountain.

"Why did your Queen keep Marie?" Believer's voice was not threatening but it was firm.

Cassadan smiled at the question. "I believe our Queen was fascinated with her. When Marie came to us bearing the offering, she also offered her own life to obtain forgiveness for the goddess. It was a very endearing gesture. Taunwee forgave the trespass and asked only that Marie stay and serve her until your wife comes to claim her this afternoon. Queen Taunwee has forgiven much and asked for very little. Is the blood of our people not worth a day in the service of our Queen?" This last statement was delivered with an almost offended tone. The tiny figure stared up at the giant cloud of a man, confident in his position.

Believer cringed beneath the words and indignant stare.

"Forgive me," he rumbled, ashamed. "A soul is priceless, Cassadan, no matter the size of the body that holds it. When I was first created, I was a cloud bird, only a little taller than you. I rode upon my Sky's shoulder just as you rode upon Reese's shoulder as you entered this room. I meant no offense. Your Queen has been most merciful." His frown slit his face from side to side as he added miserably, "I simply worry for my wife, Cassadan. I love her. I do not want her upset further if I can find a way to avoid it."

"You are an interesting people," Cassadan said as he stared up at Believer, fascinated as he watched the ever rolling clouds crash about inside his form. "Of this one thing you can be certain. We do not wish to upset your wife. She killed thousands on accident, we have no desire to provoke her intentionally. Taunwee is wise, not foolish."

"Of that, there is no doubt," Cornelius agreed.

Rain

Let Sleeping Lions Lie

R AIN LAY IN the bed, asleep and at peace, surrounded by those whom she loved. Those who also loved her.

Her mouth was parted, head tilted to the side, held in place by her horns. The horns emerged from each side of her head just above the hair line, jutting out horizontally for two inches, before turning forward and then straight up for six inches ending in wickedly sharp points. The tips of the horns were blue in color, darkening down the length of the horn to glossy, onyx black at the base, the color merging with that of her hair.

Her skin was a ghostly, pale silver and her lips were pale blue. Her body was long, lean, and muscled like a predator designed to run down prey. She wore two sashes of black fabric across her chest to cover her breasts and a silver chain around her waist from which hung a long black loin cloth. Her long mane of beautiful black hair was piled at the headboard where it had been combed out during the night by Mary and Cathryn. Mary had sung and trailed gentle fingers across her face until her voice gave out, then Cathryn took over doing the same.

Cornelius and Believer had risen early and left to tend to the needs of the Kingdom, which left Dan as the only male in the room. He stood guard by the door and watched over the eight women lying around Rain's body. The twins, Izzy and Lizzy, rested on the far left side of the bed, shifting and twitching in fitful sleep. Bethany was snuggled up to Rain's left leg sleeping soundly, but her tail would occasionally reach over and brush Rain's leg, sometimes coiling possessively around an ankle or foot for a moment before dropping back to bed.

Rain's tail was not so free to be about its own business. Emma was sleeping at the bottom right corner of the big bed with her arms around Alana, but in her hand she held the tip of Rain's tail. Even in her sleep Emma did not fully release her grip, and the tail did not seek to gain its freedom. It wouldn't. It couldn't. It didn't want to be free. Emma held the end of a long, black velvet leash. She had the Black Lion by the tail and she would not let her go. Emma's magic, her love, rolled down her hands, flowing through the tail and into Rain. Rain lay in the wash of that love and slept in it, dreamed sweet dreams in it, was filled by it.

Jane lay spooned up to Rain's right side, one leg curled around her right leg, an arm slung over her hips, her head resting on her flat, muscled stomach like a breathing pillow. Jane herself was awake but totally relaxed, unguarded and open. She was at peace.

Reassured by the rhythmic up and down of Rain's constant breathing.

Reassured by Dan, who was watching.

Her mind wandered free, played, and drifted. *Daydreams.*

Now that Rain was a god much had changed. Along with her fantastic, new body came fantastic, new blood. Jane and Dan loved the new blood. To call Rain's blood glorious was an insult. Even "divine" seemed a slight to them. They loved her new blood, but with the new blood came new problems. Her blood had a greater effect upon them, but their bite also had a much greater effect upon her. Now, when she was bitten, Rain seemed to lose all restraint. And if all restraint was lost, Rain would have whatever she wanted.

Jane and Dan had both been facing an awkward, sexual relationship that seemed completely unavoidable since they had to feed. Jane had been finding "this situation" less than appealing. She loved Rain but not in that way. She'd become bitter and angry about all of it.

And then the world turned upside down. Last night Jane was given exactly what she thought she wanted—Rain's blood—with no strings attached. In a bout of guilt-ridden depression, Rain had, in a very real sense, killed herself. She separated her soul from her body and fled, condemning her soul to a self-imposed exile in a place where she thought she could do no harm. She'd left behind instructions, like a will, concerning what she wanted done with her soulless but still living body, saying, "Let my Beloved feed daily. I will never run dry. I will never die." Her body had become nothing more than a big, eternal, god-flavored juice box.

During the weeping chaos Rain had left in the wake of her departure, Queen Cathryn had become unhinged. In a frightening panic, she had gathered all her children together, refusing to let them leave the room. Most of those Cathryn though of as her children were mentally unstable and prone to sudden acts of self-destruction, just like Rain. Cathryn had sent David and Dana and Ryan and Sky to their own rooms with guards to watch them as they slept, but the rest she had put in her own bed where she could watch them herself during the night. Everyone had been accounted for except Mary, and Cathryn had sent Jane to find her and bring her back before someone else told her the horrible news of Rain's death.

Jane found her in the gardens. Mary had joined in with a group of worshipers who'd gathered around a statue of their new Goddess. They were dancing in circles around the stone likeness, happy, singing, and blissfully unaware. Jane had stood at the edge of the clearing and watched in wretched, guilty silence. Rain had known how uncomfortable she'd been with the situation they'd been in. Jane pondered in her keen vampire mind how much that disquiet had influenced her decision to kill herself. 1%? 3%? 20%? *More?* These thoughts spun through her mind as Mary had sung, danced, and worshiped with these people, unashamed to belong to Rain. Jane listened from the shadows as Mary worshiped, happy to love her, holding nothing back.

It was torture.

Mary had no idea that all that she loved was already gone, and that the girl she and the others worshiped was now nothing but a memory. Rain was dead. Dead and gone. That body in Cathryn's bedroom might be breathing, but it was as empty as the stone statue Mary and the others danced around. For three minutes that felt like three eternities, Jane listened, feeling worse each minute, cursing herself, cursing Rain, and cursing Dan when his voice in her head urged her to calm down, and cursing this new "situation" she found herself in.

She wanted her old "SITUATION" back!

She ground her teeth and fought to hold back bitter, bloody tears for another agonizing minute, and then she moved. She stepped out and joined Mary. Jane added her own voice to Mary's song and poured out all her pent up emotions as she worshiped Rain with Mary. She knew Rain was gone, and only a rock heard her voice, yet she gave herself to it with all her heart. Jane danced and sang and loved

Rain with Mary for what she was sure would be the last time. She prayed silently for another chance and did not care that Dan heard her thoughts.

When Mary stopped dancing and began to call up her magic, Jane wondered what was happening. Mary's magic was so powerful that everyone had to back away from the clearing. Jane worried that Mary was about to hurt herself, but then she spoke, sending out all that power into the night, wrapped in just three words, "I Love You."

As Jane studied Mary, and what she'd just done, she found herself strangely envious. *Jealous?* And then she became mad at herself. Angry that she NOW wanted what she couldn't have. She didn't just want the blood, she wanted the girl! But Rain was gone! It was too late. Jane fell to the ground weeping, covered in her own blood that poured from her eyes. Mary had been the one to pick her up and take *her* to Cathryn.

But Rain did return.

Whatever Mary had done in the garden had reached her. That one touch had been enough to rouse her and bring her back. Now Jane had a second chance and she was glad to have it. So very glad. The thought of getting up and going to Dan passed through her head.

Dan spoke into the quiet of her mind, "No. Lie still for me, Jane. I'm right here, and you're right where I want you to be and right where you want to be. You're so close to sleep, you were almost dreaming. You know how I love watching your dreams. Dream for me."

She did as he asked and emptied herself, riding the rise and fall of Rain's breathing as she let her mind drift to wherever it wanted to go—a ship set free of its moorings, cast adrift upon the night waters of her mind.

In the past six days they'd all changed in unexpected and frightening ways, but none so much as Rain. She lay there, pinned to the bed, arms and legs weighed down by clinging lovers and loving children, her head held by a loving mother. A mother she had not known only days ago. The pills from the drug study had given her the ability to remake herself, but she'd also been changed by those who clung to her like living extensions of her body. They'd pushed at her with their own needs, magic, and desires over the past six days.

Emma's love, Mary's prayers, Bethany's darkness and need for a mother, Cathryn's grace and her longing for a child to love, Jane's love for Dan which had brought Rain to Believer (her husband). Believer's faith had changed her too. Believer saw beautiful things inside her soul. Things worth keeping in the world. Things worth loving. Not just darkness and pain. And if he saw it, it must be so, because Believer did not lie. He couldn't. And so she had changed.

Rain allowed herself to be changed by all of them, letting it happen little by little as she struggled through each confusing day. And now they all lay around her.

Their hopes and dreams wrapped around a girl who believed she began life as an errant dream spawned from a sick girl's mind. A dream that took that sick girl's life and lived it as her own. A dream who believed she was a witch. A witch that told a story about Godly lions and lambs. A story she believed. And because she believed, she had changed again.

The Black Lion, the flesh of fantasy come to life, lay in bed and dreamed sweet, peaceful dreams while the rest of the world wished her ill, praying and cursing her in a thousand different ways, in a hundred different tongues. All the hateful magic in the world could not touch her because love held her by the tail.

She slept.

Ryan and Sky

Good Morning America

SKY DRAGON, LUCIUS, and ten black clad guards escorted Sky and Ryan through the trashed house that looked as if it had been the site of a frat party gone bad, minus the beer cans and cups. Broken glass crunched underfoot. Decorative display cases lining the hall had been smashed to get at antiques and valuables. Clothes and a hundred other items were strewn up and down the halls and throughout the house from weak-willed people who'd become little better than grave robbers during the harrowing night, dropping stuff here and there as they had grabbed other "better" stuff.

Dozens had looted and quickly fled Amen Hale, but many more had chosen to stay. Whether they stayed because they had hope or were simply too grief-stricken to flee didn't matter once she returned. The faithful, the indecisive, the uninformed, and the heartbroken had been equally rewarded, though none of the Children of Amen Hale had felt the least bit like celebrating.

Weary servants were already cleaning in the stairway, their movements slow and dispirited, but faces brightened instantly upon seeing the sharply organized group pass by. Men and women stood straighter, tucked in, and smiled as they curtsied or bowed. Many of those not currently cleaning or working elsewhere in the house had gathered together in the Entry and Cathedral Halls, discussing the events of last night and who was gone.

Conversations stopped as they entered rooms filled with people who watched them as they passed, hope and questions in their eyes. When they paused to survey the damage in the Cathedral Hall some of the children rushed forward and pressed flowers into Sky's hands and a few of the men and women of standing approached Lucius or Sky Dragon with what they felt were important questions. Children with flowers for Sky, questions for Sky Dragon, Lucius and the others—but no one dared approach Ryan. No man, woman, or child came close to him, asked anything of him, or dared to meet his eye for longer than a moment.

Ryan caught the looks out of the corner of his eye or when he turned suddenly and surprised them. Wary, fearful looks for him. Ryan didn't blame them. He felt he more than deserved it. Much had changed since yesterday. Inside Amen Hale and inside himself. When Cornelius ordered ten guards, Lucius, and Sky Dragon to accompany them, Ryan hadn't objected. After yesterday he was more willing to let others help him keep Sky safe and help keep him under watch as well.

They passed through the kitchen then turned down the small hall in the back and stopped before a plain, white door upon which four hands had been traced with a black marker, beneath which Rain had scribbled a rhyme, creating this doorway. Lucius placed a hand on the door and white light flashed around the edges. When the door opened, the storage room that should have been there was missing; the open door now led to Rain's old bedroom at her and Ryan's parents' trailer.

Ryan held Sky's hand as they stepped into his sister's old room with the others. He was ready to be home. He wanted to sit on the couch with his mom and dad and maybe watch a college football game. Maybe he and Sky would go back to his bedroom after breakfast and make love, if the guards would give them the privacy, that is. He wasn't sure that they would.

Last night, when they all had thought Rain was lost forever, Queen Cathryn had nearly gone mad. She'd been convinced that the rest of those she claimed as her children were either about to kill themselves, be murdered, or be stolen away. She tried to keep all of them there with her in her bedroom. When Ryan and some of the others pointed out the danger of keeping him and Sky and David and Dana so close to Emma, she'd relented and let the four of them go, but under guard. He and Sky had slept in their own bed, but with a guard standing at the foot of their bed, instructed to watch over them all night to make sure that neither he nor Sky tried to hurt themselves during the night.

"Stay here until we make sure the house is safe," Lucius ordered. He gave the two frightening men at the front of the guards the nod and they took off, moving like well oiled machines, weapons held at the ready, each step precise as they glided down the hall.

The other guards from Amen Hale watched the flowing, almost dance-like steps with open awe and envy. These two men were professional soldiers who'd been captured when they had attacked Amen Hale Tuesday night. Rain had given them a choice: die and become dinner or serve her. They'd chosen to "be all they could be" in the Black Lion's Army. She'd made them vow to serve her and she'd marked both men in a frightening way—they each had one solid, black eye.

Ryan frowned and watched as these hard men treated his parents' trailer like hostile, enemy territory and said not a word about it. It was hostile territory. Nothing was the same.

Sky gripped his arm tighter but didn't say anything. She'd been shaken by yesterday as well. She'd only said six words all morning, but they were all Ryan needed to hear. "I love you," she had said when she first woke, startled to find the soldier still standing at the foot of their bed, followed a second later by, "I gotta pee."

One of the maids had been summoned to escort Sky into and out of the bathroom. The guards had taken the Queen's orders to watch them to heart. Cathryn had made herself very clear. Frighteningly so.

The older of the two professional soldiers slipped back into the room a few minutes later. He was a big, powerful, thick necked man whose preferred breakfast cereal was most likely a box of rusty nails.

"The living room is packed with people. The parents are giving a TV interview with a network reporter. The reporter is sitting with them on the couch and the cameras are on right now. It looks like live, national morning news. They have security. American military and FBI. If we're going in, we'll have to secure the area first."

Sky Dragon's eye ridges dropped. "We should leave. It's not safe here."

Sky shook her head, choosing suddenly to voice her opinion. "No. We need to stay. Ryan's not doing well. He needs to see his parents."

Everyone looked at Ryan. Wary and weighty stares. Ryan bore their inspection in stoic silence and waited for others to determine what was up and what was down. He didn't trust his own best judgment at that moment to be the right judgment for anyone, even himself.

"Sky Dragon, watch them," Lucius ordered, then he and the rest of the men from Amen Hale all dressed in black and armed with automatic weapons poured out of the bedroom and into the hall. A minute later Ryan's parents were there, in Rain's bedroom, hugging their son, their new daughter-in-law, and Sky Dragon, who made a show of being uncomfortable with the contact.

"Why are you guys doing a TV interview?" Ryan asked once the hugs and greetings were exchanged.

"We felt like we had to," his mother answered.

"They keep saying so many horrible things in the news," his father added. "Your mother and I didn't want the only things being said to be lies, so we agreed to talk to them this morning." He paused and gave Ryan a cautious look. "If you feel up to it, I'm sure they'd love to speak to you and Sky. But don't feel like you have to."

Ryan didn't answer. He looked over at Sky who was thinking hard.

"We should say something to them. But we will need to be careful," she said firmly, her mouth pressed into a tight line. "Very, very careful."

Ryan raised an eyebrow, not understanding. "Careful?" he asked.

"Careful with you, Ryan. We will need to be careful with you." She stared at him, concern mixed with fierce determination on her face. She meant to keep him safe.

Ryan's dad, always quick on the uptake, picked up on the mood. "You sure you're feeling up to this, Ryan?" his dad asked.

Ryan caught the eye of the mutant, thick necked soldier with the one, disturbing, blacked out eye. "You know how to do a sleeper hold, to knock someone out but not kill?" he asked the man.

"Yes, Lord Ryan," the man answered.

Ryan had everyone's attention now.

"Get a couple of the chairs from the kitchen table. Sky and I will sit in those while we do this thing so you can stand behind me."

There was total quiet in the small bedroom.

"On whose call should I make you safe?" the man asked. Understanding what he was being asked to do.

"Lucius, Sky Dragon, or Sky," Ryan said without hesitation.

The thick-necked man left, going to prepare the chairs as Ryan had requested.

"Good Lord, Ryan! What on earth happened?" his mother asked, unable to hold it in any longer.

"I'm dangerous, Mom. And I'd rather be safe than sorry." Ryan gave his mother a reassuring smile as he took Sky's hand. "Now let's go talk to America. Who do you have out there, Bryant Bumble?" he joked lightly. "You like him, or is it Katie Communist?" Ryan poked fun at various media personalities and tried to relieve some of the tension he'd created as they walked down the hall and into the living room that was packed to overflowing with film crews, cameras, and attendants.

The black outfitted men from Amen Hale had supplanted the other soldiers and FBI agents that they'd sent outside the trailer. There was no undisciplined crowding or shouting as Sky and Ryan emerged. The room was subdued and quiet under the pressure of black clad men with automatic weapons trained on them. A huge surprised smile jumped onto Ryan's face as he walked up to the silver-haired man he recognized from Fox News.

"Tony Kane! Now that's cool," he said as he shook the man's hand.

Beside him, Sky smiled as well, her eyes on Ryan's face. She was happy to see him happy. So were his parents.

Cameras were rolling, catching it all on film. Tony smiled and shook and greeted. It wasn't just Fox and Fox News in the crowded trailer. ABC and CBS had already had their morning stint with Mr. and Mrs. Bryant, but the remainders of their crews and talent had been pushed back into the kitchen on the other side of the bar.

Mrs. Bryant narrowed her eyes at the cameramen from those other networks who'd climbed onto the kitchen counters to get a usable angle over the heads of the crowd. Soon people across America and around the world were watching Ryan and Sky on multiple networks. All of it live, uncensored, and totally raw as news-starved networks cut into regularly scheduled shows and broadcasts.

After the usual introductory greetings, which Sky Dragon refused to take part in, Tony began with some fluffy, feel good questions.

"Did you and Sky travel here through a magic gateway?"

"Yes," Ryan answered.

"What's it like to travel by magic, passing through a doorway or archway that your sister has made with her powers?"

"To tell you the truth, it doesn't feel like anything," Ryan said. "You walk through and you're there. No goose bumps. No static charge. No drama. I know that's kinda boring, but it's the truth."

"That's all right, Ryan," Tony assured him with feeling. "We want the unembellished truth, and I think America trusts you to give us that. Did you know we were doing these interviews with your parents this morning?"

"Nope. We just popped in for breakfast. And I wanted to see my folks."

"You haven't had breakfast yet?"

"No." Ryan narrowed his eyes at the kitchen mess himself. "But we'll eat when we go back to Amen Hale."

"Can you tell us about your trip to the Bahamas yesterday?"

"It was nice," was Ryan's plain, empty answer.

"Before we went to the Bahamas we went to the movies," Sky supplied happily, looking away from Ryan's face long enough to give the camera over Tony's shoulder a chance to capture her beautiful Asian American face.

"It was the first movie I've seen since I was little. And the beach was great. We went snorkeling." She looked back to Ryan and her dazzling smile lit up when she saw he was smiling. It made for quite a pretty picture.

Tony asked Sky a direct question, trying to keep her engaged. "Is Ryan getting used to flying with you, Sky?"

Sky answered without looking away from Ryan's face. "Yes," was all she gave.

"Today is your fourth day as a married couple. Are you both adjusting well to married life?"

"Yes. We get adjusted as often as possible," Ryan replied. There was a good wave of genuine laughter that filled the trailer and Sky leaned over and kissed him and touched his face.

"Ryan, why is that soldier standing behind your chair?" Tony asked.

Sky stroked Ryan's arm soothingly, glanced at the soldier looming large behind Ryan, then gave Tony an unfriendly glare before turning back to Ryan's face.

"He is there to keep the world safe, Mr. Kane," Ryan answered.

Tony left that vaguely threatening answer alone and moved to his next question. "What's it like for the average person living inside Amen Hale? What do they do? How are they treated? Are they happy? America would like to know."

Ryan considered the question for a moment before recusing himself. "Honestly, I can't tell you. I'm not a regular person of Amen Hale. I'm Royalty. I am 'Lord Ryan' and my wife is 'Lady Sky.' You'll have to ask one of our men what it's like to live there."

"Can I ask the soldier behind your chair what it's like to live in Amen Hale?"

The camera zoomed back, showing Ryan, Sky, and the imposing soldier who stood behind Ryan's chair, poised like a waiting avalanche. The camera closed in on the man's face and his one solid, black eye. The dark orb moved in tandem with his other piercing, gray eye. The eyes went in a hypnotic, disciplined circle, darting from the back of Ryan's head to points off camera and back again. The man looked lethal and disciplined. Everyone could see that this man was a killing machine, set behind Ryan's chair like an open bear trap, tensed and ready to snap at any second. Two big, powerful hands rested on the back of Ryan's chair, framing his face as he stared calmly into the camera.

Along with the romance, the scene held a spark of danger, present and real, not far off and distant. People watching in homes across American and the world didn't dare blink. They leaned in toward the images on their screens.

"That man is busy," Lucius answered the question before Ryan could voice his reply, his tone making it crystal clear to Mr. Kane that further questions about the soldier behind Ryan would be ill advised.

"Can one of your other men talk to us?" Tony asked.

Lucius was standing off camera to the side of Ryan and Sky. "Mitch! You like to talk. Come here, sit, and speak to America."

One of the men, presumably Mitch, walked over and handed Lucius his weapon then stepped into frame and sat cross-legged on the floor, folding himself neatly at Ryan and Sky's feet. From his sitting position he gave a quick deferential bow of the head to Ryan and Sky then faced Tony Kane and his camera. He was a young man, early twenties, dark eyes, clean shaven with a plain, round face. He was wearing the black leather of the Amen Hale security forces. He seemed altogether plain, ordinary, and unremarkable. When he spoke, people who watched for such things noticed that there was no quaver in his voice, no rocking, twitching, or wandering of his eyes. His comfort level was obvious. His confidence apparent. It was this confidence, along with what he said, that made him seem not so plain and far from ordinary.

"Hello, Mr. Kane. My name is Mitch Greer. My place of service in Amen Hale is Security."

"Does everyone in Amen Hale have a place of service?" Tony asked the man.

"Yes. We all work together. Some of us take care of the food, some clean, some provide security, and some look after the Lords and Ladies of Hale."

"Are you happy, Mitch?"

"Yes. I love living in Amen Hale. It's like no place on earth."

"What's different about it, Mitch? And please, take your time with your answer. America wants to know."

Mitch took a moment to assemble his thoughts then started talking, answering the question as he wanted.

"In Amen Hale we don't think of ourselves as Americans. We call ourselves the Children of Hale and that's what we're like. Like a family. Just a really big one." His smile broadened. "Don't get me wrong when I say family. I can guess what some people are thinking. We're not some backwoods, hillbilly commune with a psychotic, religious leader spouting drivel about the end of days and calling himself "the messiah" or looking for the Hale Bop Comet. And we're not a polygamist compound where one crackpot gets ninety-nine wives and the rest get to deal with it. That's sick. That's not us. It's like a real family in Amen Hale. I've always hated the waste of government. We don't have any of that. We have a real King and a real Queen, who do the best by us they can. It might sound weird to you, and to some people out there in TV land, but I love our King and Queen, and I'm not ashamed of that."

The man gave Tony a smug smile and then gave him the rub, "Can you say as much about your representatives in congress? Or your senator, who probably just got busted for high treason? Or your local sheriff? Or your president?"

"I hear you, Mitch," Tony agreed, his own face disappointed.

At last count twenty-five Senators and thirty-one members of the House had been indicted for their association with the secret organization knows as "The Order." Not since the Civil War had there been this little trust for the American system of government. There were ongoing protests in most cities and even some riots over the corruption and scandals that continued to come to light by the hour, as news leaked out to the media and yet more names and facts were released of current and former public servants and once respected historical icons who'd betrayed their own country.

"I have to say, I don't *love* any of them." Tony declared firmly, "and I respect all of them a hell of a lot less today than I did just a week ago. Could you tell us a little more about your King and Queen?"

"Never." Mitch's eyes narrowed, and a cunning smile stole onto his face. "The questions were for the average man inside Amen Hale. If my Lords wish to speak of themselves then that is for them to do, not me. All I will say is this. I love them. They are good people."

Tony nodded, smiling sheepishly as if he'd been caught trying to steal a cookie. He pressed on with a different question about the common people.

"Can people inside Amen Hale leave if they want to?"

"About fifty people left yesterday. Mrs. Bryant said that the news people, people like you," he gave Tony an accusing glare, "have been telling lies about us. I'm sure they've had some of those people who left us on TV doing it too. I'm not a math genius or a banker, but if you pay someone for an interview they'll make sure you get your money's worth. I'm sure most of what you've heard is crap."

"Like what?" Tony urged.

"Like that last question you just asked!" Mitch's expression darkened. He was angry as he answered. "Can people leave if they want to? You make it sound as if Amen Hale is a prison. You *do* know that we don't go out and grab people off the street and haul them in against their will," he challenged. "Every person in Amen Hale asked or begged to get in, and they were told right up front what it would be like. I don't have any respect for people who leave us after they begged to get in and made vows of service that they don't want to honor. It's like getting married and deciding after the honeymoon that there's things about your wife that you don't like, so you ask for an annulment. It's not right, but it does prove one thing."

"And what's that?"

"That they didn't truly love us in the first place." Mitch seemed to realize that he was getting too personal and stopped himself, putting on a smile as he concluded, "Those who wanted to leave were allowed to go."

"We know that most of those inside Amen Hale are witches or hold to the Wiccan lifestyle. Are you a Wiccan, or an atheist, a Christian, or of some other belief or faith?"

Mitch clammed up instantly. "My faith is my business. Not America's." Without another word he stood and walked off camera.

Tony was a bit surprised by the abrupt departure but recovered quickly, getting back to Ryan.

"Would it be all right if I ask you some religious questions, Ryan?" he ventured.

"Ask away, Tony, but I've got my limits too," Ryan answered.

"Everyone does," Tony agreed with a nod.

"We already know that you're a Christian, Evangelical Baptist by denomination. You've gone to church three times a week since you were born. You play the guitar in your church's youth department and you've been actively involved in evangelistic efforts. You worked for Teen Explosion and summer youth camps. By anyone's definition you're a good, solid, Bible-believing, God-fearing Christian. Has any of what you've seen in the past few days made you doubt your faith?"

Ryan laughed, smiling as he answered, "No way. God is still God. Strange things are happening, but for every strange thing I see that makes me question what I believe I see something else that makes me believe even more strongly. Even if I am a mess I know that all is well in my Father's house."

"Some people are saying that a real Christian wouldn't live in Amen Hale. And that you should have nothing to do with your sister and the others inside of Amen Hale."

"Cool," Ryan said with no emotion.

"Cool?" Tony made the word a question, prompting Ryan to explain in greater detail.

"The religious uppity-ups way back when said the same thing about Jesus when he hung out with tax collectors, sinners, cripples, and lepers. So yeah. Cool."

Tony pushed deeper. "Do you feel strange living there, being surrounded by witches, bloody human sacrifice, and other things that most people would call evil? You're a Christian, wouldn't it be more normal to live in a Christian atmosphere?"

"Answer me this," Ryan challenged, leaning in toward Tony. "If you were me, and Sky were your wife, where on earth would you take her to keep her safe and make her happy? The U.S. government has tried to kill us twice so far. What government would you trust?" Ryan challenged. "Who would you go to?"

He turned to Sky, looking at her as he continued to speak, "Men are greedy, souls are dark, and I love her." He reached out a hand and brushed back some of Sky's beautiful blonde hair, revealing a worried face that studied his every move. "I live in Amen Hale to keep my Sky safe from the world." Ryan closed his eyes and rubbed his temples as if he had a headache. "And I must live there to keep the world safe from me."

Sky reached over and placed a hand on Ryan's brow. As soon as she touched his head she was out of her chair. She knelt in front of him and placed her hands flat on each side of his face.

"Is he all right?" Tony asked, rising from his chair. "Should we get him a doctor?"

Ryan's eyes snapped open, looking very surprised and he shook as if he had a sudden chill. Ryan's mother knelt with Sky and they shared a whispered conversation. Sky began rubbing Ryan's arms and face, and his mother fought her way into the crowded kitchen to fetch a warm rag that she handed to Sky, who wiped at his brow while the cameras continued to film everything and America continued to watch from the uncomfortable edge of their seats. After a few minutes Sky seemed content with her ministrations and Ryan's condition. She settled back into her seat beside him.

"Mom, could I have a cup of hot coffee?" Ryan asked his mother who was off camera. "Sky gave me brain freeze." He laughed as if it were funny but Sky didn't laugh.

"You were hot, Ryan," she said, totally serious. "Too hot. I won't let you burn to death like Rain did," she said fiercely. The smile slid off Ryan's face. Of course the cameras caught everything. Even the tears that Sky hid from Ryan.

Once Ryan was nursing his mug of steaming joe, Tony resumed.

"How's your sister doing?"

Ryan and Sky's faces fell even further at the question.

"She had a very rough night," Sky answered the question. "But she's doing better now."

"How are you doing, Ryan?" Tony asked.

Ryan changed positions, uncrossing his legs and sitting forward, but as he did so the mug he held began to slip from his grasp. He juggled it for a moment, then caught the bottom of the mug with the tip of his finger as it headed toward the floor, causing the cup to spin, sending the hot coffee spiraling out!

The mug and the coffee froze in the air as if frozen in time.

Ryan sat in his chair staring dazedly down at it. The hand he'd been using to hold and then grab at the errant cup still outstretched. The liquid spiral of black coffee hung in air, vertically orbiting its coffee mug core. The bright lights of the television camera made the individual drops shine like tiny java jewels. The reaction of everyone in the room was complete and utter silence.

Ryan's flat, monotone voice was horribly frightening as he spoke into that silence, still staring down at the mug.

"I had a rough night, Tony. I think I need to go lie down. I need to sleep. Please."

The big man leaned over the back of the chair and slipped his arms around Ryan's head. All of America watched in horror as he squeezed. Ryan's eyes fluttered, then shut.

His mother cried.

Sky cried.

The coffee and the mug hit the floor with a crack and a splash.

David and Dana

Sleeping Angel

D AVID AND DANA and their sleepy maid Angel stepped outside their bedroom door reluctantly, the three of them emerging like timid animals from the
safety of their warren, driven out by hunger and the need to see what further disasters, other than Rain killing herself, had occurred during the night.

In the wake of that tragedy, all the witches had gone mad with grief, Cathryn
among them. Being in that room with all that wailing madness had set Dana's
nerves on a fine edge. When they had tried to retreat to their own bedroom, Cathryn had refused to let them go until their maid Angel had sworn on her life that
she would stay awake and watch over them all night to make sure they didn't harm
themselves.

The three of them had fled the room, as if it were on fire. Once inside their own room they had wedged a chair under the knob of their bedroom door before they went to bed. But now they peeked out and scanned the hallway, three cautious heads whipping left and right as if they expected to see carnage or bodies piled high in both directions. There was nothing except one guard at the Queen's door.

"Great," David said, frowning.

"What!?" Dana scooted closer to him, pushing Angel further back protectively.

"I always feel better when I see Sky Dragon out here in the hall."

Dana's frown deepened as she realized the piece of the puzzle she'd missed. "Yeah. Where is he? It's only eight thirty, he's usually still out here."

"There's a guard, so the Queen must still be in her room," Angel said. She leaned around Dana and pointed to the black outfitted guard. The guard waved.

"Stay here." David told the two girls. He walked down and spoke with the guard briefly. He looked confused as he returned.

"How bad is it?" Dana asked grimly.

"Actually—it's good." David sounded surprised himself. "She's back. The guard said she came back to her body about five a.m. Everyone's still in bed except for Cornelius and Believer; they've been up for a while. And Sky Dragon left with Sky and Ryan about thirty minutes ago to do breakfast at Ryan's parents' trailer."

Dana cast an angry glare toward the Queen's bedroom where Rain and the others were sleeping.

"I hope she's got it out of her system, David, because I can't handle another night like that. Holy shit!"

David's stomach growled, joining the conversation.

Angel spoke up. "I'll go get you and Lady Dana some breakfast if you'd like to sta—"

"No," David said firmly. "I got a weird feeling that the shit's gonna hit the fan and I want us all to stay together today. We need to get out of that room, get some food, and get some more answers. But I want us to be ready for whatever might happen."

"Ready? Ready for what?" Dana asked, getting worked up. "And what do ya mean, you got a weird feeling? You're scaring me, David. What shit? Which fan?!" She threw her hands in the air, all nerved up and jumpy again.

David pulled a cigarette from his front shirt pocket and pushed it into Dana's mouth, lighting the end with a glance.

"It's probably nothing," he said to her, but his eyebrows stayed in a tight, angry bunch over his eyes.

"We're going to go downstairs and get some breakfast. Now hold my hand." He reached out and took her hand, not waiting for her comment or her say so as he led the way toward the stairs in that take charge kind of way that Dana was still getting used to seeing from David. The fiery crowns appeared atop their heads as they walked.

"Do we need the freakin' crowns this early?" Dana complained as she exhaled a plume of smoke from her nostrils and mouth. She usually never had the first cigarette of the day before the first cup of coffee. It was a bad habit to get into.

"Yes," was all David said. The burning crowns stayed. Their sleepy, yawning maid followed a few steps behind as they headed downstairs.

Byron, the House Steward, was delighted to see them enter the Dining Hall and rushed them to a seat at the High Table, as if he wanted to put them on display before the seventy or eighty people still eating breakfast. They were late, catching the tail end of open seating, which ran from seven thirty to eight thirty, but even the cook staff and servers looked delighted to see them.

The only other person at the High Table was Dr. Burgis, and he usually didn't sit at the High Table. David had the feeling that Byron had placed him there so the table wouldn't be so empty.

"I guess we did need the crowns," Dana said as she studied the room and the staring people who already looked more at ease now that someone was at the High Table. "Geez, these people are freaked out worse than I am," Dana said, keeping her voice low.

David spilled OJ on himself, surprised by Dana's admission of weakness. Of course, she only admitted she was freaked out by way of saying that everyone else was more freaked out—but still.

"You're a fighter, Dana," David said. "You're different from most of them. They can't help but look up to you. I've watched you all my life. I know. Few people are as good in a crisis as you are," David said proudly as he wiped OJ off his sleeve with a napkin.

"Stop, David," Dana complained quietly, always uncomfortable with praise.

"Lady Dana," Angel said shyly from the seat beside her, "I shouldn't be sitting at the High Table. I'm a servant. I should be sitting down below." She squirmed in her seat as she looked out at the crowd of people dining in the common seating where she usually sat.

"The Queen gave you to me, didn't she?" Dana demanded of her sharply.

Angel blinked tired, red eyes as she answered, "Yes, Lady Dana, but I shouldn't be—"

"Angel," Dana said, "you're mine. And you'll be what I want you to be. And right now I want you to be good, sit, and eat your breakfast."

"As you wish, my Lady," Angel answered meekly, turning back to her plate but keeping her head down and not looking out at the others down below.

David and Dana both noticed how nervous and uncomfortable she looked. And they'd also noticed the double take the girl server had given her earlier when they first made Angel sit with them, and then again when she delivered Angel's French toast. They were both tuned in and listening as Angel asked the girl, who was probably nineteen or twenty, for some syrup. The girl fetched it right away but gave her an overly sweet "Can I get milady anything else?" before she left.

Without saying a word about what she planned to do, Dana slid her chair back and walked to a surprised, white gloved server and had him fetch her a carafe of milk. She walked back and stood beside Angel's chair, held up the carafe and stared out at all those seated below with a challenging gaze as their strange, little maid stared down at her plate. Those already watching the action nudged neighbors, encouraging them to look up, and soon the entire Hall was quiet and all eyes watching and waiting.

Dana filled Angel's more than half empty glass of milk very deliberately herself, glancing out at the crowd once or twice as she did so, then asked, "Can I get you anything else, Angel?"

"No thank you, Lady Dana," came her quiet reply that would have never been heard if not for the odd way that whispered words sometimes carried in Amen Hale at certain times.

Dana gave the breakfast crowd one final glare before handing the milk back to the server who stood nearby. Then she took her seat again.

They ate their breakfast and were joined by Dr. Burgis, who'd been seated at the other side of the High Table for the esthetic sense of balance and not because of overcrowding. He was finished eating but sat with them to chat as he sipped on his cup of coffee.

Byron escorted the Millers, Jane's parents, to the High Table to join them. As the Millers took their seats, David noticed that Mr. Miller sat in the chair where Angel had been sitting.

"Where's Angel?" David asked, alarmed that she was gone. He quickly scanned the hall, searching for the girl. Hadn't he told her to stay with them!?

"Where is she?!" he demanded, starting to rise from his chair when Dana grabbed his arm and pulled him back into his chair.

"David! Chill!" She pointed down, under the table.

David, Dana, Dr. Burgis, and the Millers all ducked down and peeked under the table to find the peculiar, young girl lying on the floor, curled up at Dana's feet, fast asleep.

"Shouldn't we move her to a bed?" asked Mrs. Miller.

"No," David said. "She stays with us."

David had a pillow and a blanket brought for her. They stayed long past breakfast, talking, letting their tired maid sleep, and letting the worried people of Amen Hale see them as they passed in and through the Dining Hall, reassured by the sight of the burning crowns that rested atop their heads.

Black Rain

Bedroom Games

I OPENED MY EYES a hesitant crack.

A pair of emerald green eyes stared down into my own, surrounded by a hanging curtain of brilliant white and a stripe of bright, neon green. Mary. I frowned as I noticed how red and puffy those green eyes were. I seem to remember fixing them before I fell asleep. Had she been crying while I slept?

She shook her head no.

Mary was sitting at the head of the bed with my head almost lying in her lap as she leaned over me.

I felt her hands somewhere beyond the screen of hair as she massaged the raised flesh on each side of my head where the horns pushed through the flesh of my skull. I could see both horn's at the top half edge of my periphery vision.Blue bars holding the snow white shroud at bay. It made an attractive frame for my view.

Had she always been this beautiful?

I lay still and stared up at her, soaking in the sight of her above me. I wondered if my new vision of her was all because of Emma's touch? Or maybe the time I had spent as a witch had changed the way I saw everyone and everything. Or now that I was a god, could I simply see what had been hidden before? I wasn't sure. I understood Bethany and Emma, and I think even Alana, but not Mary. Why did she love me?

Her brows bunched. Nose crinkled. I knew she was listening to my thoughts.

So many others wanted you. The cheerleaders, jocks, and the rich, beach brats all wanted you, but you wanted to be with me and Bethany and Kendal. When you first met me I was little more than a walking zombie, but you didn't care. You talked to me, and carried me along with you and played with me even when I sat there like a human-sized doll. A body holding something that just wanted to die.

Mary frowned down at me and I saw the shine of fresh tears in her eyes.

Don't worry, my Mary. I want to live now.

The brimming tears retreated, the redness and the puffiness around her eyes vanished. It seemed to happen without me even thinking about it, simply because some small part of me wanted it.

She smiled down at me. Mary had sworn herself to me. She'd vowed to serve me, in this life, after this life, in the world to come, and forever. She would always be mine and I would always want her.

"Forever," she agreed, quietly whispering the word.

I felt whoever was lying on my stomach stir.

Mary sat up, and I looked down the length of my body and into Jane's lovely face. I couldn't help but smile. Behind her, standing at the foot of the bed was Dan. He was looking down into my eyes, and I couldn't look at him and not remember how he'd begged me to stay. How he'd cried. His desperate notes he'd written to me.

Mary wiped the tears away that came to my eyes as if by magic. I'd banished Mary's tears, but some part of me wanted to cry, so I lay still and let Mary wipe away my tears as I stared at Dan. I loved Dan, too. I hadn't truly realized it until last night, when everyone was begging me to stay. Everyone weeping and crying, trying to keep me from leaving. It was Dan's notes and unashamed tears that made me drop my facade and flinch and cry.

Dan gave me a kind, compassionate smile, and I wondered if he could already see it in my eyes. I looked back down to Jane and met her eyes.

"Forgive me, Jane. I love Dan," I confessed as Mary wiped at my tears. "It was his damn notes that got to me," I complained.

Mary giggled quietly, and I looked up at her.

"That's how he got Jane too."

I looked back down to Jane and found her crawling closer, her arms and legs stretched out on either side of me like a spider. She straddled my chest, tucked up beneath my breasts with her knees snugged under my shoulders. She squeezed my sides with her legs as she leaned forward until her face was only inches away from mine. Her beautiful violet and lilac eyes held me. I couldn't look away.

"And do you know how *you* got to me?" she asked.

I shook my head no, totally unable to speak.

"I wanted your blood, and you gave me what I wanted. You wanted me to love you, and I turned you away. Still, you gave me what I thought I wanted, and then you let me be. You gave me your blood, and then you left. You took away the girl and left the blood behind." Her head dropped, eyes downcast as if she were ashamed of herself. "I know it sounds selfish and stupid, and it makes me sound like some idiot guy," she chastened herself, "but once you were gone, I wanted you." She confessed, "I saw how much everyone loved you and I was jealous and angry. I wanted to love you and kiss you and—" she stopped abruptly. She was suddenly closer, her eyes staring into mine. "But you were gone, and I couldn't."

She looked so hurt I held my breath, feeling afresh the torment that I'd wrought when I had left everyone last night.

"You were gone forever. I'd lost you. And I didn't know what to do." Her own tears, red and tinged with the gold color of my blood, began to pool in her eyes.

"Breathe, Rain," Mary ordered.

I started breathing again, obediently.

"When you left, I went and danced with Mary in the garden. We danced around your statue and prayed and prayed and prayed. All I could do was pray, so I prayed. I prayed to my god. I prayed to you. I prayed to my Lion."

Red/gold tears started to roll down her face in two thick trails coming from the corners of her eyes.

"Jane was a mess," Mary whispered. "I had to carry her to Cathryn."

My heart clenched again as I imagined the scene. I reached up and cupped Jane's face with my hands and willed her tears away as well. If I was her god, then it was my right and my place to wipe away her tears. But as I wiped Jane's tears away my own continued to fall, and I did not send mine away.

"What did you pray for, my little Black Lamb?" I asked her.

She smiled at that, and it was good to see her smile.

"A second chance," she said. She moved closer. Close enough to kiss. "I will not waste what I have been given." Her eyes burned with such conviction and passion that they started to shift to red. "I want all of you that there is to have, and I'll give you all of me this time too, Rain. I won't hold back."

I closed my eyes, dizzy from the sight of her, her passion, and her magic. I could feel how hungry they were. They'd had my blood a couple of times and they'd both bitten me and given me their venom. I could feel that piece of them that they'd put into me. Jane and Dan were bound to me the same as Mary; they'd given themselves to me.

I breathed in her smell. It was so unbelievably wonderful it made me self-conscious. Crazy thoughts buzzed through my head. "Oh God! Do I reek?" and "When on earth was my last shower?"

"You smell wonderful," Mary whispered behind me. "Don't fuck with it. I like it."

Jane growled as if she agreed, a low hungry sound. She leaned in and started to rub her face against my cheek, wallowing in my tears as her body vibrated like a big cat.

I felt Bethany stir in the bed beside me. I didn't know what to do or what was about to happen. I willed her to sleep without even looking down to see if she was awake or not.

"Are you all awake now?" Cathryn's voice called out and we all turned to the sound of her voice. She'd just emerged from the bathroom, dressed and ready for her day.

Jane greeted her with a growl and a glare; she didn't like being disturbed.

"Yes ma'am, except for Bethany," Mary answered sweetly, like Jane's opposite. "She's gonna stay night night for a little while. Rain put her little Lion lights out. I don't think she wanted little eyes to see what's about to happen."

"Uh oh!"

"Uh oh!"

Two heads popped up like gophers from their holes on the left side of the pillow-strewn bed. Izzy and Lizzy. They both wore hilarious expressions and crazy bed head. Their kinky, curly, blond hair looked alive as it untangled and righted itself and even grew a couple of inches. Their somewhat unkempt, yellowed, and crooked teeth brightened and straightened as the dark circles around their eyes vanished. The girls didn't even notice the changes as they happened. They were staring at me and Jane, not each other.

"Izzy, Lizzy, take Bethany into the next room for me please," Cathryn ordered.

"Yes, mother," Lizzy answered obediently. "I got the feet, you get her head," she told her sister.

"Why do we gotta take her, Mom!?" Izzy whined. "Dan can carry the little monster. Look what she did last night!"

She held up an arm that sported an impressive set of scratches. They vanished as she pointed at them. She shot me a less than friendly look for destroying evidence.

"Girls, unless you want to join the others in what they're about to do, you should come with me."

The twins froze, turned, and looked at each other for a weird "twin" moment, then they looked back at the bed. Their eyes roved over the scene.

Jane sat up straight, still straddling me with her legs as she looked at them. My new skin was so sensitive, the movement made me aware of Jane's bare bottom that rested on my chest. Her red dress was fanned around to hide what was and what wasn't there. As if she'd read my mind, she ground herself against me and flexed. The feel of her made me growl. A low, long animal sound that seemed to fill the room.

That decided it for Izzy and Lizzy who quickly abandoned the bed, taking Bethany with them.

"Watch her tail now, girls; don't let it drag," Cathryn coached.

Their eyes were big, staring circles as they retreated.

"You can stay if you like," Emma offered as they passed by.

Izzy, who was carrying Bethany's head didn't look back, but Lizzy, who was holding Bethany's feet looked back over her shoulder at Dan longingly as she was towed from the room by her other half.

"Bye, Dan," she called as she disappeared.

"Alana," Cathryn said, "this is probably a bit much for you yet. You should probably come with me and the twins."

I propped myself up on my elbows to look down at the corner of the bed where Alana was huddled into Emma's arms, looking scared and confused.

"My little Red Lamb," I said.

She had a shy smile for me. "My Lion," she said back.

Alana's radiant, jewel blue eyes looked frightened. She scanned the room and weighed each of us in turn with her gaze. Mary for only a second. Cathryn she considered longer. She even considered Dan for a second as she tried to decide who would give her the safety and comfort she wanted. She didn't consider Jane for some reason.

She looked back to me again, her decision made. Her brow creased as she eyed Jane who sat astride me. She flicked a hand at Jane, and then her mouth popped open in shocked confusion when nothing happened.

She did it again. Again nothing happened.

The vampire sitting on my chest laughed in wicked satisfaction, immune to whatever magic Alana had tried.

"Jane," Cathryn's voice scolded gently, "be nice to Alana. She's brand new and you know she's scared. She wants Rain. Now make some room."

Jane growled but then said a grudging, "Yes, Mother. I know Rain loves her little Red Lamb. I'll share with her."

Jane looked over at Alana. "Heads or tails?" she asked, her voice only a little disappointed.

"What?"

Jane put on a patient face. "Do you want our Lion's head, or do you want her tail?" She pointed at the portions to the front and to the rear of where she sat on my chest. "We all want a piece of her, and you're gonna have to share like the rest of us. It's only fair." Jane's sweet voice made it sound like such a reasonable thing.

"So, what's it to be? You pick first. Heads or tails?" she asked again.

"Heads!" Alana snapped. "I want her head AND her arms!" She narrowed her eyes as if she expected a trick.

I was the Black Lion, but I lay there and listened to the whole thing like a mute Thanksgiving turkey, the holiday guests deciding over white meat or dark. Who gets a wing, who gets a thigh, and who gets breasts. The vampires will probably fight over the gizzard I thought. Mary and I both fought not to laugh and spoil the negotiations as Jane plated the bird.

"Deal," Jane confirmed. "The head and arms are yours, though you may want to share with Mary, she looks very lonely. Dan and I shall take the tail. Just give me a minute to make us comfortable and she's all yours."

I was still processing the "Dan and I...tail" comment when, without another word, Jane tightened her legs around me and slowly leaned backwards and backwards—and backwards. She bent her spine like a contortionist until the top of her head bumped my lower stomach. She hooked her fingers under the silver chain that supported my loin cloth and pulled up to get her teeth onto the chain right in the middle where the cloth was. She bit. The chain popped and fell away from each side of me.

She held the top of the loin cloth in her teeth as she rose up, and because of the upside down, ass backwards angle, the inside of the cloth that had been closest to *me* now covered her face, while the rest of the three-foot loin cloth draped over her head and down her back like a long sexy veil. She brought her hands up and pressed the black cloth to her face, then inhaled deeply.

Dan growled.

"Mary!" I said in a high-pitched squeak! A terrified chill tingled down my spine, and I reached up to Mary's arms for comfort as my heart started to run like a scared rabbit! I'd almost forgotten about Dan!

But before I could worry about him, Jane started to butt walk!—moving one cheek at a time down my sensitive body until she parked her parts right above mine. The black veil covering her face slid up and away as Dan pulled it from behind to show me Jane's hungry eyes.

Mary leaned over and slid her hands down my arms and moved to my chest. She pulled each of the strips of black cloth to the side, exposing my breasts. I moaned as she drew her nails up and around my breasts, up the sides of my neck, and into my hair where she grabbed my horns like a pair of handlebars. She leaned forward and I lost my mind for a moment as she kissed me exactly the way I wanted to be kissed.

"... or come with me." Cathryn's words came to me as Mary came up for air. "But one way or another, they're about to start. You'll have to choose, Alana. In or out."

"Think for yourself and make your own choice," Emma urged. "Your Lion wants us all. The vampires need to feed, and I need to feed, and Mary wants to be here, but you don't have to do this if you don't want to. We will love you, always and forever. You can go with Mom or you can stay and play, but, just for me," Emma gently reached over and turned Alana's head back toward us, "look at them and think about it."

Alana's brow was creased, an expression of reluctance still on her face, but she did as Emma asked and looked at us.

Cathryn gave her only a minute then tried once again to get her away from what was about to happen.

"If you're not sure then you should come with me, Bethany, and the twins." She held her hand out for Alana to take.

Alana looked at her hand and then looked back at us, but this time her gaze settled on Jane and Dan. Dan had eased onto the bed on his knees and knelt, straddled over my legs with his arms wrapped around Jane from behind. Jane leaned back into him as she sat astride me.

"Will you bite me if I stay?" Alana asked Jane.

Jane studied her face for a moment and whatever she saw there surprised her and made her smile.

"Only if you're very good to me." She arched a lovely eyebrow. "But Dan will bite you if you're very bad to me. So, I guess the real question is, do you want to be bad—or good?'" Jane's voice was filled with such heat I stopped watching altogether, squeezed my eyes shut, and stretched, pointing my toes at the far wall as my whole body turned into a stiff, quivering board for a moment.

"Can I be both?" I heard Alana's surprisingly clear voice ask. By the sound of her voice, her fear and confusion seemed replaced by a surprisingly daring curiosity.

"Both?" Jane said. "Oh, I don't know about that." She sounded doubtful. "You've already tried to use magic on me, so I know you can be bad to me. But can you be good?" she asked again, her voice dark, wooing, and hungry. "Can you really be good to me? I hope you can. I've never tasted Red Lamb. You sound so very—tasty."

"I can be good" was Alana's breathy reply.

"Prove it," Jane dared.

Above me, Mary stifled a giggle, then leaned down to whisper into my ear. "I love bedroom games! This is going to be fun!"

Bedroom games?

I propped myself up on my elbows to watch.

Alana's face was a mad mix of emotions, but through it all I finally saw the rise of true desire and excitement on her face as she eased out of Emma's arms and started to pull her arms out of the plain white t-shirt she wore. Her spiked pink and red hair matched the dusting of freckles across the bridge of her nose and around her eyes. The freckles, with her glowing jewel blue eyes, made her look as if she wore a magical mask. She had an alien beauty. Not entirely human. And I realized right then that Jane hadn't been kidding about tasting her. Alana was magic. She might be sweet enough to eat.

Alana pulled her shirt over her head, showing her ultra lean, runner's build and perfect, small breasts. She knee walked to Jane and stopped, waiting shyly before her.

Jane took a moment to admire her. Actually, we all did. She reached out and stroked her face with the back of her hand.

I ached to touch her too.

"EEEEE!" Alana screamed, hopped, spun, then rushed back into Emma's waiting arms, the tender, desire-filled moment completely forgotten.

"What's wrong, Alana!" Cathryn asked as she rushed to the edge of the bed to help comfort her.

"Some THING! crawled up my shorts!" she shouted. She stabbed an accusing finger at the culprit.

My guilty tail rose up from the tangle of sheets and waved at everyone.

"My bad," I confessed sheepishly from my prone position on the bed.

Alana looked shaken, and Emma and Cathryn tried to comfort her, but Mary had other plans. She wanted to play.

"Bad Lion!" Mary scolded as she stared down at me, face set in an angry pout. "There are rules in this bed, Miss Thang! That was BAD, wasn't it, Emma!?"

"Very bad!" Emma joined in, dividing her squinty-eyed glare between me and my poor, guilty tail.

"I'm sorry!" I whined, pathetically. "I just wanted to touch her too!"

I was ignored.

"What happens to very bad people in this bed, Alana?" Mary asked, trying to coax her into joining in.

"She was bad," Emma nodded, trying to help her along.

"Oh! They get bit by Dan!" Alana declared, smiling again, starting to enjoy herself after the unwanted advances of my sinister, slithery self.

Jane joined into the role play and grabbed my guilty tail like she was appre-hending a crook. She held her captive up in front of everyone and gave Tail her own evil glare. A foot of black velvet rope dangled from her hand.

"What's the deal!?" she spoke to my tail. "She bargained for the head, didn't she?" Jane gave my poor tail a shake and a growl. "I bargained for the tail, didn't I?!"

As I watched, the end of the crazy thing flopped up and down in Jane's grasp, looking for all the world like it nodded.

They all laughed, even Dan.

"What the hell?!" was my comment, which made everyone laugh again when they saw my freaked out face.

They went back to interrogating the suspect.

"I bargained for Rain's tail. I didn't grab the wrong tail did I? You are Rain's 'Tail,' aren't you?" Jane asked it.

It flopped up and down again. Positive ID confirmed. They had the right tail.

Emma and Mary hooted and laughed and Alana laughed with them. I even heard Cathryn laughing along.

"Her tail stole what should have been mine. That was bad, Dan. Very, very bad." Jane leaned back and gave Dan a kiss, then said, "Go make her pay for her naughty tail that went where it wasn't invited and left me here, all alone."

That was curiously worded, but before I could think on it, Dan started to walk toward me on his knees.

Mary got up and joined the rowdy rabble that began bouncing up and down on the bed as they decried the villainy of my lecherous tail and cheered Dan on.

My mouth was dry, my heart jumping. I turned my head to the side and meekly offered Dan my neck.

"Bite her!" I heard Alana's happy voice cry out. "But I'm next! I was bad too!"

Dan leaned over me, and I felt his cool breath on my neck. I trembled beneath his gentle touch as his hands brushed my hair away from my neck. He wrapped his arms around me, settling into position as if he meant to hold me still.

I closed my eyes, and in that moment of trembling waiting darkness, I had everyone's clothes vanish.

All the cheering, jeering silliness suddenly stopped, and then Dan bit my neck—

"Have fun, my children," I heard my mother call from what seemed a world away.

Cornelius and Believer

Bitter Medicine

CORNELIUS AND BELIEVER walked down the cobbled drive at the head of a column of black-clad security men and prisoners. Two of the men wore no shackles though they walked with the rest of the group. They were unlucky hunters who'd simply camped in the right field at the wrong time and were taken prisoner with the others who'd attacked Amen Hale.

The two hunters had been given envelopes filled with cash. Mary wrote the names of their wives on each envelope and told both of the men not to open the envelopes or the money inside would vanish. She meant this to be figurative and not literal (but the two men didn't know that and she did not over share). Mary had touched both men and knew they were horrible with money and would go nuts once they saw the cash. Mary also knew that both men had very responsible wives who were frugal with what money their boys brought home. Ten thousand dollars in cash was in each envelope. It wasn't a life-changing sum but it was a good way to say, "Sorry about that."

"Must we do this now, Father?" Believer asked Cornelius, trying to speak quietly enough so none of the guards or prisoners walking behind them heard his complaining.

"We will be as brief as possible. I've no desire to do this either, my son, but time does not stop at our wall. Delivering these prisoners gives us an excuse to broach other matters tactfully. We need to inform them that Rain has returned, lest they grow overly bold. I've no doubt that the men and women who fled Amen Hale have told of Rain's death. Now we must set that to right, before actions are taken based on misinformation."

"I see the wisdom in what we do and the need for haste," Believer rumbled softly, then added, "But if they are convinced that Rain has perished, will they not attack us once we are beyond the wall?"

Cornelius smiled. "Ahh. And here is where we must be bold." He chuckled. "You must consider the mind of your opponent. In this case, the minds of the soldiers who watch us day and night. What would they think if we stayed behind the walls like mice in a hole?" Cornelius asked. "And what will they think of our current course of action?"

Believer considered the question as they trudged along the path and Cornelius waited patiently. He felt exactly like a father, teaching a flesh and blood son. Believer was brilliant and gifted with a great deal of knowledge from Sky, all of which she'd given to him when he was made. But Believer was still only four days old and had a number of things to learn about the complexities of the world and the confusing humans who lived in it.

"If we stayed hidden," Believer began, "they would be convinced that Rain was dead and gone and therefore be emboldened to move against us. By coming out and conducting our business as usual, we declare plainly that we hold them and their power in contempt. They will no doubt 'inquire' as to the health of my wife while we make the prisoner transfer and we shall be honest with them. Yes, she died. Yes, it was horrible. And yes, she has returned."

"All of which she has done before," Cornelius concluded happily. "Very well done, my son. But don't forget, two of these men are completely innocent and need to be returned to worried families who think they are destined for our dinner table. It would be more than cruel to prolong their distress."

Believer's face showed his surprise at what he clearly viewed as an egregious oversight. He turned away, grumbling his displeasure. He kept his eyes forward as he spoke. Disappointment in himself was clear in his deep rumbling voice. "I did not think of the prisoners. I gave them no consideration and directed no thought to their needs or rights. I should have." He looked over at Cornelius, anticipating his soothing response, unwilling to let himself be easily assuaged for his oversight. "You remembered mercy, Father. As should I," Believer affirmed soundly. "Mercy and compassion and doing what is right are not of lesser import. As you say, two of these men are innocent, and an innocent life is of great value and should be treated with respect."

Cornelius left Believer to his mood although he ached to tell him many things. How proud he was that he was able to call him son. That he was happier at that moment than at any time he could recall since he had been raised from the dead. Cornelius felt hope. He felt as though he walked beside a good man. A man who called him father and was proud to do so. If this was his son, then surely there was hope for Amen Hale. And hope for Rain.

As they reached the archway by the wall, the magic portal opened for Cornelius obediently. He never doubted for an instant that it wouldn't, although he'd never before opened one of Rain's archways before.

Hillary Clinton was waiting to receive them there at the gate, as were a large collection of soldiers and FBI agents, anxiously waiting to process the valuable load of prisoners and the information that they carried. Ten terrorists in all. Six men and four women were being turned over to the American government with the understanding that the punitive portion (how long and in what manner they remained incarcerated) be done in accordance with Mary's written instructions.

She'd clearly stated how long each prisoner was to spend in a jail cell before being released and delivered to the front door of their own homes and given their unconditional freedom. She'd also made requests concerning the children of some of the prisoners. Each man or woman carried a pardon, which listed facts, details, and names that Mary felt needed to be divulged to the authorities. Having touched these men and women, Mary knew everything about them. Any secrets they knew, Mary knew. Everything she felt important to the authorities was written on the pardon, whether the prisoner liked it or not. The handwriting on each page was not Mary's; she'd dictated her words to the guards as she was touching the prisoners and sifting through their memories, but she had signed the bottom of each pardon herself.

By the Decree of Mary Fae, Child of Cathryn and Cornelius, Princess of Amen Hale, Royal Pardon is Hereby Granted to this soul. So Mote It Be.

The prisoners held these pardons clutched tightly in their hands. Mary had informed them that if they lost their pardon or defaced them in any way they would be fed to the lions. In Amen Hale, the lions walked on two feet.

"Good morning, Cornelius, Believer," Hillary greeted them both.

"Good morning to you as well, Madam," Cornelius greeted her with a small bow, and Believer gave a nod of his huge head but left the speaking to Cornelius.

"May I introduce you to your new charges?" Cornelius offered her his arm.

Hillary gave Cornelius an annoyed look. "Come on, Cornelius. Aren't you taking these old world mannerisms and this chivalry act a bit too far?"

"Hmm," Cornelius mused, "Madam Secretary, correct me if I'm mistaken, but adapting to the culture and customs of the various countries you visit is, I believe, part of your job description."

"So, do I need a calculator or a ski mask?" Hillary shot back. "You're an accountant and a crook." She smiled grimly, refusing to play into his game or give him her arm.

"And a King," Cornelius added to the list with a straight face. "A gentleman and an excellent dancer, if it's not too pretentious to say so myself. Shall I go on?"

Hillary glared. "Add scoundrel to the list."

"I suppose the ski mask could be useful for our Masquerade Ball," Cornelius conceded grudgingly, "though it would be a sin, dear lady, to cover such a lovely face as yours with the hood of a common rogue."

"Cor-Nelius!" Hillary huffed in exasperation. "That's enough!"

"Humor me, woman!" Cornelius grumped, extending his arm again.

"Fine!" Hillary relented with a growl, giving her arm and allowing herself to be escorted toward the prisoners.

Believer smiled as he followed them, a silent, cloudy, man-shaped mountain whose red eyes continually scanned the area for threats as he listened to their very interesting conversation.

"Each of these men bear a Royal Pardon." Cornelius spoke in a businesslike manner although he escorted her as though she were a debutante at a ball safely tucked in at his side. And just like that, the "prisoner dump" became a royal social call.

The grim-faced, almost hostile atmosphere of agents, aides, and others surrounding them staggered and changed to something like respectful accommodation as the music of the scene flipped from tango to waltz without warning.

Cornelius pointed to the prisoner at the front of the line and the paper he held in his hands. "Pertinent criminal information, contacts, names, numbers, and other information have been listed on each pardon to help speed up your discovery efforts. Mary pulled this information directly from their minds. The specifics concerning their incarceration have been clearly stated on each pardon. Any you wish to release early is wholly your choice, but none are to be held longer than the term stated on their pardon."

"Will you be bringing out more tomorrow?" Hillary asked.

"No. Mary has touched all of our prisoners, and these ten she deemed worthy of mercy. Of course the two hunters are completely innocent and have been compensated."

"Compensated?"

"Envelopes with cash." Cornelius pointed to the two men at the back of the line who held plump envelopes. Both men were smiling and seemed in good spirits.

"Do you as the official representative for the United States of America agree with the conditions of the pardons and the terms as stated on each?" Cornelius asked, again all business.

"Yes. Gladly," Hillary answered. "What about the rest of the prisoners, Cornelius? You're not going to have that little girl murder all forty of them, one after another, day after day in that stadium you've built while everyone watches? Please tell me that's not what you're going to do." She stared up into his eyes as she asked.

Cornelius returned her gaze without flinching. "Though you may not believe it, I was raised from the dead by Bethany Grave. In order to accomplish this deed, she made a human sacrifice of Fiona Pravaskov, a truly horrible woman. Her thug of a son, Yanosh, murdered me and was about to murder Cathryn, and then rape and murder Bethany as well. The people we have kept are of that quality. Vile. Murderers. Wicked men and women."

Hillary didn't complain that he'd avoided her question, but she did squint her eyes as she took a closer look at Cornelius's face. She took in his pale complexion, the dark circles under his eyes, and the overall weariness that he couldn't hide, although he tried.

"Are you feeling well, Cornelius? You look like hell."

He laughed, surprised to hear some honest concern on the crook's behalf. "I apologize for appearing less than dazzling, but at my age going without sleep wears on a body."

"What happened last night?" she asked. "We can't hear what's going on inside Amen Hale now that you've cleared out all of our bugs, but we still saw all of the panicked activity late last night. A number of your people left. I'm sure you know that. Are the girls well?"

"They are now. We lost Rain for a while and some people panicked."

Hillary studied Cornelius's pained face as she meshed the seemingly contradictory statement into one that made sense.

"So, Rain killed herself—but now she's back."

Cornelius lifted her hand and kissed the back of her wrist and begged her pardon. "Please forgive me for being brief, but we must go. There are a number of things that are—"

"No!" Hillary snapped, pulling her hand away roughly. "Dammit, Cornelius, we have to talk! And the President wants an official meeting later today! And there are other security problems we need to discuss that you have to hear right now! Not later, now!" With effort she forced herself to stop yelling. "More terrorists have crossed our borders. People that are intent on killing you and the girls, Cornelius."

"People are always intent on killing my girls, Hillary. Will it be another group of innocent yet maliciously misinformed 'U.S.' soldiers this time as well?" He glared at her. "Good day to you," Cornelius replied curtly.

"Father, we should hear what she has to say," Believer's deep voice rumbled before he could turn away. "You were right, time does not stop at the walls of Amen Hale. What we hear now may help prevent other problems later. You were right, Father."

"Give me a dose of my own words, will you?" Cornelius griped.

Believer lifted his enormous shoulders in a massive shrug, utilizing his non--verbal communication in what he hoped was an appropriate manner and not insulting.

"You are right, but it's bitter medicine," Cornelius complained. "So mote it be." He turned back to Hillary. "Lead on, woman!" he snapped at her. "I find myself short on charm, lacking in grace, devoid of patience, and ready to be quit of this business before it's even begun, so make haste!"

Hillary stood there, shocked speechless. Cornelius was ever the gentleman, even when all hell was breaking loose. She took stock of his condition again, seeing again how much he'd kept concealed. What he'd been through last night had battered him, and his limits had clearly been crossed. While it was nice to know that the man's facade had a breaking point, she found that she wasn't glad to see it.

Believer leaned down, putting his enormous head between Cornelius and Hillary as he said in his sweetest rumble of a voice. "What my father meant to say was, 'Thank you, Madam Secretary, please proceed.'"

"Indeed!" Cornelius growled.

A Priest, a Preacher, a Witch, and an Atheist

Bar Flies

AFTER RYAN'S "SOLDIER-ASSISTED" nap, he woke in his parents' bed with his head throbbing.

"How long?" he asked through the drum beat of his pulse. It hurt to talk.

Sky and his mother both spoke. His mother told him that he was only out for ten minutes. Sky asked him how he felt as she fussed over him.

"Headache," he answered with one word.

Sky sat on the edge of the bed, playing nursemaid. She was being crowded by his mother who obviously wanted Sky's spot. Ryan's father and Lucius were dire-faced, looming shadows behind the women. Ryan squinted his eyes against the headache and examined the circus around his parents' bed with a wry smile. A soldier stood at each of the bedroom windows, peeking through the drawn blinds with weapons at the ready. Three other soldiers stood around the room like randomly planted black trees with weapons as fruit instead of apples.

The anxious faces in the room held a mix of concern and fear—and something else. Was it excitement? Were they waiting to see what he'd do next?

Sky's face was different. Her eyes different from theirs. And her eyes were what he needed. Only hers. Sky squealed when he grabbed her, but her protests of "You don't feel well!" died when Ryan pulled her under the covers and kissed her.

The worried people hovering around the bed eventually excused themselves and shut the bedroom door. Sky and Ryan emerged an hour later, both in better spirits, though Sky still checked on him constantly.

For the next two hours, Ryan talked with his parents about what was happening in Amen Hale, about Mary, Bethany, Emma, Rain, and the new girl, Alana. At eleven thirty, they sat on the couch and turned on the television to catch a debate on CNN, that according to the menu guide, was about Black Rain and religion. They had a special guest on whom they were all interested to see and hear what he had to say.

"Our special guest is Reverend Robert Renolds, the Pastor of Branson Road Baptist Church, which is the church that Rain Marie Bryant and the rest of her family attended until this past Wednesday."

The moderator began, voice brisk and fast, setting the tempo for the debate. "Also joining our panel is Father Juan Cagulara, Bishop of the Los Angeles Diocese; Dr. Ethan Swaim from the Institute for the Advancement of Atheistic Ideals; and Mrs. Hellen Archer from Wiccan America, an organization that promotes Wiccan beliefs and Wiccan rights in America."

Renolds looked uncomfortable, but Dr. Swaim scowled openly, already hostile before the discussion even began. Swaim's wire rim spectacles pressed into the flesh on each side of his massive head. His sagging jowls joined with his triple chin making his already round face look like a fleshy pie with its contents sliding off at the bottom. A large, bulbous nose hung center mass and helped to balance the rest of his larger than life features. He was a fat, ugly man, and scowling as he was made him look mean and ugly.

The priest was a small man next to the broad-shouldered Renolds and the morbidly obese Swaim. His bright, trusting smile, dark, Latin complexion, and white collar made him seem innocent and childlike. Hellen Archer, the Wiccan, was an attractive, older woman who held herself with poise and politely nodded to the camera as she was introduced.

"Mrs. Archer," the moderator began, "there's been quite a lot of media coverage about this internet-driven movement to kill the Black Witch and her Coven. Witches are being encouraged to cast spells and use magic, and pagans urged to pray to whomever or whatever they pray to as part of a combined spiritual and magical attack. Do you have any comment on this effort and those who have already joined it?"

She gave a dismissive hand flip. "Cooks, crackpots, and teens with too much time on their hands and too little understanding of what they're doing. But that's the internet for you. True Wiccans focus on sending out positive energy so we get the same returned. 'Harm none' is one of our core beliefs. Wiccan America would never support any effort that seeks the harm of another person."

The moderator gave Archer a broader question. "What does the rise of the Black Witch mean for the Wiccan faith? Is she and her coven vindication? Is she a new standard bearer? A new leader for your religion? Or is she an absolute disaster?"

Archer smiled. Her voice was pleasant, and unlike the moderator, her words were unhurried. "The Wiccan faith was the fastest growing religion in America before this started. I can't see that changing because of what's happened. As far as Black Rain goes, she is a very dangerous and a very sick girl, not a leader of our faith. If there is a hell," she paused and winked at Renolds, "the doctor who did this to these kids should be thrown into the deep end, head first."

The moderator and the cameras turned to Renolds, catching him red faced and scowling at Archer because of her wicked wink.

"Pastor Renolds, Rain Bryant grew up in your church. Did you know that she was a witch while she attended your church Sunday after Sunday? Do you allow witches in your congregation?"

"It wasn't like that!" Renolds affirmed soundly. "And she wasn't like that."

"Tell us then, Pastor Renolds, what was she like?"

Renolds took a calming breath then started talking. "Rain Marie used to be a happy, normal girl. She was a little rebellious and loud at times, but that's normal. She was a normal, happy girl." He repeated himself and shook his head, genuine anguish showing. And perhaps a little guilt. "I watched her grow up in our church. Rain was fine up until two years ago when she had an abortion. Of course, she didn't tell anyone what she'd done; she just came apart and none of us knew why. Our church prayed for her when she was hospitalized. The doctors looked for head trauma and tested for drug use, but they finally said that it was a psychotic break. For months Rain wouldn't speak a single word and would hardly move and all she'd wear was black. If her parents took away the black clothes she'd walk around nude, so they let her wear black. Rain came to church with her family every time the doors were open and never caused a problem. She sat on the last row and spoke to no one except her family, and sometimes not even to them when she slipped into one of her catatonic states. Her parents told me that she was dabbling in the occult with some of her friends in the trailer park, but she never brought that stuff to our church until this past Wednesday. Before then she was just the sick daughter of one of our most faithful families, the Bryants."

"Do you feel like you've failed the Bryants, Pastor Renolds?" the moderator asked astutely.

"Absolutely. If I could go back, I'd do more for the girl. Dig deeper. Pray harder. Whatever I had to do." He sounded miserable.

The moderator turned to the priest. "Father Juan, we understand that the Pope himself has called today," the moderator held up a piece of paper and read directly from it, "'A day to pray for righteous judgment to fall upon the wicked. A day to see the wicked pulled down to hell.'" He addressed the priest, "The Pope did not say her name outright, but everyone believes he was referring to the Black Witch and the others in Amen Hale. Was he?"

Father Juan's smile was wide and calming. "A great deal of fear and confusion has gripped the world over the past few days. It's understandable. We are all shaken by what these scientific breakthroughs suggest. It raises questions in the educated and the illiterate alike. In the panic, fear, and uncertainty, people are hearing what they want to hear. The Holy Father did not say her name. You will have to ask him personally for more clarity than that, but it seems clear to me."

Reverend Renolds started chuckling, smiling broadly and the moderator turned back to him.

"What's funny about that answer, Pastor Renolds?"

"Oh, I had an ethics teacher in college who once drew a square on the black board, then he drew a circle inside the square and asked all of us in the classroom if we were looking at a square or a circle. He insisted we choose one or the other and made it a one question quiz. After some debate, half of us went with square and the other half wrote down circle. When we got our papers back we all got zeros. When we complained he told us that the ethical thing to do was to call him a liar. Instead we chose circle or square. Choosing to accept a lie is the end of ethics."

"Are you calling the Holy Father a liar?" asked Father Juan, his smile turning into an angry flat line.

"I'm not the one drawing a circle inside a square," Renolds answered smugly.

"Father Juan," the moderator cut in before the priest launched an angry retort, "has the Pope seen the pictures out of France that claim to show Black Rain's new form?" Picture in picture on the screen showed the images as he continued. "If these images are to be believed, she now has horns and a tail, and we've been told by experts who've examined those images that she's now seven feet tall. Reports from those who attended the disastrous wedding in Amen Hale last night have corroborated the photographic evidence. And, as I'm sure you know, those same guests who've been interviewed have described their meeting with her. Her odd eyes that they say are so disturbing. And that she now claims to be a god. Has the Pope seen these new images, and what does he think of them if he has?"

"I'm sure his Eminence has seen these new pictures," Father Juan replied unhappily.

The moderator continued with the priest, "There are many people who believe that this poor girl was demon possessed before she took the pills; that something happened back when she had her abortion and went insane. They say that the demon within her has finally taken its true form. What are we to believe?"

The moderator leaned in, pressing his point. "Is she a demon?" He almost demanded, "Is she just a poor, sick child who took these pills and is simply changing herself into new shapes because she's mentally ill? Changing her body over and over like a regular, teenage girl changes clothes two to three times day. Some of the people of Amen Hale are worshipping her as a god now. America, and the world, wants to know what the Catholic church's position is. Please don't be evasive, and tell us plainly what this girl is."

"I am glad to answer this question and will do so plainly and simply," Father Juan affirmed with a nod, apparently thinking himself up to the challenge.

"Let us say that Dr. Swaim, our atheist guest, took these mind-altering pills and gained telepathic or healing powers, and then, as an experiment in irony, decided to journey into the depths of the rain forest where he flamboyantly displayed that power to an undeveloped tribe. I'm sure he would have no difficulty convincing them that he was a god. Soon they would all bow down to him, and in short order he would have them happily laboring to fulfill his will."

"I suppose I would make a rather impressive Buddha," Swaim chuckled, amused by the idea.

The priest continued, ignoring Swaim. "There is a desire inside every man to believe in something greater than themselves. From the beginning God has made us with this inborn need." The priest's face fell. "It would be a sad fate for the poor, deceived natives to worship Dr. Swaim as god. As it is sad for any who would bow down to a sick girl and call her god. To have that empty space inside a person's soul that cries out to be filled with God's presence instead be filled with a lie is a horrible thing. To murder someone's body is horrible, but to murder someone's soul is far worse. One death lasts but a moment, but the other lasts an eternity." Father Juan's face was grave.

The moderator turned back to Renolds. "Do you think she's murdering people's souls, Pastor Renolds?"

Renolds looked green around the gills. "If she's actually telling people she's a god and letting them worship her, then yes."

"And people think of Christians as being tolerant!" Mrs. Archer interjected firmly. "It's nonsense talk like that that will cause people to act like idiots. Do you want the scared villagers to grab the pitchforks and torches?" Archer challenged. "It may just be a simple misunderstanding anyway. In the Wiccan belief system all females are considered daughters of the Goddess, and therefore we are all gods. When we worship the goddess we worship one another as much as she who is from the beginning and in all things."

"With all due respect, dear lady, this situation is different," Swaim said kindly, but firmly.

The moderator turned to Dr. Swaim. "You've been very patient, Dr. Swaim. In what way is this different?"

Swaim's original frown stole back onto his face as he began. His big body held an equally big voice, colored with a cultured, gentlemanly southern drawl which added an eloquence that caught at the ear.

"I've listened to our guests debate religion. And rightly so, because this is a religious forum." His big head dipped in acknowledgement of his surroundings. "Normally, a fella of my par-ticular way of thinking would be out of place in this arena. When I die, I expect nothing but the end. No judgment, just the end of life. I find the thought comforting." And he smiled, as if to prove his words true. "I don't believe in God, the Devil, heaven, hell, demons, angels, or the boogie man," his smiling face fell and his voice darkened, "but I find myself here, at this table. An active participant in a debate on religion, and I hate that I am here!"

He leaned forward, radiating outrage as he stared into the camera. "These pills have given the minds of these disturbed adolescents the ability to do just about anything. They are being called "Believing Pills" because it makes whatever you happen to believe in come true. Whether Black Rain believes in the Wiccan dogma is highly questionable based on her actions. I'd say that the girl surely believes in God. And then there's her brother Ryan and his new wife, Sky. They both believe in God. And if they believe in God, will that then make him real? If these 'chemically enhanced' children gaze up at the clouds and expect someone to be up there looking down, will he be there, simply because they believe he is?" His ugly but expressive face added to his words, further captivating his audience.

"And if these teens believe in hell, will that make hell real? And what if this girl, or her brother, or one of these other teens believe that when this fat, old man dies he will then be judged by God and rewarded or punished for all eternity?" Hanky in hand, Swaim reached up and wiped a sheen of sweat off his face. "Whether God existed yesterday may not matter if these teenagers make him real today."

He pursed his lips and arched the fat over his eyes where eyebrows would have been, "As an atheist, I find my peaceful death and quiet eternity in grave peril." He smiled wickedly. "But I am not alone in my predicament. What of all those Muslims, Hindus, Buddhists, and other religions? If the only way to get to this newly imagined God is by doing it the good old 'Baptist' 'Bible' 'way'," Swaim made air quotes with fat, pudgy fingers as he said each word, then stabbed an accusing finger at Renolds, "the way they grew up learning! Their pastor no doubt insisted his way was the only way, the *exclusive* way to get to heaven."

Swaim's big, resonant voice became a mocking representation of a hell-fire and brimstone preacher as he bellowed out, "BROAD is the way and WIDE is the gate that leads to destruction, and many there be that go in thereat! And narrow the way and straight be the gate that leads to life, and few there be that find it!" His impassioned mini sermon delivered, he smiled and summed up his point of view with a personal touch.

"It would seem that the rest of the world is in the same boat as this fat, old atheist. Tis not the Suwannee, the southern gentleman shall say, but the river Styx that now guides our way." He opined poetically in his close.

The camera panned out enough to reveal the utterly shocked faces of the moderator and Hellen Archer. Even Father Juan and Reverend Renolds looked somewhat shocked by Dr. Swaim's surprising and rather animated oration.

"That is a disturbing picture you paint, Dr. Swaim," said the moderator, clearly unsettled.

"I hate to say it," the fat man said, "but things would have been much simpler if these unfortunate children had died in that limo that blew up. This would have ended Wednesday."

"You're a vile monster!" cried Mrs. Archer, incensed. "You want Ryan Bryant dead because he might create heaven!"

"No, Mrs. Archer," Swaim replied gravely, "I would kill him with my own hands because he might create hell. The man that saved billions from an eternity of burning torment. I'll take that as my legacy." Swaim smiled at Archer wickedly as she withered under his gaze and the crushing weight of his logic.

"You're a witch, Mrs. Archer. If my fears are justified we shall be sharing the same fate. Perhaps we'll even be cell mates." He chuckled grimly. "Hell may have its small comforts yet," the fat man leered.

Archer paled visibly, eyes wide and unblinking, too shocked to respond.

Renolds and Father Juan began yelling at the same time.

The moderator tried to regain control of the group as the program cut to a commercial.

The Bryants and Sky were debating what they'd just seen when Lucius rushed through the front door of the trailer.

"Everyone to the bedroom now!" he shouted as he rushed through the room toward the bedroom. "Everyone comes! Everyone!" His words came from where he'd disappeared down the hall while "everyone" jumped up and pushed to follow.

"Move! Move! Move!" bellowed the professional soldiers as they urged the others along while they covered their retreat. In less than a minute they were all panting, standing inside the crowded storage room closet that had no business being behind Rain's bedroom door.

Once the door shut and they were waiting in the darkness, Mr. Bryant asked the question they all wanted to know. "What's happening out there?"

"Helicopters," Lucius said. He reached out and opened the door, a door that now opened to the kitchen storage hall in Amen Hale instead of the hallway in the Bryants' trailer. Lucius explained as they all stepped out into the hall.

"There were two helicopters coming in a little too low and a little too fast for my liking. It may have been news choppers, but it looked like an attack approach to me and to the sergeant up the pine tree across the street with a pair of good binoculars. May have been nothing," he confessed, "but I'm not risking it."

"Good!" Sky Dragon said. His eye ridges were locked into angry, downcast slants. "I wanted Sky home anyway. After what we just saw on the television I don't want her going anywhere. And now Mr. and Mrs. Bryant can talk to Rain and help with Ryan and Sky."

"I wonder if the trailer's still there," Mrs. Bryant fretted quietly.

"It's just an old trailer, hun," her husband comforted and gave her a squeeze. "I worry about those boys standing guard around the trailer. I hope they're all right."

Sky was stuck to Ryan's side, and he was holding her pressed tight to himself. Neither had said a word since jumping up from the couch.

"What on earth did you see on TV?" Lucius asked them.

Sky Dragon spoke up. "Humans are insane!" he growled. "Some Catholic religious leader called 'Pope' has people praying for grandfather God to judge Rain and the witches because they think she's a demon who doesn't believe in God, but the rest of the world wants Rain, David, Ryan, and my Sky dead because they do believe in grandfather God. This is bad, Lucius. Very bad."

Sky Dragon snapped his jaw shut and snorted an angry breath out his nostrils before continuing. It was a peculiar, dragonish gesture which was unlike Sky Dragon, who usually made every effort to look and act human.

"I'd be surprised if they didn't attack again soon. But this time we need to be ready." Sky Dragon's eyes began to glow a brighter red, as if he expected the attack to come at any second.

"The dragon's right, sir," said the big black soldier who also had one blacked out eye. Another man Rain had captured and let live because he'd agreed to serve her.

"I was standing behind the couch and saw the newscast. It was bad," said the soldier.

"Threat assessment?" Lucius asked the man.

He smiled. "A hundred percent, sir. We'll be hit within twenty-four hours. If I'm wrong I'll let Bull choke me out."

Bull chuckled.

Ryan laughed. "Oww!" he winced as he brought a hand up to his temple.

Sky Dragon growled.

They headed out of the hall, out to the kitchens of Amen Hale.

Chef Tanner

A Cheerful Heart

CHEF TANNER WALKED past the cooks, bakers, other chefs, and assistants who bustled about the busy kitchen until he reached the back wall. He'd been given the use of an isolated and out of the way upright freezer to house his special meat. Tanner had just extracted a human leg and kicked the cooler shut when people started to emerge from the storage hall in the back of the kitchen.

Tanner stood there, the weighty severed limb held in the crook of his two arms as the group stood there, gawking, and in obvious dismay at the grisly sight that greeted them.

"Can I give you a hand with that?" Ryan asked, totally straight faced and serious for a moment before he burst out laughing. He collapsed to the floor of the kitchen, both hands grasping his head, pressing in, as if his head would burst if he didn't hold himself together. Laughing as he writhed. Mad, insane laughter.

He was still laughing and crying in pain as they carried him out.

Chef Tanner hadn't laughed at the time, but he did later. He laughed quietly off and on for the rest of the day. Those working with him would hear him mutter, "Can I give you a hand with that?" And he'd start to laugh again, shaking his head, smiling, taking pleasure in life's little surprises. He muttered and laughed and smiled as he cut and flayed and brazed and broiled and baked human flesh.

The Hillmans

Making the Best of Things

"OH MY GOD, Mike, look out my side, there's nothing left!" Hanna Hillman told her husband as the helicopter they'd been rushed into climbed higher into the air.

Mike leaned across his two youngest daughters and looked out the window beside his wife. Below, the blasted remains of the Bryants' trailer and the remains of the helicopter that had crashed into it were still smoldering. He spotted a trail of fire trucks and ambulances heading in their direction, lights flashing as they came. The helicopter lurched forward, and Mike settled back into his seat.

Only moments ago he'd been sitting in his own living room with Hanna and the girls, watching the news, when they had heard a huge explosion. A minute later, soldiers were pounding on the front door of their trailer telling them they needed to get into a helicopter that was landing in the field by the Park Clubhouse.

The FBI man sitting beside the pilot shouted back to them, "The soldiers on the ground think they got away before the blast. There are no bodies inside the trailer."

He was holding his hand cupped over his earbud, trying to hear his phone conversation over the roar of the helicopter.

"Where'd they go? Amen Hale?" Mike shouted back.

"We think so."

By reflex, Mike looked around at his family, wondering not for the first time what he'd do if he lost them. His two youngest daughters sat huddled between him and Hanna, holding onto each other. What would happen now? What would they do? Who was after the Bryants? And would those same people come after him and his girls or Mary next?

"Where are you taking us?" Mike shouted up to the FBI agent.

"We can place you in a safe house until we're sure things have settled down and you can obtain some safer housing than that trailer. We have safe houses all over the country."

Hanna Hillman shouted up to the man, "Can you take us to Amen Hale?"

The agent looked back at her. His face said what he thought of the idea but his mouth said, "Yes ma'am, if you want. But I doubt it would be any safer there than the Bryants' trailer was. And it's not a place I'd want to take my children. Especially my young, beautiful daughters," the man added with a straight face, then said, "It's your call."

Mike and Hanna had a quick whispered discussion and came to the same conclusion quickly.

"You got a safe house in Hawaii? Or Key West maybe?" asked Mike.

"Hawaii! Hawaii! Hawaii!" Kaylee and April both started to shout.

"I want one of those magic doors installed so Mary can come visit whenever she feels like it," Hanna said, face set in stubborn lines Mike was all too familiar with. "She'd enjoy seeing Hawaii too. And so would Bethany."

Her husband gave her a helpless face. "Woman! I don't think they sell those things at Home Depot yet."

"I don't care. I want one."

"Yes dear. Soon as we get there and get settled I'll get on it."

Katie Linn

Bunnies

MARCIA CASTILLO'S GRADUATE thesis had been grandly titled "Manipulation and Pacification of Mentally Challenged Adolescents." It went into her file. It helped her get to where she now sat. The only female in an exclusive men's club.

She sat between two of those "men," both older than her by thirty years. She was a valued and trusted part of the team. Marcia was proud of herself. The three of them were in the observation room, seated in expensive and quite comfortable leather chairs, peering through a massive ten by four foot section of one way, see through glass observing two of the teens.

The other side of the dark room in which they sat was filled with dozens and dozens of monitors, showing every inch of the facility from cameras located in every room. Troy Dyal, the facility director, sat on Marcia's right while Dr. Ogburn sat on her left. Ogburn was a psychiatrist who'd been deeply imbedded in government projects for so long he jokingly said that he was little better off than the teens they were holding, only he was standing on this side of the glass.

"Some jobs you can't walk away from once you reach a certain level of trust," Ogburn had told her after she'd been added to the team.

Marcia tried not to take it as a threat, but as advice. If she stayed too long and worked too deep she'd be in the same boat. The thought of that amount of trust being hoisted upon her young shoulders didn't bother her in the least. Ogburn's job was to study and supervise the other researchers, who were working directly with the teens who'd taken Dr. Burgis's mind-altering drugs. Dyal's job was to keep them secure and safely under control. Marcia's job was both simple and simply impossible.

She was the pretty face for an ugly place. She was supposed to keep the teens "manipulated" and "pacified," but that was incredibly hard to do when she couldn't force them to take their meds or impose other, harsher control measures. It was further complicated by the lack of environmental control.

They had two teens in isolation and four in a communal group, Katie Linn, Susan Palamino, Shikith Bowls, and Alfred Freeman were housed together. The girls were no problem, but Alfred had become a huge a problem. Along with his dangerous, physical abilities he also found ingenious ways to listen in or otherwise ferret out information that should have been shielded from the group. Thanks to Alfred, some of that sensitive information caused a complete meltdown yesterday. Any trust and good will Marcia had managed to accumulate turned inside out.

Of course, finding the hidden cameras in the bathrooms this morning hadn't helped, especially since Marcia had sworn to the girls just yesterday that there were no cameras in the bathrooms. It was incredibly hard to recover from that type of blatant betrayal. The group was now convinced that they'd been lied to and were nothing but prisoners – which of course they were – but Marcia's job, the aforementioned "manipulation" and "pacification," had become a lot more challenging now that her subjects knew that they were being manipulated and pacified.

Dyal and Ogburn had been intensely concerned that Alfred would make an escape attempt after yesterday's incident, and they'd concocted what they believed was a brilliant plan to guide the event. This morning they attempted to lure Alfred into attempting a prison break under controlled and safe conditions. It backfired horribly. Alfred hadn't cooperated with any of their designs. The attempt ended with one of their own guards losing control of himself and trying to kill Alfred and killing another guard instead.

Alfred hadn't tried to escape, but after provoking him so thoroughly they all agreed that it was time to move him into solitary confinement and further restrict his freedom. He was angry and dangerous. Of course he had every right to be angry. But as all the teens now knew, they no longer had any RIGHTS.

"She's painting that rabbit again," droned Dyal.

It was Katie's third outlined rabbit in the Rec Room where the teens spent most of their time. Earlier she'd painted one of the unusual rabbits on the outside of the two-way glass. The rabbits were always left empty, painted only in outline. When Marcia asked about the peculiar outline style, Katie informed her that the rabbit was invisible, and that therefore the only way to paint him was to trace around him.

"She's painted that rabbit in every room she's been in today. What do you make of that, Dr. Ogburn?" asked Dyal.

"Just being herself," Dr. Ogburn answered. "Katie is the only true schizophrenic in your group. The rest are troubled, but Katie's a horse of a different color. She should improve after Sunday when she's back on her meds."

"Katie seems calm and responsive today," Marcia commented as she looked through the glass at her charges. "And her word salad wasn't too pronounced when I spoke with her earlier. What I'd love to hear is your theories on Susan's change in attitude. She hasn't cussed at a guard since last night, when she and Katie had their unusual midnight chant meeting under the blanket. And I haven't been spit at all day, and that's got me worried." Marcia sounded disappointed.

Dyal and Ogburn couldn't help but laugh. Susan did love to spit at Marcia.

"I agree," said Dr. Ogburn. "Her good behavior is out of character. With what happened yesterday she should be acting out. And we have the odd resurgence of her musical abilities to consider and her detached, almost intoxicated state. I don't think it's imagined either. I've been watching her closely and she's not faking it."

The three of them looked through the glass, eyeing the subject of their discussion. Susan was sitting on top of the pool table in the Rec Room scribbling in her notebook with a couple of instruments scattered around on the green felt.

Ogburn continued his analysis. "It seems that the effect of these pills may ebb and resurge. Once these new areas inside the brain are stimulated it may be impossible to completely shut them down again. It doesn't bode well for releasing them any time soon. Even Shikith may have a resurgence and redevelop dangerous abilities. I wish we'd taken another MRI yesterday while Susan was in her downturn."

"Dr. Tachi will not allow another MRI so soon," Marcia reminded him.

"Tachi," Ogburn grumbled.

Dr. Tachi was an outside (non-government) physician who'd been tasked with the teens' welfare and medical treatment. At times Marcia was truly glad to have the man around when her conscience became unsettled, but at other times, like when he refused to let her use the mood-altering drugs she wanted, she found the man's intervention a pain. Tachi had argued that the teens' systems needed a few days to clear the drugs Dr. Burgis had been giving them, and that any pills they introduced this soon might have harmful interactions.

"When will you extract Alfred?" Ogburn asked Dyal.

"Five. Shift change. We'll be able to double the guards throughout the facility just in case. We'll also chip him again and that's sure to be a fight unless he's unconscious."

"Will the guards shoot to kill if he tries to escape?" Marcia asked.

"Yes," was Dyal's short reply.

Katie finished her third rabbit. It was an outline. This one painted in profile with one ear up and attentive and the other drooping. She gathered her paints and other junk into her shoulder bag and shuffled over to the lunch table. She picked up two bottles of water, walked across the hall to the small kitchen, opened the tops and dumped the water into the sink, rinsed the bottles, then filled them both with water from the tap.

"What are you doing, Katie?" came the flat monotone voice from the intercom.

She ignored the voice and the queer look from the guard who stood by the door as she shuffled back into the Rec Room and up to the lunch table. It was eleven, but Katie was still wearing her pajamas.

Another guard standing by the table spoke to her. "Why are you still in your PJs, Katie girl? Shouldn't you go get dressed?"

Katie looked at the man and frowned.

"Pajamas. Pajamas. Pajamas. Why change my pajamas? Do the dirty, old men want to see me naked again?"

"No!" he answered, shocked and embarrassed. The man's eyes turned accusingly toward the one way, see through glass. Most of the guards were unaware of the shower and bathroom cameras until yesterday.

Katie fired more questions, all run together, in a rushed unbroken chain. "Are my parents coming to see me? Because I know they want to see me. And they should be able to see me. It doesn't make any sense not to let them see me. Why you won't let them see me? I'll change and let the dirty, old men see me if that means my parents can see me. So, are my parents coming to see me? Are they? Are they? Are they?" Katie demanded.

"Well, not yet, honey." the guard answered sadly.

"Am I going anywhere?"

"No," the guard answered, then turned and walked away, not wanting to face her or her questions.

Katie gave his back an angry glare and turned back to the lunch table. She grabbed two tuna salad sandwiches and dropped them into the huge bowl of salad meant for the entire group. She chucked the bottles of water into the bowl of salad as well. Then she picked up the whole bowl and drug her feet over to the pool table.

"Susan," Katie called to her.

Susan didn't look up. She was sitting Indian style in the middle of the pool table, scribbling in her notebook.

Katie threw a cherry tomato at her.

"Hey!" Susan shouted, her head snapping up.

"Time to take our food. Let's go, go, go," Katie told her and pointed with her head toward the door.

Susan got an odd expression. "Time to? But we just—"

She got beamed with another cherry tomato.

Surprisingly Susan sat there and blinked. She was silent and pliant, not cursing and violent. She got down off the pool table, and Katie pushed the bowl into her arms, turned, and headed out of the room. Susan followed along behind her carrying the bowl of salad without a word. She didn't ask, "What's up with this big freakin' salad?" Or "Why the hell did you throw a tomato at me?" Or even, "Where the hell are we going?" She followed without question. This was strange behavior for both girls, too purposeful and directed. Too assertive for Katie, and too accepting, cooperative, and pliant for Susan.

The black door (one down from the Rec Room) opened suddenly and Marcia came rushing out. She quickly caught up to Katie and Susan and matched their pace, walking beside them as they headed down the hall.

"Katie, Susan, you girls going to go eat in your room?" she asked sweetly.

When they didn't respond, Marcia asked, "Can I join you?"

Katie stopped and her salad-toting shadow stopped as well. Susan stayed quiet as Katie dug into her art bag and came out with a pen then reached over and grabbed one of Marcia's hands. She turned it over and began to draw on the back of her hand and wrist. Marcia let her draw, fascinated by the odd behavior. Katie looked intense as she concentrated on her work; each movement of her hand was perfect and quick. In only two minutes a tiny piece of art was born on the back of Marcia's right hand. A bunny with dark little eyes.

"Ooh! One of your rabbits. And it's so beautiful! I can't believe you did it so fast. Thank you, Katie, that's so very sweet!" Marcia beamed as she admired the bunny, her tone overly complimentary, as if Katie were a little child who needed to be praised more than anything else in the world.

"Not sweet. Mean. Mean like you! Crunch! Crunch! Crunch!" Katie bit the angry words at her, snapping her teeth at her, her face pinched and fierce.

Marcia snatched her hand away and took a step back. Katie had been her most passive charge, and she was astounded to see a spark of true hate in her eyes, but even more troubling were the eyes themselves. They were glassy and unfocused. It reminded Marcia that Katie was dangerous in ways unlike other children, as were all the teens in this facility. The thought stiffened her resolve. This was why Katie was here. Why they were all here. They weren't stable, and she had her job to do. Trying to build from zero was possible, but not if you didn't do anything. She plowed ahead with faked emotional distress.

"Please, Katie! I didn't know about the cameras in the bathroom and shower! Honest! I've told them not to do that anymore. It was a horrible invasion of your privacy!" Marcia added some tears to her efforts.

Katie turned to her salad-toting follower.

"Spit on her!" she ordered.

Susan had her arms wrapped around the big salad bowl, but she reared back obediently, preparing a good juicy projectile. Marcia turned away and retreated before she caught it in the face. She still caught it, just not in the face.

The two girls proceeded down the hall and into Katie's room. Her room was one massive, art studio with dozens of projects in various states of completion from one end to the other. Katie dropped her art bag and made a beeline for the wire frame bunny she'd constructed that morning.

The bunny was shaped out of four, wire clothes hangers. She'd used a pair of sculpting tongs to bend the metal ingeniously, crafting a wire frame rabbit. Katie grabbed the bunny and dropped him into the salad bowl, like an ingredient in her own insane salad.

Susan followed Katie over to her bed and both girls sat, facing each other at the foot of the bed with the bowl of salad placed between them. Katie took a tuna sandwich and a bottle of water out of the bowl and set in on the right-hand side. Then the other sandwich and water bottle went on the left. She took a couple of minutes to balance the bunny in the middle of his bed of salad to her liking. It looked like three people sitting down to lunch. Katie, Susan, and the bunny. When those tasks were complete, she reached to the bed behind her and dragged the end of her thick comforter off the bed and covered herself and Susan letting their backs make the outside corners for their own little tent.

"Well, now we know who the salad was for, her bunny," Marcia sighed as she stared at the bank of monitors displaying three angles of Katie's room. "I didn't think Katie had it in her to be so—*angry*." She looked up and noticed the two older, leather necked men eyeing her and she hardened instantly. "Her eyes were glassy again!" she fired at them, going on the offensive. "If I didn't know better I'd swear she was taking something. Maybe that's what they're up to under that stupid blanket!" she muttered defiantly. "I want Tachi to run her blood this afternoon."

"Don't let her anger unsettle you, Marcia," Mr. Dyal said. "We knew they'd be upset after yesterday. The anger I understand, but this behavior doesn't seem normal. I wonder if it's schizophrenic nonsense or if there's some purpose to her actions. Maybe she is up to something under that damn blanket." He arched an eyebrow and played with the controls as he zoomed the camera in on the thick spread covering the two girls.

"I wouldn't worry too much," Ogburn said. "Katie's suspicious. Which explains the water. She thinks we're trying to drug her. And come Sunday there will be drugs in the food. And she's no doubt very angry about the cameras as Marcia mentioned. Katie values her privacy. And now she feels unsafe, betrayed, and threatened, so she's grabbed a friend she feels she can trust and went to hide under a blanket. All these pieces of crazy make perfect sense to trained eyes, Dyal. You've got enough on your plate for today; focus on Alfred and Benjamin."

"Have they made a final decision on Benjamin Grant?" Marcia asked.

"Yes. We'll do that tonight as well," said Dyal. "If all goes well with Alfred," he added cautiously.

"I won't be sad to see it done," Marcia said firmly. She'd worked with Benjamin only the first night he'd arrived, and that was more than enough. She still had purple bruises on her arms from where he'd held her and forced a kiss from her before letting go. She refused to go near him, especially after he attacked the female soldier yesterday. He'd grabbed her and pulled her into an unused room before anyone could stop him.

Once they forced opened the door and the other guards saw what he'd done, two of the men had opened fire, both with pistols. The bullets seemed to hurt him at first, but the more they fired, the less effect they had. Backup arrived and Benjamin cooperated, walking to an isolation cell with his hands up, covered by soldiers armed with flame throwers and toxic gas guns.

"According to Dr. Burgis's nurse, he was an amoral monster before he took the pills," Ogburn mused.

"Doesn't matter now," Dyal said. "He's too dangerous to let live and the decision's been made. But I must say, Tachi surprised me. I didn't think he'd be able to make a call like that. Especially this early." Dyal stood up and frowned at the two-way glass where the bunny was painted on the reverse side. Removing paint from two way glass was bound to cause problems.

"I hope she gets off the rabbit fixation soon. She's painting up the walls. The place is going to look like a daycare," Dyal complained.

"Bullet holes and bunnies," Marcia mused darkly. "I don't think it will be mistaken for a daycare, Mr. Dyal."

Cathryn

A Mother's Work Is Never Done

PENNY CAREFULLY HANDED the sacrificial blade to Queen Cathryn.

"Thank you, Penny." Cathryn smiled at the girl. "Now go down to the kitchen and tell Chef Tanner that Bethany will be down shortly to eat her lunch, and tell Chef Andre that we will all dine at the High Table. When Bethany comes down, sit with her and keep her company. That's all. Please send Merrit in on your way down. He's the guard standing out in the hall."

"Yes, Queen Cathryn." Penny turned to go but her eyes flicked back to the gleaming blade in Cathryn's hand, then to Bethany, who lay asleep on the couch. Her brow creased in worry as she slipped from the room, wondering why the Queen had called for the blade if Bethany was asleep.

Penny hadn't been the only one giving the blade a curious stare. In Izzy's case it was a hungry stare. Izzy had been excited since Cathryn mentioned using blood to wake Bethany from her magic-induced sleep. Izzy, and Lizzy to a lesser extent, had a desire to cut themselves. Izzy was a serious cutter. A suicidal cutter. She'd tried to kill herself many times over the years, and she'd succeeded once since coming to Amen Hale. After Bethany had raised her from the dead, Cornelius cast a spell upon her and bound her by it. Izzy could no longer cut herself. Now, if she wanted to be cut, she had to come and ask the Queen to do it for her. In this way she had a safe outlet. And as Cornelius had explained it to Cathryn, "Who else could I trust to put a blade to one of our girls?"

Merrit entered the room, taking in the disturbing scene there in the parlor as he went to his knees before Cathryn. "Queen Cathryn, Penny said you wanted me?"

"Yes, Merrit. Would you please tell the Prison Keeper to ready a man for Bethany and have him taken to The Hallow. She'll be there as soon as she's done with lunch."

Merrit hesitated, his eyes lingering on different points. There was no shortage of troubling sights to snare the eye. Last night's rumors had spread through all Amen Hale that the Queen had gone mad with grief at the loss of Rain. Cathryn knew about the rumors, and she saw that fear mirrored in Merrit's eyes as he stared at the blade in her hand.

Just then a particularly loud scream came from the bedroom, followed by a rumbling growl that had to be Rain because even the air in the room on this side of the door seemed to vibrate.

"Stand still, Child of Hale." Cathryn told the now half-panicked guard who looked as if he wanted to go check on the bedroom to see who'd been stabbed. "What's happening in there is not for your eyes to see. And Bethany is asleep. She's be-spelled, and I'll wake her soon. The blade is for me and the twins, and the cutting we do will not be fatal. Be at peace. Now go and see the Prison Keeper," Cathryn made that last a firmly worded order, not a request.

"Yes, Queen Cathryn," Merrit replied obediently.

Cathryn could still see the tightness in his eyes as he shut the door. Word had indeed spread of her condition.

"Hanna," she called to one of the two maids who lingered at the edges of the room, ready to serve.

"My Queen." She rushed forward and knelt.

"Stand outside the door. Keep everyone out. I will have no distractions while I hold a blade to flesh that I love."

"Yes, my Queen," she replied instantly. Cathryn was pleased to see no trace of doubt in Hanna's eyes as she went to the door.

"Izzy—"

"Yes!" She shot out the word before Cathryn could start her sentence. Izzy sat on the edge of her chair, her gaze locked onto the blade. Her right hand (her knife-wielding hand) rubbed and massaged her left wrist which wore a latticework of scars from past cutting. After escaping from the sexual tension in the bedroom, all that pent-up energy seemed to have shifted to darker needs in Izzy.

But Cathryn had important things to say before she began any blade-work, no matter how "ready" Izzy was to be cut.

"Izzy," Cathryn began again, her voice firmer, to get her attention.

Izzy met her gaze, looking away from the blade.

"Lizzy," she added to make sure the other girl knew she was included in what she was about to say.

"I know that you'll enjoy what I'm about to do. But I don't want you to think that this is all that I have in store for you when you come to me for release."

Release. The mysterious word said so little. It was like a blank check for the mind. Izzy and Lizzy turned to each other and shared one of those inexplicable twin moments, identical expressions staring into identical faces and thinking identical thoughts before looking back to Cathryn, heads tilted at identical angles.

"We need to wake Bethany. This will be a quick, simple thing. But when you come to me in need, what will be done will be done for you. To meet your needs and not another's. And it will not be simple."

Lizzy's face showed distaste but her eyes still honed in on the blade Cathryn held. She looked as if she hated it but longed for it as the same time.

"Lizzy, do you want to join your sister in this?" Cathryn asked her.

"I've never cut myself just for me," Lizzy said. "Izzy's done it to us lots of times, but I've never done it." She gave her sister a guilty glance at this small declaration of independence then looked back to Cathryn.

"I'm scared," she confessed.

"Scared of what, Liz?" Izzy asked her sister softly.

"What if I like it!?" Lizzy complained, not happy at the likely possibility.

Cathryn knew it was a moot point. This desire was born in Lizzy when she was pulled from her sister's soul. But she didn't go into those facts. She was gentle with Lizzy, guiding things, while seeming to guide nothing at all.

"It's not all bad, Lizzy," Cathryn assured her. "There is good that can come of this too. If you find pleasure in it, then you will understand your sister more, and you'll be able to share in this part of her life. But this is simply solved. Just watch us," Cathryn gave both girls a reassuring smile, "and if you want to join me and Izzy, then join us, my daughter."

"Us?" Lizzy said. "You're going to cut yourself too!"

"Mother," Izzy cut in. For the first time the word 'mother' sounded natural in her mouth. "Can we get started?" She twitched impatiently in her chair.

Cathryn nodded, looked down to Bethany's sleeping body stretched out on the couch, and frowned.

"Damn. I'd hate to ruin the couch."

"Would you like her moved to the floor, your Majesty?" asked Beth who hovered nearby, ready to serve her needs.

"Please, Beth. And maybe a few towels for the floor," Cathryn suggested as she looked at her plush, white carpet with worry.

She was about to cut herself with Izzy and Lizzy, but Cathryn was already bleeding on the inside. She was putting on a brave face but she was hurting. Rain's return had restored a measure of hope, but not enough. What she'd endured last night had broken her, and she did not feel whole in body or mind. Losing a child was worse than all the hell her mother had put her through as a child. Worse than losing Cornelius. Worse than any pain she could have ever imagined.

She'd always wanted children and dreamed of what it would be like to have a child to love. She wanted to keep them safe, keep them happy, keep them fed. Those maternal instincts surged within her. She wanted to heal them when they hurt, to hold them when then needed to be held, to counsel them when they needed her wisdom.

But when she stared down at Rain's empty, soulless body she knew that she was going to lose them all. One by one they'd kill themselves, be murdered, or be taken from her. Last night she'd lain in bed wearing a determined face for those of her children whom she could deceive. Mary could feel the complete loss of all hope, and she cried and did the same. Jane and Dan could see in her eyes and face the abandonment of any thought beyond a rudimentary, miserly hoarding as she gathered her remaining children into her bed.

She'd practically bitten poor Cornelius's head off when he tried to crawl into bed, and she'd not have allowed him in if not for Bethany's weeping for her father. Cathryn despised her own weakness. She never wanted to lose hope like that again. She had more than one child and she loved them all. She wanted to fight to the last so long as even one remained alive.

She was thinking again. Functioning again. Taking care of her children and planning again.

As a mother, she felt satisfied with the morning's accomplishments.

A little orgy to keep Rain too busy to even dream of running away or hurting herself, to feed Jane and Dan, to feed Emma, and to entertain Alana and Mary.

A little blood to wake one be-spelled child. Easily done.

A little cutting to help satisfy the self-destructive desires of two more of her children. Also, easily done.

And for herself, a little cutting, and some of Bethany's special attention to fix what was torn inside, so she could love her children more and never again give in to despair.

So long as one lived, her soul lived.

Black Rain

A Lion Lying with Lambs

ALANA RODE DAN'S body in the bed beside me. Dan held his hands up for her to hold onto for support as she labored, moving and working at her own pace and guiding her own pleasure. She was so close to where I lay her knee pressed up against my ribs. I was close enough to touch them, so I did.

I ran my hand up the length of her leg, feeling her toned muscles strain and flex as she lifted her body up and down the length of him. My hand slipped down and in between the two of them with my palm up and stopped with Dan's shaft resting between the V of my middle and index fingers. I felt the rise and fall of flesh, up and down, up and down. The sound of her flesh slapping my palm, the sticky moment as that flesh pulled away from my hand and Dan's body, rising up for another satisfying plunge back down and another smack of flesh to hand. My hand.

I watched as Jane slipped up behind Alana and wrapped her arms around her. She moved up and down with her for a while as her hands roved over Alana's thin athletic frame, but soon she rose up to Alana's neck. Alana's jewel eyes snapped open wide as she felt Jane there, and she settled down, trapping my hand between her flesh and Dan's body. She was trembling and her blue eyes shone brighter as Jane pulled her head back enough to kiss her before moving back down to her neck again.

Alana had stopped moving, but Dan began to move now, thrusting himself in and out of Alana, gliding up and down between my fingers and into her body faster and faster. And then Jane bit down, sinking her teeth into her neck and Alana screamed at the ceiling and wrapped her arms around Jane's head, holding her to her neck as below her Dan growled, thrusting up, his body stiffening as he came. I felt the pulsing of his shaft as his sperm rushed into Alana's body.

Dan's eyes stared up into Jane's burning red eyes as she drank from Alana's neck, and the look they shared as they shared her body and blood was too intimate. I had to look away. For some odd reason I needed to give the three of them some privacy, so I extracted my hand that held a little extra "Dan" on it and I turned to my left side.

Mary lay on the other side of my body writhing in pleasure at what I was do-ing to her, or what my tail was doing to her. Her eyes were closed, a smile on her face. I wondered what she was feeling and if I was hitting the right spot. I wasn't as experienced as Mary. I didn't know for sure. I let Mary's thoughts slip into my mind, and I found myself in two places at once.

"two places at once" (two places at once) "two places at once" (two places at once) "two places at once"

My own thoughts echoed back and circled again and again as Mary listened to my thoughts and I heard her listening to my thoughts, back and forth.

"Hello, my Lion" (Hello, my Lion) "Hello, my Lion" (Hello, my Lion) "Hello, my Lion" (Hello, my Lion)

Mary's thoughts became mine then echoed back again.

I laughed at the strangeness, and my own laugh echoed around between the two of us. Mary laughed as well, between whimpers and grunts, as my tail was still hard at work and seemed doggedly determined to make her scream. Our thoughts continued to echo, over and over, until I shielded myself from hearing the echo, which also helped Mary.

"Oh that's better," she purred beside me.

I heard her thoughts, but what I wanted was her feelings so I could know if I was hitting exactly as I should. The feelings of her body slipped into my mind as if I'd put on a second skin and I began to feel my own body, plus everything Mary felt. My tail adjusted itself automatically as it tapped into this new treasure trove of information and redoubled its efforts until it was making both of us twist and squirm. I felt Mary's body as if it were my own, so I felt my own tail pushing in and out of her as if it were pushing in and out of me! I felt the tail and moved the tail, but there were times (like this) when my tail seemed to have a very determined mind of its own.

"Oh my God!" Mary screamed and writhed and swore as she had her orgasm, but my tail didn't relent as it moved and adjusted and drove for more. "Oh SHIT! RAIN! SHIT!" Mary cried.

"MAAARY!" I cried as I felt her and came with her, squirming right beside her.

Mary felt my orgasm and I felt hers and mine—which meant she felt mine, and hers again! (a second time for the same bit of magic!) and then I felt her doubling down on her happy, which set me off again with a whole new orgasm which only complicated things further!

"OOh! Rain, the damn thing's not stopping!" Mary shouted between stuttered pants and screams.

"Oh, Oh, Oh, Oh, Oh TAIL! Stop! Stop! Stop! Stop!" I cried and begged as I came with Mary again as our orgasms echoed back and forth as our thoughts had only moments earlier, trapping us in a twisting knot of cussing, pulsing writhing screams as we came over and over and OVER AND OVER AND OVER!

"THERE!" Emma growled as she yanked my tail out of Mary's body like you'd snatch a power cord out of a wall socket.

Mary and I collapsed onto the bed and lay there gasping and panting. As soon as I was able to form a lucid thought, I pulled my senses back into just my own flesh while I had the opportunity. My tail started to snake its way through the sheets, back toward Mary's opening, and Emma grabbed it again.

"Hey! Stay the hell outta there! Bad tail!" she scolded it. "Go play somewhere else!" She pitched it over her shoulder then looked down at Mary who lay there like a dead body, limbs spread out like limp spaghetti, eyes closed, her whole body covered in a glistening sheen of sweet sweat as she breathed in and out.

Emma stared down at Mary's body and liked what she saw. I noticed the hungry gleam in her copper gold eyes. I looked over and saw a smile spread on Mary's lips. Her eyes were closed, and she panted in complete exhaustion, but Emma was touching her so she knew what Emma was thinking.

Mary rallied her strength enough to move her legs up and spread herself in the exact way Emma must have been fantasizing about. Mary was amazing in bed because she knew your thoughts and knew exactly what you wanted, and she did it, exactly as you liked it. Her pleasure was self-assured because she felt your pleasure and satisfaction as her own so it was a win/win for Mary, who also experienced her own body's pleasure as a bonus.

Emma lowered herself to Mary and took my tail's spot with her mouth, but then she gasped and reared up, eyes wide with shocked surprise! My tail had found a new place to crawl into and I smiled at Emma as I felt it explore her body.

I felt all of it. And all of it felt good.

My new skin was extremely sensitive; even casual touches felt sexual and pleasurable, but erotic touches quickly brought me to that strange moment when pleasure overrode all the senses as everything being done in and through and to my body made my flesh sing or shout or shake or laugh or even cry. It seemed like I had a variety of different responses in this moment of release, and I found that I enjoyed all of them.

I'd lost track of how many of these moments I'd had since Dan first pushed his teeth into my neck while Jane took advantage of her portion of body that she'd bargained for. For some time I'd had two or three people touching me, holding me, kissing me, sucking on my breasts, running their tongue up and down the length of my body or into my body.

I rested and listened to the sounds of pleasure around me; the only part of my body touching anyone was my naughty tail, but even my tail seemed sated. It rested inside Emma's body, not disturbing her too much while she took advantage of Mary in her weakened and worn out condition. Tail had the right idea and I did the same. I lay back and stretched and purred like a contented cat as all around me in the bed my lovers made noises that made me smile.

Mr. and Mrs. Bryant

One Cut Too Many

R YAN LAY ON the floor of the kitchen, clutching his head, laughing, then moaning in pain as Sky and Sky Dragon knelt beside him.

"Where is Princess Rain!?" Lucius shouted, then looked around for anyone who could answer the question among the crowd of stunned workers.

"I believe they are still in the Queen's bedroom, if not on their way down for lunch," replied Chef Tanner as he stood there, still holding the human leg he'd taken from the freezer. "I was told they would be dining at the High Table shortly."

"I'll carry him," Sky Dragon said as he scooped Ryan up into his arms and rushed out of the nightmare kitchen. Mr. and Mrs. Bryant, Lucius, Sky, and most of the security team followed them out, scattering the people in their wake as they stampeded through the Cathedral Hall.

Before they gained the stair the front doors blew open, admitting a raging mass of swirling, angry clouds that had two, burning, red eyes.

"Sky!" Believer's deep voice rumbled, obviously relieved that she was alive.

"Ryan's hurt! We need Rain!" she shouted as she followed Sky Dragon up the stairs with the others.

Believer's shape defined as he glided thorough the Entry Hall, arms and legs becoming distinguishable from the mass of clouds as he joined the others already heading up the stairs. As they reached the top of the stairs and rushed down the hall, a tingling, crawling sensation began to slide across their skin like the disciplined marching of little, magical ants. The feeling grew stronger as they crew closer to Cathryn and Cornelius's bedroom door.

Hanna, one of the maids, stood outside the door, her arms spread out and blocking the entry.

"Ryan's been hurt! Open the door!" Sky Dragon shouted to her and gestured with his dragon head for her to get out of the way.

Hanna stood her ground. "The Queen bade me let no one pass! She's cutting on the twins and needs to be careful with the blade!"

"Get out of the way!" Mrs. Bryant shouted at Hanna.

"Stand aside, Hanna!" ordered Sky Dragon, grimacing as Sky's panic and Ryan's condition pushed at him.

Hanna looked stricken with indecision herself, but still her feet remained resolutely planted before the door.

"Allow me, my brother." Believer spoke and stepped forward. He stopped before Hanna, settled himself, and backed up. Cornelius slipped out of Believer's cloudy body, deposited there before the door looking a little off balance. He gave his damp clothes a shake and ran a hand through his wet hair.

"Well, that was certainly quicker than walking, but next time a little warning would be appreciated before you swallow me," he complained conversationally as he surveyed the scene with Hanna guarding the door and Ryan hurt and lying in Sky Dragon's arms.

"Make her move so we can take Ryan to Rain!" ordered Mrs. Bryant.

"She's cutting the twins, my King. Queen Cathryn ordered me to keep the door safe while she did so," Hanna told him quickly.

"Is that Bethany's magic?" Sky Dragon asked.

"Is it?" Cornelius looked at the door, suddenly worried. "Why do I feel Bethany's magic?"

Ryan moaned and Sky and Ryan's mother shouted at the same time. "Open the door!"

"Right away, ladies," Cornelius complied. "Excuse us, Hanna," he asked politely.

Hanna quickly stepped aside, glad to be out of the way.

Mrs. Bryant rudely blew past Cornelius, throwing the door open and rushing inside, but she froze only a few paces in, as did everyone who entered behind her. They piled up like a traffic jam in the small foyer as they surveyed the scene.

Bethany sat on the floor with Cathryn in her lap, holding her upright with one arm wrapped around her shoulders to steady her. She and Catheryn were both covered in blood. Izzy and Lizzy were lying on the floor a few feet away, passed out or dead. Scattered beneath the group were dozens of white towels, many specked and some completely soaked through with various shades of mottled red. The ruined, white towels looked like bandages covering wounds on the pristine, white floor.

Bethany's eyes watched the group as they charged into the room, but she didn't stop licking at the ten-inch gash that ran down the length of Cathryn's left arm. The grizzly scene silenced everyone, and they remained silent as Lucius stepped forward and knelt beside Izzy and pressed a finger to her neck.

"She's alive," he announced, sounding surprised as he eyed the amount of blood on the floor. He did the same for Lizzy and nodded again.

Cathryn's eyes were closed and she swayed unsteadily as Bethany continued to play with her blood. They all watched as Bethany licked her way up the gash again, collecting the fresh welling with her mouth which she then spat into her cupped palm. She lifted her hand and rubbed the blood through her hair as if she were applying hair gel. Her actions had a certain feline quality to them as she groomed with the blood.

"Bethany, what are you doing to your mother?" Cornelius asked carefully.

"I'm eating my mother's sins," her sweet, little voice answered. If spoken by another child, of another mother, in another place, those words would have come out as "I'm combing my mother's hair" or "I'm painting my mother's nails". But Bethany Grave was the Red Witch, her mother was the Bloody Queen, and they lived in Amen Hale.

Cornelius remained calm and took it all in stride. "What happened to the twins?" he asked.

"They needed to be cut, so Mom cut them. But one cut didn't do it for them." Bethany frowned down at the two unconscious, greedy girls. "They begged and begged, so she cut them again and again, but the fourth or fifth time was so deep I had to heal them or they would have died." She shrugged. "Cathryn and I played in their blood for a while as they watched. They liked it. They liked to watch us play. It was kinda—different." Bethany didn't look like she wanted to explain how. "I let them get as close to dead as I dared before I healed them. They weren't scared at all." She furled her blood caked brow and shook her head. "I'd of been scared out of my mind." She made a funny face and then laughed at her own wit. No one else laughed but she didn't seem to notice.

"Before they passed out they asked me to leave them the scars if I could."

"Why?" Cornelius asked, then winced, wishing he'd kept his mouth shut instead of asking for more details.

"They said they wanted to be able to touch the scars later and remember the cuts. The twins really are crazy," the bloody, little girl declared, nodding her head sagely, as if she were a paragon of mental stability herself. Then she licked at the blood that had welled from Cathryn's arm while she'd been distracted, making a satisfied "mmm" sound at the red bounty she found waiting for her.

"Stop it, Bethany! Where is Rain!?" Mrs. Bryant demanded, stepping away from the others in the foyer and pushing past Cornelius.

"Another mom!" Bethany's happy voice chirped. "Do you want me to eat your sin too?" she asked.

Mrs. Bryant took a step back, shaking her head. Her face drained of color, and she dashed to the edge of the room and vomited. The other chamber maid, Beth, grabbed one of the cleaner towels from the floor and knelt beside her, trying to be of some comfort while Mr. Bryant stepped further into the room and spoke to Bethany.

"Bethany," he said, "Ryan's hurt, can you heal him?"

"NO!" Mrs. Bryant screamed from where she knelt by the wall.

"But Ryan's hurt!" Mr. Bryant shouted back. "He needs help."

"No! Not her!" she screamed, rising and rushing back toward Bethany. "Not her! Not like that!" She spat into the towel the maid had given her, trying to clear her mouth. "He doesn't need this kind of help!" She growled and pointed to the floor. Her pale, colorless face had done a 180; it was flushed with color now, ugly red and sweating, etched with hard, angry lines.

The last of Bethany's bloody, good cheer vanished, and she frowned as she noticed Ryan in Sky Dragon's arms.

"Ryan's hurt? I can heal him. Watch." Bethany placed a finger on top of the gash on Cathryn's arm and brought the finger down the length of the cut. As it passed, the flesh knit together perfectly as if she simply zipped the gaping wound closed. There was no scarring at all, just seamless, beautiful flesh.

"No!" Mrs. Bryant insisted. "What you're doing is evil, Bethany. This is evil." She pointed at the twins. "All of it is evil. You shouldn't be doing this. These sick people have pulled you into this filth and filled your head with lies." She gave Cornelius a hateful glare. "Now they have everything! Everything that was mine!" she accused viciously. She pushed her husband's hands away as he tried to comfort her.

"Margret, calm down," Mr. Bryant tried again to wrap his arms around her, but she thrust him away.

"No! I'm through with this!" she yelled at him. "And I'm through being polite and reasonable as they do this to us!"

"Be reasonable, Mar—"

"Reasonable! Reasonable! You always say that damned word! Do you even know what it means?!" she shouted, not letting him speak. "This isn't reasonable or Christian or even human! This is wrong! Rain, Ryan, Mary, and Bethany would all be going to church with us this Sunday if not for them! We'd all be home right now if not for them!" She pointed at Cathryn, who still sat on the floor beside Bethany, eyes fluttering wildly as if she wanted to wake but couldn't reach the surface from wherever it was she'd sunk to.

"And we would still have a home to live in if Rain had never come to this godforsaken, evil place to light that horrid candle! And Ryan wouldn't be sick! And everything would be back the way it's supposed to be!"

"Let me heal Ryan, Mom!" Bethany shouted into her rant.

"Yes, let her!" Sky pleaded. "Ryan doesn't mind."

"Please, Mother," Believer added his deep rumble.

"NO! NO! NO!" Mrs. Bryant screamed. Tears started to pour from her eyes as she reached the next phase of her breakdown. "Rain can do it, or we'll just take him to a hospital like normal people and pray! Yes PRAY!" she shouted at Cornelius who took a step away from her. "Normal people go to a hospital when they're sick! They don't cut people or kill them to make someone else better! I don't want Ryan healed with this, *this evil!*" she hissed and pointed to the bloody towels again.

Mrs. Bryant turned away from Bethany and approached the huge, floor to ceiling, golden doorway that protruded from the wall on the side of the room. The gleaming monolith was impossible to miss, and for anyone who'd never entered the room before and become adjusted to its presence, it tended to stagger the mind and suck in the imagination.

"Is Rain through this!?" She pointed at the colossal, golden doorway that currently led to nothing but a bare wall.

"Someone open this stupid thing!" she commanded, looking back toward Cornelius and Bethany.

"So, my magic's good for opening doors and stuff but not for healing Ryan," Bethany said, drawing attention back to herself as she stared at Mrs. Bryant.

"She's just upset, Bethame," Sky Dragon told her. "Her house was just destroyed, and Ryan is hurt. She's upset. And she is not feeling well, Bethany. She's— freaking out."

Bethany considered Sky Dragon's words and nodded, somewhat mollified.

"Okay," she said to Mrs. Bryant, "so you're freakin' a little, I get it, but let me heal Ryan," Bethany asked again.

"No." Mrs. Bryant remained steadfast. "I want Rain to do it."

"So mote it be," Bethany said grimly, giving her a flat, hard stare. "Have Rain do it then. I wouldn't want Ryan tainted with my nasty, magic germs."

"Bethany, it's just that I don't want—"

"I know what you want!" Bethany shouted. "Now go get what you want! But remember, you asked for it. Rain's in the bedroom with her lovers." She pointed to the white door across the room. "But the last thing she needs right now is for you to yell at her. Unless you want her to die, like you want me to die," Bethany's angry eyes accused.

Mrs. Bryant looked shocked, shocked at many things, but she answered the last part and not the rest.

"I don't want you to die, honey. I just want you away from all of this," she said calmly, sounding more herself and less crazed.

"Leave me alone." Bethany turned her back on her and snuggled into Cathryn's body. Cathryn was just as bloody as she was and still out of it, so she voiced no objection, and she wouldn't have objected anyway. Bethany's tail, which had been keeping a low profile up until then, wrapped around the two of them.

With nothing left to be done, Mr. and Mrs. Bryant walked to the bedroom door, turned the knob, and stepped inside.

Jane

Sharing Love and Shaping Fate

T HE OTHERS HEARD nothing through Cathryn's thick bedroom door, but Dan and I heard Rain's mother out there going postal. We stopped having sex and started to hustle! Dan left me and appeared on the other side of the bed where Mary was and placed a hand on her arm. Dan and I listened (and Mary through us) as Rain's mother wigged out, bashing poor Bethany for her bloody work with Cathryn and the twins.

Mary did the talking, urging Rain to clean us up and get us dressed before her parents barged in, but she wisely said nothing about what was happening out in the parlor. One minute we were all naked in the bed, covered in sweat and other fluids from sliding around on each other, and the next, we were all clean. Our skin, hair, teeth, and everything else. Then our clothes appeared on our bodies, cleaned and perfect as well.

My red dress and necklace appeared, somehow simply there and in place on my body. Dan's form-fitting black pants and open fronted gothic jacket materialized on him as well. Emma's white pants were suddenly there, like a second skin. Her ruby belt, red boots, and her red and white flap of cloth with a collar that she used as a top appeared as did Mary's white dress and Rain's loin cloth and top. Everyone was dressed except Alana.

I wondered why. Of course the pajamas she'd worn to bed last night wouldn't do, and before that she'd been wearing a wedding dress. NOT a pleasant memory! She didn't have anything pre-made and ready to wear. Rain had thought of something I'd missed, and I was super glad she had. Even with her parents about to bust in on us, Rain remembered. It reminded me of something very important. Rain loved her little Red Lamb. Shit, she wasn't alone. I think maybe I did too.

"*You do,*" Dan spoke his commentary into my mind as he listened to my unguarded thoughts.

"Yeah. Maybe," I grumped back inside my head.

"You do," Mary said out loud. Backing Dan up, listening in on both our thoughts through Dan.

I growled at the both of them. I didn't like getting double teamed by the two people who had the keys to my brain and everything in there that even I couldn't see.

"What?" Alana's scared voice asked. She sat on the end of the bed with Rain between us. Her head snapped toward Mary then toward me because I'd growled. She saw my angry face and turned to Rain, concerned.

"Do what? Why did she growl, my Lion?" she asked Rain in a worried rush of words.

"*Now you've upset her,*" Dan griped at me inside my head. Not happy.

I shot him a silent glare, my eyes flashing bright red.

"Your mother and father will be in any second!" I snapped at Rain, my voice clipped and angry. "Make something nice for Alana to wear!"

Rain and Alana both studied me with their alien eyes. Rain's frightening, hot red dots floating in darkness and Alana's radiant, jewel blue. They both considered, weighed, and wondered.

"Emma, taste Jane and tell me what's made her sour," Rain asked Emma who was standing right beside me.

"I think I already know," Emma answered, voice happy, already smiling as she reached over to my frowning face and ran a finger across my fiercely frowning bottom lip. She stuck her finger into her mouth and smiled.

"Jane's in love with Alana," she announced happily to the room.

"It's just because her blood tastes so good!" I argued like an idiot, embarrassed at having my feelings blabbed to everyone.

"Jane-e, Jane is ly-ing!" Mary sang out happily.

I turned away from all of them and faced the wall as they laughed at me, and for some damn reason I started to cry! Why the hell was I crying!?

Emma put her arms around me. "What's wrong, Jane?" she whispered.

I whispered back. "How could I love someone I just met! She doesn't have your magic. And she's just a silly girl, even if she is a witch. She's not making me feel this way. Her magic isn't that king of magic, so this doesn't make any sense. I'm not gay, Emma!" I stared at her hard, daring her to argue the point!

"Sometimes people fall in love at first sight," Emma whispered, keeping her voice low. "You're one of those people."

I shook my head no.

"It happened with Dan."

"The Midnight books and the pills did that!" I argued. "And Dan's freakishly, pretty eyes!" I added. "And his damned, romantic notes!" I threw my lame excuses at Emma as I peeked over my shoulder, only to find Alana's bright, blue eyes staring right at me.

She was smiling as Rain whispered into her ear like a gossipy school girl! Of course I heard her.

"Jane's so adorably cute when she gets flustered, isn't she?"

I quickly turned around and faced the wall again. I strained to hear the conversation and frowned when no further words came. I peeked again, too quickly for them to see me move. They were still talking! Impossible! Rain had to be using magic to keep me from hearing!

My heart raced as I wondered what they were saying. I watched as Emma reached out and ran a finger through the golden blood that trailed down my cheek. She tasted it and made a surprised, hungry face, which she stifled and tried to pretend hadn't been there.

"What?" I whispered, half afraid of what she'd say.

She looked into my eyes. "You've got it bad, girl." And I could see in her eyes that she wasn't lying. She wasn't even exaggerating! If anything she was holding back because she didn't want to scare me.

"Shit," I whimpered quietly and cried some more as Emma held me.

I'd noticed Alana's fascination with us yesterday in the Hallow as Dan and I fed on Rain. I'd seen her watching us from high up in the balcony where she sat beside her guy with the stand out, blue hair. He'd been disgusted, but she'd been enthralled. She had wanted us before she became a witch. Before she died and became whatever she was now, because she was more than a witch.

Dan and I had shared her in every way we could. We both slept with her. We'd shared her body and her blood, pressed between the two of us, and we both agreed that the Red Lamb was lovely, delicious, and absolutely ours. Now there were two people on earth who could keep us alive with their blood, and she was one of the two. We could drink deeply of Alana's sweet blood in a way that would kill us, drive us insane, or at the very least knock us out cold for days if we tried it on Rain.

Dan and I had put ourselves into Alana in the same way we had with Rain, giving her our venom. We didn't want to change her into a vampire, but we did want to make her more ours if we could, as we had with Rain. Alana's blood and heart were magic in some very strange ways and we knew there was a good chance she'd be immune to our magic, but we still tried. We meant to keep her.

And I was officially over my girl-on-girl issues and my sharing issues. I'd shared Dan with Rain, Alana, and Mary and I hadn't freaked out. Of course Dan had shared me as well, but he was sharing me with girls and not guys. I wasn't gay, but Alana made my mouth water and my heart race in ways that I couldn't understand and didn't really want to because it might mean I really was gay. Or at least bi. I loved Dan, but I'd kiss Alana any time she wanted me. She was ours. She was ours, and all of us were Rain's.

This strange world into which I'd fallen made sense. I was still a little freaked out by how I'd ended up in a orgy with my husband as the only guy and me being cool with it, but I was. I was happy with all of it. Now Dan and I just had to keep all the people we loved alive.

"What type of clothes do you want me to make for you, Alana?" We heard Rain's words again. The gossipy part about "me" apparently done for now, Rain was back to business. Emma and I turned and faced them.

Alana was looking around at the rest of us, embarrassed now that she was the only one still naked.

"Would you like me to make a pretty dress for you? Part of you used to be a dress. Or do you need a change?" Rain gave her a knowing smile of having been there and done that. "Sometimes when you change your soul and your body, like you did, you also need to change how you dress to match the new you. When I changed to this," she motioned to herself, "I left my black dress behind because I was no longer that girl. I'm the Black Lion now, and this is what I wear."

"Can I pick anything?" Alana asked.

Rain nodded. "Whatever you like. You can even go nude if you like. Whatever feels right to you."

"I want a dress, but I want it clean and simple. And different," she added. "I don't want it to be like other dresses."

"Simple but different," Rain mused, bringing a hand to her chin. "What kind of different and what color?"

"I don't want a dress that's too showy or too plain. And I want it to be white. Only white."

The bedroom door opened without a knock, and Rain's mother and father stepped inside and stared around the room.

Alana pulled a sheet up from the bed and covered herself. Rain soothed her, whispering that it was "all right" and that these were some of her new parents.

"New parents?" Alana asked as she tucked the blue sheet around her.

The sheet changed color from blue to a bright, diaphanous, white and the cloth re-formed even as Alana fought with it, separating, coming apart and sliding across her body like a living thing as it reshaped itself into a knee length, Greek style garment that swept across her front and over one shoulder leaving her sides mostly exposed. White, open toe sandals with white ankle ties and a white sash as a belt finished off the Greek attire. For Rain, it was modest, but the material itself was so sheer you could practically see right through it. Rain stood up and pulled Alana to her feet and turned to face her parents, who stood by the door, tight lipped as their eyes circled the room. They were both trying to understand exactly what it was they were seeing.

Emma and I switched roles and I held and comforted her. She was dying to go to both of these people and wrap her arms around them, even though she didn't know them from the man in the moon. Something about being a witch had opened her heart to these people and made them into her parents. I hated it. The last thing Emma needed was another set of standoffish, horrid parents.

Emma held back and stayed in my arms. She didn't know how she'd be received. They might not want her to touch them. Mrs. Bryant's gaze swept the room. Once she reached us she frowned at Emma's hoe-ish attire and actually curled a lip in disgust as she stared at the blood on my face that I'd boo hooed in my fit of embarrassment. She was done with blood.

She joined her husband who stood before Rain and focused her attention on her daughter. They had to look up to meet her eyes, as she towered over all of us in the room. Rain held Alana to her chest with one arm, and Alana held the tip of Rain's black velvet tail to her own chest as she watched these too new people with her brightly luminescent, jewel blue eyes.

"How are you feeling, honey?" her father asked her, doing his best to give her a kind smile and not freak out.

"I feel strange, Dad," she answered honestly, but her honesty didn't help her father's fragile control. Dan and I could see how badly the poor man wanted to break down, cry, or shatter into a million pieces.

"Are you still my little girl?" He stared up at her.

"Forever and always," Rain answered.

"Are you in any pain, honey? Does this hurt you?" He looked her up and down.

Rain gave her father a small smile. "Sometimes I hurt so bad I cry, sometimes I feel good, and sometimes I feel so good I cry. It's just a body."

Her mother took a step closer and stared into Rain's frightening eyes for a moment then looked away, disturbed.

"I never thought I'd say this, Rain, but I miss your black eyes."

"*Bitch!*" Dan barked in my head, though his face to the room stayed smooth as unliving stone.

"They're just eyes, Mom," Rain said, cut by the comment. Embarrassed and heartsore, she looked away from her mother's face. Rain was sensitive about her eyes.

"Mary, go shut her up!" I growled in my head.

Mary left Dan's side with a cheerful "Hi Mom!" and rushed toward Rain's mother with her arms out, but froze, totally surprised as Mrs. Bryant stepped back, holding up an angry finger and giving Mary an absolutely hateful glare.

"Ryan told me!" she snapped at Mary. "He said that you did something to Rain. Something that caused THIS to happen! How could you!?" she yelled. "What did you do, Mary? Answer me!"

Mary flew backwards as if pulled by an invisible cord, landing in Alana's waiting arms. Alana held onto Mary. Her utterly baffled expression plainly said that she thought this woman was out of her mind to refuse the affections of Mary.

Rain reached down and wrapped her long arms and her tail around both girls protectively and nuzzled the tops of their heads in a somewhat feline way. Her parents took a step back when she lifted her head and looked at them with her frightening gaze. She answered her mother in a firmer tone.

"What's done is done and cannot be undone. And whatever Mary did, I took the first and the last steps of this journey myself. No one made me do this, Mother. I did it myself. As within, so without. If I act like a god and present myself as a god and answer prayers as a god, it was only a matter of time before my insides changed to match my outsides. I'm still Rain. But I'm also a god. I'm not the Lord God, but I am *a* god. And I'm still your daughter."

Rain's parents were quiet for a moment. They looked at each other, then they both stared around the room again. I read their unspoken words and thoughts.

Right now they were thinking about what they saw when they first entered. Alana had been naked. They knew what we'd been doing.

"Ryan's hurt. Can you heal him?" her mother asked suddenly. I heard in her voice the dull sound of resignation. Acceptance of loss. She was focusing on Ryan now, no longer concerned about her daughter. She couldn't see her little girl in what stood before her, even if it did call her Mom.

"Just bring him in and I'll heal him," Rain said.

"It won't cost him anything spiritually to have you heal him, will it?" her mother asked, raising an eyebrow. As if she were dealing with Satan and needed to keep her wits lest she be tricked.

"Ryan belongs to God, Mom. Just bring him already." Rain sounded tired.

Her mother called for Ryan.

Sky Dragon came in, carrying Ryan in his arms, followed by Sky, Believer, and Cornelius.

Emma and I moved further away from everyone, holding ourselves up against the wall as our side of the bedroom filled with activity.

"Put him on the bed," Rain told Sky Dragon, then turned and handed Alana and Mary off to Dan.

My Dan didn't have quite the reach that Rain had but he still did a good job of holding both of them.

"Fix him, Rain. Please!" Sky begged as she stroked Ryan's hair and quietly cried.

Rain walked forward and looked down at Ryan. Whatever she saw didn't make her overly concerned. She turned and studied Sky and was hugely surprised by something she saw. Surprised and happy. She turned and looked at Cornelius and frowned, then looked at the rest of the people in the room one by one and I could see by her face that she was seeing inside each of them, to what was inside their bodies and maybe even inside their hearts or souls. When she reached Believer she looked him up and down, smiled, then slipped into his waiting arms.

"Rain!" Sky barked. "If you're through strutting around, get your butt back over here and fix Ryan! Hold your husband after you fix mine!" She was out of patience.

"Sorry! I still get distracted easy, Sky," Rain said as she hustled back to Ryan's bedside looking suitably chastened.

"What's wrong with him?" Rain's mother asked. "Can you tell us that much before you work on him?"

"He's bleeding inside his head, but I'll fix him," Rain said. "Ryan's got work to do. He's got a wife to take care of and a baby on the way."

"Baby!" came the surprised shout from all over the room.

"I'm pregnant?" Sky asked, one hand dropping automatically to her stomach but the other stayed on Ryan's forehead. She wanted to be happy about the baby but couldn't with Ryan hurt and dying.

"Holy crap! A baby!" Mary charged over shouting. "Let me see! I wanna see! Please! Please!"

We watched as Mary touched Sky's stomach, anxiously waiting for a second opinion from a different doctor. After a moment Mary's face lit up. "Oh wow! She's so small." Mary wrinkled her nose. "Well, she's not a she yet." She raised a finger. "But she wi-ll beee." In sing song she added, "And Ry-an's going to be a da-ddy!" Mary stopped the song cold and declared. "But, Blessed Be! She's tiny! She's only an hour old!" Her white hair fanned around as she turned to Sky, leveling a sideways look of naughty insight. "You guys must really be FA-REEKS! What kind of people get busy in the middle of the day!"

Everyone laughed except Rain's parents, who didn't see the humor in the situation. Mary joked with Sky and looked at the tiny new life inside her and tried to predict what name they would call her with her magic. Sky couldn't help herself; she smiled, quickly becoming enthralled by the idea of finding out the baby's name before she herself had even chosen it.

I held onto Emma and we laughed along with everyone else. And it felt good to laugh and smile. I stared across the room and watched Dan as he held Alana. She was smiling and laughing and leaning back into his arms, enjoying the feel of him and the joy of laughing. Dan's eyes were on me as I looked from him to her.

I was caught in a confusing ball of emotions and not sure quite what I felt or should feel. His arms lifted and he placed his hands on either side of Alana's face and started to turn her head to face me. I saw what he was doing and went to turn away.

"*No, Jane! Not yet! Let her catch you, then turn away. She likes to catch you watching.*"

Without questioning his motives I did as Dan asked, waiting until Alana's blue eyes were on me. I showed the appropriate, small amount of surprised embarrassment at getting caught staring and some completely genuine confusion before I turned away and back to Emma, who was watching me curiously, already onto my game of catch and be caught.

"Rain, is anyone else pregnant in this room?" Mary asked as she looked down at her own stomach. "I'm too freaked out! I can't see into myself!" She certainly sounded freaked out.

"Pregnant?" Mrs. Bryant spoke up. "Why would you or the other girls in this room be worried about getting pregnant, Mary?" She turned and eyed Dan and the rest of us.

"You're not pregnant, Mary love," Rain told her. "There will be no more un-wanted life created inside Amen Hale. Life will come only as it is wanted and sought for and not before. After my accident with the Children of Glass I set it so from wall to wall, but my spell wouldn't have prevented Sky and Ryan's baby girl from coming. She is not unwanted, and I don't even think she's accidental."

"Ryan, get up and see to your pregnant wife," Rain said before her mother had a chance to open her mouth and ask more questions. Her words were spoken casually, but that was all it took.

Ryan opened his eyes and Sky helped him sit up on the edge of the bed. We all enjoyed seeing his reaction when Sky told him he had a child on the way. Mrs. Bryant knelt with Sky and Ryan, rejoicing with them, happy and talking about the baby. It seemed as if this small, new life was the glimmer of hope she needed, a lifeline to cling to that might lead to happiness, beyond what she saw in this room. Something to help her cope with the loss of her daughter. I could see it in her face. With each passing minute Rain was more dead to her than the one before. And now that she had the grandchild, it was a simple thing to move her affections over to this new, little life. Rain would be gone. Lost. Jill was here. Fine by me, I just hoped she'd keep her mouth shut and not upset Rain anymore than she already had.

"What's wrong, Jane?" Emma asked me.

"Rain's mother has given up on her. She's already moved her affections over to Jill. Look at her."

If she didn't want Rain, that was fine. I wanted her. I'd love her. We all would.

Rain's father was handling things far better, or at least far different. Rain's mother spent her time hovering over Sky, Ryan, and the new, little life they shared together and only spoke to the rest of us in passing, but Rain's father spoke to all of us.

Rain introduced Alana as his newest daughter and of course he was charmed by her instantly. Then Rain led him to Emma, and even after he was warned that if he touched Emma he would love her as a daughter forever, he still opened his arms for her. Emma practically ran to him.

Four daughters, Rain, Mary, Emma, and Alana surrounded him. He was a nice man, but I didn't see him as a father figure. Nor did I claim his hag wife as a mother. She was nothing but a big, fat problem. I did claim Cathryn, and Cornelius to a lesser extent, if I were to be honest about it. I had my own parents out there somewhere in Amen Hale, worried and no doubt waiting to see me at lunch. I didn't want anything to do with Mrs. Bryant, but Cathryn was mine.

"*Ours*," Dan spoke into my head, agreeing with me.

We moved out to the living room where Rain woke the twins, revived Cathryn, and cleaned the blood off the floor and off of her angry, little lion cub who didn't want to get clean; she wanted more blood. Cathryn was smiling, no trace of last night's horrible ordeal showed on her face. She actually looked years younger and at peace in ways I'd never seen her before, but she also looked focused. Her eyes sparkled and I could see that she was steeling herself for the tasks ahead, even as she took care of us right now and loved us.

My game of peek-a-boo with Alana was a constant thing; one part of my mind dedicated itself to the task. I'd let myself get "caught" a few more times in different ways. I was constantly aware of her eyes, where she stood, posing myself perfectly to catch her attention with Dan coaching me.

I was entirely engrossed, watching Alana when Emma snuck up behind me and kissed me on the neck like a vampire! By the time I figured out what she was doing it was too late to do anything about it. Alana was watching me and I saw the concerned and surprised look on her face. I knew what she was seeing.

My face went slack, my mouth parted, and my eyes half lidded as Emma's magic gripped me and took me, pulling my love for Alana into herself. I'd seen her thinking about it since she tasted how I felt. She did not remove the love I felt for Alana because it was in me and there was more made every second, but she brought it into herself and copied it perfectly, making it her own. In this way she could share in my crazy high of new love. Instantly, all my butterflies, the anxious, aching desire, stupid confusion, even the worry and almost painful, expectant longing to touch Alana were Emma's. She also had my thirst for her wonderful flavor swirling in her head and heart.

I'd closed my eyes at some point, but when I opened them Emma and I were cheek to cheek, both staring into Cathryn's face.

"Mother," we both said, as if we were joined of mind and not heart.

She smiled at us knowingly. "Come, my lovesick children. It's far past time; we must go down to lunch." Cathryn was still studying us as she called out, "Alana! Come here, child."

Alana came quickly with a bright, "Yes, Queen Mother."

I watched Emma blush crimson beside me and I felt the butterflies in my stomach and the aching desire to kiss and bite. I leaned toward Alana and breathed her in, then stumbled, dizzy and disoriented and found myself caught in the air before I hit the floor. A surprised and delighted Alana lifted me up with her power and set me on my feet where Emma put her arm around me. Half to steady me and half to steady herself.

Cathryn was watching us. "Alana dear, your sisters are besotted with you to the point that they can barely walk."

Emma and I both looked down and away at the same time, in the same way, and we both heard the blue-eyed girl giggle, delighted at our reaction.

"As you're responsible for this you'll have to escort them to dinner. Hold their hands and use your magic if you must, to help them down the stairs and get them to the table. And it would probably be less distracting to everyone at dinner if you sat between the two of them. That way they won't have far to look to see you."

I cast a quick glance across the room to find Dan and Mary. Both of them were smiling back at me, both knowing what I was doing and thinking, both of them sharing our high. She had her arm resting on his, and it looked as if he was escorting her to lunch as they walked out of the bedroom. Like a couple on a date.

I thought there would be a mountain of awkwardness to climb over after we all slept together. Everyone being with everyone and all the things that could go wrong. Hurt feelings, personal issues, disappointments, jealousy over this or that. But there was no weirdness or awkwardness at all. I was the one with the most issues, and somehow I'd handled them.

I loved Rain. I loved Emma. I loved Alana. And I loved Mary. So I shared the man I love with the girls I love. Since this started I'd fought against anything and anyone who tried to love me or have me love them because I wanted to save all of myself for Dan. All of my heart I hoarded back to lay at his feet. And here I was, in love with all these other people. And loving them with Dan. And sharing Dan with them.

Alana took my hand in hers. My feet left the floor as her magic picked me up. I floated beside her. Just as with Rain, now that Alana's blood was in me, her magic worked on me. Emma was on her other side, also holding her hand and floating an inch or two above the floor. The three of us held onto each other as Alana guided us out of the room, chatting with Emma as we ghosted down the hall.

I took a moment to speak to Dan and Mary in my head.

"Kiss him for me, Mary, and keep Dan happy while I'm playing with our little Red Lamb."

"Mary said she will and that she loves you too, Jane. And I love you too. Do you remember lunch yesterday, what Rain said just before you bit her?"

Curious. Why bring that up now? I recalled her exact words from my memory.

"'Please let it be beautiful for the ones I love.' Have you figured out what she meant by it?' I thought to him.

"Mary explained it to me. Rain was praying to herself, and she answered her own prayer. Didn't this turn out beautifully? You were wondering earlier how this could happen without problems. Rain made it beautiful."

What Dan said made sense. All of us together in bed had worked out because Rain willed it so. Just that easily she'd made what should have been a colossal nightmare into something—beautiful.

I wondered with a sudden chill how much of my life was mine to control and how much now danced at the end of Rain's smallest whims. As she willed it, so it was. It was frightening. There was a time when she couldn't affect me, touch me, or change me, but that was before I started drinking her blood. Now her magic worked on me. She could make me into whatever she wanted.

My anxiety began to mount as I thought again about what I'd just done. I'd shared Dan with others. And I'd had sex! A bunch of sex! With a bunch of girls! I thought about what I was doing right now, going off to chase after this girl who was holding my hand. She was a G-I-R-L! I would have never done this. This didn't seem like the "me" I remembered being. Did I control a damn thing anymore or was I simply a puppet on Rain's string!?

What was she turning me into!?

"Jane? Are you okay?" Alana asked. "Your eyes are all red!"

We were stopped halfway down the stairwell, floating in air. There in front of us at the foot of the stair was Mary. She had a hand on Dan's arm, whispering to him. As soon as I saw them, they both looked up and—they were in my head.

Dan spoke, telling me what Mary wanted to say.

"Mary said to take a fucking chill pill and stop wiggin' out. Her words exactly. I'm sure you can tell. She said, and I'm just the messenger here, 'It's a little late to cry into your beer about having someone else shape your path when you're the one who started it all.'"

"Jane, you all right?" Emma asked.

"No," I growled as I dropped Alana's hand, landed on my feet, and ran down the stairs to Dan and Mary.

"Me!" I shouted. "How the hell did I start this!?" I demanded as I got into Mary's face. "And when the hell did I shape anyone's destiny other than my own and maybe Dan's!?"

Mary kept one hand on Dan, angry herself as she shouted back. "Rain would have never fallen in love with Believer if your magic hadn't of changed her! After what she'd been through with her abortion, that kind of love didn't even exist for her! Her heart was dead! *YOU* changed *HER!*"

I growled and showed some serious fang, causing some of our gathering audience of onlookers at the end of the landing to blanch, but Mary just kept going, unafraid.

"Ryan would have never gotten with Sky! Lucius would still be G.I. Joe! And Rain would have never fallen for Emma if you hadn't of fallen for her first! *YOU!*" She jabbed a finger at me, "fell in love with Emma when you were twelve years old. Emma followed *YOU* here! And Emma took me when I touched her and saw how much she loved *YOU!* You shaped everyone's destiny, Jane! And when Rain came to rescue you from the soldiers who stole you from the crypt, she prayed that you would be okay. I saw that prayer in her mind and learned from it just how to compel her into becoming a god with a prayer of my own. So you helped make her into what she is! You changed her!" She finished her rant, her green eyes glowing like mad. A crackling haze of green energy buzzed in the air around her as she breathed in and out, trying to control her own anger and power.

Mary was right of course. But Rain had so much control over Dan and me. And she was so powerful. And her blood was in us and our venom was in her connecting us in weird, freaky ways. Now that I was thinking of her, somehow, I knew that she was happy right this very moment, very happy. I realized that I was smiling, happy, simply because she was, and my borrowed joy imploded and turned into fear that stabbed down into my guts like a blade.

I wondered how much of me was still me! I was scared and I didn't know what to do. Dan couldn't stop this or change this, and neither could I. Mary reached up and touched my face, no longer angry as she spoke to me.

"Jane, if she's your god, you should trust her and love her and let her make you into what she wants you to be. Didn't she just die and give you her body for an eternal chew toy? And 'Please let it be beautiful for the ones I love' isn't a bad thing for your god to wish for you."

I thought about what I'd done in the garden with Mary. How I'd prayed to Rain. How I'd danced and sang and prayed and wished and hoped for a second chance to love her. I'd meant every word at the time. It made me wonder if I was like those people in hospitals. People that pray and promise God this and that and the kitchen sink when they're sick, only to pitch it once they were feeling better. Was I like that? Was I that shallow? Was Rain my god or wasn't she? Was she Dan's god, I wondered suddenly. Dan still stood beside Mary, her hand on his arm as he looked at me and raised a lovely brow.

"I know you won't give me a straight answer, you'll just say whatever you think I need to hear," I told him.

"Is Rain Dan's god, Mary?" I asked her as I stared into Dan's blue-green eyes. Mary was a witch. She could be vague and tricksy but she couldn't lie outright.

She smiled at my cunning, though I could see she was happy to answer. "Your mind is free, Jane, and your imagination unbound, but Dan's has a different flavor. His mind is wired differently from yours. He's analytical and organized and steadfast. He doesn't think she's a god; he thinks she's a beautiful girl with powers, but that will change eventually, and there's not a damn thing he can do about it."

Dan frowned. A real frown, not pretend or halfway.

Mary stepped closer to him and closer to his frown. She spoke to me as she reached up and played with his hair and stared into his angry eyes. I could see it, and I knew Dan could see it. Mary loved him too.

"Dan will believe as you believe, Jane," she said this as she gazed into the eyes of the man I loved. "You are his window into a world that his mind cannot see, make sense of, or imagine. You are his faith, Jane, and through you he will believe, whether he likes it or not."

Mary made a face, as Dan thought something to her but not to me.

"What did he say, Mary?" Emma asked. She and Alana had been standing on the last step, listening intently, whispering together as they tried to follow along with our half spoken, half mental conversation.

"Dan's whining about being changed, just like Jane was earlier. He's pissing and moaning about his 'free will' being violated."

Now it was Dan's turn to growl and show some fang, but Mary ignored him too.

"He's asking me why it's not enough just to love Rain as a girl."

"Because she is more than a girl," Alana affirmed soundly. She looked impatient as she turned her eyes on me and I felt her magic wrap around me and lift me off the ground. She brought me back to her side and took my hand again.

"Enough already," Alana admonished, as if I'd been misbehaving. "I'm supposed to take care of you and bring you and Emma to lunch. Now stop being silly and let's go." Her strange, blue eyes looked into my face, and just like that, I wanted her. Whether it was from Rain or Emma or Dan or even myself, it simply didn't matter. Alana did it for me.

I felt my own heart speed up and my thoughts went to weird places and flashes of memory danced through my vampire mind with a vivid crispness that was both startling and painfully arousing. Memories of me and Alana and Dan. My hand went to my face and I frowned as I recalled that I had dried blood on my face again from crying.

That can't be pretty to look at.

I wanted to be pretty for her.

"Emma, do you have a napkin?" I asked nervously and a little too quickly. "Or something to clean me up with?" I managed to slow to human speed as I pointed to my mucked up face.

Alana passed her hand in front of my face and the dried blood that I'd cried came away from my skin and floated in the air between us. She made a small move with her hand and the flakes fell to the floor. Emma reached over and fixed my hair a little and adjusted me.

I looked back toward Dan and Mary, surprised to find them already gone. I'd been so distracted I hadn't noticed them leave. I felt a completely illogical wave of dread well up inside me when I didn't see him. Had he left me!?

"DAN!" I shouted in my head.

"I'm right here inside you, Jane," Dan's words came into my mind. "I'm here and I love her too. Don't be ashamed of how you feel about Alana or embarrassed or worried about me being jealous. I can feel you holding back because of me. Don't. I'm in you and a part of you, Jane. As you love her, I love her too. As you kiss her and hold her hand,

I'm holding her hand. Don't forget, your lips are my lips. I'm the one that's out here not sharing, as Mary pinches my ass."

That made me smile which made Alana and Emma smile.

"And that made Dan smile," Dan added to the list in my head. *"Oh! Wait! and that made Mary smile, and some red-haired, shriveled old woman out here in the Dining Hall smile. Man, I really hope she doesn't pinch my ass."*

Meridith and Ambrosia

Mothers and Daughters

"COME ON THEN you lot!" shouted a girl standing by the telly, waving her arms about as if she were signaling for a plane to land in the field. "They got some woman doing an interview that says that the Black Witch is dead! It worked! She's dead! The Black Witch is dead!"

Meridith and Ambrosia gave way to the mad stampede of tittering women, all fighting to get close to the tiny telly with its twelve-inch screen to see what was happening. Being older and slower and having no desire to be bashed about by the crowd of pushing, jostling women, the two grand dames hung back. They squinted their eyes and watched the younger women with sour expressions. They both felt like old wolves, too long in the tooth to go in and fight for a scrap of flesh and forced to wait at the edges, until someone else saw fit to share some scraps of what they'd heard once they'd had their fill of meat.

"Think they're so smart, do they? Hmm!" Ambrosia frumped. "Come on then. I've a thought!"

Without another word of explanation, Ambrosia waddled off. There was nothing for Meridith to do but mutter and complain as she followed. Ambrosia led them around the throng of almost three hundred women, all packed in front of the telly like sardines in a can. They came up from behind the television stand where there was no crowd at all.

"Just like listening to a radio," Ambrosia whispered with a smile at her own cleverness.

Meridith and Ambrosia faced each other and cupped their hands around their ears as they leaned close to the back of the set and listened.

"...and the last time you saw your daughter, where was she?" a male voice was asking.

"She and Emma, the Love Witch, were sitting together in one of the chairs. My daughter was beckoning me to come to her, but I couldn't. I ran out of the room. I couldn't take anymore," a woman's voice answered, sounding emotional.

"And why couldn't you go to her?" the male voice asked.

"Because if I did, I'd belong to Emma too. Just one touch and she would have owned me as she does my daughter and the others."

"And the last time you saw Black Rain?" he asked.

"She was lying in her cloud husband's arms. Dead. Or brain dead anyway."

"Are you sure this wasn't a trick? Some type of subterfuge? A coma perhaps?" the male voice pushed.

"I told you what happened! I was there!" was the woman's angry reply. "I saw the girl fall apart. She was crazy before all this began, but there at the end she was absolutely delusional. She'd accidentally stepped on some bugs earlier in the day that she thought were fairies in disguise. She went crazy with grief thinking she'd killed little people. It was heartbreaking watching those poor, desperate people try to humor her and play along with her mad fantasy, making up drivel on the fly to try and talk her down. They actually formed a line. One by one they begged the poor girl not to kill herself, but she wouldn't listen to anyone. Hell! I waited my turn. I begged her not to do it! It was an emotional, ugly scene. Rain stayed until the vampire girl fetched Emma, but she killed herself before Emma could touch her and stop her. Emma is the glue that holds that nightmare place together. Like a spider in the middle of a web, she traps everyone with her magic and holds their hearts so they actually want to stay there. And that Mary, she's Cathryn's little spy. She reads everyone's minds and tells Cathryn and Cornelius what everyone's thinking. And if anyone has a problem with the way things are done, that monster child Bethany will kill them and eat them."

"Mrs. Ainsley, we're just trying to make sure we understand. Black Rain isn't actually dead. She's just asleep."

"You tell me," the woman challenged. "When Mary Fae arrived and touched the body she screamed like a banshee. She said there was nothing there, no soul inside the body. She screamed over and over like a broken record '*Rain's gone! Rain's gone!*' I know you're trying to see some trick or cunning deception, and believe me, I can understand that it seems impossible for this particular girl to actually be dead, but she is." The woman was certainly convinced. And convincing.

"But her body is still alive?" The news man continued to probe for a weakness in her story. "Perhaps she'll just return?"

"She left her body behind to feed the vampires who were addicted to her blood. She loved them and she wanted to take care of them. She tried to take care of everyone but herself." The woman sounded sad and tired.

"When you say that she loved the vampires, do you mean she loved them as friends or was this a sexual relationship?" the man asked.

"She loved them every way she could, the boy and the girl. Especially the girl. Rain was bi-sexual. But it's not like she had a choice about being bi; once Emma touched her she liked girls, it's as simple as that. She sat across a table from me and told me herself that she didn't have a gay bone in her body until Emma touched her. She loved Emma, she loved the vampire girl, she even loved my daughter.

"She was shy in some ways and brazenly bold in others. She didn't care about nudity in the least. She preferred to be nude. Her idea of formalwear was a loin cloth. But when it came to things of the heart she was shy and awkward. It was endearing in someone with so much power. She had a good heart. And she loved my daughter more than that shit of a boy who tried to marry her. I wish we could have helped her. I wish she would have listened to one of us."

"You do sound sad that she's gone, Mrs. Ainsley." The man's voice sounded compassionate.

"Of course I am. Lots of could haves and dreams are dead now. It's sad that she's gone. I watched the girl make a golden gateway in the Queen's bedroom that opened onto the surface of Mars. Rain and a frumpy, old maid walked through that gateway. I have no idea what they did there, but when they came back that frog of a maid had turned into a beautiful girl, like a princess in a story book. It makes me wonder what else she could have done, what could have been."

"Did you see the news interview that Rain's brother Ryan and his wife Sky did this morning?"

"No. I didn't, I was traveling here. What interview?" the woman replied.

"How did Ryan look last night? Was he sick or unstable in any way?" the news man asked instead of answering her question about the interview she was unaware of.

"How did he look?" she scoffed. "What do you think, you idiot!? His sister just died! Of course he looked like hell. But the whole place was falling apart when I left. Mary stabbed herself right in the heart with a pair of scissors she found, but the little witch Bethany healed her or brought her back. It was total madness there in Cathryn's chambers. The whole place was coming apart. I just wish I could have gotten out with my daughter."

"This morning during his interview, Ryan said that Rain was doing better now."

"Did he say that she died last night?"

"No. He said that she had a rough night."

The woman barked out a joyless laugh. "Yeah. Well, technically the boy didn't lie. I guess you could call it that."

The television broadcast broke for a commercial.

The gaggle of women in front of the telly began talking all at once. Lots of excited, self-congratulatory banter drowned out any voices of caution or sadness at the grim news. Most of them were excited by the stink of their own power. Many were already bantering about who they should curse next and whether they would die as swiftly.

Ambrosia frowned as she studied her friend's dour face.

"Now you can't have it both ways, girl!" she scolded. "Ya wanted her to go quickly and quietly and without a fuss, and she did. It's over now. All the same, I'm still glad we didn't spit at the poor child."

"Says you," Meridith said. She held out her hand and tugged up her sleeve to show Ambrosia the hair woven charm bracelet she wore. It was fashioned with her own hair mingled with strands of her granddaughter Cricket's hair and her daughter Robin's hair. The silver, blond strands and the rich brown stood out of the dull, gray band as plain as day.

"You gave a charm to Cricket then," Ambrosia said, not really surprised, but then she noticed the brown hair woven into the circlet. "And to Robin! There's no way she'd have put it on!"

Meridith smiled a thin, grimly satisfied smile. "Cricket loves me more than her mother. She plays games and acts otherwise so her mother doesn't find out. She's very good at it, my little Cricket. She tied the charm around her mother's ankle when she wasn't looking. I told her what they were and why I wanted her to wear it."

Ambrosia shook her head and huffed out a big sigh. "So that's why you didn't spit. Only someone innocent can stand in for someone guilty. Dammit Meridith! You could have told me what you were really about!" She bit back further angry words.

"I've only spat at two people in my life, Am, and they both deserved it, but this poor girl didn't. And I'll take what may come back at my girls for what they did, but shouldn't have done."

"But why let Cricket spit into that damn thing!?" Ambrosia demanded. "You could have just told her not to do it, and then had her sneak that bracelet onto her mother's ankle. Why'd you let her spit into Mab's Cauldron, Meridith! This isn't fun and games. Any fool can feel the darkness we've brewed here this day!" Ambrosia reached into her handbag for a napkin to dab at her eyes. "I'm not half the witch you are, but even I know this is far from done, no matter what that woman on the tele says. Now whatever harm comes back will be threefold and doubled again."

Just an hour earlier the women of The Wicket Street Knitting Circle had formed two, long columns. Individually or by pairs, they'd walked forward and spat into the big, black cauldron, prepared to hold the combined curse of their coven. A curse of death for Black Rain, her coven Star Night, and her home, Amen Hale.

Meridith had watched as her daughter and granddaughter stepped out to add their curse to the foul pot. They'd been smiling and holding hands as they approached the cauldron, walking between the two long, rows of women that her daughter so wanted to impress. Cricket hadn't looked about as she walked beside her mother, taking in the approval of crowd, nor had she searched through those faces for her Ganna. No, she'd gazed up adoringly at her mother the whole time then told her that she loved her before the two of them, together, spat into the Cauldron.

She'd done exactly as her Ganna had told her to do in hastily whispered words when they had first met this morning. The poor, deluded fools around Meridith offered her sympathy, thinking that she wept to see her daughter and granddaughter do evil, and she let them think what they would. Robin had looked away from her daughter's face to seek out her mother as she and Cricket walked together. She saw her mother's weeping face, then quickly looked down at her daughter, who looked up at her and nowhere else. Only her. Oh how she'd smiled and even cried, she was so happy.

Robin wanted her mother to suffer for what she saw as the wrongs of a hard childhood. So Meridith gave her what she wanted. Robin wanted her child to love her more than her mother. Meridith gave her that too, with Cricket's help. Robin always had a hard time standing on her own and she wanted to join the crowd, be a part of this day's doings, and Meridith did what she could to let her have that as well and still not suffer for her having what she wanted, even if what she wanted was evil.

"Real magic's often hidden inside other workings, Ambrosia," Meridith said confidently. "I've known witches who could make a rose grow on cursed ground and bloom on a blackened eve."

"And is that what you've done then?" her old friend asked.

"Aye, I'm pleased with what I've wrought." Meridith nodded, then scratched at her chin thoughtfully. "I just hope I don't go bankrupt when the bill comes due."

Benjamin

Circling the Drain

BENJAMIN WALKED IN the courtyard outside his room, a small, enclosed space with ten foot high walls. A gleaming spiral of barbed wire lined the top that was so new and bright it was hard to look at without squinting. At the four corners of his out-door prison area were towers, each holding a soldier with a huge sniper rifle trained on him. He had no idea what kind of bullets those guns used or if he could handle being shot by one of them, let alone four at once, but he didn't want to find out. The handguns hadn't hurt too bad, but these weren't regular guns.

Benjamin wasn't too surprised they'd put him in prison after what he'd done to the girl soldier he caught and the lady he'd scared the first day he was there. He understood why they were treating him like a prisoner but felt he should be given some mercy or a little extra leeway or some understanding - or something! He'd taken those pills and he was a bit off, like the rest of the kids in the drug study. He wasn't in control. He wasn't responsible for what happened. He wouldn't have done that if he hadn't have taken the pills.

And the girl lived. He was pretty sure she lived anyway. He should spend time in a mental hospital, but not prison. He wanted out. He was sick of this and he was scared. He'd asked to see his parents and a lawyer, but the only person who would talk to him was a shrink. He didn't try to talk to the soldiers; they wanted to kill him. They were upset because of the girl, but still, he was a minor, and he had issues. It wasn't his fault. What the hell was wrong with them!?

His stomach growled as he circled the empty cube. The long barrels of the four sniper rifles followed his every move as he circled his bare rectangle of earth. He didn't even have a chair out here now; they'd removed anything he could throw or use as a weapon. Inside his room he still had a TV with video games and movies, and they'd told him that any book he wanted they'd download onto the Kindle that was there with the rest of the electronic stuff. He was smart enough to see that they wanted to keep him occupied and waste his time.

Benjamin was getting desperate. He wanted out. He knew most of the others were probably already here; they just weren't telling him. He'd seen Katie, Shikith, Susan, and Alfred when they first arrived but not since. He wanted to be put back with the rest of his group. The girls wouldn't mind. He'd be nice to them.

He circled the small, square yard, frustrated and frightened, but not knowing what to do about it. He hadn't eaten since the incident with the female soldier because he was scared of what they'd put into his food. He was hungry. He didn't understand why they were so upset. The girl lived. Maybe they'd ease up in a few more days and then he'd risk the food. Maybe.

Peffan

Gift Exchange

"THE ENTRANCE IS right there." Peffan pointed out the small gap between the vegetation from his perch atop the dash console of the truck.

"Thank you, Peffan, that driveway is nearly impossible to spot."

Mr. Thorpe decelerated. He turned the 28-foot, white, box truck onto the dirt road that ran down to the cemetery behind the old, burned out church. Thorpe kept his speed to a crawl and rolled his window down, occasionally leaning out to look down at the dirt trail and the tires, keeping watch for small moving things in the road and in the air that might not be what they seemed. He had no desire to hurt one of their new, little neighbors now that he knew they were people and not bugs. And Thorpe had no reservations about their humanity, even if they weren't human.

At first they saw nothing but motes of dust glowing in the sun on either side of the tree, shaded path, but as they passed some invisible, magical line, the air shimmered, and each drifting speck became a tiny, winged being. Thousands filled the air on both sides of the drive and high in the air, creating a living tunnel of tiny creatures. Their quickly beating wings appeared as colorful, iridescent blurs behind each little, human figure.

Through his open window Thorpe could hear the soft hum of thousands of those tiny wings. A dark cloud of the creatures hovered above the tombs, covering the graveyard in a roiling half shadow even though the morning sun was high and bright in the cloudless, blue sky. The small beings flew along with the truck, easily keeping pace as they crowded the passenger and rear window. They held tiny hands to their curious eyes as they peered into the cab.

Suddenly all the faces began to look worried, then bolted from the glass in a mad, colorful flurry!

"Stop!" Peffan cried out. "Stop Mr. Thorpe!"

"OH!" Thorpe cried and stood on the brake as men waving their arms wildly on the trail jumped out of the way. Loud sounds of thumping and rolling came from inside the trailer as the load shifted due to the sudden jerky stop.

"I can't believe I did that," the old man scolded himself even as he stared back out the window, distracted again by the curious faces, already returning now that the danger of "impact" was past. "I bet I made a god awful mess back there. Them boys won't be happy when they go to unload."

The old man gathered a few things from the truck. "Let me go talk to'em." Thorpe carefully opened and shut the door, being mindful of the Twilins as he began his apologies to the men of Amen Hale who were still picking themselves up off the ground.

Last night, Peffan had appeared inside the cab once Benson and Thorpe were miles down the road, making things too inconvenient to turn the truck around and take him back. Both men had been tight lipped at the outset of their journey, suspicious and careful with details about Amen Hale, but after ten plus hours they'd both said far more than they'd intended. It was hard not to.

For every small revelation they shared, Peffan reciprocated much more. Both Benson and Thorpe felt a fair amount of empathy for Peffan and his people after hearing how they lived, and Peffan felt the same for them, especially poor Mr. Thorpe, who was already bent and troubled with the ravages of old age. Peffan had spent more time in the presence of humans in the past ten hours than he had in the past five hundred years combined, and most of that time was casual, unstructured, and enjoyable.

He'd been free to "sightsee," as the humans called it. Benson and Thorpe had been friendly and accommodating at every stop. They had bought him sunflower seeds and purchased him the fruits he said he enjoyed. Their trip was simple and they did unglamorous but necessary things.

First, they stopped at a local dump and disposed of the garbage that had been loaded into the truck. After the dump they stopped at a twenty-four hour car wash to clean out the back. Then they went to a number of docking bays and stores to pick up pre-ordered supplies and to leave orders for others to pick up later.

Peffan collected information, storing the pertinent bits and pieces in his head to share when he returned. And he'd studied Benson, the twenty-year-old boy in whom his Queen had shown an interest, as well as Mike Thorpe, the crusty, old veteran who did most of the driving and dealt with the vendors.

Peffan found to his great surprise that he liked both men. The trip had been the adventure of a lifetime for Peffan and he was sad to see it end. He gave the envious Twilin faces pressed to the glass outside the truck a companionable wave as he looked over to Benson and shook his head, amazed and amused that the boy was still asleep after that jerky, shouting stop. He'd fallen asleep only thirty minutes ago, leaning against the passenger side door.

As Peffan stared at Benson he had a daring and horrible idea. One his Queen would either be pleased with or kill him for. A handful of Taunwee's other attendants flew through the open window and landed on the blue, vinyl seat beside him. Peffan ignored them, keeping his eyes on Benson as he teetered on what to do. The last time Taunwee had shown any interest in love, the object of her affections had been another Child of the Dawn who eventually rejected her.

Peffan was young the last time he'd seen true green in the Queen's hair, but he could still remember the sight of it, and the sight of her. It was the happiest he'd ever seen her. The Twilin mothers told stories to their bits as they put them to bed, telling them that one day the Queen would wear green and that she would sing and dance and play like a child.

The six Twilins standing nearby said nothing as they watched him. It was considered the height of rudeness to interrupt someone when they were weighing their future, as it was plain to see he was now doing. Peffan's sense of self-preservation and the needs of his own house weighed on his mind as he flew out the window, but when he spotted Reese in his line of flight he landed on the now familiar perch and started hashing out his plan before he could stop himself.

When Peffan suggested before all her people, that she, Queen Tauwnee, The Twilight Star, come and wake the boy from his slumber inside the filthy, human vehicle and speak to him alone for a time, her hair had flashed to rusty orange streaked with murder crimson. She managed to restrain herself from lashing out violently, not wishing to shock her human guest, but the girl would leave soon, and the Twilins knew what the Queen's displeasure meant.

Taunwee asked the human girl her thoughts on Peffan's ludicrous suggestion. She'd been asking the girl about most everything, all night and all morning, and the girl never failed to surprise her with her answers. Taunwee asked about his suggestion but Marie spoke about Peffan himself, who knelt before the Queen, weeping brokenly, but silently, his small shoulders shaking, face hidden by his hair.

"This Twilin knew what he said might make you mad, and he still said it, Queen Taunwee. Either he wants to embarrass you before all your people or he loves you more than he loves himself. He risked everything he has just now, before everyone. I think he is very brave."

Taunwee saw the truth of it. It was too simple to deny. Strange and alien colors crept through her hair that left even her oldest attendants confused as to what she felt, how to react, or what to do. Taunwee found herself forced into a moment of rare self-examination. What was wrong? She was not stupid or lacking in insight. She was a thousand times wiser than any human, but this girl child had seen in a second what she had been blind to. Or blinded to, she thought as she faced herself. Blinded by pride.

The Children of Dawn were a very proud and arrogant people. If there was one, great, character flaw common to her race, it was pride. Taunwee considered this and what she'd become and what she should do about it. Her next words were not spoken in anger. Her hair was a mix of colors, too varied to name, too tangled to interpret with any certainty.

"What of his suggestion, Marie? Tell me what you think of his unusual proposition."

Marie smiled then, eyes twinkling, "I like to watch men sleep. The few men that I've had, I've watched."

"Tell me why," Taunwee asked.

Marie blushed deeply, looking up and around at all the thousands of Twilins listening raptly to her every word. She pulled herself together and spoke as if she performed a penance, pouring out her secret self as payment for her Lion's sins. She'd done so all night long, for questions just as personal and embarrassing, holding nothing back no matter how self-defacing. Complete honesty was what she gave, which was good, as Taunwee would have sensed anything less in an instant.

"Many reasons," she said, taking a moment to sort them in her mind before she began. "I like being awake as a man sleeps, so I can watch him as I want," she declared boldly, "for as long as I want, in the way that I want and without him seeing me do it. And I like to watch a man as he dreams. It's like seeing inside his head without him knowing you've seen his secrets or what troubles him. I think a man is at his most beautiful when he's asleep and calm and still." She wore a smile, caught in the happy memories, her face open and easy to read as she spoke.

"I had one man who'd let me wake him with kisses and my body. It was my favorite part of the day with Clive; he was always sober in the morning and kind to me." Marie stopped there, her mood darkening with the memories of that relationship. She decided to sum things up. "In my first life I was drab and plain, Queen Taunwee. I was shy and ashamed of myself for no good reason. I did not love myself, and the few men that I gave myself to were bad men. I knew they did not love me, but I still loved them," she confessed without tears. "The only one to ever love me as I was was the Black Lion. Those men did not love me, but she does."

Brown and green and cotton candy pink and even some blue streaked through Queen Taunwee's hair.

"I have never watched a man sleep," the Queen confessed, quite surprised to realize that she hadn't. After twelve thousand years of life she'd done just about everything imaginable with a man or a woman, Roe or Dam, but she'd never intentionally watched a man or a Twilin male sleep.

"I'm sure Benson will be very interesting to watch. Don't deny yourself the pleasure," Marie said sincerely, eyes large, head nodding.

"And should a gift be given to Peffan for his brave service?" the Queen asked her.

Marie's shook her head no right away, surprising Taunwee yet again.

More blue.

"He did what he did because he loves you. He brought you a gift; let him have the joy of seeing you take pleasure in it."

"Is that true, Peffan?" Taunwee asked. "Is there no gift you could name? Another child?" she suggested. The greatest gift she had to give was the gift of life.

Peffan shook his hand no, eliciting surprised gasps from the Twilins watching raptly.

"My Queen, Reese said he would wait thirty minutes and some of that time is now lost. I would not have you miss a minute more."

"Rise," she told Peffan as she walked toward him.

He quickly got to his feet, ready to take flight and lead her to the sleeping boy, but then he noticed that Taunwee was walking toward him, eyes fixed upon *him*. The Queen stopped a hand's width from his face, then brushed his green hair out of his eyes, leaned in, and kissed him. It was a good, long, deep kiss, not the quick there and done given for the women seeking a child and a mate.

When Queen Taunwee stepped away from the dazed Roe she seemed happy with his awed expression. "I don't want you watching me. I will have privacy as I watch him sleep. No consorts. No guards. No attendants." She spoke these words over her shoulder, then turned back to Peffan. "Just me and the boy. So go enjoy my gift with your Dam, and I'll go enjoy yours with my human Roe."

She took off, completely alone, followed a respectable distance by a stunned cloud of attendants and consorts and guards.

Peffan's Dam, Camas, flew to his side, weeping with joy and relief. Hundreds of Twilin voices shouted to Peffan and called him blessed or crazed, mad as a rabid bat, or similar shouts of well-deserved honor or good natured jibes as he held his very proud and smiling Dam, but one calling voice caught everyone's attention.

"Where will you go?" Marie asked them.

The shouting voices of the Twilins hushed to hear what Peffan and his Dam would say to this human girl they were all so enamored with.

"Go? What do you mean?" Peffan asked.

Marie pointed around. "Where in all of this will you go? The magic will fade if you wait."

"She's right," Camas said, frowning. "We didn't expect this. There's no place for us to be alone, Peffan."

"Come to me. I've a place for you here." Marie resettled herself on the ground and made a place like a cloth cave with her dress that was perfectly spacious for the inch and a half tall couple to spend some quality alone time in.

Peffan and his Dam entered their shelter and made love in the folds of Marie's dress as the Queen of the Twilins watched a young man sleep in the cab of a rental truck.

Caught Unaware

"Benson," Taunwee whispered for the third time, hoping even as she did so that his fitful sleep would continue.

The boy moaned, then burrowed further into his borrowed, black leather jacket. His dream continued. His eyes moved about behind the lids. He frowned. Not a pleasant dream, despite her whispers. She watched. Every few seconds a new expression would begin to form, the lines in his face starting to shape an emotion that often slipped away. His mouth sometimes moving, perhaps half muttering a word before going slack.

For the past fifteen minutes she'd done as Marie had suggested. She watched him, exactly how she wanted. She'd done so, unhurried and alone. Her guards ensured that there would be no curious faces pressed to the glass. She was alone. Just her and this boy, who thought she had a pretty name.

Taunwee looked away from Benson's face and gazed around the alien environment, giving it her scrutiny for the first time. The cab of the truck did reek of the old man and his cigarettes, but it also smelled of other things—paper, engine oil, gas, food smells. She noticed the open bag of sunflower seeds. The back half of the long bag had been squeezed into the crack of the seat in the middle of the bench, no doubt positioned there for Peffan's benefit.

After another quick glance at the windows to assure herself that she was alone, she flitted over and snatched a crumb from the open end of the bag. She sat on the sticky vinyl beside the bag and popped the tiny bit of nut into her mouth. She'd gone without eating for years and the flavor filled her mouth and made her sigh happily as she chewed.

Taunwee did not have to eat, and eating made certain unpleasant things necessary, so from time to time she simply abstained. Her first meal should have been greens or soups or nectar—something light. This was a bad idea, but the pulpy nut tasted so wonderful she went back to the crinkly plastic container for another sunflower seed.

As she looked into the bag she spotted a salt crystal. She picked up the crystal with her small fingers and held it up to the light, admiring the beauty of its refractive sparkle for a moment before popping it into her mouth like a piece of candy. The quick spike of salty flavor made her wings shake, but she dug into the bag and retrieved another salt crystal and ate it as well.

She stretched extravagantly and smiled, enjoying her privacy and her little, hidden indulgence and the boy. She began to lick the oil and nut crumbs from her fingers.

"Hello," said a voice behind her.

Taunwee spun around! She froze, wings out, knees bent, ready to fly.

Benson was watching her. His eyes were open and his face calm except for one line that crossed his brow. He made no move to get up or go anywhere. He was still squished up against the door, half buried in his leather jacket.

His eyes stayed on her.

Taunwee remained still, her eyes on him.

"Why do you want me, Queen Taunwee?" Benson asked.

She stood straight and retracted her wings, brushing green hair out of her eyes.

"How do you know I'm Taunwee? I could be any Twilin girl," she said, voice arrogant, angry with herself for being caught unaware. And by a boy. And by this boy! What good was watching someone sleep if they catch you!?

"Did you like the sunflower seeds?" he asked.

"I shouldn't have eaten them," she said with a sneer.

"Why?" he asked. "You were enjoying them. You were smiling."

"It does not matter," she said firmly.

"It matters to me."

"Why?" she demanded.

"Because you're even more beautiful when you smile."

And she had no words to answer that.

Susan, Katie, and The Rabbit

I Believe

"I BELIEVE. I BELIEVE. I believe. I believe. I believe. I believe. I believe. I believe."

The three voices blended together as they chanted under the blanket. Katie and Susan had been at it for almost two hours and both girls were soaked with sweat, dizzy and lightheaded. Neither could tell exactly when the Rabbit had started chanting with them, adding his higher pitched somewhat whiny voice to the mix of voices. Rabbit stopped first, then Katie.

"I believe. I believe. I believe. I believe." Susan's hands were still wrapped around Katie's hands, which were wrapped around the cup, which held the pills. Susan rocked back and forth as she chanted, dragging Katie back and forth with her.

"I believe. I believe. I believe. I believe."

"Susan!" Katie shouted and Susan finally opened her eyes and stopped chanting.

"Are the pills ready?" she asked.

"Yes. But hurry!" said the Rabbit urgently.

"Rabbit said they're about to come in here!" Katie warned as she retrieved her pills from the cup. "We need to take the pills right now!" She put action to words, downing the first two and chasing them with a swallow of her bottle of water.

"You were chanting too well! And too loud. Dangerous. Ve-ry dangerous! They're probably too strong," the Rabbit complained. "But that doesn't matter, they'll be here any moment, Susan. Take your pills! Hurry! Hurry! Hurry!"

It was dark under the blanket, and Susan was dizzy and couldn't see the Rabbit. She felt the cup get pressed into her hand.

"Here! Swallow!" Katie ordered.

Susan raised the cup to her mouth and dumped in the payload of pills and began to fumble around in the dark for her bottle of water to help her wash them down.

"Here!" The bottle was pushed into her grasp.

Susan twisted the top and stuck the bottle into her mouth as the blanket was snatched away roughly. She swallowed, getting the pills down just as someone grabbed the bottle of water from her hands. She was still blinking in the bright light as hands grabbed her and hauled her from the floor and dropped her into a chair.

"Get off me! Leave us alone!"

Susan's head was spinning, but she heard Katie yelling and someone else, a man, yelling further away.

"What the hell are you doing to the girls!" It was Alfred.

Susan's eyes focused just in time to see a needle crammed into her vein by a man in a white lab jacket. Three guards held her in the chair as the doctor extracted blood.

"No! Get off me! Stop! Help!" Katie fought in her chair.

"Katie!" Susan shouted. "They just want blood! Stop fighting. Stop!"

Katie looked around the doctor to Susan.

"Why!?" she shouted, breathing hard.

"Just let them have their blood, Katie, and stop fighting. Trust me!"

Katie didn't really have a choice. The guards had taken advantage of her distraction to wrap her up. Soon the needle was in her vein. They drew three dark red tubes from each girl.

Dr. Tachi was there in the room supervising what was being done.

"What have you girls gotten into?" he asked. He held up the little painted paper cup. It had been crushed during the struggle. Then he held up Katie's small bag of white and blue pills. She'd made enough for one more day for her and Susan and those were still in the bag.

Two guards were on each girl, holding them in their chairs. Lots of people had crowded into the room. Standing with Dr. Tachai was Marcia, Mr. Dyal, and Mr. Ogburn along with three other doctors. At the door of their room a dozen soldiers held weapons, pointing them at Alfred, whom Susan caught a glimpse of past all the bodies.

He was standing out in the hallway. Just knowing he was out there made her feel better. Knowing that someone else saw what was happening to them.

"Alfred!" Susan called. "Don't let them shut the door!"

"I'm right here!" he shouted back. "I can see you!"

"You crushed our cup," Katie accused angrily as a soldier wearing gloves bagged the flattened item like crime scene evidence.

"What are these pills, Katie?" Tachi asked with exaggerated patience.

When Katie didn't answer, Tachi picked up one of the pills and studied it, frowning. He applied a little pressure and the white pill crumpled. He took out one of the larger blue pills and did the same and it collapsed, showing an empty hollow middle. Tachi looked relieved as he gathered the pills and went to talk to the other doctors.

Marcia came and stood between the two chairs and looked at them, frowning like a disappointed parent. "The doctors were worried you may have taken something or swallowed something bad for you. We had to do this. It's for your own safety." Her voice was firmer, and she wore a less friendly face than she'd shown before.

"So," Susan said, curling her lip in disgust, "are the gloves off, bitch? You through playing your nice girl games?"

Marcia sighed. "We're just trying to take care of you."

"If you want to take care of us," Susan said with a smile, "then start by giving us our sandwiches and our water."

Marcia stood there frowning suspiciously.

Susan tried again, this time cursing as she usually did. It seemed that Marcia couldn't understand her without every other word being an insult so she used a dialect Marcia responded to.

"Snap out of it, bitch. Go over there and pick up our sandwiches and our drinks, you dumb whore. We just got blood raped by your goons and we need to eat. Unless you plan to have the guards hold us down and shove something else into our bodies we don't want shoved in, why don't you make yourself useful and go get our food? Or should I start screaming rape and see if Alfred comes to help us? I hope he breaks your neck first."

Marcia shot a worried glance toward the door where Alfred stood.

"No need to get Alfred riled up, Susan," said Dr. Ogburn, the head shrink. "Marcia, do as the girl asked. Go get their food. They do need to eat after having blood drawn."

Marcia stalked off toward the bed, where the soldiers had stacked all the things they'd collected when they'd raided the girls' blanket party. She grabbed the two tuna sandwiches, still in their wrappers, and the two bottles of water. Most of the salad was stomped flat and all over the floor. She looked at the salad bowl.

"There's supposed to be a wire rabbit. Where's the rabbit?" she asked a nearby soldier.

"Maybe it's under the bed." The man resumed his search as Marcia took the girls their lunch.

Katie and Susan sat in their chairs though the guards had moved away. Katie rubbed at her wrists where they'd restrained her, staring down into her lap and looking traumatized.

"Here's your food, Katie. And your bottle of water." Marcia set the items into Katie's lap and gave Susan her food as well. Katie noticed that the Rabbit she'd drawn on Marcia's hand was gone.

"Munch. Munch. Munch," Katie whispered quietly with her head down. Unmoving. She watched from the corner of her eye as Marcia rubbed at her stomach, as if she were hungry.

"Munch. Munch. Munch."

"Munch. Munch. Munch."

"Munch. Munch. Munch."

"Eat, Katie," Susan told her. "You need to eat. Eat!" she ordered.

Katie began to unwrap the sandwich obediently. Both girls kept their heads down and ate their food in silence as the curious doctors and psychiatrists watched their every move, wondering what was happening with these two girls. And they had another mystery. The wire bunny was missing.

Bree

Trapped in Time

Bree Shellhouse gazed around the palatial Banquet Hall of the Builtmore House in absolute ecstasy. Bree had no idea what strange confluence of events had transpired to make this trip possible, but whatever it was, she was glad to be out of the house and standing where she stood.

She was also glad to be given some privacy and some peace. Her mother was letting her wander the place all on her own—or almost on her own. The man who followed her kept at a discreet distance, pushing an empty wheelchair. Someone to collect the body if she dropped—when she dropped. It was only a matter of time.

"Excuse me, dear, how big is this room?" asked a plump, cherry cheeked woman in a blue dress who walked at the head of a small group of other plump ladies.

Bree curtsied. "The Banquet Hall of Builtmore House is three thousand square feet, ma'am," she gladly told the inquiring woman.

"How do we get to the gardens from here?" asked another woman.

Neither of them commented on her pale, sunken cheeked appearance, thinking it part of her costume.

Bree pointed helpfully. "Just that way, ma'am. Though it is a bit of a walk I'm afraid."

To Bree the long hall seemed to stretch a thousand miles off into the distance, but the gaggle of women seemed unintimidated as they lumbered off in the direction she'd indicated. Bree sat on a nearby bench and watched them go, envious of the vitality these old women possessed. She gave directions to another passerby.

People had been asking her questions and directions since she first walked onto the property dressed in her nearly historically accurate, blue gown, servant's apron, and bonnet. The bonnet helped hide her bald head. All her clothes were vintage or things she'd made herself by hand. She'd had no problem coming up with an ensemble that worked for this unexpected trip.

By Bree's estimation the Builtmore House in North Carolina and the Hurst Mansion in California were the only two, modern American castles. The good ones, at least the ones she really liked, were all overseas. Bree loved the sense of safety that seemed to fill her when she stood inside a structure like the Builtmore House.

She liked anything solid and permanent. Monuments, obelisks, or any object that felt like an anchor stuck deep into the bones of the world comforted her. Castles were that way. They resisted the flow of time and continued on for ages and ages. She loved the big, European castles like Neuschwastein, Mount St. Michael, Lowenburg, and even the tiny castles like Swallow Nest, perched on a cliff overlooking the Crimean Sea.

It wasn't just the castles that she loved; she also loved the history and the romance of the age in which the castles began. She loved simplicity. She hated TV. To the horror of her friends, she despised cell phones. She hated the internet (though she used it). Her brother Luke was practically a cave dweller, playing World of Warcraft, wired to his computer and trudging through that fantasy land for hours at a time while the real world slipped away.

Bree liked the real world and the real things in it, things she could still touch, smell, see, and enjoy. She took a deep breath and tried to lock the particular scent of the place into her memory. She turned about on her bench and studied the beautiful tapestry mounted on the wall behind her. She squinted, trying to see the fine stitch-work and puzzle out how it had been done.

Bree loved to make things with her own hands. She honestly thought she'd been born in the wrong time. A sad cosmic screw up. Her own attempt at fixing this screw up had led to the greatest adventure of her short life. Five months ago she'd run away from her parents, her doctors, and everyone else and hid away in a monastery. The Sisters of Peace.

She had searched for months before choosing the enormous 1920s brick building in Chicago and the Anglican Monastery that called it home. They had gardens within the walls where they grew their own food, kept chickens for eggs, and made cloth and dresses by hand. They even had a room filled with old looms and did weaving the old fashioned way.

The elderly women at the monastery treated her like a long, lost daughter who had found her way home. She'd been so angry at God and the world when she ran away, but her time with the Sisters had changed that. She enjoyed the prayer times and quiet times with the old women as much as she did the weaving and gardening. Bree found peace for herself there within the four, solid red brick walls of the old monastery.

She hid with the Sisters for three months before her father tracked her down and took her back to the doctors, back to what he insisted was her home. He would have never found her, but she'd left too many bread crumbs behind at the public library. She should have never used her own library card.

Bree got to her feet and walked along the grand halls, dreaming of castles and kings and simpler things. She also let her mind wander to her newest interest—a piece of the past that was here in the present, the Kingdom of Amen Hale.

Her father had been with a group that went inside a few days ago and he'd told her a lot about it. Not all of it had been good, but she strongly suspected he was coloring things darkly, trying to discourage her interest in the place. She'd been caught by her parents doing research on her brother's computer just last night. They were worried she'd try to run away again, and they were right to worry. She was as good as gone already.

From everything she'd heard about Amen Hale, once you got in, no power on earth could get you out. Amen Hale seemed like a special place, a fine place to finish her journey. A nice place to lay down her bones and become part of the ground. To Bree, Amen Hale sounded like a wonderful place to die. All she had to do was find a way in.

She walked as she thought.

The man in the suit followed with the chair.

Donald Claus

Last Day at the Office

THEY MET THIS morning two hours before dawn on a dead end road. There was nothing there except a long, metal tool box. Donald had been paid good money to do this job. Up front. Clean. Even if he were double crossed, the money was already his, safely tucked away, placed into nurturing off-shore accounts that would plump and swell over the next twelve years. He'd arranged things to his liking. The funds would be made available to his four children discreetly when they reached the age of twenty-two. It was his money, free and clear. He could have bailed on the job and run with the cash, but should he make that choice his family would be the ones to suffer while he enjoyed his retirement in tropic seclusion.

Only two other men showed at the predawn meet, their headlights joining his and illuminating the metal box and its contents. Donald could tell the other men were professionals. Killers. Who knew, maybe there were supposed to be ten men at the meet and only three had showed. There was no way to know.

There were ten weapons inside the box. Did that mean ten snipers? The weapons were all different makes and models. Each with special (non-metal) rounds, specific for each weapon, taped to the stocks. Perhaps the principal party simply desired to be accommodating, making sure each of them had, in hand, a weapon they felt familiar with.

Each of the men chose a different weapon from the box. Maps were provided as well. Detailed maps. Clearly marking security measures they needed to avoid and highlighting ideal vantage points from which they could fire. Within the box were other goodies as well. A tarp with the matching roof pattern was there in the box along with other convenient toys and gadgets. None cheap. All professional.

One of the other men who introduced himself as Grady Mange summed it up nicely. "Makes me feel stupid for not asking for more money."

Mange wore denim overalls. He was in his fifties, his face lined and weathered. He looked as if he should be on a farm in the Midwest, wrangling a combine down endless rows of corn. At least that was what he looked like until you saw him fish into the box and select his weapon and quickly scan the map and pick his perch.

Mange spoke first, "Once we fire, the game will be over. Wait till we have at least two targets in view. Clock starts at ten, we go if we have more than one target in sight, but if it gets past eleven, even one target will do. As long as we give it a go they should leave our families be. I'll take that tall cypress tree." He pointed to the map, claiming his spot. "Don't get caught going in. See ya in hell this afternoon." He tipped his hat, walked to his old pickup, placed the weapon and gear in the back, and drove off.

Donald followed suit; he pointed to the map. "Roof's mine, and I got the tarp to match. Start at ten, two's a go, after eleven any target will do. Careful going in." He echoed Mange exactly, turned and walked his gear to his shitty Enterprise rental.

Smith was still standing at the box, eyeing the map as Donald pulled away.

Donald wondered casually if Smith would bail. It didn't really matter. His business. Donald was in and so was Mange. Of that, Donald had no doubt.

After the quick predawn gathering, Donald drove to a nearby hotel and enjoyed an early morning romp with two very high-priced whores he'd paid for in advance. He took the pleasure of their delightful company with no condom. A first for him. As a married man he'd rarely cheated and had been careful and paranoid as hell when he had. But not now. No fear. No stress. No guilt even. STDs did not frighten a man who had death's shadow lying long across his path. He'd never stare into his wife's eyes and worry what he might have brought home. He was done. The game was over. Donald felt that a part of him was already dead.

The girls treated him oddly. Strangely respectful and submissive. Was it simply because they were well paid or was the shadow of death something that could be felt on his skin? Seen in his eyes. Heard in his voice. He'd certainly heard it in Mange's voice this morning. He wondered if these two girls had seen the look before? Other men on a last romp.

Donald showered, dressed, and went to work for the last time. The map was incredibly helpful, detailing the best way to get past security. By nine thirty he'd crawled out the window on the second story of the big, brick home four properties down from the Hale House. He eased out to the edge of the tile roof under the cover of the tarp. It matched the orange clay roof tiles perfectly. He managed to get set up and comfortable in no time. He sighted down the barrel of his rather plain, no frills, 50 Cal. rifle from under the cover of the tarp. He had an excellent angle and comfortable perch.

The human heart beats 72 times per minute. He would have three, maybe six minutes, before the U.S. gunners tracked in on his position. He'd get off at least two or as many as five shots. That gave him between 216 to 432 heartbeats once he pulled the trigger. He sighted down the weapon, scanning.

He saw what appeared to be servants, gardeners, and occasionally black clad guards but none of the targets. His angle was of the back portion of the house where most of the activity was. He checked his watch: 9:42. Start at ten, two's a go, after eleven, anything goes.

He took the last few minutes to admire the beautiful trees. Oaks and cypress mostly here by the river with a few other hardwoods mixed in. It really was a great view from up here. Donald thought about Mange's cool parting words, "See ya in hell this afternoon." Spoken so casually, like it was no big deal. Perhaps it wasn't. Hard to be afraid of the unavoidable. He and Mange could talk over how things went when they got there. Compare shots. Discuss how things may have been better this way or that. Lament a miss or a jam. Perhaps bitch about Smith being a puss if he bailed. Bitch about the untested rounds.

Donald picked up one of the rounds and felt the odd ceramic head. Maybe they'd be too light and sail high or wide. Perhaps all three of them would end up firing and firing and none of them would hit a damn thing. He chuckled at the thought. That'd be a screwed up deal.

"See ya in hell this afternoon." He thought on it some more. Hell. The place seemed more real now. The world around him, less so. He wondered what the view would be like in hell. Did they have mountains? He hoped it wasn't too over-crowded. Donald liked open space. Not a big fan of crowds.

He looked over at the river. The St. Johns. A big river. A weird river, flowing north the way it did. *Won't see one of those again.*

He took a long, satisfying, almost gloating pull from his canteen. "Aaaa." He nursed the canteen, even dropping a little water on the roof to watch as it snaked down the orange tiles. An extravagant waste. One he could afford. After a few more idle moments of strange contemplation and idle gazing at the world of the living, Donald got into position, sighted down his weapon, and waited for the chance to send one of the primary targets to hell before he arrived there himself.

Black Rain

Cassadan's Offer

KNEES IN THE seats of their chairs, Bethany and Penny leaned forward, practically lying on the table while they gnawed their ribs. The girls were starry-eyed, staring down the length of the table at the Twilin. He spoke with Cathryn and Cornelius, seated comfortably before them in a perfectly sized chair that appeared on the table out of nowhere.

I hadn't made the chair with any stray thought of mine, though I was sure I knew how it had come into being. Bethany's birthday gift, her magic bloodstone bracelet. She must have been worried about the Twilin having to stand for so long without a chair. One of the kisses I'd placed on the stone had come out, finding a way to surprise her, and make her smile.

I kept an eye on the Twilin, but mostly I stared past him and watched my birth mother as we ate. We'd sat as far from her as possible at Bethany's request. I had no idea what my mother had done to wound Bethany so deeply, and I hadn't asked—yet. Part of me hoped she still loved us.

My father, Ryan, and Sky had looked across the expanse of the High Table and met my gaze a number of times during the meal, but my mother had not glanced my way even once. Believer's red eyes watched me watching my mother. He worried over my heart ache, just as he watched and worried over Bethany and little Penny as well. A husband and a father.

The girls slid back into their seats and placed their bones, and mine, in what they'd playfully dubbed "the cemetery." Bethany had growled when the red coated servants tried to remove the plate that held our finished ribs, so the plate stayed, and our bone pile grew.

The "Memphis Dry Rubbed Man Ribs" we were enjoying had been Chef Tanner's best creation to date. I had no idea how he cooked it, but the dry, sweet meat melted in my mouth like fleshy candy, almost making me swoon. The food went a long way toward lightening my mood, which had darkened considerably since meeting my "birth" mother.

The Twilin caught my eyes as he rose from his seat. He bowed to Cathryn and Cornelius, making his farewells. Unfolding a pair of beautiful blue and gold wings from his back, he leapt into the air. He flew gracefully down the length of the table and landed in front of our little family.

"Greetings, Believer, Prince of Clouds," the tiny man bowed to Believer, then to me. "Greetings goddess. I am Cassadan, attendant of Queen Taunwee, the Twilight Star."

"Hello, Cassadan," I said. He stared at me, taking in my appearance as I did the same to him.

He was very handsome and his movements seemed delicate and smoothly perfect, not sharp or twitchy. He wore a pair of exquisite, white, knee-high boots over a pair of sky blue pants with a long-sleeved, black top that shimmered like silk. The white lace at his cuffs reminded me of the black dress I'd worn as a witch. Beautiful, shoulder length, silver hair and a youthful, angular face gazed up, carefully calm, as he stared at my horns then peered into the depths of my frightening eyes.

His eyes were not irregular; they seemed to be the most ordinary part of him as he watched me reach out to the white dish he stood beside and bring a piece of candied bone marrow to my mouth. I made some room as Bethany (who'd abandoned her own seat) squirmed her way in front of my chair like a wriggling fish. I saw her little maid's longing eyes as she remained in her own chair, watching and wanting to come closer as well. Bethany's tail had wrapped itself around her wrist and was tugging at her already, urging her to follow.

"Come on." I waved her over as well and she slid out of her chair with a bright smile and scooted in beside Bethany. The servants quickly swooped in and removed "the graveyard" and the other plates to make room for the girls, who rested their chins and fingertips on the edge of the tabletop and stared at the Twilin with big, dreamy eyes.

"Hi," Bethany said shyly.

"Hi." Penny, just as shyly.

I put a hand on Bethany's head. "This is Bethany," then touched her maid, "and this is Penny."

Cassadan did a magnificent bow to the girls. "Greetings, ladies. It is a pleasure to meet you."

"When did Queen Taunwee expect us to arrive?" Believer asked, taking Cassadan's attention.

"Soon," was Cassadan's vague reply.

Believer started to discuss the particulars of how long we would stay, the special items they'd requested for restitution, and who would be going with us.

I only half listened, my attention captured by an older, female servant with a bad limp on the far side of the hall. As she walked her stride changed, leveled. She kept going—minus the limp.

Bethany reached over to the dish and grabbed a handful of brown marrow bits. She urged Penny to try one, and soon both girls were munching away as they listened to Believer and Cassadan talk. They seemed content just to watch him, fascinated that he was real and not something from a movie or a storybook. All of the hurt that had rested on Bethany's face was gone, replaced by joy and wonder.

"Would you like a piece?" Bethany pushed the candy dish an inch in Cassadan's direction.

His tiny features sharpened into larger focus as I squinted down at him, my eyes perfecting as needed. The suspicious arch of his delicate brows made me laugh.

"It's candied human marrow," I explained to our guest with the happy laugh still in my voice. "You don't have to eat it, but you're welcome to it if you'd like to give it a try."

"I've had marrow before," he said. "Many, many times. But it's been hundreds of years since I've had human marrow." His wings snapped out suddenly, making the girls jump.

Cassadan leapt into the air and hovered over the bowl. A colorful blur shimmered in the air on each side of his frame where wings beat faster than the human eye could follow. I heard the soft hum of his wings accompanied by a feather light breeze that glided across my sensitive skin. Bethany and Penny watched with rapturous delight as he pulled a small, shining knife from inside a boot, leaned head first into the dish, and cut off a convenient sized piece. Cassadan landed, snapped his wings shut, and took a small, experimental taste.

"Excellent," he declared with a judicious nod, then took a bigger bite and amended that to a bright-eyed "Fantastic!"

Cassadan studied the white dish's disturbing design as he munched happily on his marrow.

"Any bowl in Amen Hale that holds the flesh of man will be made in this fashion," I told him.

He showed no reaction to the fact that we were eating human flesh and bone. His acceptance of this would have made me worry, once upon a time, in another life. But not now. Who was I to judge this man or his people?

Cassadan stepped closer to the man-carved dish, studying it with renewed interest. The two-inch high, marble figures that made up the dish stared down at the Twilin with dark, dour faces, as if he were an interloper into their miniature world. With the heads facing down, the lip of the dish ran along the artfully crafted plane of muscled shoulders and outstretched arms. The marble figures were all male, standing side by side, arms held out but bent at the elbows and interlocked with the figures on either side.

As I stared at it, the dish defined, lines and details too small for the human artist to create taking form on the marble figurines. As I looked for more detail, more detail was simply there because my eyes sought it. Similar things had been happening to objects, and even people, since I woke this morning.

Teeth, hair, eye lashes, genitalia, and toenails took form, each of the figures different and unique from any other. Names began to ghost through my mind. I did not call their names, but I did wonder what each of these names (names that I did not call) would need. Feelings and thoughts, cares and concerns, hopes and dreams, each set unique, stretched out behind each name—

A soft, cloudy hand covered my eyes and all I saw were clouds.

"My love," Believer's deep voice soothed. "You lost yourself as you stared at the bowl."

The marble figures had not come to life, but it was disturbing to see again how easily I reshaped what I saw and how easily my mind wandered. When I was a witch the same thing would happen. I'd fall into a daydream right in the middle of things due to some shock or surprise, wild colorful daydreams with baton twirling girls, marching bands, and acrobatic midgets.

I did not want my accidental daydreams or nightmares given life. I was very glad that I'd given myself a measure of protection here in Amen Hale. Here at least, life would only come when, and as, I called for it. No more accidental life.

Believer took his hand away and I looked again at the white dish and the twenty-two male figures who wreathed the outside with their joined bodies. I knew each of their names, but thankfully, they did not know mine. Not yet. Perhaps one day they would live, but it would be my choice and no accident.

Believer turned my face away again to face him, and his worried, red eyes.

"Thank you for helping me. I need you," I told him and pressed my face into his huge, open palm, breathing in the smell of him. The clean, wonderful, familiar scent of spring rain filled my lungs and cleared my head. He moved his hand and pulled it through my hair.

"You smell like home," I told him. "I missed your smell so much."

He smiled for me.

Bethany tugged on my arm to get my attention.

"Can we go with you to see Queen Taunwee!?" she asked, her voice an excited plea that quickly turned into a rapid fire "Please! Please! Please! Please!"

Believer grumbled, "Little One, Cathryn sent a man to The Hallow for you to sacrifice. The guards holding him have missed lunch waiting for you."

Her pleading eyes turned onto me, not as a sister, but as a child to her mother. Somehow, it felt right to treat her as my child, and that was what I tried to do.

"Are you still hungry, Bethany?" I asked, knowing that she could not lie.

Her angelic face frowned.

"This will be dangerous, Beth, we don't want any more accidents. And I don't want to keep the Queen waiting."

Her countenance fell even further and her eyes teared up. This part of being a mom sucked! I soo wanted to cave!

Believer came to my rescue, his tone kind but parental. "Your mother is right, Little One. We must go, and you must feed."

"If you would allow me to serve you," Cassadan offered with a small bow. "You have no need of an escort, goddess. You are expected and very much anticipated. If it would please you, I can remain behind with the Princess and bring her to join you once she has finished with the sacrifice."

Of course the girls loved this option, erupting in cheers, but Believer and I frowned.

Cassadan quickly dropped to one knee. "Forgive me. I presumed too much. I shall escort you to the Queen instead."

I smoothed Bethany's beautiful head of black and red hair and kissed the top of her head.

"Do you have children, Cassadan?"

"I had two," he answered, "and two grandchildren."

"Had?" I made the word a question.

"A lightning strike hit our warren. I and my Dam are a house unto ourselves now." He noticed the girls' sad faces. "It happened many years ago." He tried to take some sting from his dire tale.

"You had a daughter?" Bethany asked.

"Sons," Cassadan answered. "But I had a granddaughter. Her name was Caitrin. Her name meant 'pure.'"

Bethany continued to ask Cassadan questions about Caitrin which Cassadan seemed only too happy to answer.

What color was her hair? Her wings? Was she small, like me? Did you sing to her a lot? What games did she like to play? Did the boys pick on her? The questions she asked seemed to interest him, and Cassadan seemed to enjoy the remembering and the telling as much as the girls enjoyed the listening. The more I heard, the less I worried about Cassadan and the more I worried about Bethany. She liked Cassadan.

Taunwee

Salvation

Being caught enjoying a rare moment of unguarded, private self-indulgence by the boy who was "supposed" to be sleeping had not been how Queen Taunwee intended to begin things with Benson. Actually, the Queen had absolutely no idea how to begin. In the past, if a human or Twilin male drew her interest, she would simply allow "said male" to approach her, and then would graciously "deign" to accept him into her bed. Barring that, she would simply take whom she wanted by force of will or force of might. Even other immortal beings she'd shown an interest in over the millennia she won or lost while using guile, cunning, or force.

But her old tried and true methods of courtship were not possible with Benson. He belonged to Amen Hale. Taunwee could not take him from this girl goddess by deceit or violence. To do so would be madness. For the first time in her existence, Queen Taunwee, the Twilight Star, had to woo, and win, her Roe.

She'd been aloof and haughty at first, finding herself annoyingly tongue tied. She was not sure what to say. She did not want to scare the boy off by seeming too harsh or too alien—so she said nothing, or next to nothing. Benson didn't seem bothered by her reluctant manner or her near silence; he simply filled the quiet void between them with his steady voice. Unlike her own people, and most every other human she'd ever encountered, he was not afraid or overawed by her presence—though he did appreciate her beauty.

He complimented her, but not in the ways she was so accustomed to hearing. Compliments from her own people were placating emptiness, shameless groveling, or sycophantic maneuvering in her ears. Her Twilins were so familiar with her, they were blind to her and she to them. The many compliments she'd received from humans in past ages counted for even less, most of them praising her beauty as they prostrated themselves with their heads buried in the dirt.

Benson's compliments were different, well considered and purposeful. And they did not come every time he opened his mouth. Taunwee marked each one as he spoke about the common things of his human life, and occasionally about her.

She had never before been so self-conscious of her changeable hair. She kept glancing down at it, fussing with it, brushing it back behind her. She could tell by the way the boy stared as she did this, that Peffan had, indeed, informed Benson of this aspect of her nature. This boy possessed this knowledge, and here she stood before him, G-R-E-E-N! And not merely green; she herself had never seen such a shade! It made no sense. What did it mean?

She tried to work up her anger at Peffan to force some other color into her hair and mute the pure color, but it only got worse. Brighter green. This made her frustrated and even more unsettled. She felt exposed while the boy was not. Taunwee was completely alone, nervous and hesitant to speak, horribly embarrassed by her hair, hopped up and heady on sunflower seeds—and counting his compliments.

And that was how they spent almost forty-five undisturbed, wonderful minutes, until Reese started shouting for Benson to drive the truck into the garage from some distance away.

"When will I see you again, Benson?" she asked as Benson turned the key in the ignition. The truck engine rumbled to life.

"I hope I see you as soon as I park this truck, but I don't know." He gave her a small incline of the head. "I am a servant, Queen Taunwee, and I must go where I am sent. I'll be back as soon as they let me return."

Her Twilins beheld her hair as Taunwee flew from the window of the truck. Bright green, perfect and pure, shown in the sun, trailing out behind her. The gentle hum of wings and soft murmur of thousands of hushed voices which had filled the clearing like a babbling brook EXPLODED! Deafening cheers and wild rejoicing filled the air.

The unexpected, swarming buzz of activity and the sudden eruption of thousands upon thousands of shouting, happy voices startled Reese and his men. They quickly gathered into a tight, protective knot, as if preparing for an attack.

"Keep your hands off your weapons!" Reese ordered his men, shouting to be heard over the din caused by countless, rejoicing voices. "Stay calm! I said hands off weapons, Martin!"

Reese and the others watched silently as the Twilin Queen and her encircling entourage flew past where they huddled on the trail before the truck. She landed on a stump directly in front of the gateway arch and watched them from her woody pedestal.

Benson honked the horn, causing the men of Amen Hale to jump and squeal like a bunch of frightened, little girls. Once over their surprise, they of course cursed or threatened to kick his ass. Reese and his men moved off the path and let Benson drive the box truck into the garage, then quickly followed, retreating through the gate and into the safety of Amen Hale.

Taunwee sat on the oak stump and watched Benson drive the rental truck through the gap between the joined trees. Once they entered, her curious and rejoicing people closed in and crowded around the opening. They were careful not to block her view or enter the gate themselves, though Taunwee could tell that they wanted to. They longed to. They wanted to keep Benson with her as much as she wanted the boy by her side.

Taunwee stared though the tree-formed window into Amen Hale and observed how the other men of Benson's kingdom eyed him warily as he climbed out of the truck. Benson had a clipboard in hand and a bag slung over one shoulder. He walked to a desk and separated papers from the clipboard into various bins before walking to Reese, his superior. He spoke with Reese briefly, then walked into the whispering gauntlet of other men who were milling about. The men bombarded him with questions and Benson answered some of them as he passed by, but only in passing as he strode purposefully along, walking in her direction.

Could it be this easy? Had her attempt at courtship been successful? She'd sensed no moment of victory or domination or even surrender during their time together. Perhaps he merely wished to speak more. Her heart beat faster as he approached. Both excited and uncertain.

"Stay," she told no one specific (and everyone in general) as she snapped out her wings and took to the air, leaving her frustrated attendants and consorts behind on the stump. She hovered in the air before the open gateway, waiting for Benson to come to her.

His eyes locked on the tiny, beautifully formed female before him, wearing a white, diaphanous gown. He smiled brightly, oblivious to the men he walked past and their faces. Her hair shone in the rays of the near noon sun. Behind her, the Twilin people rejoiced and roared as if watching a pairing, the Roe walking out to take his Dam.

"Good thing you got a needle dick," a rough whisper.

Benson froze as he passed the last group of men.

"Bug-Fucker!" a second whisper from the same voice.

Benson's brows dropped, his face flushing red. Just behind him stood a large, blond-headed boy with two other men, all three struggling to suppress their mirth. Without warning, Benson whirled, pouring all his twisting, furious momentum into his fist, which he aimed, not at, but through the much larger boy's head. The crushing blow connected. The blond boy's flailing arms and body collided with his two companions. All three men ended on the floor of the garage, the entire group felled by one blow.

Taunwee quickly waved with both hands behind her to keep her consorts from rushing forward. They would want to protect Benson, who was already under her care. She did not want them killing his adversary (who may already be dead) or in any way interfering. She did not turn away from the sight for a second but waved her arms as she watched.

She did not notice her hair or she might have been more alarmed. It had not gone red or orange or blue with curiosity, but white. Fear. Pure as fresh, fallen snow. Afraid for Benson, not herself. Her people had never seen this. The Twilin race went silent, their quiet dread joining their Queen's as they watched and waited.

The two other men scrambled away on hands and knees as Benson advanced and stood over the much larger boy, fists clenched, angry, lungs pumping in and out like the bellows of a war machine. Reese and others had come running, but Benson wanted the boy to get up and fight.

The boy he'd struck did not move.

Benson straightened and stepped away.

Reese glanced out toward Taunwee, where she hovered, alone, not more than twenty feet from where he and Benson stood. He scanned the sea of miniature, hovering bodies that stared into the garage from beyond the gateway, watching his every move. The roaring cacophony of jubilation had vanished, leaving in its place a deeply threatening silence and the steady hum of countless wings.

Under the scrutiny of tens of thousands of Twilin eyes, Reese knelt beside the downed boy and checked the damage, then motioned a couple of his men to come. He stood and kept his eyes on Taunwee as he spoke to Benson in hushed whispers.

The men lifted the unconscious boy. Blood seeped from his nose and mouth, making a red trail as he was carried away. Benson nodded to something Reese said and started forward again, passing through the gate and walking the last twenty feet to stand before her.

He did not kneel and she did not ask him to. She wanted to ask him many things, but no thought of abasement or homage entered her mind. Her eyes focused on his still trembling hand. The quickening of combat. She knew that the flush of it and anger and outrage still coursed through his human body. He was not used to this.

The white leeched from her hair as the poison of fear left her body, green taking its place.

"Did you hurt your hand?" she asked.

She didn't have to know what the boy he'd struck said, and she was sure, without really knowing why, that Benson would not tell her even if she did ask. So she did not ask. Even though she wanted to know.

He nodded in answer to her question, not speaking, still breathing hard. Catching his breath.

"Give it to me."

Benson held up his shaking hand, palm down, and she landed on his wrist and walked down to his bloody knuckles. She hadn't used her powers to heal a human for three thousand years. And she'd never done anything over so small a hurt. It was childish. Foolish. But she did not care. That boy had surely said something foul about her. About her and him together perhaps?

She dropped to her knees there on the back of his hand, leaned forward and rested her palms on his first and second knuckle and used her power. The broken bone on his pinky finger popped back into place and knit together, as did the cuts in his flesh from the boy's teeth. She was so close, she simply could not resist leaning forward that last, short distance and rubbing her face in that gap, between those two knuckles. She breathed in her human Roe and tasted his skin with her tongue, enjoying the sweet, salty tang of his sweat.

She stopped suddenly, feeling the eyes of all her people on her as she acted the fool with her butt stuck high in the air behind her. She stood as demurely as she could manage, then turned to face Benson. Her hair seemed one dimensional now, a solid color, shifting through different shades and flavors of the same color with her mood. The dark, hungry shade of a moment ago was now replaced with the brighter glow of new, rye grass.

Taunwee noticed with a twinge of alarm that Benson's face was red. Redder than before! Was he still flushed from the fight or—was he blushing?

"Benson!" Reese called from the other side of the gate.

Benson frowned in annoyance. "They wanted me to tell you that the Black Lion will be here soon. And Queen Cathryn wanted to thank you again for your warning."

"Benson!" Reese called again. "Get back inside! Now!"

Quick flashes of bright, cotton candy pink flashed through her hair, as fast as strobe lighting.

"You should go," Taunwee said petulantly, narrowing her eyes in Reese's direction. "Go to the Queen that you love!" She snapped her wings open, kicked off against his hand, pushing it down as she leapt into the air.

She did not leave, but hovered before him, already regretting her words.

Benson leaned closer until his eyes were only inches away, radiating challenge and other emotions that Taunwee could not decipher in her own confusion.

"The *other* Queen that I love," Benson corrected, then turned and walked back through the gate.

As soon as he was inside, Reese closed the gateway. The image of Amen Hale vanished, leaving nothing but twisted trees framing a picture of the woods beyond.

Taunwee was in love. She reveled in the glow of it. She felt light, pure, clean. Not since before The Fall had she felt so innocent. So childlike. Wrapped in the warm comfort of Benson's last words, she floated back to Marie and settled on her knee like a weightless piece of pollen. He was her Roe.

Marie studied her and her hair, then asked, "Did you enjoy watching him sleep?"

"He caught me," Taunwee answered, narrowing her eyes at the girl.

Marie's smile widened, not fooled in the least. "Did you enjoy getting caught?"

The Queen smiled and then laughed.

Marie laughed with her.

The Twilins in the meadow laughed with Marie and their Queen. No more joyous sound had ever been heard in the Summer Court of the Twilight Star. Ever called the Quiet Court. Summer had come at last, the Green Queen had come. But every child knows that after summer—comes Fall.

"CRACK!"

The sound of a gun rang out, so different from the sound of laughter. By the time the last of its echo had vanished, so too had the rejoicing and laughter. Marie's body fell, pinning a number of Twilins beneath her. The night air filled with the screams of her people and the shouted commands of her consorts. Taunwee picked herself up from where she'd fallen and leapt into the air to see for herself what was happening.

Marie's hands and legs were twitching, but she'd been shot in the head. A round hole was in her temple near her left ear. Blood and brains were strewn out behind her head and an endless line of dead and wounded Twilin bodies followed the path of the killing shot, as the bullet traveled in, across the crowded field, and out away from the Beloved of the Black Lion.

The chill knowledge filled Taunwee as she looked down at Marie. She could not heal this. Perhaps Marie's goddess could or this Princess Bethany that Marie had told her about. The child who raised the dead so easily. This was far beyond her. All she could do was keep the body safe and keep Marie's soul close and wait for help.

Taunwee's magic held sway in this field and her power prevented the entrance, or exit, of spirits that might harm her children or pull a soul down into the earth. She spent no time seeking the shooter, her people would be doing that already; she focused on Marie. With her power she gathered Marie's shocked soul together, restoring awareness and cohesion as she tied her ghost to her body to keep her from drifting away or down.

Marie's soul stood beside Taunwee in the graveyard, a ghostly apparition that matched her physical body in appearance and dress. She looked down at herself.

"Is that me?" Marie asked, surprised.

"I'm sorry, child. It is," Taunwee answered calmly, not sparing the truth. "You've been killed, Marie. Shot in the head. We are looking for the shooter now."

"What will happen to me now, Queen Taunwee?" Marie asked.

"Don't worry," Taunwee assured the girl's soul. "Angels, even fallen ones, are very good with souls. I will not allow you to go anywhere or drift away. Benson said that your Lion will be here very soon. If she does not put you to right, then surely she will call Princess Bethany and she can raise you from this death."

"My Queen!" a guard shouted. "A car approaches!"

An early eighties station wagon with blue, faded paint and a ladder tied to the rack on top barreled down the dirt path. Flying and wingless Twilins rushed to avoid the speeding vehicle as it raced down the trail and then kicked up a massive cloud of dust as the driver stood on the brake right beside the graveyard.

The car door swung open and a tall, wild looking man stepped out. He had nappy, unkempt, shoulder length hair and a wild mustache and beard to match. He wore a long-sleeved, flannel shirt and jeans. He could have passed for the usual type these mountains sheltered—if not for the mark, carved onto his forehead. For everyone who saw it, it was different. Whatever was most disturbing, vile, abhorrent, that was what they saw. For many it was a swastika or a big, ugly 666 or even a pentagram carved into the flesh of his forehead. For others an upside-down cross or the words PEDOPHILE, SODOMITE, or RAPIST spelled out on his forehead.

Cain rushed up to the old, rickety gate and swung it open and strode over to the body. Twilins rushed and tumbled over one another to avoid his path and he seemed utterly unconcerned by the swarm of creatures that surrounded him. He was not concerned by Taunwee either. Very little troubled Cain, except life itself and his lot in it. Cursed by God in many ways, he also was protected in one very important way. No one was allowed to kill him. Any who tried, died.

"Who is he!?" exclaimed Marie's soul as she watched the man stride through the crowd and right up to her body. "What is he doing!?"

"Why are you doing this, Cain!" Taunwee asked, ignoring Marie's questions. "You have never been a pawn in Lucifer's games. From the beginning, ever you have stayed apart. Why hurt this child?"

The one known as The Wild Man or, The Wandering Man threw Marie's body over his shoulder as if she weighed nothing. He seemed in a hurry, but spared a glance over his shoulder for Marie's soul and Taunwee, even as he walked toward the gate, dragging the weeping ghost of Marie along with him and her body.

"When they take her to her proper place, will this new god make war with our old one?" Cain's voice graveled out in hillbilly English.

"Proper place?" Marie's soul paled. "What is he saying!? Don't let him take me!" She wailed, even as she drifted along behind her dead body, tethered to it by unseen ropes.

"Why take her to the darkness!?" Taunwee cried out, following along with them. "WHY, CAIN!? You have killed no one since your brother, and that was done in a moment of anger! This is not anger, Cain! This is hate! GREED!" Her angry voice accused as she followed him in frustrated impotence. Unable to stop him.

Cain cringed, guilty, at her voice. He cursed in the first language of men as Marie's dress caught on the hinge of the gate and slowed him down. He moved as if he thought someone might gain the ability to hinder him at any moment or stop him from doing as he wanted. Ever before, Cain had worn no expression other than fatigue or stoic acceptance, but Taunwee saw in his eyes the faint glimmer of hope balanced by the darkness of ugly shame. And fear.

For thousands of years he had traveled and been solitary, avoiding man, eschewing violence entirely. He did not need to raise his hand to defend himself ever again. God protected him. The few times she'd seen or heard of Cain making contact with others was to offer some assistance to lost or injured travelers, who feared and loathed him even as he helped them and often cursed him as soon as he departed. Since losing his temper with his brother and spilling his blood upon the ground, he'd been the most gentle soul to softly tread the earth.

Cain spoke as he rushed across the open grass toward the waiting station wagon. "If you want answers, ask the darkness yourself." He pointed off to the tree line with his free hand, the other held the body draped over his shoulder.

Off in the shadowed trees dark shadows were pushing up from the ground like snakes. Red, hot, baleful eyes stared back from the shadows. Screams were beginning to rise from all directions. Twilin screams. Tens at first, then hundreds, then more. Blurs of flashing lights began to shoot by as her horrified Twilins charged toward the safety of the clearing and the graveyard. The safety of her Summer Court.

"No! Leave me alone!" Marie's soul self cried out desperately, helpless to stop what was happening as she was tugged along with her body. "I don't belong to you! I don't! I belong to the Black Lion!" she wailed.

"Shut up!" Cain shouted. "You shut up!" He opened the back of the station wagon and threw in the body. Marie wailed as her spirit passed through the side panel of the station wagon following her physical self into the vehicle. Cain closed the back door with a slam.

Suddenly the driver's door swung closed, pushed by a handful of determined Twilins. Other small forms were already inside the vehicle. The car roared to life, the horn honking and honking to warn Twilins in the road to stay clear. Cain rushed forward and started pulling wildly at the locked door handle as the vehicle sped away, flying down the dirt road, throwing up enough dirt to bury a small human child let alone a Twilin.

Taunwee's victorious shout joined that of many others. Cheers mixed with the screams and desperate cries coming from the woods.

Cain cursed and ran down the dirt choked trail in hot pursuit, but as the station wagon reached the tree line, a huge wave of dark shadows, thirty feet high, swept over the car and passed into the ground. The vehicle slowed, then stopped. Cain slowed, then walked at a leisurely pace down the trail, toward the waiting vehicle.

Taunwee's attention turned to her own people's plight. Those far down in the valley would never make the shelter of the Summer Court in time, but they tried. There was no other place of safety. She watched the woods as her people continued to run the gauntlet of hungry shadows, zipping through the trees like streaks of light, trying to keep from being snuffed out. Beautiful candles, being swallowed by the darkness.

Those within the graveyard crowded in. Every Twilin who could fly flew. The ground was still covered in some places near the fence two and three Twilins deep as her people trod upon one another as they climbed to safety. The weeping and wails of horror and loss were there, but the sound was not overwhelming.

From birth, each Twilin child was taught that one day all life would end. Their light, and their life itself, was a borrowed hope. A spark, or a glimmer, thrown off by one of the Shining Stars, given as a gift, to be loved and treasured while it lasted. One day that spark would go out, either by accidental death or it would be blown out by The Shadow or burned out by the Glory of God. The Twilin people had witnessed other kingdoms, the realms of other exiles, vanish or be destroyed by darkness or light. No being in the field was surprised that the end had come, but they still fought to keep their small individual sparks alive for a short while longer. Roes clung to their Dams or bits, weeping or simply holding each other.

Queen Taunwee's oldest servants and advisors gathered around her, all grim faced, stoic, accepting.

The end had come.

Her people looked to her hair, expecting to see pure white or defiant red or inky black. The Queen wore green. Gray streaked it, but mostly still green. This calmed her people more than anything else. Green. Love.

A small child was forced past the guards and consorts into the circle of open space they held around Taunwee. Forced between their legs by the press of the crowd like a squeezed grape, she fell at Taunwee's feet. The tiny face of the terrified bit stared up at her. She was filthy, tear streaked, trembling. No children had come near her for over three hundred years and she had not borne a child herself for well over three thousand.

As she gazed down at the child she wondered why she had ever ceased to create life herself. A regret. Taunwee knelt and gathered the clinging bit into her arms and stroked her tangled, golden hair and cooed to it softly. A gentle noise like a sweet tinkling of bells.

"What will the demons do next, Great Mother?" asked the bit with bright, staring eyes.

She would have given Benson a child. Benson cared so for names, perhaps she would have let him name their child. Taunwee answered with the truth.

"They cannot pass through the graveyard from below or come past the fence, but they will not have to, spark of my life."

They all smelled the smoke. Rising from the nearby trees as one by one flames licked at their trunks, rising from the ground itself. Taunwee stood in the midst of her people with defiant, bright green hair, now streaked and seasoned with grey and black. Her people would die today. When her children were gone, the demons with flesh and form would come for her. Taunwee wished she could burn with her people and simply die.

"Let me through!" Taunwee heard a Dam arguing with one of her consorts. "That's fine! You may kill me—after I see her!"

Taunwee recognized the voice.

"Bring the Dam!" she ordered, still holding the bit in her arms.

Deeka held an object wrapped up in a cloth, clutched tightly to her chest. Was this another motherless bit?

"My Queen," Deeka lifted her chin and spoke boldly, "I have a plan." Deeka unwrapped her burden and raised the diamond cup that held the goddess's own tears.

"What salvation can I find in this cup for my children, Deeka?" Taunwee asked her quickly.

The attendants and consorts nearby went still, and that stillness traveled outward like a wave even as thicker smoke began to drift across the graveyard. The eyes of the Twilins turned inward and fell upon the glittering cup.

"Why did the Wandering Man kill the Black Lion's beloved with a gun!?" Deeka declared fiercely. "He could have killed her with his bare hands or with a knife, but he did it with stealth, before she could cry out or pray. He did not want her to pray! He was afraid her goddess would hear! I think he was even afraid of her soul praying or calling out. That is why he came quickly into the graveyard and bore her away before she thought to do so."

"But how does this help us, child? We are not the Black Lion's beloved."

Deeka held the cup out to her. "You will be."

They exchanged burdens. Taunwee took the cup from the Dam's hands and handed her the bit from her own. Taunwee, The Twilight Star, sank to both knees in the dirt and gazed into the glittering depths of the cup.

"What is it like to love her, Deeka?" Taunwee asked.

Deeka knelt beside her. "Drink deeply, Mother, and let us pray to our goddess together."

When Taunwee still hesitated, Deeka reached into the cup with one hand and dipped her fingers into the tears and brought them up to Taunwee's lips. Taunwee shivered as Deeka's fingers brushed her lips, then she raised the cup, and drank deeply—

Donald Claus

Enough to Make a Blind Man Blush

D ONALD SQUEEZED THE trigger. "Bang!"

The pretty, olive-skinned girl spun in two complete circles before she fell to the ground, a full six feet from where she'd been standing on the path with the others. Another shot rang out from somewhere; Donald didn't look away from what he was doing until he was done reloading. He settled and another shot sang out from a different direction and the tall man with black, spiked hair and one, creepy, black hand went down.

"Atta boy, Smith," Donald said, surprised to hear the third gunner join in with him and Mange.

Through the scope he scanned for the girl he'd already hit.

She was *the* primary target. He'd hit her square in the heart, but he wanted to give her a second round to be sure. He saw the small, black girl on the ground as the guards rushed around aimlessly, but there was no sign of his target. He could feel the seconds slipping by as he panned left and right through the scope, up and down, left, right, up, down.

She was gone. Vanished.

Another shot rang out. And then another.

"Great!" he muttered as he repositioned and took aim at the back of the house where people were charging out the main doors. There was no end of ready targets and some already down. A tall girl stepped out of the house, white pants, red boots, a tattoo on her forehead.

He sighted on the tattoo and fired.

Her head shattered in a sea of red. The girl's body dropped awkwardly, limbs twitching.

Other shots cried out after his. Donald reloaded and quickly settled back to the scope.

"Whoa!" he said, as the woman with horns on her head charged out the back of the house, looking like a silver she demon. Her red, hellish eyes promised horrors untold.

He lined up, crosshairs in the scope on her red eyes.

He fired.

Nothing happened.

The tarp was snatched away. Bright sunlight blinded him. A hand with an iron grip closed around his right wrist and a second grabbed his belt and hoisted him into the air. He was flung about and shaken like a rag doll. He heard his rifle skitter down the side of the clay tile roof and caught a sun blurred glimpse as it slipped over the side of the roof.

Donald groped for his backup weapon in a shoulder holster with his left hand, but before he could clear the holster he was airborne. Thrown from the roof. Everything slowed down, and at the same time, everything sped up. Donald's body dumped its hoarded reserves of adrenaline and unleashed every scrap of biochemical magic at its disposal in a final, last gambit, to slow down the world by speeding him up and sharpening his senses to a razor's edge.

Donald saw his attacker as he flew through the open air, away from the red tile roof. She was beautiful. Long, black hair, a beautiful, red dress that matched her bright, red lips and glowing, red eyes. She vanished into thin air.

Donald had time. He was able to smile, sad to see the girl go. He did not need to look up to see the sky as his body shifted his gaze for him, slipping into a horizontal orientation as he fell. He stared straight ahead and studied the sky. Three, puffy, hand-sized clouds and a matching number of contrails in various stages of dissolution marred the pristine plate of blue overhead.

Everything he saw was rendered in vivid detail and color. The edge of the roofline and the leaves of a tall oak popped into his periphery vision as he fell. The leaves were so green. He was picking up speed. Donald wondered if that part of him that lived on after death would continue to fall at his current speed and velocity after impact or if he'd stay with his body for a while and slowly seep his way down to hell. Things were certainly going slow. Maybe it would take the same—

The smacking impact drove the thought from his mind and the air from his lungs in a woosh! The ground continued to give at his back as he sank deeper and deeper. The sky overhead took on the shape of a body sized hole. The open imprint of bright sky above him shrank as the edges of his grave closed in and covered him.

Instead of grave dirt, water buried him alive, surging into his empty lungs as they recoiled from the impact of the landing. He'd just started to choke as incredibly powerful hands pulled him from the pool and threw him over a shoulder, and then he was moving again, flying through the woods faster than he could have ever imagined possible.

The water in his lungs was expelled with bone jarring, lung clearing jolts as he rode upon the shoulder of the female vampire. One final incredible leap through the air and he was over the Cursed Wall and inside Amen Hale. His mouth filled with sandy grit as his silver fillings and two crowns turned to white sand in his mouth.

The blurring movement stopped and he was flung to the ground to land beside Mange, who'd swapped out his overalls for camo, green fatigues.

"Mange," Donald greeted the other man, then spit more sand out of his mouth.

Mange nodded as he swirled his own tongue around, probing his mouth for sand and stray, non metal portions of costly dental detritus that where now loose and unhomed. A small mound of white, ceramic teeth bits already rested before him. His bloody arm hung limp at his side and his knee seemed to be useless now. Metal pin perhaps? Donald guessed.

A pale man stood with the vampire woman in the red dress who'd captured him. Both the vampires. Donald studied the pair.

A scream pulled his attention across the lawn. Right away he felt a twinge of disappointment. The Red Witch, the little, olive skinned girl he'd shot first was on her feet and very much alive. A crowd of people stood around her as she worked on Smith, who was held upright by a dragon headed man.

She snatched a dagger out of Smith's chest and then dropped to her knees in front of him, letting his blood spray onto her as she released one, long lungful of air in a scream of blind fury, then slashed up with the knife. She plunged it into Smith's groin, twisting and gouging.

Donald's skin prickled first, then his body flushed with a sick heat as if he'd suddenly become feverish, and then goosebumps shot up on his arms and neck. His heart hurt. A dull ache. It wanted to leap in his chest and race like a frightened rabbit, but it couldn't. His reserves of "fight or flight" mechanics were expended. He was numb. There was no escape. The chill seeped into him from the ground and hummed in his bones as Bethany's black magic poured over the land of Amen Hale.

"Lucky bastard," Mange muttered as he eyed Smith's bloody ruin. He spat out more sand.

They watched as the man with the burr cut, black hair and one, black hand was helped to his feet by the tall, demon woman with horns and a tail. And then the small, black girl stood up as well. The Red Witch quickly got to her feet and checked both the man and young girl herself, then nodded to the woman with the horns.

The two of them vanished, as did Mange. Donald searched around until he spotted them on the porch, where he'd head shot the girl in white pants. Mange floated in the air, arms and legs pulled out in tight X, held by some invisible force. He remained grim faced and defiant as the little, blood drenched girl cursed in his face. Mange cursed right back.

Donald could see the white of the girl's bared teeth standing out from the blood on her face. She threw the blade on the ground and the clang of fine steel rang out across the clearing. Mange went quiet, eyes wide with horror as his head began to redden and swell grotesquely. Many of those nearby began to back away, their faces masks of horror as Mange's head continued to swell grotesquely.

"POP!" With a sickening noise, Mange's head exploded in a shocking sea of red.

Donald turned away and laid back on the cold ground and studied the sky some more. He'd seen enough. His brain had seen enough for today. It wanted to stop seeing these things. He felt as if he might be in shock as he stared at the sky, picking out shapes among the clouds again as he waited for his turn to die.

Black Rain

Blood and Ashes

Bethany MOVED AS if speed was deathly important. She cursed and swore and launched herself at the first shooter that Sky Dragon held, hacking and slashing in a frenzied rage. The thing was done almost before it began and Penny and Lucius were back with us, both of them raised with just the one human sacrifice.

As soon as she'd checked on them to make sure they were all right, Bethany turned to me. I saw the horror in her eyes.

"Something's wrong, Rain! Something was trying to keep me from raising them!" She looked down at the ground, her bare feet stepping up and down as if poisonous snakes slithered through the earth beneath her. "I can feel them down there!" she hissed. "Whatever they are! Lots of them! Amen Hale is fighting them, but they won't stop! They're trying to pull the souls out of Amen Hale!"

I moved us before she finished the sentence. Bethany and I appeared on the porch, along with another of the snipers Jane and Dan had caught. Bethany utterly destroyed this next man in a shower of blood, bone, and gore so horrendous that many of our own people simply couldn't cope and fled or got sick on the spot, or combined the two and retched as they staggered away.

Only the most determined remained on the porch when Bethany started slitting wrists. She called for two or three people to gather around each of our dead. Dana was dead. She caught a bullet in the gunfire. Angel (her little maid) and David were first to hold out their wrists for Bethany's blade, letting their blood and love cover their dead.

Mary, Cathryn, and Hanna did the same for Emma. I knelt beside Alana, wrist out, waiting for Bethany to come and was surprised to find Jane and Sky facing me, both kneeling on the other side of her body.

"Part of Alana is mine," Sky said as she put her wrist out beside mine. She was sick with worry as she stared down at this girl who, in every way that mattered, was her daughter. I heard my mother's acid voice complaining about the blood and calling Sky away until she was hauled away by Ryan and my father.

And then Bethany arrived. Sky flinched but didn't cry out when the blade went over her wrist, and neither did I or Jane. My golden blood mixed with Sky's red and Jane's own mixed blend of gold and red. The blood covered Alana's face and the horrible wound in her neck where the bullet had ripped into her. Last of all Bethany called for Cornelius and drug her blade down both of his forearms and then did her own.

"Please! Give her what strength she needs to save the ones we love!" I prayed to myself, over and over as I watched.

I heard others weeping and praying as well. Some of them were praying to me, like Cathryn, Jane, and Mary, while others like Sky and my brother and father who stood nearby prayed to God. I could hear those prayers offered to me like small whispers in the back of my mind, echoing and at times even mixing with my own prayer to myself.

Bethany and Cornelius pooled their blood at her feet and she dipped the blade in the blood before she began. She filled herself with all the dark magic she could call forth, supported by all of our combined blood, tears, hopes, and prayers, as she began her chanted spell.

"Blood! Blood! Blood! Blood!
Let this blade now spirit be!
Bathed in hate and love and need!
Pierce the shadows in the deep!

Pierce the hands that grasp and seek!"

"As Above!" She cried out, thrusting her sacrificial dagger high into the sky with both hands.

"So Below!" She growled as she turned the blade over in her hands with the tip pointed down to the ground.

She tightened her two handed grip on the handle until she trembled.

"IN YOUR FACE!" she screamed, then dropped to the patio floor and drove the blade straight down into the pool of blood at her feet. The blade went into the cement clear to the hilt and straight down into something else as well. There was a trembling in the earth beneath our feet and a high pitched keening surged up from the ground itself.

"Now Let Them Go!" Bethany cried out once again and twisted the blade while it was stuck into the concrete patio.

The blade turned as though it rested in hot butter and not solid stone. Again the ground trembled, and more frightening cries rose from the ground. A foul, sulfurous wind arose, gusting across Amen Hale, pushing people about and raking through the trees like claws.

I wanted it to stop. I wanted our walls and borders secure, and our earth to be proof against these unseen enemies. I willed the wind and noise and any spirit, demon, or angel that wanted in, to stay outside of Amen Hale! Silence and stillness descended just as Bethany spoke.

"Arise," she commanded, her voice a hoarse whisper after all the shouting.

I watched the rend in Alana's neck mend, and then her chest rose with a sudden inhalation of air. Alana's glowing, jewel-like eyes snapped open and then she started to gasp, pulling in more air as if she couldn't get enough into her lungs. Her hands clutched at her own throat in panic as if she were still wounded and needed to hold herself together. The three of us calmed and soothed her as the others did the same for Emma and Dana as they arose.

I was still working with Alana when I felt a strange stirring within me. Anxiety flooded through me. Somehow I knew that someone who loved me was in trouble. I shot to my feet, thinking in horror that we'd lost someone.

"Are they both back!?" I looked over to where they lay. "Emma! Dana!" I called out.

"Emma is fine," Cathryn said calmly.

"Dana's here too!" David shouted.

"Don't shout, David!" Dana growled. "No shouting. Now get this filth off me," she mumbled as she touched her bloody, sticky face. She began to cry and curse at the same time.

The blood on her, David, and Angel vanished before I turned my eyes away, still looking for the cause of this feeling within me. Behind me, my tail whipped about in angry agitation, keeping others at a distance as I turned in circles. Scanning. Seeking. Someone who loved me needed me! But who! I could practically hear them SCREAMING my name! Was it one person? A thousand?

I didn't know!

"What is wrong, my love?" Believer asked, growing alarmed by my obvious panic.

"Bethany!" I shouted. I didn't see her anywhere. "Where is Bethany?"

"Bethany is inside me," Believer rumbled, putting a huge hand to his chest, "with Penny. Both of the girls are fine."

A bloody head, eyes half lidded, pushed out from the clouds in Believer's chest and regarded me wearily.

"I'm good, we're good, all good in here," she said, half asleep already. "I'm just tired. Really, really tired." She narrowed her eyes at me, coming more awake. "You good? We good?" Her alarm growing, she pushed her head farther out, looking left and right with worry. "We okay?"

I leaned forward and kissed her bloody forehead.

"Go to sleep, my little Lion," I told her. "Sorry for waking you, and don't worry, we're all—good—out here."

It wasn't a lie, those of us on the porch were, but someone, somewhere, most certainly was not! I hid my panic from her.

"Good," she mumbled back. Her eyes fluttered closed as she sank back into the clouds of Believer's body. I watched as the last, long strands of bloody hair disappeared into the swirling clouds of his barrel-like chest.

I started to pace as the urgent call for help squeezed my heart in an ever tightening fist.

"What's wrong, Rain?" Mary came up to me, seeing the distress on my face. Jane appeared by her side.

"I don't know! I don't know!" I practically wailed, which got everyone's attention.

They all started to circle the wagons, gathering around me, worried I was about to go nuts and kill myself again. Believer's deep voice, Cathryn's voice, Mary, Jane, others called out. They spoke, but I could not hear the words. I pressed my hands over my ears to shut out the sound as the aching, desperate need inside my heart made me start to cry myself.

And then I heard it.

"Dear goddess, come save us! The demons! They are killing the Twilins! They are killing your children!"

I do not know what had changed, but when I opened my eyes, no one could look upon my face. Everyone turned away as my gaze passed over them. I didn't bother to explain what I knew or what I was doing, I simply acted.

Taking Dan and Jane with me, we vanished off the porch—and appeared in an INFERNO!

I screamed and began to dance from foot to foot as smoldering cinders and ash blistered my bare feet, while my legs and back were scorched by lapping flames all around me. Smoke blinded me. For a panicked second I wondered if I'd made a mistake and sent us straight to hell.

Jane and Dan grabbed me and moved all of us forward about ten feet, getting us free of the flames. The damage and burns we'd all taken when I first popped us in here vanished. I coughed and rubbed at my eyes.

With a thought I extinguished all the raging fire for miles around in every direction and sent the thick smoke that hung in the air into oblivion. With the smoke gone, I was finally able to see the graveyard and behold the last stand of the Twilins.

They'd taken shelter within the fenced in area of the graveyard. There was still a lot of movement at the center, bright colors of Twilin wings flashing brightly in the air above the middle of the cemetery, but those by the edges hadn't fared as well. The fence-line around the cemetery looked scorched like the burnt crust on a pie.

Everywhere my vision passed I saw the small, singed bodies. They lay at my feet. I looked back to the burned and blackened sticks of what was once the trees on each side of the gateway. A larger pile of bodies lay there, as if they died trying to get through or hoping that the portal to Amen Hale would somehow open.

I could see where we'd tread upon the dead. Three sets of footprints crunching through the snow drift of ashen bodies. I turned about, letting my eyes drift down the trail and across the once high, weedy grass that ran up to the fence of the overgrown cemetery. Tiny bodies lay everywhere on the brown, burnt landscape. The dead covered the ground. There was no place to step without crushing bodies beneath our feet. The only thing my mind had to use as a comparison was the old, black and white footage they'd forced us to watch in history about the Holocaust. The Holocaust had been six million lives, burned or butchered, and I wondered if what I was seeing right now was worse. How many had died? How many yet lived? For every one that still lived, how many more had died?

"Rain, are you all right?" Jane asked gently.

"No," I answered.

She was watching me, but Dan was scanning the wood behind us. His eyes glowed murder red, brows angry, jaw clenched tight.

"We can't help the dead, Rain, but we can help the living and those who've been burned," Jane encouraged.

I turned to see what Dan was watching. Off between the burnt and blackened trunks of trees not more than twenty feet into the tree line, shadows moved.

They were man sized, ghostly and mostly transparent, except for their eyes, which glowed red. Farther back into the distance swam a mass of inky darkness dotted with countless sets of side by side red dots.

Thousands upon thousands of shadows, too many to count, were ghosting through the trees. The creatures were circling the woods around the clearing with the graveyard, turning the Twilins' protected patch of earth into the eye of a demonic hurricane that wanted to rush in and suck the life from the small island of creatures that remained.

"What the hell are they, Rain?" asked Jane.

"Demons. Or demon shades. I think." Guessed. Who knew.

"Rain, Dan thinks this it too much of a coincidence for us to be attacked in Amen Hale the way we were, while at the same time these creatures attacked here. If these are demons, does that mean that the Devil wants us dead?"

I shrugged and answered absently as I stared about. "Maybe. But he'd have to pick a number and wait in line. Witches want us dead, governments want us dead, churches want us dead, my own mother wants me and Bethany to die. Lots of people want us dead. The Devil may just be a two bit thug, sending out his goons for a hit simply because others have paid for his services."

Dan nodded; he seemed to consider this a valid point of view, but Jane gave me a nasty look, like I was in denial.

"Something's happening." Jane pointed back toward the Twilins. "They've seen us."

The Twilins in the graveyard were stirring, crying out for help. Their voices and weeping had been hidden by the crackle and pop of the burning woods when I had first arrived but now the noise was heartbreaking. Wails, weeping, cries of hope and hopelessness from countless numbers of suffering people.

One of the Twilins left the safety of the cemetery and started a labored, halting flight across the burnt clearing toward me. My periphery vision spotted an inky, man shaped shadow as it detached itself from the woods, moving to intercept the tiny creature. Fury surged through my whole being. The strength of the emotion was beyond anything I'd ever imagined before or dreamed myself capable of.

I found myself standing in the field with my hand closed around the shadow's neck. It was insubstantial and not solid, but somehow my hand gripped it firmly, finding substance where none existed. My fingers around its throat were causing its red eyes to bulge and its very manlike mouth to grimace in pain. It had all the features of a human face and nude male body, but everything about the creature was dulled and leached of color, leaving its skin an ashen gray. The only color came from its bulging, red eyes.

The Twilin flew right past me and my demon captive but quickly backtracked and landed on my shoulder, crawling forward and clinging to my neck, panting.

It was a female. She did not speak, she simply held onto me as shakes wracked her body. My sensitive skin could feel her labored breathing and the tiny nails on her tiny hands as she dug in like a frightened cat.

"Release me!" hissed the demon shadow. "You can do nothing to me, you stupid child! I cannot be killed! I am eternal!" It spoke in a thin hiss, as if my hand on its neck constricted its air.

Which was weird. I was sure that this thing did not breathe "air." The mechanics made no freaking sense to me, but one way or another, a furious god's hand wrapped around its throat apparently hurt plenty. I squeezed harder.

The demon's eyes bulged, ghostly hands scrabbled at my wrists and arms ineffectually, finding no purchase, while my hands had no difficulty touching him.

"That's just nasty," Jane said as she passed her hands through the shade's midsection slowly, finding nothing solid.

Another Twilin joined the first, making a stumbling crash landing on my shoulder. A boy, or a man this time. I looked down and watched him as he struggled to get his damaged and uncooperative wings to retract, then fell over onto his back a few steps from the trembling female. Soot covered the man's face, burns marred his clothing and skin.

He lay there and stared up at me, looking done in, and somehow content. After surviving all he had been through, it seemed as though he was now ready to die. The unbelievably, powerful feeling of fury I felt earlier was matched and then exceeded by compassion for this tiny being and his people.

As I studied him, the burns on his face and hands healed, the soot that covered him vanished, and his clothes mended; a few seconds later he was pristine. The weariness I saw in his face was still there. It was not something that could be fixed by healing his body or mending his clothes. I could see that. He needed more, much more, and my heart broke to give him and this trembling girl what they needed.

I heard a gurgling sound and looked down to find that I'd squeezed so hard the head of the demon now hung from a wispy disgusting string that resembled its fleshy equivalent. The demon's body still struggled, alive, independent of the head, and the head stared up at me, still defiant and very much alive as well. I grabbed its body with my other hand and pulled the two halves away from each other then cast them behind me in separate directions.

"Remain in this useless condition until the day of judgment. So mote it be."

That said I stepped up onto the air a few inches above the ground and did the same for Jane and Dan. I did not want us to tread on the dead all the way to the graveyard and the waiting Twilins. I glanced back behind me and saw that a dozen or so dark shapes had gathered around the remains of their fellow. I watched as they set the head atop the shoulders of the ash gray body. The shadows backed away as one, removing their support.

The head fell to the ground.

I turned my back on them and continued on, walking over the ashes of countless thousands, and as I walked, I wondered—was it all my fault?

Sky

Airing It Out

MRS. BRYANT HAD me sitting at a table on the patio. She was making me drink hot tea as she looked at my wrist where Bethany had cut me. She wasn't happy with me. She wasn't happy with anyone. Ryan and his father came out of the house and headed to the table where we were sitting, and they looked like they were arguing.

"I know you think of that girl as your child somehow, but you should have let the others do it. You're pregnant, Sky; you can hurt the baby."

"You don't think I hurt her, do you?" I asked, suddenly worried. I had forgotten about the baby. I'd jumped right in and done what I felt I had to do. And Alana was my baby too—but I guess she was right, others could have done it. I did need to remember I was pregnant. Growing a baby inside me was more dangerous than making one myself. I guess I needed to be more careful.

"Maybe I should go see Dr. Burgis."

"Not him," Mrs. Bryant scowled. "I don't want that man coming within a hundred yards of you or the baby. You need a real physician, Sky, a prenatal doctor. And you don't need this type of stress so early in your pregnancy. The first few weeks of gestation are so important. You don't want to lose her. That can happen if you—"

"Stop it, Mom!" Ryan growled as he and his father joined us at the table. Both of them glared at her as they settled into their seats.

"I'm just trying to help," his mother said defensively, then turned back to me. "I bet your mother could help us find a good prenatal doctor in Ormond Beach. We can get you checked out and make sure everything's okay. And it would be more relaxing there with your mother. Less stressful."

It was the fourth time she'd suggested we go to my mother's. The first time she said we should go because I hadn't seen her in a while, the second because I needed to tell her about the baby. Right after the shootings it had been because it was too dangerous to stay here. Now it was because I needed a special doctor and a stress-free place for the baby. Stress free? She didn't know my mother! And I liked Dr. Burgis.

Ryan answered before I had to. "Mom, Rain's done something around Amen Hale with her magic. Mary's not sure anyone can get in or out right now. We'll have to wait until she gets back before we go anywhere. And if we did go anywhere, it wouldn't be to her mother's house. We'd go someplace where no one knows us and no one's looking for us." Ryan looked over at me. "Maybe another tropical island somewhere. Tahiti or Hawaii or maybe Australia."

He gave me a smile.

I shrugged. I didn't really want to go to any of those places. Especially Hawaii. I didn't like Hawaii at all. And it was such a small dot of an island. I didn't know how hard it would be to find it in the middle of all that ocean.

"What about your headaches?" Ryan's father asked him. "I thought it wasn't safe for you to be away from here."

Ryan rubbed at his temple as if being asked about his headache brought it back.

"I said that *before* I walked through Emma's brains scattered all over the back porch." He looked sickened by the memory of it. Maybe about to throw up.

"Think about something else, Ryan. Anything else!" I told him. I didn't want to think about it either. And if he threw up that would make his head hurt more.

"I can't get it out of my head," he said, closing his eyes and looking ill.

His mother made a suggestion of her own. "Tell me what you and your father were discussing before you sat down. You looked interested in whatever it was he was saying. And here! Drink some tea, " she ordered as she set a cup in front of him and filled it from the little pot of hot tea the servants had left on our table.

"Oh." His eyes popped open and he made a face. "That." He still looked sick, but a different kind of sick. More grossed out than throwupy. "Dad was telling me about you two walking in on Rain earlier. He said that Alana was naked when you first walked into the room." Ryan stared at the cup, watching as his mother poured the tea. He held the cup carefully with two hands. "Dad said that Rain was in the bed, having sex with all of them, at the same time!"

The three of them shook their heads like triplets, Ryan, his mom, his dad, all with the same pinch brow, sickened expression.

"When I woke up, I thought we were all in the bedroom because of me and my headaches. And then we all started talking about the baby. I didn't think what else might have been going on in there. Rain, Mary, Emma, Jane, Dan, and your Alana," He gave me a look that I didn't understand, "all of them, rolling around in the bed at the same time. I saw Jane and Emma making eyes at Alana and kissing on each other during lunch, and I saw Mary walking arm in arm with Dan and sitting with him at dinner, but holy cow!" He rubbed his head with one hand, carefully holding his cup with the other. He took a sip of tea.

"She was happy," I said. She had been happy. Not sad, happy.

"Who?" demanded Mr. Bryant.

"Alana." The three of them gave me a worried look I didn't like. It was dangerously close to the "crazy girl" look I hated so much.

Whatever look they were giving me, it didn't change the fact that Alana had been happy. During lunch she was practically glowing as she sat between Jane and Emma. Alana was happy with her life and that made me happy too.

"Rain is married but she's acting like a—" Mrs. Bryant stopped herself before she said something ugly, then turned suddenly and shouted at Mr. Bryant without warning. "And you didn't say a single word!" she snarled. "I kept waiting for you to say something! But you were all smiles, as if she hadn't done anything wrong!"

"Margret! Why don't you use your head for a change instead of acting crazy!" Mr. Bryant told her with a little anger of his own for the first time.

I wondered if I could sneak away.

Mr. Bryant kept going. "Think about what we saw when we walked into that room. Rain didn't blush or seem upset, not the least little bit. There wasn't any hint of shame on her face."

"Are you blind!?" Mrs. Bryant shrieked back. "She couldn't even look me in the eyes. She was ashamed!"

"She looked down because you said her eyes were ugly," I spoke up in Rain's defense. I'd been right outside the door and I saw and heard what she had said to Rain.

"I did not say that!"

She yelled at me just like my mother used to. She looked half ready to hit me. And I was sure that wouldn't have been good for me or the baby! I scooted to the edge of the bench as she glared at me.

"It wouldn't have done any good to say anything to her about who she was sleeping with," Mr. Bryant said with a calmer voice, trying to bring the tension level down a notch. "She doesn't think she's done anything wrong."

"You should have said something, Tom!" Mrs. Bryant insisted stubbornly.

"Rain hasn't been well for years Margret, but these pills have made it worse. She believes she's a god now." He pointed up toward the house. "There are people up there, on their knees right now, praying to her and praying for her. They've got a place in the garden with a statue of Rain," he waved off to the left, "over there somewhere. A woman invited Ryan and me to come with her. She said that they gather three or four times a day to worship our daughter. A young girl came up to me and asked if I would sign her prayer book. Her prayer book was filled with prayers to the Black Lion."

Mr. Bryant faced his wife dead on, as if daring her to argue his point. "Rain has bigger problems than who she's sleeping with. You saw what she's turned her-self into. You saw what she and Bethany were eating." He leaned back in his chair. He seemed spent. Spent and sad. "I still love her," he said, "but I don't think she's the same little girl we started out with; she thinks she is, but she's not. My Rain wouldn't let people pray to her and worship her. This girl isn't my little girl any-more."

I didn't like what I was hearing. There was a lot I wanted to say, but I didn't bother. I didn't think they'd believe me or want to hear anything I had to say any-way. I wished Ryan and I could leave.

"But you didn't even try to tell her she was doing wrong," Mrs. Bryant began again. "She's married to Believer, and I actually care about him!" she added bitterly with a sharp glance at me, as if I didn't. "Rain has no business what-so-ever sleep-ing with Jane's vampire husband! And she certainly has no business sleeping with Mary; she's practically her sister for heaven's sake!"

Ryan slipped his hand into mine, looking sorry he'd brought the subject up. He looked like he wanted to run away too—finally. Maybe we could sneak off.

"On top of everything you didn't do, you let that girl touch you. That— *Emma!*" Mrs. Bryant said the name as if it were some nasty thing stuck on her tongue. She turned back to me and Ryan, pinning us with her angry glare. "Have either of you ever let Emma touch you?" she snapped.

Her yelling reminded me of my mother. Maybe they switched places. Maybe I should go visit to see if my mother was calm and sweet and nice now that Ryan's mom had become all mean and nasty. But if I did go, I didn't want Ryan's mother to go with us. Too stressful for the baby.

"No ma'am," Ryan answered, as I shook my head no. "Not even before she became a witch," Ryan added. "Not even at Rain's wedding. And Mary's gone out of her way to keep Emma away from both of us. So has Cathryn and Byron and Hanna. All the servants are super careful with us when it comes to Emma."

Mrs. Bryant turned her angry gaze onto her husband again, lip curling in disgust. "All that effort to keep people away from her and your stupid father agrees to let the girl give him a big, sloppy hug! Are you looking forward to the next orgy, Tom? Are you ready to crawl in bed with them? Maybe you'll be so sick in the head from touching that girl that you'll even touch your own daughter," she accused boldly, staring at her husband, daring him to deny it.

I stopped breathing altogether as I waited for someone to say something.

Mr. Bryant just stared at her.

"Hey!" Ryan rose to the defense of his silent father. "Cathryn and Byron have touched Emma and they don't sleep with her." Mr. and Mrs. Bryant both turned to look at him, and after a few seconds Ryan seemed to reconsider his statement. "I don't think they do anyway," he added lamely.

It all blew up! A three-way yelling mess.

I went straight up, leaving my seat and simply going away from all the angry sounds. Mrs. Bryant was freaking me out, and like she said, I needed less stress. There were so many things making her angry that it made me dizzy. She was angry at Mary, at Rain, at Emma, angry at whoever blew up her house, at me (I was sure), at her husband for not doing some stuff and doing other stuff, at Cathryn—

I crashed into what felt like a brick wall made out of air.

I was falling.

Falling.

Taunwee

A Prayer to the Goddess

"YOU ARE A fallen angel. You turned away from the White Lion, who is pure and perfect and all-together wonderful. You left Him to seek your own way. You left Him because you wanted to be a god yourself. You made yourself a people, you built yourself a throne, and for thousands of years you have received your worship. Why would you bow down to the Black Lion, who is not pure or perfect, when you have refused the White Lion? Will you not pine for your throne, hunger for your worship? What has changed in you, Taunwee? Why should I make you my own?"

"I was made a servant of the Most High God. I watched as He created the firmament and fashioned the Heavenly City, the Paracoleese, the Saracoleese, and the Holy Mountain of Zion wherein were fashioned the Jade and Twilight gardens. One hundred billion angels he formed as his Heavenly Host, of many shapes and kinds. My voice and my song joined the Host of Heaven in praise, as God created the Earth, hung it in the black void of space, and filled it with such things as pleased him.

"I, and some others like me who tended the Twilight Garden, sat in a window sill and stared down on the Earth on the day He made man, placed him in an earthly garden, and gave him dominion over the Earth. We were curious. All the angels were. Some of us were confused, while others became angry. We thought that man was to be God's crowning creation, something greater, stronger, higher, wiser, and nobler than we ourselves—but he was not. He was less and weaker, made without power, formed in ignorance and forced to learn day by day. We did not understand.

"And God loved man. And man loved God and worshiped him and brought him gifts and did many other odd things that we did not understand. Man was strange, but exciting in both his weakness and his strangeness and his worship. Many of the angels began to emulate the man and worship God in the manner that he did, and this pleased God. In the Twilight garden, I and my Sill did this as well, and we glorified Him. Time and again I left the garden and journeyed to stand before the Great White Throne. I knelt with others upon the sea of glass to offer my worship. I knew the pleasure of worship, and it was sweet indeed to my taste. Very, very sweet.

"But this new worship made Lucifer, the Covering Cherub, jealous. He stood above the Throne of God and watched us. He did not join us on the sea of glass, he did not learn the joy of giving worship, he knows only the hunger for receiving it. When war came, God let each of us choose. It was a choice we could make only once, and one that could not be unmade. I thought within myself, if it is sweet to worship, how much more so must it be to be worshiped. I chose to fall and turn away from the one who made me, but I did not follow Lucifer as did most of those who fell. I chose my own path, made my own people, built my own throne, and received my own worship."

"And was it as sweet as you dreamed it would be?"

"It was sweet, but it was also bitter. I could not forget the pleasure of worship. I could not forget the face of God nor the glory of the Heavenly City nor the splendor of the Twilight Gardens nor the peace of being clean. If I could go back and choose again, I would have stayed. I would have gone back to the Twilight Garden and continued to make my journeys to rest my knees upon the sea of glass, bringing Him my voice, for it was sweet indeed to praise Him. I have made me a people to love me and worship me—but I have tasted your tears; I know that I cannot love them as you can. I was made like Him, you were made from Him. I have learned that I cannot become something that I am not. I am not God. I am a servant of God. My people whom I have made need a God to love them, to care for them, to save them. And I need a God to love and worship. I long for a home. Please, Black Lion, save me. Dear Goddess, please, save me! I offer myself and my children to you, for I have tasted you and long to be yours."

"I accept all you offer, and I will be your Goddess. I will receive your worship, and I will help you forget. You will remember the God who made you, but you will not remember his face. You will remember the Heavenly City but only as shapes and forms. You will remember the Host of Heaven but dimly, as a dream. The hidden things and mysteries that man must not know will be as shadows in your mind, both known and unknown, that they do no harm to others. And I shall give you a new name that bears no shame, for you shall no longer be The Twilight Star that fell but will be Taunwee Calla Hale, my pure and lovely star, clean and perfect before my sight. I will be your Goddess. I will love you and keep you and shed my blood for you, and you and your children shall be my own."

Cathryn

The Other Queen

Cathryn stood by the patio doors and watched the last of the stragglers file out of the house. She and Cornelius had ordered the people of Amen Hale to gather in The Hallow until Rain returned, but as always, a few had stayed behind. She cleared the nursery, ordering those there to bring the infants and toddlers with them. Next she emptied the kitchen of those few chefs who thought "everyone" surely applied to everyone except them.

"We shall recover as best we can," she assured the scandalized men and women in their tall, white hats as they rushed about, turning off burners, throwing perishables into coolers, moved to tears over sauces left to congeal as they filed out the door. The only people left behind were the Bryants and those taking care of Sky and Ryan.

After Sky's headlong crash into whatever invisible dome Rain had placed over Amen Hale, Ryan had caught her with his own magic a second before she hit the ground, but in doing so his own headaches had returned and put him on his back once again. Bethany healed Sky's injuries and did what she could for Ryan, but neither of them were doing well. Due to Mrs. Bryant's badgering, Sky was petrified she'd harmed her unborn child and insisted she stay abed, and Ryan's mind seemed to be wandering badly.

To complicate matters further, Mrs. Bryant had degenerated into a screaming shrew with nothing but hateful and hurtful things to say. On Cathryn's orders, Believer had picked up his mother-in-law (begging her pardon and gently asking her understanding as she screamed and even began to curse). He carried her to the room she'd been using as her husband followed, silent and brooding. Dr. Burgis gave Mr. Bryant some valium for his wife and encouraged him to get her to take the pills, which enraged Mrs. Bryant even further. The two shut the door on their room still arguing.

Cathryn left Willomena and Dr. Burgis at Sky and Ryan's bedside, and Believer had insisted on staying and guarding the hall. He wanted to make sure Mrs. Bryant stayed well away from his Sky. Though he'd had only kind words for the woman, her attitude toward Rain and Sky was causing him to reevaluate his opinion of Sky's mother-in-law.

"The kitchens are empty, your Majesty," Chef Tanner said as he passed by.

"Thank you, William," Cathryn said.

He bowed and walked away. Cathryn prayed under her breath as she watched him go. She called each of her children by name, asking for safety and protection. All of them were so fragile and so very good at hurting themselves. Only moments ago she had watched her children die before her eyes. The shootings and resurrections, the new threat posed by the demons, Rain and the vampires disappearing, and then Sky and Ryan—all of it had crushed the calm she'd fashioned for herself with this morning's bloody work.

Cathryn had narrowed her goals for the day. Other needs of the Kingdom still pressed at her, but all she truly cared about was making it through this day without losing any of her children.

"Please, my Goddess, don't let my children die today!" That was her goal and the prayer constantly hovering under her breath.

Cathryn stepped away from the doors and onto the back porch. She wrinkled her nose at the sour stench of vomit yet to be dealt with. There was still blood and bits of flesh and bone scattered everywhere from the shootings and the sacrificed shooter Bethany had destroyed there on the porch. The red stains pulled at her eyes. Her mind filled in the blanks where the bodies of her children had lain. She passed a nest of soapy buckets, mops, and cleaning gear, abandoned by servants pulled from their work to obey the summons to The Hallow.

Cathryn felt the wild urge to run down the trail and push past those few people ahead of her to get to her children who were already there, waiting for her. She forced her feet into measured, graceful strides. She was the Queen of Amen Hale. She wanted to bring calm not panic. She didn't want to relive last night. She could not give in to despair.

"Please, my Goddess, don't let my children die today!" she prayed as she walked down the path.

Cathryn turned at the sound of rushing feet coming up from behind her. She was surprised to find Reese and one of the other, young guards named Benson rushing down the path from the Gateway Garage. They came to a panting halt before her where both men slipped to a respectful knee. The Twilin, Cassadan, was planted on the young man's shoulder; he'd been hunkered down, gripping his mount's flannel shirt as he ran but now that they'd come to a stop he stood and bowed.

"My Queen," Reese began, "Lord Cornelius was correct, none of the gateways are working. Not the gate at the wall or the gate to the Twilins' home in the graveyard."

Cathryn nodded, releasing her irritation at finding yet more people still creeping around the house that was supposed to be empty. Where he'd been and what he was doing made sense, but something was off. Reese seemed nervous as he knelt before her, which was very unlike him. He was one of their most trusted guards. And she knew that he was one of Rain's. She'd seen him kneeling and praying to her. She turned her attention to the Twilin. She noticed blood on his fine clothing. She'd been told how he'd made Bethany invisible during the attack, keeping her from being shot more than once.

"I apologize for the inconvenience, Cassadan, but you'll have to stay with us until Rain returns. And before I'm busied with other things, I must thank you for keeping Bethany safe and hiding her during the attack. I will seek opportunity to show Queen Taunwee my favor. But you will tell Reese what might be done for your – wife?"

"My Dam," Cassadan supplied the correct Twilin word as he bowed. "Thank you, Queen Cathryn. It will be an honor to stay until the goddess and the vampires return."

Cathryn looked away, turning her head down and to the side where her eyes fell upon the blood of her children, spilled out upon the path right at her feet. She closed her eyes as her stomach roiled and her flesh prickled with colliding sensations. She felt someone reach out to steady her. She leaned upon the arm heavily.

Benson stepped closer, taking more of her weight. She hadn't realized she was so worn.

"Please, my Goddess, don't let my children die today!"

She prayed out loud.

She silently scolded herself for her weakness. She'd been caught up in other things and her mind had momentarily voiced its background mantra. Cathryn opened her eyes; she stared straight ahead as she kept the prayer playing like music in the back of her head.

"Benson. Escort me."

"Yes, my Queen."

Cassadan left Benson and flitted over to Reese's shoulder. The tall and the small exchanged a mystified look between them and fell into step. Neither of them were quite sure of what to make of what they were seeing. How did this happen? Did Benson cause this? Was it magic? Was it fate? Would Queens continue to fall into this boy's arms everywhere he went? They followed Benson, mystified, as he walked down the cobbled path with one of the Queens he loved hanging on his arm.

Susan and Katie

Rock On!

ALFRED AND SHIKITH stepped out of Katie's room but left the door open for the guard to see in. They stood just outside the door, sharing some very concerned eye contact. They didn't try to hide their shared concern from the guard seated in a chair out in the hall. No need. He had the same concerned look.

Inside the room Katie was busting up pieces of the mirror Alfred had smashed when he destroyed the hidden cameras in the bathroom. She had the pieces in a bin breaking them down into smaller pieces with a hammer. These smaller, shaped pieces she was gluing to a globe she'd removed from its stand and painted over. While Katie was lost in her art, Susan was dancing around the room with boundless energy to some music in her head because none was playing inside the room.

"Someone needs to stay with them while they're like this," Shikith said, as if it should be obvious.

"What am I?" The guard, a guy named Sherman, gave the pair a defensive put upon look. "I'm watching 'em. Along with who knows how many people in the camera room. If they do something—"

"Enough over sharing, Sherman," came the monotone voice from the hall intercom.

"See what I mean." Sherman gave them a blank face.

Alfred frowned. "I saw how you pushy bastards handled the girls." He looked up to the hall camera mounted on the wall. "It could have been handled better. Next time, come get me or Shikith and let us take care of the girls." His voice was angry, accusatory.

"So you agree with our actions," the monotone voice sounded smug, "just not our methods."

Alfred and Shikith both shared some pained eye contact. To agree with anything these bastards did for any reason felt like treachery of the worst possible kind, but the girls had certainly gotten into something. They were high as kites. Shikith gave Alfred a nod, looking nauseated. Alfred had the displeasure of putting it into words for both of them.

"Yes. We agree. But if something like this happens again, do you agree to let us handle it?"

"Handle it, Alfred?" the monotone voice mocked.

"Do you think *now* is the best time for you to be a smart ass?" Alfred asked the voice. "That's not very smart."

"You're right, Alfred," Dr. Tachi's voice quickly spoke up, easily recognizable on the intercom, "now is not the time to be a smart ass. And Dr. Ogburn is sorry."

Sherman, who'd been battling a cold since they arrived, choked, trying to hold back a laugh, and then he exploded, blowing snot all over himself. His hands came up in time to snare the ropes of sticky goo. He stood up like a half frozen statue, holding his hands a few inches from his face, cupping the mess. One thick, sticky rope connected hands to nostril and beyond, as if anchored to something deep inside his skull.

"Jeasus!" exclaimed Sherman as he stared into his cupped hands with huge, watery eyes. His delight at hearing Ogburn put in his place was replaced by angry embarrassment.

"Just go, Sherman, I'll watch the girls," Alfred said as he took a cautionary step back from the man.

Sherman, moving hands and head together, managed to look up at the camera on the wall. He wasn't supposed to leave his post.

"You can't very well stay like that," said what they all now knew was Ogburn's monotone voice.

"Alfred and Shikith can take care of things while you—" Tachi's voice began.

"I told you not to push that!" an angry Dr. Ogburn shouted.

"I'll push whatever I—" The intercom cut off, and so did the argument between Tachi and Ogburn.

Hearing the argument had revived Sherman's good cheer in spite of his circumstances. "It's snot a pretty picture, is it?" He managed to crack a joke in a nasally voice as he headed down the hall toward the bathroom, laughing to himself as he walked away hunched over, hands still tied to his face.

Near the end of the hall the room with a black door on the other side of the Rec Room opened. All the teens knew that their jailers sat in that room and observed them in the rec room through the large section of one way glass or on the countless cameras that were even mounted in their bedrooms. Dr. Tachi and Marcia stepped into the hall and made equally disgusted faces as Sherman ambled toward them and then stopped before the bathroom door just across from the Rec Room.

"Please Sherman! Allow me." Dr. Tachi rushed to open the door for the man.

Once he was inside they continued on, with Marcia extracting some hand sanitizer from her purse for Tachi, which he thanked her for and used. The pair stopped before Alfred and Shikith. They both ignored Marcia but eyed Tachi with something almost akin to hope.

"Believe it or not, we are here to help," Tachi gave them both a tired, imploring stare, "even Dr. Ogburn, though I'm sure you'll disagree with me on that point. But the fact of the matter is, if you are willing to help us, then I would love to let you. So," Tachi's eyes challenged, "was that offer you made a minute ago for real or were you simply trying to prod Ogburn into an argument?"

"What, exactly, are you talking about, sir?" Alfred asked respectfully.

"The girls are not like you, Alfred. You have internalized, stabilized, or in some way adapted to Dr. Burgis's pills far better than Susan and Katie have." He turned to Shikith. "And you only took the pills for one day, which was very fortunate, considering your accident."

Shikith nodded in agreement, not wanting to remember the crash. Her mother had made her drive home from the doctor's office that first day, even though she told her she was dizzy. "You need more practice if you expect to get your permanent driver's license," she'd said. Shikith was driving on the freeway, terrified that the other cars were getting too close. And then they got closer. She became even more panicked. The cars in front, beside, and behind her drew even closer, as if her car were a magnet pulling them in. The other drivers started honking, cutting their wheels, even putting on brakes—and then they hit. The horrible sound of the crash was the last thing she could remember before waking up in the hospital with her broken arm.

"It's time for Susan and Katie to start taking meds," Dr. Tachi said. "If we try to slip the meds into their food they may simply stop eating, so I've decided that the direct approach would actually be safer. They'll get the drugs, and since they'll see when it happens they won't have to fear eating the food or feel like they can only drink from the tap. This is the point where doing the right thing is hard."

Tachi fished inside his lab jacket and pulled out two sealed syringes. "They will fight us when we try to give them their meds. It will traumatize them," he said straight faced. "I'll have guards hold them down and then I will forcibly inject them because it's the right thing to do. Or you can make good on your offer to help." He handed the two syringes to Marcia and fished into his lab coat again and came out with a small pharmacy of bottles, one after another.

"Hold out your hand, Alfred," Tachi ordered.

"Yes, sir." Alfred held out his hand as ordered.

"What are you doing!?" Shikith demanded, staring from Alfred to the pills Tachi began to count out into his open hand.

"What I can to help. Just like you're going to do," Alfred replied stiffly. "Unless you want it to go down the other way."

"Shit," she whined. "I don't want to be no traitor bitch like her!" Shikith turned her angry gaze onto Marcia who had the gall to look hurt.

"It's called being a friend," Tachi corrected gently.

Shikith whined but stuck out her hand anyway.

Susan and Katie

White Rabbit

A FRESH-FACED SHERMAN JOINED the others who watched the two heads bobbing around under the blanket. After being told their options, Katie had grabbed her notepad and a furious Susan. "Need some time. A little time. Fifteen minutes. I'll talk to her. Calm her down. Chill her out. Make it happen. Captain." She dumped that on them, pulled Susan to one corner of the room and huddled under a blanket for a little over fifteen minutes. The waiting crowd was surprised as the girls emerged from their blanket cloister in what seemed like high spirits.

"Deal, deal, deal. Let's make a deal," Katie said as she approached, snapping her fingers repeatedly as she said, "Tell'em, tell'em, tell'em."

A smiling Susan laid out the plan while Katie continued to snap away.

"We'll take your shitty medicine if you'll dance and listen to my shitty music. I want to karaoke! I wanna sing, and everyone has to dance while I sing."

"Deal," Shikith agreed quickly. "I'll dance with you guys."

Susan shook her head. "Not just you. Marcia, Dr. Tachi, and Sherman too, everyone boogies or it's no deal."

Everyone quickly gave their consent once the girls agreed that they could stop dancing and leave "if they chose to" after just one song. Susan and Katie also had to agree to take their pills *before* the party started. Deal made, all parties agreeing to the insanity, Katie and Susan started snapping out directions, ordering everyone around as they prepared the room to "get groovy."

Ogburn's monotone voice complained to Tachi over the intercom about coddling the patients and continued to complain about the problems this delay was causing with the rest of what was scheduled for the day. Everyone seemed more than happy to ignore Ogburn as Katie and Susan handed out tasks.

Alfred was put to work hanging Katie's hastily finished, home made disco ball from the ceiling. A ruler stabbed horizontally into one side at the equator sported her tiny pin fan she used to dry arts and crafts projects. The miniature fan, secured to the ruler with a hair scrunchy, acted like a little airplane engine and rotated the globe in a nice, steady spin as it hung from the ceiling.

Sherman secured four, narrow beam flashlights and colored filters to place over the heads of the flashlights. Katie had him move a heavy pot filled with sand so that it was directly beneath the globe. She stuffed the flashlights, butt down, into the sand and aimed the beams up at the globe overhead. Two female soldiers entered and helped move the furniture and scattered art projects to make the room party friendly. They did a sound check to make sure the cued up songs on Susan's iPod would still play on the badly abused equipment and speakers they'd carried over from her room.

Once everything was arranged and it was obvious that the girls were just stalling, Dr. Tachi called Alfred and Shikith over and gave them the girls' pills which he'd been holding onto. The two helpful soldiers and Marcia gathered around, the three women giving the girls encouraging smiles. Shikith's murderous scowl soured the positive "female energy" as she glared at the others. Alfred couldn't help the grim face he wore as he held out his open palm to Susan.

"I don't like this, but we can't stop them. Doing it this way is better than having them hold you down and use needles. But if you want to fight, I understand." Alfred studied the girls, trying to get a feel for what they really wanted. They were out of it, but he could see that they were angry. It made the odd smiles they wore and this acceptance all the more strange. He knew something had to be up but had no idea what it could possibly be. With raised eyebrows, he presented Susan with her handful of meds but closed his hands around the pills before she took them. Shikith did the same.

"Alfred, Shikith! We had a deal," Marcia reminded them in a scolding, parental voice with her hands on her hips.

"Give the pills to Marcia," said a glassy eyed Susan as she patted Alfred on the cheek and gave him a wink. "You don't want to pill me, so let the bitch do it. Don't fight, Alfred baby, get groovy."

Katie spoke to Marcia in a rapid spill of words. "We don't want to take your pills. Alfred don't want us to take your pills. Shikith don't want us to take your pills. You're the one who wants us to take the pills, so you need to give us the pills. We're ready to take the pills. I'll go first."

Marcia frowned suspiciously and spoke in a rush, "Why do you want me to give you the pills? Alfred and Shikith can give you the pills. Dr. Tachi can give you the pills. Why do you want me to give you the—" She stopped and clamped her mouth as she realized she was talking just like Katie. Sherman, Katie, and Shikith started laughing.

"Do your job," Alfred said, not laughing.

He extended his hand to her and she backed away as if he held spiders instead of pills. This whole crazy business had her hackles up. She wanted no part of it. She wanted both troublesome girls held down, injected full of drugs that Tachi refused to let her use. She wanted both of them turned into compliant little zombies that would do whatever she asked!

Alfred grabbed her hand and quickly forced his payload of pills into her palm.

"Susan's pills," he said, then backed away.

Dr. Tachi, Sherman, and the two female soldiers all stared at the gape mouthed Marcia as she tried unsuccessfully to get Alfred and then Tachi to take the pills. Shikith surprised her, grabbing her other hand and forcing Katie's pills into her other palm. She flashed white teeth in a wicked smile before she walked away. She obviously expected something bad to happen as well.

"Stop acting like a child and give the girls their pills," Ogburn's monotone came across the speakers and everyone smiled.

Marcia forced herself to be calm. She was painfully aware of the cameras that were recording everything she did, or failed to do, all to be replayed and reviewed—for who knew how long—by who knew how many.

Katie and Susan stepped up to her, smiling. If Susan had come up to her and spat in her face or cussed her up one side and down the other, Marcia would have been put at ease, but no—the girl was smiling. That was so wrong!

"Gimme, gimme, gimme," chirped Katie happily, like a baby bird asking her momma for a fat, juicy worm.

It gave Marcia a chill. This was the girl who was so paranoid about being slipped meds, she only drank from the tap. Marcia readied herself to throw the pills in their faces and storm out.

"Chicken shit," said a smiling Susan, who then spat right in her face.

Blindly, with her eyes closed tight, Marcia held out both pill-filled hands and the girls took their pills. Once her hands were empty, she cleared the spit from her eyes. Everyone in the room watched as the girls knocked back their pills a couple at a time, taking swigs off their bottled waters. Once they were finished, Marcia gave them both an evil grin and made for the door, only to find a stone-faced Alfred and a frowning Dr. Tachi blocking her way.

"Just one song and then you get the hell out of my way!" she hissed at both men.

"Only if you dance," Alfred answered stone faced.

"You made a deal, lady, now go get your groove on."

Susan's amplified voice came from the speakers as she spoke into her microphone. "Loosen up, Marcia, it's gonna be painful to dance with that stick shoved up your ass." The room broke into hysterics, the teens laughing, Sherman, Dr. Tachi and even the two female soldiers laughing as well. All at Marcia's expense.

Marcia seethed! She was tired of being the object of everyone's laughter and abuse. The two women had obviously been sent in by Ogburn or Dyal to liven up things. Nothing happened by accident or coincidence in this place. Even now, this room was a test tube. Marcia was incensed at the injustice of the situation. At the coercion from all the men—Tachi, Dyal, Ogburn, even Alfred! They would have never done this to another man! She was supposed to be the one inflicting the humiliation, not the one receiving it!

She turned on Susan. "You better go ahead and sing your song, Susan!" Marcia yelled. "You'll be out like a light in about three minutes!"

Susan nodded as if she agreed, then pushed play on her sound system. Psychedelic music filled the room. It was familiar to all, a famous seventies tune from Jefferson Airplane—White Rabbit.

Alfred hit the light switch by the door, plunging the room into darkness; the only illumination came from the nest of flashlights shooting out their multi-colored, neon beams in the middle of the room, reflecting off the rotating, broken glass disco ball overhead.

After a brief moment of stunned awe at how Katie had transformed the room into a night club, everyone except Marcia started to dance. The psychedelic ball was the perfect match for the drug hazed, seventies tune coming from the sound system. The music and atmosphere were tied together by Susan's vocals, which were absolutely amazing.

As Susan finished the last line of somewhat altered lyrics, she slumped and sat on the stage, as if she were about to fall asleep, just as Marcia predicted. Everyone stopped dancing except a smiling Katie who pogoed away, bouncing up and down in the middle of the room like she planned to go all night long. With or without music to dance to. With or without anyone else to dance with.

"Dance, Rabbit, Dance!" Katie cried out as she bounced, drawing sympathetic glances from those standing around. In the awkward absence of music, Alfred was about to surrender control of the light switch to a smugly smiling Marcia when Susan's somewhat slurred voice spoke up though the sound system.

"You can't leave until you dance, Marcia." She struggled to her feet, pressed a button on her handheld remote, and started in on the next song.

It was a high energy, contemporary dance number and she struggled with it at first, but by the end of the song her energy was back, her voice strong and power-ful. The energy only built as she launched into her next song. The lights stayed out and the party went on.

While the same in basic tone and texture, Susan's singing was far superior to the original artists on every song she voiced. She sang and danced with an ability, pathos, and energy beyond anything a human artist could possibly hope to possess. The room pulsed with the energy of her music and presence.

Marcia had been lingering by the door, watching for Susan to slump over and frowning because she wasn't. And frowning as she tried to resist the urge to join in. She stayed there, unwilling to walk out the door even though it was no longer guarded. She tried to keep her scowl and fight whatever it was she felt, but the siren call of the music was not something she could resist. She joined the others, throwing off her suit jacket and dancing to the music, forgetting her problems and bitter disappointments as she let herself go.

Dyal and Ogburn watched with their cameras for signs of drowsiness in the girls. They waited to see if the drugs were taking effect.

After fifteen minutes of non-stop singing and dancing, Dyal and Ogburn sent soldiers to end the party. The dozen soldiers they sent joined the party. They re-loaded and tried again, but this time they cut the power to the room first, and then stormed the room with soldiers wearing protective head gear to block out the sound of the blaring sirens and gas masks to block the fumes which filled the room.

And then the party truly was—over.

The Shellhouse Family

Foiled Family Fun Day

T HE THREE SUVS barreled down the twisting road at a stomach turning pace. What had been considered a complete waste of time and resources, going to check on an abandoned graveyard in the Smokey Mountains, had turned into a mission of the highest priority quite unexpectedly.

The original mission had called for a car and two men to come and take pictures of the graveyard and look around, simply for the sake of thickening up a back-file. It was a throw away errand, handed down to satisfy the government's insatiable hunger for information on the Black Witch and her origins. They'd given it to Shellhouse and his office since he was close to the graveyard, and he was one of the few agents in the country to have actually been inside Amen Hale before.

He'd gone in with the Secretary of State at the first official meeting between Amen Hale and the U.S. Government, but that meeting had been a disaster. When the King of Amen Hale had mentioned that they could cure cancer but wouldn't, he'd lost control, right in the middle of an official state meeting, surrounded by hundreds of people. He'd interrupted everything and begged them, then and there, to heal his daughter.

Surprisingly, he hadn't been reprimanded for the incident, but he had been removed from the detail working in Amen Hale. He was transferred into an open position in Raleigh-Durham, North Carolina.

In a way it was a huge promotion, and in another way it had been a demotion. One way or another, Randolf Shellhouse was now the Acting Director of the Raleigh-Durham Office of the FBI, and he took this trip as an opportunity for a free, family vacation for himself and the Assistant Director. It also gave him an opportunity to do something for his dying daughter while he still could. It gave her a chance to see the Biltmore House, which she'd always wanted to see, and to see a place that was somehow connected to Amen Hale at the same time, which she had an unhealthy interest in. He hadn't told his daughter about why he'd been reassigned, or anything about his incident in Amen Hale, but he hadn't been able to keep from answering all her other questions. What he'd seen inside Amen Hale was all supposed to be kept secret, but what loving father could refuse the questions of a dying daughter?

The day had begun wonderfully. The caravan had left early that morning and stopped in Asheville, where the two families toured the Biltmore House for a couple of hours, reserved the rooms they planned to use that night on the return trip, and ate lunch at the Biltmore House Hotel that overlooked the mansion and gardens.

By one thirty they were well on their way to the remote, country graveyard. Should anyone check the GPS signature on the three SUVs, it would indicate that all three vehicles did indeed go to the graveyard. The plan was to let the junior agents in the lead vehicle take care of business at the graveyard, while Shellhouse and Loraina Tally, the Assistant Director, let their children stretch their legs and play while they picnicked out by the road.

They had a nice, propane grill loaded in the back of the lead SUV. They had a cooler filled with hot dogs, burgers, steaks, and corn on the cob, already shucked and wrapped in tin foil and pre-seasoned for the grill. A bundle of citronella, tiki torches lay in the back of the SUV, snugged in beside the photo equipment the other agents had planned to use to photograph the empty graveyard.

"I told you why!" Randolf shouted.

"I won't let you take our children there!" Randolf's wife, Abby, shouted right back. "Not if she's there!"

"We're on N-Sat now!" Randolf pointed to the roof of the vehicle angrily. "They'll see! Even if all we did was pull to the side of the road and let you out on the curb, they'll see." He pleaded, "I'd be lucky to just get demoted!" Randolf wanted to look at his wife, but he couldn't take his eyes from the twisting, mountain road for a minute.

His wife and kids had hushed up, as they'd been trained to do, when his phone rang. Their silence only made it that much easier for them to listen in, as analysts informed their father that they now believed the Black Witch was at the graveyard, just a few miles down the road. If there had been a gas station, a restaurant, or any kind of dwelling he could have stopped at, he would have stopped, but there was nothing. They were only a mile away. The few driveways they passed were dizzying trails climbing up steep inclines or dropping down frightening grades, disappearing into the forest as they headed to some unseen homestead lower down or up the mountainside.

For now, Shellhouse was being congratulated by Washington for his uncanny foresight in personally overseeing this mission and for coming in force. If he were fortunate, and if his wife didn't ruin it, this could end up as a shining gold star on his record instead of the biggest blunder he'd ever stumbled into. Their kids heard the call and understood that this could go one of two ways for their father and all of them, except Bree, were trying to reassure their mother.

Randolf Shellhouse took a deep breath and did the only thing he could do: he threatened his wife's security and hoped the threat held. "Honey, it's your call," he said, tight lipped. "If you want me to stop, I'll stop. We can get you and all the kids into one truck and send you home. But before you say anything, be sure you don't hate me later for not telling you to shut up and suck it up. Don't blame me if we don't retire with a Director's pay grade. That's all I'm saying."

He shut up and waited.

Abby remained silent. Thinking.

"We'll park the SUVs well back from the cemetery. Luke," Randolf called to his oldest in the second row seat, "here, take this!" He waved him forward and handed him his iPad. "Zoom in on that flashing dot."

Luke did as instructed and handed the iPad to his mother.

"Is this what's there right now?" she asked as she studied the aerial picture on the screen.

"No. It's Google earth," Randolf answered. "The image was taken within the past two or three years. But you see how the cemetery is way back from the road. We'll leave the trucks by the road and walk down. You'll be a good two hundred yards away. That's two football fields away."

"I know what two hundred yards is, Dolf!" Abby snapped, giving him a nasty look. "Fine!" she conceded then turned to face her oldest daughter in the seat behind her. Her eyes promised unmentionable parental torment. "Bree, if you get out of this truck you better bring a bottle of BBQ sauce because I'll eat you myself if the Black Witch doesn't!"

"Luke," Randolf growled, "keep ahold of Bree. No matter what your mother says she's not going to listen. She's your responsibility. I don't care if you have to tie her up to keep her still, you do what you have to do to keep her in this truck."

"Why wait," said Kip, their youngest girl, still reading her book in the third row seat while being slung around on the curving road.

"Rope her," agreed Skip, Kip's twin brother and ever dependable wing man. Skip was seated on the bench beside Kip as he played his hand held video game.

A blind man could have felt Bree's tension as she sat there in her seat. She was a silent, coiled spring.

Luke stared at his sister, then gave his mother a questioning look.

"Leave her be unless she tries something."

"Mom's in denial." Kip.

"Sad. But true," wing man echoed.

Bree

Quietly into the Day

THE GPS STARTED to beep, announcing that we'd reached our mysterious destination, and Dad slowed down and then pulled into the grass in front of a burnt out church. It couldn't have been a large building even when it was standing, but now it was nothing but a collection of sooty, black sticks. The charcoal framework that made up the ghost of a steeple still sat upright in the middle of the rubble, clearly marking the ruins as having once been a church.

An unnatural blanket of white fog clung low to the ground beyond the ruined church, obscuring what lay beyond from view and giving the place a frightening, otherworldly cast. Fog should not have been possible on this warm and bright a day at almost two in the afternoon.

"Is that smoke from the fires? Did this just happen?" Luke asked as he eyed the blackened structure. "The church was still standing in the Google earth picture."

"The church burnt down more than a year ago," Dad answered as he got his things together. "And the forest fires that were burning earlier went out about an hour ago. This is something else."

My heart sped up a beat. The other two SUVs pulled in on either side of ours.

"Now stay put," Dad ordered as he was getting out of the truck, his voice already slipping into "FED Mode."

"We love you. Don't do anything stupid," Mom managed to say before the door shut in her face.

We all watched him walk away. Even Kit-Kat (as I referred to the twins) were nervous and alert, their faces pressed to the glass as my father, Loraina, and the other two men from the first truck huddled together in front of the vehicles, talking on their phones. In the steamy, tense silence, I watched and waited until Dad closed his phone and they got moving. One of the agents stayed behind, standing in front of our vehicles while Dad, Loraina, and the other agent walked toward a weed-strewn driveway that ran beside the burnt out church. In the SUV next to us we could see Loraina's kids as they pressed their faces to the tinted glass and stared out, just like us.

"Is the Black Witch really here, Mom?" Kip asked, sounding scared.

"I hope not," Mom answered. "Why don't you two come up here with me? We may have to wait a while."

"Hey! There's someone out there!" Luke shouted making us jump.

I pushed in beside my brother who gave me some window space. A young woman in a red dress and a young man in black pants and a black jacket stood in front of our father and the others at the start of the weedy drive. My heart sped up as I watched, but with excitement, not fear. My brother said the words out loud as I said them silently to myself.

"It's the vampires! It's Jane and Dan Simmons."

"Everyone stay still and be quiet," my mother ordered.

A terrified "Kit-Kat" clambered over our chair and into the front, attaching themselves to Mother like a couple of blond-headed parasites. Watching the twins made me sad. They were so very—*unique*. I'd never met a couple of kids like them before, and I'd miss them. I'd miss everyone, but my leaving wasn't something I could change.

When and *where* I left, now that I could change. I had no intentions of dying in a hospital. Three months to live, with the last month nothing but drugs and pain. No thanks. I'd choose three minutes that mattered over three months that did not.

"Don't get any ideas," Luke said as he scooted closer to me.

"I'm just going to lie down," I said.

Mom, Luke, and Kit-Kat eyed me warily as I pulled my jacket around me, as if I were up to no good. Which I was.

"Stay away from the door!" Luke ordered roughly.

"Can I lie on the floorboard at least?" I asked weakly, playing on his sympathy.

"Are you going to be sick, Bree?" Mom asked, beating Luke to the question.

Luke went toward the back to retrieve my official barf catcher. Worried faces all around now. Our dad was outside talking to two vampires, and here I was, the center of attention because I might barf. That was so wrong.

I took the stupid bucket Luke proffered.

"I'm lying down." Actually, I did feel like I was going to be sick, but that was another problem altogether.

I slid down onto the floorboard and covered myself with my jacket. Luke threw his jacket on top of me as well, which was sweet of him to do, and it also helped hide me nicely. I slipped my hands under the driver's seat and pulled the black box a little closer. I'd watched my father put it under the seat this morning, and he'd already opened the box and took out one of his guns before getting out of the car, but I knew there was more than one gun in the box.

My hand slipped inside and I felt around blindly until I found the small gun. I broke out in a sweat as I felt the grip and shape of the handle without seeing the weapon. This was way worse than anything I'd ever done before. Worse than running away. I could get Dad into so much trouble. Maybe I wouldn't even have to use the gun.

I pulled it out and fumbled with a latch on the side until the clip slid out into my hand. I dropped the clip back inside the box and pushed it back under the seat. I slipped the empty gun into the inside pocket of my jacket. I promised myself that I would leave it in there. I didn't want to touch the thing again.

I quickly moved onto the more sane portion of my plan and fumbled out the lighter and the fat smoke bomb I had purchased at the last gas station we stopped at before we left Asheville. I held the fuse to the lighter and thought about what I was doing one last time.

Tomorrow was the first Sunday of the month, chemo day. In all likelihood it would be the last day I'd be able to walk on my own. I might not even wake up. At best I'd be bedridden for the next week, sick as a dog, and then go home and be sick as dog and maybe last another couple of weeks and then die at the next treatment, unless I lingered, hooked to the machines with a morphine drip, slowly rotting away. The thought made me feel sick. No. I had time for one, last adventure before I died. I clicked the button on the lighter. The fuse hissed to life in a bright, blue sparkle.

Luke had all four doors open and greenish smoke was still billowing out of the SUV. I heard Mom's voice from what seemed a far away place. My stomach clenched and I threw up again. All my lunch was in the grass and I could see blood mixed in with it.

That was new.

"We'll get you to the hospital!" Dad said as he dropped to the ground beside me. I felt him slide his hands under me and start to lift me up.

"No!" I said as loudly as I could, then threw up again as he held me.

More blood.

I looked up at my father. He paled at the sight of the blood and hugged me tighter. I felt him stiffen. He pulled away, giving me a surprised look. My head and eyes and mouth still worked, but my arms and legs seemed to be done. They lay around me like useless pieces of rope. All I could do was watch as my father ran his hands across the front of my sweater, then reach in and draw out the gun. He gave me a look that said everything.

"Sorry, Daddy."

"Bring her to the Black Lion," said a pretty voice.

"Will she help us?" Dad said, sounding angry.

"I don't know."

Dad picked me up and I saw that it was the vampire girl who had spoken. Jane was standing right beside us.

"Hello, Bree." She smiled at me.

"Hi, Jane." I smiled back.

She reached out and ran her hand over my bald head. Her hand was cool and so soft it made me smile again. "Wow," Jane said as she stared down into my eyes, obviously seeing something in me that fascinated her.

"What?" asked my father. "What is it?"

"Let her say goodbye to everyone, and then bring her to the graveyard if you wish. Or let her say her goodbyes and find a peaceful spot under the trees. Choose, but don't put her back in the car. She doesn't want to die in the car."

"Not in the car." I agreed with Jane.

She smiled at me, then vanished.

So I said my goodbyes.

I started with Dad, and he was easy; we'd already talked a lot about my leaving. We didn't have a whole lot to say. Then I said goodbye to Kit-Kat. "I'll miss you two the most," I told them. "You're the coolest people I've ever met." My mother cleaned the blood off my face and clothes as she cried. She asked me three times if I was sure I wanted Dad to carry me into the graveyard where the Black Witch was. I told her I was sure, all three times, and not to worry three times as well. I told her

I would see her again one day. When Luke came up to me I asked him if he could go get Hadden, Loraina's son.

"Why?" he asked. "You hardly know him. You just met him today."

"I think he's cute. He's been nice to me all day. And I've never been kissed." He looked as if he were about to say something but stopped suddenly, then turned and went off to talk to Hadden.

Mom handed me some mouthwash she'd wrangled up from somewhere and I started to cry. All this time, no tears. Mom gives me mouthwash. I cry. It made no sense.

I was still in my father's arms, but I didn't want to kiss Hadden while I was in his arms. I asked him to give us some privacy. Mom laid down a blanket for us and Dad had Hadden sit down with his back against a tree and he set me in his lap. Everyone walked away and gave us some space.

I looked up into Hadden's face. He forced a grin and brushed back his ridiculously long, bleached blond, skater bangs and stared into my eyes. While not a total jock, he was in good shape. He had strength in his brown eyes and in his jaw that clenched tight as he stared down at me.

"Well, now you know my secret. I was dying to ask you out."

He laughed, then he wiped at his eyes. He was crying.

"I wish this wasn't happening," he said, then made a horrified face. "No! Not the kiss! I mean—" He swallowed, "You know. I wish we had a chance to do, to be, more. I—" He choked up.

I waited for a minute then asked, "Would you have gone steady with me Hadden?"

"Yes."

"And if everything worked out?" I asked. "And some other girl didn't steal you away?"

"Or some pretty boy didn't steal you away," he fired back.

I smiled. "Yeah. What would have happened?"

He pulled me a little closer into him. "We would have gotten married."

He leaned in and put his face on my cheek. His skin was so warm, and he felt so alive. It made me wonder if I felt cold. He slid his lips up to mine. His upper and lower lips slid around my bottom lip—and that was how we started.

We kissed for a while.

Then we talked for a while longer.

I asked him what our first child's name would be if it were a girl. We argued for only a moment before he let me have my way and we settled on "Peace." But then I gave in and let him have his silly boy name, "Keenan."

I asked him how often we would have made love. He didn't even blush as he answered me.

"Some days we would do nothing but stay naked in bed from sun up till sun down. But other days we would just hold hands and go places or sit on the couch together and hold each other as we watched TV or read books. I would have made every day as special as I could." He leaned in close, his tears falling on my face as he stared into my eyes and said the words, "I love you, Bree."

I was getting dizzy. Weaker.

"I love you too," I had to take a breath, "Hadden."

"Now kiss me—and remember me forever."

A boy I loved, a boy who also loved me, kissed me goodbye.

Hadden called for my father.

The person who came for me wasn't my father. He wore white, and he was smiling. He captured my attention.

"Who are you?" I asked the man.

"I've come to take you to your Father—and to show you His castle. I hear you like castles."

I arched a brow. "I saw the Biltmore House today. That's a castle." I frowned. "But it didn't have a garden for vegetables like they did at the Sisters of Peace. They had lots of gardens, but not useful ones with fruit you can eat."

He reached down and took my hand and lifted me to my feet.

"In your Father's castle, there are wonderful gardens, and a tree which grows twelve different kinds of fruit."

"Wow. Do they all taste different?"

He laughed. "Yeah, they do actually." His huge smile made me smile as well, but then my smile faded. I swallowed.

"If I went there, do you think my Father would let me work in the gardens?"

"Yes, Bree. I'm sure he would. He loves you. Are you ready to go?"

"Yes. I am."

Dan

Doubts

T HE BOY CLUNG to Bree's body, refusing to let go. Jane revealed herself, stepping out of her hiding place behind a nearby tree. After a few reassuring words to the frightened family and the nervous FBI agents, she knelt beside Hadden and told him about the angel she'd seen. The agents and the girl's family listened in. Hadden let go.

The girl was lifted away, her lifeless hand slipping through Hadden's fingers as her father rose to his feet and walked away with his child. Jane went with the family, following them back toward the vehicles, still answering questions about what she'd seen. Hadden waved off his mother's sympathies and remained where he was, leaning against the trunk of the tree, head tilted back as he gazed upward, doing his best to deal.

Jane was with the family, but a portion of her mind was contemplating Rain and something she was fond of saying, that love and death often found her and revealed themselves to her in unexpected ways at unexpected times. Jane was wondering if what she'd just witnessed was a strange coincidence or if her new "goddess" was pulling the fickle finger of fate to draw love and death together. Drawing those two forces to this remote and unlikely place like bees to a flower.

She thought of the love and death in the graveyard behind us. Rain's new love for the Twilins and the countless numbers of tiny dead bodies we'd seen and even stepped on. Then there was the love and death out here with Bree and Hadden. Then Jane included me and her in this litany of cosmic conundrums. A freakily euphoric thrill shot through her as a new revelation dawned inside her head.

Dan and I are in love (and death) at the same time, forever and always. So that means that everywhere she goes, we will be exactly what Rain needs and wants—and we'll be called to her.

She continued her weird, religious ramblings, taking the same pieces apart in her mind and putting them together again and again in different ways like a four year old with a pile of Legos. That portion of her mind wheeled away, happy in its insanity, while at the same time she conversed with the grieving family.

This strange, new religious fervor had come on suddenly, born out of her guilt over Rain's attempt at suicide. It was terrifying to see the changes inside her mind as she made a happy place inside her head and filled it with different thoughts about this girl like a room filled with furniture. Part of me was more than a little jealous, but another part of me couldn't help but be happy because she was happy.

Sharing Jane's body and her unbelievably strong emotions that made my own seem so drab by comparison had never been quite so—strange before. While I wasn't altogether comfortable with it, her changes made sense on a completely practical level. The facts were simple:

We could no longer eat human blood.

We needed to adapt to our new prey.

After a difficult start, Jane found a way to adapt.

She needed help getting over her sexual issues, and seeing "this situation" as a religious experience turned out to be the crutch she needed. I didn't like it, but I didn't think less of her for it. I considered it an unfortunate but necessary realignment of her nature. That part of her hunter/predator, instinctual, inner self (that once focused on humans) now helped her hunt and feed on new prey. Two girls. The only two girls on earth with blood sweet enough to drink.

Plainly put, Jane had fallen in love with her food. In Alana, her new instincts had brought on a wildly, intense romantic attraction that took my own breath away as I experienced it (and greatly enjoyed it) through her. It was an almost comical, manic, clingy, I want to keep you close, pet you, touch you, kiss you, and most definitely eat you alive! type of relationship.

I loved both girls too, but for regular, human, "guy" reasons and not because I thought one of them was a god and the other a "Red Lamb," whatever the heck that meant. Yeah, I'd seen angels and demons today, but there were logical explanations for that now too. Perhaps the angels and demons were made by someone whose mind had already become what Rain was reaching toward. Evolution in fast forward.

The facts were simple. Dr. Burgis made these pills which caused all these changes. That was science, not fantasy. I knew that Jane wanted me to pray and worship Rain with her—but I couldn't do it. To me, the idea of Rain being a god was sad. Rain was a sweet, but crazy girl, who had taken crazy pills, made by a psycho doctor. Logic was logic. Facts were facts. Even if her blood did taste like the blood of a god that didn't mean that she was one. Humans tasted like shit to us now, but that didn't mean that they were shit, it just meant that they tasted like shit.

Black Rain

A Million and—One

W E SAT BENEATH a white canopy of softly glowing clouds which concealed the graveyard from the helicopters overhead and the federal agents out by the road. The Twilins who could be saved I'd restored, and those who'd died at the edges of the fence, in the field and surrounding woods, as well as those scattered all down through the valley, I collected.

Clouds of ash, tiny bones, and burned bodies joined others who looked as if they'd only fallen asleep. They all came to my call, drifting through the air on currents of my will, gathered from all directions to the place I'd prepared. I, Taunwee, and thousands of weeping Twilin survivors watched as the ten foot, deep grave filled to the top with nearly a million, tiny dead forms and a snow fall of ashes made of friends, children, fathers, sisters, brothers, dams, and roes, some who died together, some now separated forever.

I tucked the earth atop the grave like a warm blanket, then made it scarred and weedy to match all the rest of the neglected graveyard. A chipped and weathered headstone rose up from the ground to mark the spot as I wanted, inscribed with these simple words:

A Million Pieces of My Heart

The Twilins were not angels like Taunwee, powerful and eternal, and they possessed no immortal soul as did humans, who came from God and were a part of his soul. Each of their lives was only a borrowed spark of spirit from Taunwee herself, which gave them life and breath but not the potential for new life. At least, not without help.

Their limited creation did not diminish their uniqueness as individuals nor their capacity to feel, love, hope, suffer, and dream; it only meant that their end, when it came, was simply the end. Though they did not age past youth, the Twilins were a temporary people and fragile. Only Taunwee herself seemed to place any value upon them, until now that is.

Now, the Twilins were mine. Their adoration, praise, and worship were mine— so too were their tears, suffering, and loss. Only a tenth of the Twilins remained alive from those who'd managed to reach the safety of the graveyard. Little more than a hundred and eighteen thousand tiny beings. Never had so many seemed like so few to me, but even with almost a million lives given to the open earth, to me this grave was incomplete. The body of someone I loved, someone I'd given my own name, was missing.

Taunwee explained what had happened to Marie, being careful with her words but unsparing with her honesty. Her frank talk marked her as other—not human—but I loved it. I loved her and her differences, even her size and I told her so. This pleased her and her people—my people.

My clouding of Taunwee's memories hadn't changed her from what she was or taken from her the edge and mannerism she'd adapted over the ages. She was now as she had been, but now she was mine—as were her children.

"Lucifer spoke to Cain and bid him kill your Beloved and steal her from the graveyard. He has set a trap for you."

"What kind of trap?" I asked the tiny angel who stood upon my knee.

"A trap meant to pierce your compassionate heart. A trap that only works because you love. The Devil knows you loved Marie more than your own soul. He hopes you will try to deliver her from where he has taken her."

"And where has he taken her?" I'd asked, though I already knew.

Taunwee must have heard as much in my voice. Her lovely face frowned. Her hair, which had been varied shades of green, now grew locks of black and white.

"My Goddess, I drank from your cup. I tasted your tears. I know how much you loved Marie. I loved her too."

"Tath!" cried a young dam from somewhere by my feet, surprising us both.

"Tath! Tath!" Others took up the cry, along with cries of "I loved her too!" or simple laments of "Marie!"

Taunwee waited until quiet returned before continuing as though nothing had occurred.

"You cannot give your soul in exchange for Marie's." Her voice was calm and exact as a razor. "God's laws do not work in this way. Just as you could not go to Heaven and steal away one of his beloved children from that sweet rest, so too you must not go to Hell and remove one of his damned who suffers torments there. All things are made by Him, and all things that are made are made to bring Him glory. Those who seek Him become vessels of honor, unto praise, and those who turn away from Him to serve other gods or the pleasures of this life become vessels of shame, unto wrath. He will be glorified in their worship or in their judgment, but one way or another, He will have His glory. Once a soul reaches Heaven or Hell," she said sadly, "all choice is lost, fate is sealed, eternity is set. Marie turned away from God to follow another, and though we loved her, to Him she was a vessel of shame, made unto wrath, and in this way she will bring God glory for all eternity."

How could a loving God send a good, kind, beautiful person like Marie to a horrible place like Hell? The truth of Taunwee's words chimed perfectly with the knowledge already inside my head like matching tolls of twin, grim bells. It wasn't pretty, but it was true. It was all right there in the Bible. I'd heard all of this stuff before, but now I stared it hard in the face for the first time. Now it was personal. All those years of church that I remembered from Rain Marie's life had left its mark in my mind. Preachers, Sunday school teachers, Bible memory games as a child, all of it accumulating within her heart. All of it was in my heart as well.

"Marie is in hell," I said the words out loud. My voice cold. Distant.

"Where she must stay." Taunwee's voice was insistent, but also pleading. "Please, I beg you my Goddess!" She went to her knees there upon my knee, color leaching from her hair, the green and black becoming the white of fear.

The Twilins were watching and listening to our words. Weeping began to spread through the thousands and thousands who stood around me. They feared that I would go and save Marie. Bible verses popped into my mind; I did not want them to, but still they came. I did not want to face this truth. I did not wish to think about or know what was happening to my sweet, little lamb, right now, at this very minute. My lamb who loved me and trusted me.

My Marie

"shall be reserved in chains in everlasting darkness."
"where there shall be weeping and wailing and gnashing of teeth"
"where the worm dieth not, and the fire shall not be quenched"
"and all idolaters shall be cast into the lake of fire and brimstone, which is the second death."

The sounds of keening and weeping became so loud that it pulled me from my black thoughts of hell. I found myself surrounded by utterly distraught multitudes. An entire civilization, a mass of tiny men, women, and children who needed my help, and needed me to put their lives before my own sorrow and loss, and before Marie's tormented soul. The weight of their need and sorrow pressed on me harder and deeper than my sorrow for Marie.

"Forgive me, my Marie," I whispered.

"Thank you, my Goddess." Taunwee's hair was shock white and she was trembling where she knelt. One bright lock of green remained in front, which reminded me of Mary. Mary, my prince. Mary, whose love brought me back from my own red world of hell. She'd been able to save me, but I could not do the same for Marie.

"How can I be a god if I cannot keep my own lambs safe from such an end?" I asked.

"This place is His." Taunwee gestured around the burned and ruined graveyard. "You walk in another man's field and fall in love with another man's disobedient children. Children that are a part of Him. Though you love them, and they you, it is His field and they are His children. Make your own field. And then make your own children. Make them from your own heart, and those children and that field will be yours alone and no others."

"And what about you and your children? And what of the lambs I already love?" I leaned close and stared into her small beautiful face. "What of Bethany and Emma and Mary and Cathryn? What of Alana, my little Red Lamb whom I love? What of them?"

"I do not know," she admitted, "but neither do I know how you came to be. You are impossible, and yet you are. I've no need of faith." She reached out and ran her tiny hand across my pale, silver cheek. "I can see you and touch you, and I know that you are real. How can a girl become a god? I do not know. My ignorance does not trouble me. I believe in you. You will find a way to save those that remain. I do not know how, yet I believe you will."

"So mote it be," I said.

"So mote it be," Taunwee echoed.

"So mote it be." The words from voices rose around us, rippling out like a wave to a thousand, then ten thousand, and then all. The Twilins fell to their knees where they could find space or raised their hands to me as they hovered in the air. They made a sweet sound that sounded like singing bells that was so sweet it made me cry.

Taunwee joined her people, and for the first time since she fell, she worshiped. Not knowing what else to do, I simply watched them and received their worship.

The demons that circled the clearing became more active, drawing closer and hissing, as if annoyed by the Twilins' singing or by me being worshiped. Or both.

"Determined bastards, aren't they?" I growled.

"They have probably already slain our children at the other steadings." Taunwee's voice was angry, like mine.

My eyes narrowed in anger as I watched the circling shadows. I knew from Taunwee's mind that there were a dozen Twilin steadings which were protected like the graveyard. Places that might yet harbor survivors. I wanted to travel to those places and see if any were left alive, waiting to be rescued, but I couldn't go anywhere and leave the ones I already had. I wasn't even sure if Amen Hale was safe for them. The demons had been trying to claw through the ground there too. I felt like a mother hen sitting on her eggs with a million, red eyed weasels circling the coop.

"What are you thinking?" Taunwee asked in her concise way.

"How to do a thing," I said.

Taunwee nodded. Not put off by my short, almost nothing answer.

"How large is the Earth?" she asked suddenly. Her face, calm as always, betrayed nothing of where she was going.

"It's not large. You know that."

She nodded, then pointed up. "And the sun?"

I turned my gaze to the hazy, golden ball shining through the blanket of concealing, white clouds that canopied the clearing. As I stared at it, the knowledge came to me, and as it did my own world changed and shrank. I knew the sun's depth, character, and dimensions. My eyes altered as I looked upward. I studied the curling flares upon its surface for few seconds. Kinda pretty.

I frowned and looked back to Taunwee.

"It's very, very small," I said, honestly disappointed and more than a little frightened.

Taunwee nodded. She seemed very patient. "Now think about your problem again. But think as a god, and not as a girl. Your problem only seemed large, my Goddess. It is very, very small." Now she smiled.

I considered her words carefully before I acted. I decided it was both good advice and very bad advice. I loved thinking like a girl, acting like a girl, and being a girl, and I didn't know if I would still be able to be "that girl" if everything in my world kept shrinking. I felt like Alice in Wonderland eating the cake that made her grow, only if I kept growing and growing I'd became more like Horton the Elephant and the entire world where I'd stood before would seem like a speck clinging onto a dandelion, filled with tiny voices of little people.

I loved Black Rain and I didn't want to lose her, so I saved the girl. I reached inside myself and collected those delicate, intimate, quirky, little pieces of myself that I wanted to protect and carefully lifted those parts free of my intellect and will. I felt little change other than an increased calm and a strong sense of purpose. I set Black Rain aside, to put on as a coat once my Goddess work allowed. That done and without fear, I opened myself wide to what I'd become.

It was all about size—and what was here or there or even needed at all. The solution was easy. Oddly enough, I found the answer that I needed in the middle of my fears, which no longer troubled me.

"My beautiful Star, do you trust your Goddess?"

"Yes."

"I need to see if any of our children still live in the other Steadings and Courts, but I can't leave you here while I travel abroad because the demons will destroy you. I must take you with me."

"How?" she asked.

I smiled. "I will eat you."

She cocked her head to the side, momentarily surprised, then smiled as well. "Will we all fit in your mouth?"

I saw her words for what they were, an attempt at humor. I gave Taunwee a sly smile and set to work. The red dots within the dark voids of my eyes winked out, leaving two, pitch black eye sized holes. My vision split and shifted, the pictures in my head no longer coming from my eyes but from outside my body, showing me a view of myself sitting in the graveyard with my arms around my knees drawing them up to my face, and a second view of a dark, hollow place within my skull.

It was in this darkness that I would make a place for my Twilins. First, light illuminated the darkness within my skull from up above, out of view. From my other perspective, that same light shone out of the dark sockets of my eyes as if my head were as hollow as a lamp shade.

Taunwee drew closer. She walked across my knee and leaned on my face, gazing down into one of the open sockets. She smiled and marveled at the vast expanse of space somehow held within my head. She watched the land form from the darkness far below, rising up from the black abyss to form rolling hills and dells, rills and stony projections and peaks. Vast mountains drew up on all sides giving the picture edges and walls, creating a huge, circular bowl to hold this land. A waterfall spilled from the top of the ridge in a dozen places dumping shimmering water down into waiting pools that had formed down below to receive the spill from above. Rivers snaked out across the land in bright, blue lines.

Taunwee's head darted quickly from sight to sight as forests and fields populated my world, small streams teeming with minnows, tadpoles, and colorful salamanders. Bright flowers burst into being and plants and fruit trees which should not have been growing in a tropical setting were simply there. Ripe pineapples grew beside cherry trees, both in full, ripe bloom.

Taunwee cried "Tath!" her cup too full to contain her joy. I laughed as her wings fluttered in excitement and tickled my nose as she leaned upon my face, head pushed far into the orb of my eye as she gazed about, staring down from her window in the heavens. She watched as the world took form, sharpening and completing in countless little ways as I pulled ideas and knowledge from Taunwee's own mind without her even knowing I did so.

Taunwee knew her people and their needs and I supplied those things for our children. I made a palace for my Star and her servants and created other grand homes and cities and villages which I scattered around my new world. I also made countless individual dwellings, secluded grottos, and mysterious gardens placed throughout my world like hidden gems waiting to be discovered. I created insects to eat, bees for the flowers and honey, and countless little things needed to balance and sustain the other things. I shaped a cycle of life that could exist and sustain itself, but one that was far different and more magical than that of the Earth. This was my field and I shaped it as I wanted. In the center of the garden I made a huge statue of a roaring Black Lion.

Other Twilins, too excited and curious to keep their distance, flew over and landed on my face like tiny bats, little feet and hands searching gently for footing. Others landed on top of my head. Tiny hands gripped long strands of black hair as they lowered themselves down like circus performers descending ropes. They crowded around my eyes, faces peering in from every angle; some were so curious they risked death and began to press in beside their queen, staring within at the wonder of the unimaginable.

I willed my voice to reach out to every Twilin in the graveyard. "We will leave this place together. Everyone, up and into the air. Shift to sparks and circle about overhead, but stay over the graveyard where it's safe."

The world seemed to flip upside down as thousands of tiny, winged bodies began to rise into the air all at once before suddenly "popping" like popcorn, shifting their shape into fast moving balls of light.

I had an odd moment of feeling like an elementary school at a car line as determined Dams crowded in, combing through my hair to claim their little bits. Since I stepped foot into the graveyard the little ones had come to me. Some came of their own desires with their Sire's blessings but I'd seen others sent by weeping mothers who thought some extra measure of safety might be found in the shelter of my hair. I'd welcomed my infestation of beautiful dime-sized children, all of them hiding, playing, and even sucking on my hair over the past hour.

I smiled reassuringly as Dams collected their precious bundles, held their bits to their chest, and took flight, the two transforming into a single sphere of light before joining the ever growing ball of circular motion overhead. It was a beautiful process. Twilin mothers often called their bits "spark of my spark" and in this transformation, when they shed their physical forms, the child's spark once again returned to its mother, living in her as she flew. I knew from Taunwee that as they were joined in this way, each bit would feel and know exactly how its mother felt, all the love, anger, disappointment, or pride. It was good, and sometimes bad, but that was the way of most things.

"What of our flightless ones who have no wings?" Taunwee asked as she snapped out her own wings. I noticed a new color on her head. Her green lock remained up front, but apart from that, her hair was now a radiant, spun gold.

"Everyone will fly, with or without wings. Lead them in, my Star, but tell them to be patient." I arched an eyebrow. "I may have a huge head, but I still have a small mouth."

Taunwee didn't question me, she simply curtsied where she stood upon my knee, then bounded into the air. The terrified, wingless Twilins began to rise into the air, arms thrown forward, doing the Superman for a moment before suddenly popping into brilliant balls of colored light. In only a few minutes one hundred eighteen thousand and eighty three sparks of light circled over my head in a weird, glowing doughnut. If I had seen this from any distance and not already known what it was, I would have sworn that I'd seen a UFO.

I stood and stretched, and my poor tail swished about behind me, practically rejoicing at the freedom of movement. It was disorienting to be able to move without having to worry over the little bits who'd fallen asleep in my hair and those traumatized Twilins who seemed unable to keep from touching me.

After a few deep breaths, I leaned my head back and opened my mouth as wide as I could. I blessed my new unshakable calm as a ribbon of light broke away from the doughnut and sped toward my open mouth like a glowing arrow. A steady stream of tiny lights disappeared into my mouth, only to emerge out of the mouth of the roaring lion statue inside my own created world. In only ten minutes the last of my new children vanished from the sky above the graveyard and flew out into the warm welcoming glow of the world I'd created.

I watched the Twilins as they landed upon the soft, green grass in a strange, new world and stared upward in both fascination and fright. The inside bowl of my skull seemed countless miles away, high overhead, and capped my world like a white, skeletal sky. The random pattern of growth plates, little ridges, bumps and depressions in the bone providing that element of detail once given by stars and constellations that filled the night sky, but the details of this sky would be revealed in the day and hidden in the night.

The ball of light I'd created acted as a sun for my new world. It would rise, set, and warm my world as it followed its path across the dome of my skull world, providing life to the plants, trees, reptiles, bugs, and everything else. I felt the beautiful connection that all the life down below held to this glowing ball, as if it were the battery snapped into an electronic device, giving the world below the ability to live and thrive.

I watched within, pleased to see that Taunwee was taking charge, speaking to everyone and keeping them together instead of letting them scatter to the four winds. Taunwee stood at the base of the statue, addressing the Twilins who covered the land before her. Some of them were weeping even as she spoke, still lost in suffering and grief for loved ones lost in the burning, but others were overjoyed, smiling with wonder filled faces. Many dams clutched tightly to their bits with one arm and their roes with the other as they studied their surroundings with either relief or suspicion, as if they worried the place may collapse or turn out to be a trap.

I could feel them within me. A multitude of sparks of life, each one unique, each one possessing his or her own heartaches and joys. I felt each of them, my heart and mind expanding to touch these people. The outside world shrank again as I held them, felt them within me—and I knew them. I was the soil upon which their feet stood and the blades of grass upon which they sat or leaned as they listened to Taunwee. My breath of life was the air they drew into their lungs and breathed out again. I held them within me, sheltering them, giving them the life they needed and in turn feeling the life they yet enjoyed and cherished.

Though they stared and wondered at all that was happening around them, so too did I, but the wonder I felt was not born from the place I'd made or the people who now filled that place, it was within the hearts of those people.

Gratitude - Wonder - Awe - Joy - Sorrow - Heartache - Guilt - Envy - Excitement - Peace - Despair - Hope - Fear - Hate - Adoration - Love - Worship - Weariness - Shame - Anger - Greed - Lust - Longing - Pride - Hunger –

I felt unable to comprehend this mountain of emotions or to know what to do with it, though I wanted to do both. I wondered at the odd flatness I felt in their emotions, if it was something to do with the manner of their creation. Whatever the cause, I didn't fault them or Taunwee for it, they were still precious to me. I was not bored with them or disinterested because I now knew so many similar, little lives with similar problems. Quite the contrary, I found each and every one of them fascinating.

Is this what it means to be God? I wondered.

"Please, let this be beautiful," I prayed to myself. It seemed appropriate after doing what I'd just done. If ever there was a time to pray, surely this must qualify. Before I turned away, I sent my voice into my world for all to hear and a hundred thousand faces turned, some looking up to the skeletal sky while others looked toward the statue of the Black Lion.

"You are in my field which I have made and where is that shadow that shall pass the gate of my jaws to steal you away from me. I am the Black Lion. I am the one who holds you, guards you, and loves you. So mote it be."

Cain

Cheers

THE WEATHERED, OAK door of the Spinning Wheel Tavern swung open, and a huge man filled the doorway. His face was hidden, his body backlit by the afternoon sun pouring in from behind. Conversation ceased as the dozen or so men and women within turned and squinted at the imposing silhouette. The outlined image seemed as big as a mountain. A mountain wearing a cowboy hat.

The hatted head turned right, then left and looked about the bar, hesitating in the doorway as if unsure he really wanted to come inside. The silence would have been complete if not for the juke box blaring a country song at full volume. He stepped inside and quickly made for a table in the corner, hidden in shadows, as far from the current collection of denizens as he could get.

"Now that's a big ol boy!" Dee's face was locked in a huge grin. "You orta go say hi, Tan. Maybe you could settle down way back in them mountains with that big ol, tall, lo-ong grizzly bear."

The three men seated around the table laughed as Tanya paled at the suggestion, obviously not feeling up to the challenge. She slid closer to Punk Boy and pulled his arm around her like a blanket, eyes averted from the shadowed corner.

"You seen this guy before?" asked a smiling Punk Boy, pointing with his head in that direction.

"Shit no," his buddy Corbel answered, "and I've seen every hillbilly these woods got to show. Even the ones who only crawl out of the woods once or twice a year show up at the feed store."

"Naw man," Jerald grinned, "that ain't the kind of cowboy someone's likely to forget seein. He can't be from around these parts."

They watched as the waitress walked up to the man, spoke briefly with him, and went to the bar. The bartender got busy filling a pitcher. As nothing more spectacular seemed to be eminent, and watching a man drink beer alone in a corner was dull, people got back to doing whatever they were doing.

Cain drank his beer and tried to forget what he had done.

One pitcher.

Two pitchers, a trip to the restroom.

Five pitchers. Another trip.

"Honey, I'm gonna need to see money before I can get you another round." The saucy little waitress stared expectantly at the mountain of a man, huddled around his empty mug.

The man didn't respond.

"Hey! I need you ta catch up your bill, buddy!" she shouted at the man.

Still no response.

She swept out a hand and hit the brim of his hat, knocking it off his head.

Cain jerked awake, reaching up for his hat then looking around drunkenly.

"Whersss m-my hat?" he asked the wide-eyed serving girl who stared at his forehead. Cain fumbled into his pocket and came out with a wad of bills he held to the girl. Her hand trembled as she took the money and retreated to the bar, whispering to the bartender.

The bartender brought the next pitcher to the table himself. The hat was back in place on Cain's head. The little waitress stayed away from Cain's table, but as she went around the room she whispered to everyone else in the bar. The bartender made a phone call.

Six pitchers, and another stumbling trip to the restroom.

Seven pitchers.

Sheriff Pemberton stepped into the Spinning Wheel, gun drawn and held in an easy grip down at his side. He was an old man, not a black hair remained on his head, but his hands didn't shake and his voice was still strong.

"Which one of you boys is drivin that old, blue station wagon parked out front?" he asked the room. When no one owned up he began calling the names of the men he recognized, sending them out one by one as he stood there at the entrance. As each of them left, they warned Pemberton about the man in the corner, even the men who didn't like him, even the ones who hated him.

"I hear ya, Jerald, now get the hell out and stay out."

"But—"

"I said get!" Pemberton gave the other man such a glare he high tailed it out the door. The sheriff had kept an eye on the man in the corner the whole time, but he hadn't moved a muscle other than mug to mouth.

Shaw, the bartender, came back into the bar through the back door, face as white as a sheet. The sheriff knew with one look that there was no talking the man out of his own bar, especially after what he'd no doubt already seen in the back of the station wagon out front. Shaw fetched his shotgun from behind the bar and edged around the room until he had the man seated in the corner in his sights.

Pemberton walked over and cautiously eased into the seat across from the big man.

"What's your name, son?" he asked the man.

"Cain," came the deep, regretful rumble from where the man hunched in on himself, hat low, hiding his face.

"That girl out there the first person you ever killt?" Pemberton asked.

"No, sir."

"Who was the first then?"

"My brother—Abel."

Pemberton's eyes widened. He gave Cain a closer look. It couldn't be—or could it? He looked again at Cain's hat that sat low, resting atop his bushy brow, hiding his forehead from view.

Pemberton had been hired on by the good folks of Elsworth County after the fancy, big city sheriff they had brought in got caught messing with the town's married women. After that, the county decided they needed a much, much more seasoned man with a little religion as opposed to someone who'd be sneaking in when others were out, stealing something more precious than a man's money. Pemberton was a retired Brethren Preacher, born and raised local, and he fit the flavor of the moment to a tee. He'd been the sheriff for the past six years.

"How'd you kill your brother?" Pemberton explored.

"We got to arguing out in the field one day. I shudda let it go. He tried to get away from me, but I was mad." Cain sniffled. "I kept hittin him." Cain wiped his nose with the back of his sleeve.

"Bring us another pitcher, Shaw," ordered the sheriff.

Eight pitchers.

Sheriff Pemberton finished praying with Cain and got up from the table. His big, old Bible, the bindings tattered and frayed, lay open before the huge man. Tears and beer had fallen all over the pages, making a mess of some of the underlined passages. Cain's eyes were blurry as he stared down at the book.

Pemberton reached down and thumbed the pages where Cain was reading in Genesis over just a page or two.

He took out his pen and circled Genesis 9:6:

"Whoso sheddeth man's blood, by man shall his blood also be shed."

The sheriff did what no regular cop would ever do. He set his loaded gun on top of his Bible and backed away.

Shaw set a last pitcher of beer on the edge of the table.

After sharing a look, the two men stepped out of the bar together.

Flashing lights from six other police cars greeted the two as they exited. State troopers and police from the two neighboring counties had descended on the Spinning Wheel Tavern.

"Shaw, go on around and watch the back," Pemberton ordered the barkeep. "But whatever ya do, don't shoot at him, ya here. If he comes out, just leave him be. If he shoots, you run and hide. You understand me, Shaw?"

"Yes, sir." Shaw nodded gravely, then took off to do as he'd been told, ignoring the other cops who called for him to stay put.

The state troopers argued. The two other sheriffs argued. The local drunks who wanted to go in and drink argued.

"My county, my call. If you got a problem with that, hit the road."

They heard a lone gun shot inside the bar about five minutes later. When they went in they found no bullet hole and no blood. Cain was simply dead. They were at a loss as to what had actually killed him, but good money was on alcohol poisoning. Nine pitchers, they said, may have been one too many.

Marcia

Visiting the Grays

THE SOLDIERS AND other staff who'd been caught by Susan's powers and slung around like dancing puppets for nearly an hour were overflowing the facility's small infirmary. The beds and couches were being used by those who'd suffered more serious reactions to being gassed into unconsciousness. Everyone who seemed likely to keep breathing on their own had been placed in the long hallway outside the infirmary. Marcia lay there on the hard tile floor, a pillow under her head and a warm towel wrapped around her pounding head. She didn't feel well. She felt sick and weak.

"Marcia," Dyal's ugly voice intruded into the throbbing darkness. "We need someone to ask Gannon to come inside. It won't be safe for him in his courtyard when we start with Benjamin."

She resisted the urge to cuss him out, tell him that she was going to file a report that would see him fired within a week, or simply threaten to kill him herself, which would get her fired.

"Be mad at us later, Marcia, but go take care of Gannon right now. This is no time to be childish." His voice was abusive and belittling.

"Childish." That was what Ogburn said. It was the hot button word he told Dyal to use. She knew the tricks herself. His use of the word was too perfect to be accidental. Could they—

"Do I need to send one of the guards or—"

"I'll go!" She pulled the towel off her face, ready to cuss Dyal out right then and there, but one of the medical interns had stepped up and was leaning in, whispering something urgently to Dyal. It was the man who had checked her out when she first arrived at the infirmary.

Dyal glanced down at her and gave her the strangest look, then took the doctor by the arm and walked him away, both of them casting suspicious glances at her as they whispered their way down the hallway together. Marcia had no idea what the hell that was all about. It seemed as if they were cutting her out of the loop of information now. She was no longer in the know. That wasn't supposed to happen! She was part of the oversight!

Feeling robbed, and bullied once again, she tried to get up only to fall back onto her pillow, head pounding like a drum. She hated this pounding in her head. She hated Dyal. She hated Ogburn. She hated Dr. Tachi, who hadn't let her use the drugs she wanted to from the beginning. God, she hated all of them.

After two more failed attempts, Marcia finally got to her feet, staggered into a bathroom, and got herself presentable. When she came out she noticed that the hall was empty of gas victims and was now filled with soldiers wearing gloves, scrubbing off all of Katie's artwork up and down the hall. They were attacking the walls as if the bunnies were dangerous. She looked down at the back of her hand, relieved to see that the bunny Katie had drawn there was already gone. She'd washed it off without even realizing it.

Marcia stepped into the open courtyard where Gannon the Gray, her most docile charge, was enjoying some afternoon sun with his wife. Gannon had the easy grace of someone who truly knew how to enjoy doing nothing. He lay in the hammock, shirtless, the disembodied, beating heart of the girl he loved lying on his bare chest, glistening and moist with blood.

The cleaning staff came to his room twice a day, and Gannon also showered often (with Kim) and he kept damp towels handy, but blood was a constant part of his life and he'd simply accepted it and managed it as well as he could. Dried, bloody stains were everywhere in the room, but the heart itself never dried out, never stopped beating, and most of all—it never left Gannon for more than a couple of minutes.

If someone removed the heart from the room, the organ would vanish after two minutes and reappear with Gannon. If the heart was dropped into an incinerator and obliterated, it would reappear in two minutes, restored and beating, lying right in his lap.

Gannon's story was a true fairy tale, Grimm Brothers ugly style, where the endings to the stories were not quite so Disney. His story started as most cliché fairy tales did—boy meets girl and falls in love. They came from different worlds. She was rich, he was poor. Desperate to stay together, they found a way to get into Amen Hale where they planned to get married and live happily ever after (Disney version).

Only, once there, Gannon found that he hated the place, but tragically, Kim did just the opposite; she fell in love with Amen Hale and the people she met there. She even changed her name to Alana, wanting a new name for their new life in this new magical place. When she refused to leave Amen Hale, Gannon left her, breaking all his promises. He'd left her standing at the altar with a broken, bleeding heart. Alana chose that moment to become a witch of Amen Hale, and in a fit of grief driven madness used her new power to rid herself of her broken heart, which still loved a boy she now hated. She cast the despised organ from her own chest with her magic and cursed it to follow Gannon until the day he died. Without a heart of her own, Alana dropped dead, but the heart lived on, as it apparently always would.

Horrified, Gannon ran from the bloody heart of the bride he'd spurned only to find that he couldn't get away. It followed him. He threw the heart away only to have it return, appearing right beside him. He cut it to bits, burned it, stomped it flat, only to have it reappear, whole, healthy, and lying in his lap each time he destroyed it or threw it away. The heart found ways to express how much his actions hurt, but it still forgave every offense, no matter how vile—and it never left him. Gannon fought it, but at some point he simply snapped. By the time he had arrived at the facility he was already broken. From the first day here, he'd introduced the heart as "My wife, Kim."

Gannon lifted the heart from his chest and held it to his ear, listening. "No. Of course not," he said, giving Marcia a friendly wave as she neared. They'd run a number of tests, but the scientists had been unable to determine if Gannon was actually communicating with the heart or if he was simply imagining her words in his head. The beating heart showed no discernible pattern, but if you asked anyone who spent time with the two of them they'd swear that the heart was most definitely aware, alive, and quite communicative.

"Yeah, she's cute, but she's old. Er." Gannon gave Marcia an apologetic glance as he whispered to the heart then set it back upon his chest and spoke to Marcia. "Sorry about that. Kim's a little jealous." He gave the heart a narrowing of his eyes but a playful smile turned up the ends of his mouth.

Marcia played along. She actually enjoyed spending time with the two of them, though the heart did frighten her when it moved suddenly. It even spat at her once, sending a fresh squirt of blood from one of the open valves that ruined her suit. It was her own fault. She'd placed a hand on Gannon's arm to offer some sympathy and got herself hosed for it. She'd learned her lesson. Marcia kept her hands off Kim's husband.

"Why would she be jealous of me?" Marcia said. "You're right, I am old."

Gannon's look turned more somber. "You're old-er, not old, Marcia. And you're beautiful. Kim misses having a body. She doesn't want her old one back, and you're the only girl we get to see. You remind her of what she's missing."

Marcia blinked in surprise. Where was this headed!? Was every single one of her charges going to go crazy today? She'd only just gotten out of the infirmary a few minutes ago, determined to do this one, small task before going home and things were already getting weird. She didn't feel up to this if it was going to get weird. She took a step back.

Gannon sat up, coming to life as he watched Marcia back away, looking sick and afraid.

"Give me a minute," he said to the heart. He left Kim on the hammock and got to his feet.

"Marcia. Are you all right? Sorry if what I said was a little weird," he apologized. "Really. It's cool."

His sincerity and unfeigned compassion was so different from Dyal's calculated ugliness. Her eyes began to tear as her emotions fought with reason, and in the midst of that she swayed, suddenly very dizzy. Gannon stepped closer, as if to catch her from falling, but Marcia put a hand out to stop him.

"No. Don't. You'll make Kim mad," she warned. "And I don't want her mad at me, Gannon. This is the only place I get treated halfway decent. The others are so mean to me."

Gannon took a step back, his frown deepening as he re-evaluated Marcia's condition silently. She looked and sounded a mess, but he didn't know what to do for her. He glanced back over to the hammock. His internal clock knew the two minute leash was running out of slack. He walked over and grabbed the heart and returned to Marcia.

"Marcia, you need to move Gannon and Kim indoors where it's safe," Dr. Ogburn's monotone voice came over the intercom.

Gannon looked up to the camera mounted on the wall. "Safe?" he asked. "What's up, doc?"

"Ask Marcia, Gannon, but move inside for now."

"No problem," Gannon answered, agreeable as always. He strode into his room and Marcia followed, pulling the courtyard door closed behind them and locking it with a key.

"I'll unlock it once it's safe to go back outside."

"Do we get to know what's going on?" he asked.

"Might as well tell you I guess. You two are the only ones stable enough to actually tell the truth." Marcia looked at the heart Gannon held in his hands and spoke directly to it. "And yes, Kim, that includes you. You're a sweetheart next to our other patients." She rubbed her temples as she continued. "Unfortunately, one of the teens who took those pills will be getting put down in a few minutes." She said it plainly, not shading the truth with niceties.

"Like a rabid dog." Gannon grinned. "Is it the bastard that put those bruises on your arms?"

"Yes," Marcia confirmed. "I didn't tell you before, but he caught one of the female guards yesterday and raped her."

Gannon noticed how Marcia rubbed at her bruised forearms, remembering the contact. It was easy to see how much that encounter still affected her.

"Sorry I didn't tell you sooner. I didn't want to upset you," she apologized.

Gannon, ever trusting, nodded his easy acceptance.

"That kid is a monster. And from reading Dr. Burgis's files we think he may have been one even before he took the pills." Marcia felt strange. She'd never been gassed before but she didn't understand why her legs would feel so weak. Her whole body was weak and sore, like she'd been running or working out.

Gannon grabbed a chair and dragged it over for Marcia. She immediately let herself drop into it.

"So. You and the doc wanted us indoors," he said, not as if he truly wanted to know but as if he wanted to keep talking for Marcia's benefit. "I take it they're gonna use some major firepower on this kid. Are you worried you might not be able to kill him? Is this guy anything like the Black Witch?"

Gannon twitched and looked down to the heart in his hand as if it had shocked him. He lifted the heart, pressing it to the side of his head again, listening to the beating pulses that conveyed words and thoughts only he could discern.

"Fine," he replied to the heart with a little attitude, "I'll call her the Black Lion, but only for you. And, yeah, I know." He took the clothes out of another chair and drug it closer, sitting beside Marcia. He balanced Kim on the arm of the chair, considerately keeping her in the middle of things. Marcia wordlessly offered him a wet towel that was hanging on the back of her chair, getting the back of her blouse wet. Gannon took it without comment and started wiping himself down.

"What'd she say?" Marcia asked.

"Huh?"

"Kim," Marcia asked, "when you two were talking, you said, 'I know.' What did she say?"

"She said that if this kid really is like the Black Lion then we're all going to die. And she wants you to stay in here till it's over."

"Why?" Marcia asked, eyes tight with the pain in her head. She felt like she needed to go lie down.

Gannon gave her a level look. "That guy's already tried to get you once, Marcia. This is the perfect place to hide out. He won't look for you in here. Kim's worried about you, and so am I. And you don't look like you're feeling too well."

A huge boom and a series of crashes shook the building. Marcia let out an undignified squeal and drew her feet up into the chair. "It's started," she said in a hushed tone, looking about like a frightened mouse.

"Nope," Gannon said, flatly denying the obvious.

Marcia smiled in spite of her fear and the pain in her head. "Then what was that noise?" she challenged.

"I dun-no, maybe someone's moving the furniture around next door," Gannon said innocently. He lifted the heart to his ear then rolled his eyes as he listened. "Don't fuss at me, woman!" Gannon argued. "Of course it was stupid. It was supposed to be stupid. It got her mind off what was happening. Look at her." He pushed the heart in Marcia's direction as if it had eyes then brought it back to his ear. He continued listening, occasionally nodding.

Marcia smiled at the attempted humor, but before she could say anything, gunfire and other explosions started to vibrate the floor and shake the walls. For a while, the three of them were quiet, all hoping and wishing for the same thing. That someone would die, so they could live.

Benjamin Grant

Burnt Toast

Dyal and Ogburn moved forward with the grim operation in spite of the difficulties caused by Susan's musical uprising and other strange and troubling developments. The fear that Benjamin's powers would continue to escalate made further delay impossible. Every hour they waited increased the likelihood of catastrophic failure.

When the attack started, Ben fled the room as they'd expected, knocked the door down as they'd predicted, and took the round from the small portable rail gun dead on, exactly as they'd hoped. Surprisingly, the super velocity hunk of metal did not pierce his flesh, but turned his entire body into a human sized projectile, crashing backward through three cinderblock walls before stopping, half buried, in the final, exterior compound wall.

The waiting forces converged and unleashed hell before he could pull himself free of the rubble. In the end, Ben, the unstoppable man, a.k.a. The Juggernaut, was dead—and yet he was far from gone. Ashes or less was what they expected, but scattered fleshy pieces still remained. All of him still seemed to be present but spread out across the blackened stones like strawberry preserves scraped over burnt toast. His substance remained, and therefore the threat remained.

Men in bio suits used shovels, sponges, and other tools to gather the remains that were mixed in with ash, rubble, and bullets. Bit by bit, they deposited Ben into three orange containers. The containers were equipped with heat, temperature, and motion detectors. If the body somehow began to regenerate as the vampires did, they would know.

Benjamin Grant, all powerful and unleashed upon society had not been a pleasant picture, but it was one that Dr. Ogburn actively fostered and promoted. Before the assault, Ogburn intentionally released details of Benjamin's assault of the female soldier to the troops who were about to conduct the operation. He'd told Dyal it was prudent, in order to foster a proper mindset among the soldiers during the euthanasia of an unarmed and apparently helpless teenage boy. He said that nothing was as unpredictable or as disruptive as the spontaneous moral eruption of men or women experiencing a crisis of conscious.

Just that morning Ogburn updated the orientation material for all those who came into close contact with the teens, including some shocking video of Benjamin's attack on the girl. The material was meant to reinforce that these kids were, in fact, incredibly dangerous and insane. The doctor wanted to be prepared and proactive. If they decided to euthanize the others, he would need people with the proper mental attitude to carry through without conflicting moral inhibitions.

Marcia

Wake Up

MARCIA WOKE TO find herself lying in Gannon's bed. Had she fallen asleep or passed out? She couldn't remember. She gazed about her surroundings in dumb disbelief, wondering why Dyal and Ogburn had left her in the room of a psychotic mental patient, hurt and unconscious. It was unthinkable. This would be the icing on the cake in her report.

It would have been a lot more frightening to wake in such a place if Gannon hadn't been asleep in a chair directly in front of her, sprawled out like a gangly, long legged, blue headed spider. He was even drooling. Marcia couldn't help but smile. He wasn't the most handsome man (or boy) she'd ever seen, but she admired his adaptability. While the others were imploding, he thrived. She could see why Kim had fallen in love with him.

She didn't remember lying down, so Gannon must have picked her up and carried her to the bed after she blacked out. And where was Kim? Marcia scanned around Gannon. She didn't see the bloody organ anywhere near him—which was impossible. Surely he'd been in that chair for more than two minutes!

Her own heart began to race as she imagined where the bloody heart must be. She recalled Gannon saying something about Kim being "jealous." With horror movie slowness she rolled back the blanket that covered her and looked down at herself, expecting to find the bloody thing sitting on her chest or lying in her lap.

It wasn't there.

She searched through the covers. She even looked under her pillows. It wasn't in the bed with her. Strange.

Marcia peered over the edge of the bed and found it lying there on the floor, beating away. Apparently it had rolled away from Gannon while he slept, but it couldn't climb up into the bed to get her. Kim didn't have a lot of mobility now, all she could do was roll a little. Kim couldn't reach her unless Gannon helped, which he wouldn't.

She stared down at the heart on the floor, wondering herself what it must be like for this poor girl. Not having a body. Living with this curse. A fresh wave of fatigue washed over her. The last few days she'd hardly slept at all, and her head still hurt so badly from the gas she wouldn't complain if the whole thing simply had to go. She drug a pillow under her pounding head, lay on her side and pulled the covers back over herself, looking down at Kim as her eyelids began to close – open – close – open –

Close.

Two men entered the room quietly, wearing protective hazmat gear. The heart moved between the men and the sleeping woman, but the men didn't approach Marcia. Using tongs, they removed Marcia's purse from the table then left silently, locking the door behind them.

Meridith

Gathering the Sheaves

AT FIRST THE witches of the Wicket Street Knitting Circle and their children had been delighted as the spirits of the woods revealed themselves, lighting up the night like fireworks streaking through the woods and gathering in the field in ever increasing numbers. They laughed and cheered as what they called "will o' the wisps" circled like a magical pyre, replacing the fire they'd just doused as they prepared to leave for the evening.

Soon it became clear that these glowing creatures that rushed to the glade were, in fact, running for their very lives. Dark, ghostly shadows moved among the trees, chasing the dots of light and devouring any they could catch, snuffing out their light before they reached the glade. Some of the women counseled flight, but the wisdom of older voices prevailed.

Twenty six women trapped in the clearing gathered around the column of circling lights in a circle of their own. Holding hands, they faced out toward the shadows and ominous, dark shapes that moved among the trees at the edge of the glade, while their weeping and frightened children clung to their legs. And so they'd held for almost two hours, besieged and hoping for deliverance, rescue, or help of any kind.

At the edge of the clearing the branches of two, old rowan trees leaned toward one another and merged, almost as if they wished to hold hands. The dense wood within the trees did not pop loudly in protest, but merely creaked and sighed pliantly as they joined to form a living arch, eight feet high and fifteen feet across. Rowan trees had a long tradition in English mythology and folklore; for centuries its wood had been used to fashion magicians' staves, druid staffs, dowsing rods, charms against witches, and tokens to ward off evil spirits. Rowan wood was even left on graves of the recently deceased to keep them from returning and haunting the living.

The women in the center of the glade who happened to be facing that portion of the tree line watched as a witch they thought was dead, a witch they thought they'd murdered, stepped through the Rowan Gate. The horned, female figure halted after only a few paces. Two burning, red dots within greater pools of darkness regarded the trapped group of women silently.

Cricket liked to read the classics and classic horror most of all. Frankenstein, the original Dracula, and The Headless Horseman were among her favorites, though she'd always thought that certain parts were a bit overdone, like the account of Ichabod Crane's knees knocking together in fright. That was completely ridiculous. She'd said so to her mother this morning in the car as she'd read that particular portion again.

"I mean, really Mom-ma!" She rolled her eyes. "How could knees actually *knock* together? That's so stupid!"

As she held her place with the women in the circle, Cricket's knees, as well as the rest of her body trembled. She craned her neck and looked behind her and caught a glimpse of the horned form of the Black Witch drawing closer and quickly turned back to the front. The view before her was no better at all! The ghostly, man shaped shadows drifting about were far from the most disturbing things moving among the trees.

Man-shaped creatures crunched about in the foliage there at the edge of the glade. Malformed, muscled nightmares, glistening with wetness too thick to be water. Some of the creatures had the faces of animals while others wore a man's face but had the antlers of a stag atop their heads. All of the man-shaped horrors were nude, grotesque, and sexually aroused. Their leering gazes and long tongued, lolling mouths promised horrors that made the darkest passages of Cricket's books seem like gay nursery rhymes fit to share with babes in cradles.

"Steady!" Meridith's firm voice commanded as the women began to gabble in mounting fear. "Stay in the circle and hold still!"

The women faced outward, toward the wood, so they were forced to crane their necks to speak with one another or simply call out blindly. The women kept a firm hold on each other's hands and kept the circle whole, each of them doing as Meridith bid them do.

"Meridith! The girl's here for blood!" cried one of the women.

"Hush up, you daft ninny!" Ambrosia shouted from her spot in the chain of women.

"Meridith! We must flee!" she persisted. "She's come for vengeance for what we've done. She'll kill us for sure!" Shannon Bristol's voice was almost a whistle, and though she urged mad flight into the night, her feet remained firmly planted.

"Aye!" Meridith shouted back. "You may be right! Go then if you mean to, but I and mine mean to stay where we stand and beg this girl for mercy. I suggest you do the same, child. I doubt the bogles and beasts in the woods will give ya a listen afore they have their way with ya."

"That's easy for you to say, Mother!" her daughter Robin cried out bitterly. "You didn't spit into the cauldron! What mercy is there for Cricket and me!?" She was breathing hard. "Just say it, Mother! SAY IT!" She went on a rant, copying her mother's voice in mockery, "I told you so! You never listen! You brought this on yourself! You've killed your own daughter with your stupid pride! Say it, Mother! Say it! I want to hear you say it before we die!" Robin ran out of breath and words.

"Look at the charm on my wrist, Little Bird."

Something in her mother's gentle voice made Robin listen, listen more than she had in years. She looked at the hand she held in her own and saw the hair woven circlet around her mother's wrist. She leaned closer, recognizing her own brown hair and her daughter's golden strands woven in with her mother's stout, iron gray strands.

"Cricket put a charm on your ankle." Meridith tightened her grip on Robin's hand. "Don't let go of my hand to look! It's there. You and she are free of any blame here, it'll be on me and my head only. I'll tell the girl so myself. Now hush up, stand straight, and mind me for once in your life without a fuss."

Robin's mind spun back to earlier that day, when Cricket was at her feet doing something. An ankle charm—

"Yes, Mother." Robin straightened up and obeyed. It was the first time she'd called her mother "Mother" without making the word a curse since she was fourteen years old.

Meridith continued to shout orders and encouragements to the other women who now clung to her words like lifelines as they dangled precariously over the hungry maw of hell itself.

Black Rain

The Devil Within

I RUSHED FROM PLACE to place, wooded fields, hidden dells, and secluded grottos all across the globe looking for survivors. The remote locations yielded nothing but dead bodies, the Twilin at those sites already slain by the demons or scattered into the woods, but in those few steadings located near people I found some to save.

I found a few hundred, traumatized survivors in a city park in Seoul, Korea. In another location I found nearly a hundred bits and few dozen, brave Dams who'd forsaken all the guidelines laid down by the Ban and sought shelter within a posh hotel. They remained invisible to human eyes, lingering in the crowded lobby, but even there they were hunted. Five, demon possessed men were there when I arrived, trying to crush the Twilins. The possessed men looked like an escaped group of mental patients as they stomped on the marble floor, upended flower pots, and trashed the furniture in their attempts to destroy the elusive creatures which only they could see.

Most of the humans and all the demon possessed fled at my appearance. I kept my visit to Cairo brief, only a few minutes in the nature reserve by the Nile, a quick flight over the city and less than five minutes in the lobby. It was quick, but I was still seen and photographed swallowing little bits of light.

Next I found nearly ten thousand in a small glen in Sweden. These Twilin had been fortunate to have a large concert happening practically on top of their protected circle. I used some tact and shrouded myself with a long, black cloak as I drew in the survivors, pulling them in with my will from all across the field. The concert goers quickly followed the points of light racing through their midst as they vanished into the caul of my hood like water down a dark drain. Young people began to gather around me, shouting angrily until I did an Obi Wan Kenobi, vanishing and letting my empty cloak fall to the ground there in the field as I traveled on. The final refuge was located in a protected wood not far from London.

What I saw when I stepped through the gate was not what I expected. Before me in the middle of the clearing was a huge, spiraling mass of Twilin sparks surrounded by a ring of women and children. I noticed without worry or alarm that the woods were teeming with many of the man-shaped beasts, lumbering monstrosities, and other smaller creatures that I'd seen at the other, more remote locations.

I also took notice of the large number of green-eyed fauns. The fauns were more bold than the other creatures, lingering closer and shooting me sly smiles with their boyishly handsome faces. They had two swayback horns at the top of their head, long wavy hair, pointy ears, Elvis lamb-chop sideburns, and tiny goatees dangling from their chins. They were human from the waist up but had the tail and the wooly, bent back legs and bottom half of a goat.

The creatures and demons around me acted as they had in every place I'd traveled so far; they moved as I moved, keeping their distance. So far, the only demon that I'd touched had been the one in the graveyard that I'd decapitated and cursed. With that one exception I'd left them be, and they'd done the same, but I didn't know if that would change here. There was something different about this place. These demons hadn't hidden from the humans but had blatantly revealed themselves.

I looked around the clearing again, noticing how the man-shaped creatures stared at the women. It appeared that these demons not only wanted to destroy my Twilins, but also wanted these women and children. But why? Either something was different about these women, about this place, or something or someone different was out there in the darkness. Maybe it was all three.

I approached the circle of women and listened as they spoke to one another, shouting encouragements or fears back and forth. Apparently they believed that staying in the circle would give them some measure of protection from the demons, and from me, and it was abundantly clear that they did recognize me.

"It's her! That's what they were doing! They were just saving us for her!" cried one frustrated woman bitterly.

"The Black Witch! The curse has come back onto our own heads! Sweet Diana save us!" said a voice teetering on the edge of madness.

"She's come for vengeance for what we did. She'll kill us for sure!" cried another painfully shrill voice before being shouted down by saner women of sounder minds.

Most of them wore common dresses or street clothes, though some wore the unmistakable gowns and robes of witches. Their dress, combined with some of the things they were saying, added to the fact that they were holding hands in a circle declared this to be a coven of witches. I wondered what they'd been up to here in this clearing tonight. Lammas was past, and I knew of no other holy day or festival for this night.

I spied a bundle of stuff left almost thirty feet outside their circle, which told me that they must have gathered around the spiraling Twilins in haste. I stopped at their abandoned stuff and casually flipped open the lid of a blue cooler and looked inside. The ice was mostly melted but the water was icy cold. A few cans of English brand sodas were down at the bottom and I swilled around until I came up with something that seemed a fair equivalent to lemon lime.

After shutting the cooler, I took a seat on the top and opened the can. As I sipped my super sugary soda, I rummaged through someone's hand bag and came out with what looked like an agenda for the day. My eyes only scanned as far as the header at the top of the page before I dropped the paper.

> Come Saturday and Curse the Black Witch and Her Coven of Darkness!
> Wicket Street Knitting Circle Coven and Guests
> Special Gathering This Saturday at the Wicket Meadow Reserve
> All attendees must register upon arrival

I stood and studied this group of women with new understanding. Now that I knew what their coven was up to, their fears and shouted comments made more sense. These women – women that I'd never met – had cast a curse upon me today. A curse meant to kill me and my sisters.

My mind flashed back to the website someone had created from the stolen security video of the Lammas celebration. The website showed me at my naming, when I lit the Black Candle and declared myself a Black Witch. They accused me of being the child of the Devil and my sisters of being my "coven of evil" and urged witches and pagans everywhere to join together to curse us. I made the connection. Today, Saturday, was the day they'd set. Today, all across the world, witches would have gathered in their special places to curse me and my sisters.

I viewed the events of the day through this new filter and weighed it out. In one form or another, we'd all died today, the curse had come, just as they'd called it. I wondered curiously how much of what I'd endured today could be laid at the feet of this group of women and others like them, all those who'd cursed us and wished us dead.

I stood and came closer to them. They were frightened by my approach but held their circle, each woman or girl gripping the hands of the women on either side, drawing strength from that continued contact. Being locked in this hand to hand position held them in a cross and forced them to face me. Even if they turned their head or lowered their eyes, there was no way to avoid me.

Quite a situation to find oneself in. What were the odds? It seemed a nearly magical manifestation of balance. They'd hidden in the woods, wishing me evil behind my back, and now they were practically forced to stare me in the face, held there by their own superstition and evil deeds. What would I do with them? What did they deserve? What did I owe them after what they'd done to me, my sisters, and perhaps the Twilin as well.

As the balance of things seemed to have pre-arranged this scene I felt obligated to carry through. Perhaps this was some strange new facet of deity that I was unaware of before now. I determined to administer an eyeball to hellish eyeball inspection, trusting that by its conclusion I'd have a direction as to what to do with these—*humans*.

The first of them I stood before was a young girl, perhaps a year older than I. She wet herself as I stood there. I watched her face, listening to the sound of pee running down her leg. I could tell that she remained in the circle only due to the borrowed strength of the others. She met my angry gaze without flinching and actually seemed to be begging me to kill her. She was a very pretty girl, her finely chiseled features seemed so delicate and fragile. It was plain to see that what she feared lay in the woods behind me. She'd rather die than face that.

I was unmoved by her plight, which didn't seem right. I should care, or feel something, shouldn't I? I realized quickly what my disconnect was. I could not see myself in her place. I was a god, not a girl. I could not imagine myself as something this small, this limited, this simple, this mortal. This seemingly insurmountable distance between myself and the girl troubled me a little, but what troubled me a great deal, oddly enough, was how very "little" it troubled me.

I knew that this should be flipping me out, and—it wasn't. I'd saved the human girl that I had been, and I knew that I could don that cloak of being once more, but the thought of doing so troubled me. It troubled me a very great deal. I knew with absolute certainty that this shouldn't be the case. I'd saved the human girl for a reason.

But why the hell would I want to be like that again? I argued. I went back and forth for a few moments, forcing myself to play both sides, but finally – grudgingly – I landed on the side of experimentation. If I put the girl on I could always take her off again, but I should at least experiment with putting the girl on and off (at least once) if only to see what the difference was. Perhaps there was no difference at all. Perhaps I didn't care because there was no reason to care?

Already hating the decision, I reached within myself and put on the girl I'd been, that shroud of innocence, jumbled emotions, fears, hates, and odd eccentricities that I'd saved from the life I was given and shared with Rain Marie. As this covering pulled tighter, I felt my perfect calm crack – then shatter! And then vanish altogether.

My existence, what I was, pulled in and changed. I, Black Rain, stood upon the damp earth, facing this girl that looked at me. The way in which I perceived the outside world before had been by simply filling the entire area with myself with my body as a focal point, but now, all of me was contained within the skin in which I stood. While outside my body I'd shrunk, my insides remained as vast and incredibly endless as it was when I created it.

Oddly, I felt as if I had two hearts, one that beat inside my chest for me alone, and one inside my head, a heart made up of thousands upon thousands of smaller hearts. Hearts that I knew. Hearts that I could feel even now. That strange flatness I'd felt from the Twilins was gone. I understood their pain and suffering now. The problem I'd felt had been with me, not with them.

I was still adjusting to this odd balance, being both big and small at the same time, when a series of grunts and hoarse calls rose from the trees behind me. The girl I stood before began to make a small, keening noise, which rose and fell as she breathed in and out. Instantly, I was flooded with compassion for the girl. I stared into her face and shared her fear.

I turned and looked off into the woods and felt a chill run up my own spine at the sight. The fear of mortality and abuse stabbed through me. The brevity of life assaulted my mind and body like a punch to the gut. Suddenly, I questioned my own wisdom in being here, alone. Perhaps I should bring Dan or Jane or Believer.

I pushed back my fear and turned back to the girl.

"I can give you this promise," I said. The girl's eyes moved from the woods behind me back to my own disturbing, red eyes. "If I decide that you need to die, I swear I will kill you myself. I will not let them have you."

The keening stopped. She nodded but said nothing, although she did relax. She was ready for the end that she felt sure was coming at my hands. It seemed odd that the quickest way to comfort her was to promise her death.

I moved on, studying one after another of these women, still trying to adjust to the way my perceptions had changed. I learned a little more about myself with each woman I stood before. My own prejudices began to surface. My likes and dislikes, and even my darker emotions and cruelty seemed to return.

"Please forgive me. Please forgive me," mumbled a woman over and over. She met my eyes, but even with all my empathy held at the ready I felt no pity for her, but at her feet was a nine year old boy. He glanced up at me, then looked away, blushing.

I smiled.

Here he was, in the midst of terror and horror no nine year old boy should ever have to see, and he's staring at me in that way. Noticing my body. Boys. I ignored his mother, who was trying to say something to me, and knelt down to stare at the boy. His name popped into my head.

"Are you thirsty, David?"

He looked up from his intense inspection of the grass at his feet, surprised that I knew his name. He zeroed in on the soda in my hand and nodded, too timid or too frightened to speak, but the offer of a soda already had him licking his dry, parched lips. I handed him my lime soda and resumed my walk and my inspection, wondering as I did so if I would have done this for the boy if I hadn't have put on the girl.

"Our father that art in heaven..." A middle aged woman who wore a witch's gown seemed to be the brightest of the bunch so far. Apparently she'd decided to change her religion. She had her eyes closed tight, making a solid attempt at the Lord's prayer.

"Esther! Blessed Be! You're a witch, now act like it and keep your wits!" came a voice from the circle.

I moved on, passing a few more women before reaching the older woman who'd just called out to Esther. She looked melted. Ice cream left in the sun. It was plain to see that she was a well to do and proper lady, but her hair, which had sat high on her head, had fallen, slipping free of its intricate entrapment so that it sat like a loosened mop atop her head. She'd been sweating profusely but unable to wipe her face, held prisoner by the women on either side. Her thick makeup and eye shadow had begun to stream down in runnels, and even her body looked to have melted down her frame and gathered into her legs and rump. The poor woman was in a state.

"Oh my," she said as I studied her. "My name is Ambrosia. How are you, dear?"

Her voice was so warm and motherly that I blinked in surprise. It was not what I'd expected. She was asking *me* how *I* was! Was this the Titanic thing? I wondered. That queer British penchant for politeness as the ship went down, musicians playing violins as they slipped beneath the icy waters.

"On the whole, it's been a really rough day, Mrs. Ambrosia. People I love were murdered," I answered in a kind, respectful voice, as to a mother. I watched her blink in surprise like I had. She had her neck bent back staring up at me, which didn't feel right, so I dropped to my knees. That put us eye to eye.

"Mrs. Ambrosia, did you curse me today?"

"No, child. I wouldn't do it. Meridith and I spoke against this business from dawn till dusk."

"But the others did curse me?"

She frowned, looking frustrated that she didn't have the use of her hands. She seemed the kind of woman who'd be busy with them right now, using them to help her talk, hold a napkin, or to adjust her bothersome hair.

"They were caught up in the hype and lies told by the news people," Ambrosia said sadly. "I know that they shouldn't have done what they did, but they didn't know the truth."

"But you, and, Meridith, you told them the truth. Didn't you?"

"Yes," she agreed reluctantly. "But what's the word of two, old witches compared to all those fools on the telly and the internet. It's a hard thing standing on your own when the whole world's gone mad."

I regarded her for a silent minute as she did the same. Her eyes slid up to the horns atop my head.

"Did you call the demons to trap us here?" she asked.

"Why on earth would I do that, Mrs. Ambrosia?" I answered her as I rose to my feet to move to the next woman. "If I wanted to kill you, I'd do it myself or take you home and feed you to my daughter." My tail swished about happily and I looked back over my shoulder and met her eyes with my own, frightening gaze. "It's a sin to waste good food, Mrs. Ambrosia."

She paled and I felt the sweet pleasure of her fear. Was it wrong to feel pleasure at her fear? All I said was the simple truth. I thought on that as I moved on. After inspecting the last few women I reached the one who had to be Meridith. She was a tall woman, but sway backed and stooped with age. Her crooked posture and advancing years did not diminish her presence in the least.

The mettle she was made of was so easy to see that I smiled broadly as I faced her. Without a doubt, this was the woman who'd saved all the fools in this field. I'd heard her strong voice when I'd first arrived, keeping them in line. She was the rock on which they'd cast themselves, hoping she would save them from the storm they'd driven into. Surely this woman, much more so than Ambrosia, had tried from sun up till sun down to keep me safe. She didn't know me, but she'd fought for me today.

I felt a deep sense of gratitude and a connection to this woman. A woman I'd never met until this moment. I wondered *again* if I would have felt any of this without that portion of myself called Rain. What would I have felt if I faced this woman as I'd been? I knew the answer to the question. I wouldn't have felt any connection at all, or empathy, or seen any wisdom in her eyes worth serious consideration. She's a human.

As I thought on it, those remaining, human pieces of myself took on a value worth more than the entire rest of the whole. Those scraps, dregs, and shadowed pieces which Rain Marie had collected in her mind and pressed into service that day in the abortion clinic, the scraps of soul that I'd despised for so long as my "miserable creation"—no longer looked miserable at all. They were still pieces of her soul. Precious, beautiful pieces of a human soul.

My soul.

If I never put the girl back on, I would have been me, but would I have been a "me" that I could love or care about? The answer was HELL NO! My mistake had been innocent, but it had been so incredibly stupid that it scared me to death. In my worry about changing too much, I'd ignorantly stripped myself of my humanity. Apparently I could live without it, but it wouldn't truly be me doing the living.

"Here now, what's this about?" said the old woman before me.

I'd wandered off in my mind, but I focused again on where I stood and those around me. I was trembling as badly as the young girl who held tightly to Meridith's left hand. I met the girl's wide eyes with my own, fear widened gaze. I felt like a little girl myself right then. A young, ignorant, stupid child that needed to mind her mother.

Earlier, I couldn't see these women as being my equals, but now I felt as if I had more in common with this girl to her right than the woman before me. I felt abused, as if I'd fought a war and lost badly, only to have the enemy make a mistake as monumentally stupid as I'd made – and somehow, someway—I was back! I had a second chance to live.

I wanted to live!

I dropped to my knees before Meridith, and with difficulty (damn horns!), I laid my head to the old woman's chest. I wrapped my arms around her, holding her as I trembled. Who else here in this place could I cling to? I did not cry, but the horror of what I'd almost done seemed caught in my flesh and bones. I'd been killed for real this time, and the truly frightening thing was knowing that I almost didn't come back. I was well and truly gone. She could have just as easily thrown out that old Rain coat. It was too tight anyway. But thankfully, as with any old coat, she tried it one last time before giving it the old heave ho.

I felt arms around me, holding me. I looked up at the old woman. "You broke your circle."

She smiled and winked. "It's just a circle," she said, quietly. The other women were gathering behind her, looking over her shoulder curiously. "The circle helped keep the weaker ones from rushing off and getting killed and kept the strong-headed ones in place and forced them to help those who were weak. Aye, lots of good can come from simple silliness for those who've a mind to use it."

Someone screamed. The creatures around us in the woods were beginning to enter the clearing.

The women descended into panicked madness.

"Bloody Hell! You've killed us, Meridith!" shouted one woman angrily. "You shouldn't have broken the circle!"

"We're done for! They're coming!" cried another. All the women started shouting, crying and begging at once. The children started to wail. One flame headed woman was bellowing, trying to take charge, pushing vehemently for reforming the circle while the others shouted back and forth. The thirty something here in the clearing sounded like three hundred. Watching the chaos reminded me of a bad episode of Jerry Springer.

Meridith released me, grabbed the young, trembling girl beside her and shoved her at me. The girl let out a horrified squeal and leapt away from me, shaking her head. She looked from Meridith to another woman who stood nearby who had to be her mother.

"Cricket! Stay beside her! And don't look to your mother for help, she's finally learned to obey! Now mind me, girl, or you'll learn for yourself why your mother thought me wicked!" The stooped, old woman actually looked evil in the darkness, as if one of the misbegotten shapes from the woods was here with us.

Cricket paled and scuttled right up to me, far more afraid of Meridith than of me. At my other side, the girl I had promised death quietly found me, touching my arm. I met the concerned look in her eyes.

"I remember," I said right away.

She nodded, then pliantly let my tail pull her down where she lay at my feet, waiting for her nap.

Meridith watched the girl with one bushy eyebrow raised then, harumphed, "That'll do." She narrowed her eyes at the three of us, "You three stay put!" She turned to Cricket's mother, "Come on!" Cricket's mother followed Meridith as she launched into the melee of shrill, female voices like a warrior wading into battle.

Cricket and I were both trembling, I felt hers and she felt mine. It was a warm, reassuring contact that I shared with the girl. I huddled closer and let myself be like her, be like this girl. We sat in wonderful, companionable fear together and I soaked it in. Soaked her in. My tail stroked Broken Beauty at my feet and I listened to the wonderful arguing behind us. I was here, and this life mattered. These crazy people mattered—because I was one of them.

I was a girl named Rain.

Within me, I felt my second heart flutter, as if asking me if I was sure. In horror at the blasphemy of my thoughts, I put a hand to my head, willing my people to be safe and well with all that I was! I started breathing once again, after exploring myself, searching each and every little life. They lived, although what just happened had not gone unnoticed. Every living thing in my world felt that moment of horrible stillness and silence, where all creation was a candle flame, waiting to be snuffed by a gentle breeze from my will. Even now many of the most sensitive of them were weeping. Taunwee herself was weeping, in fear, joy, and relief. So many were weeping.. thousands and thousands and thousands.

Trembling again at this new stupidity, I quickly amended my will and thoughts. I am a girl named Rain with the heart of a Lion. Both girl and god! All Girl! All God!

"Forever. Always. Eternally. Blessedly. Both."

I prayed to myself, held Cricket tight, and trembled.

Black Rain

Garden of Wrath

Meridith shouted down the last of the rebellion, refusing to hear any more nonsense. The beaten down women obeyed but looked upset as they huddled together and stared out at the figures still taking slow, encroaching steps into the field. The man beasts only went twenty feet into the clearing before stopping, but that short distance was enough to leave them exposed. They were no longer half hidden mysteries partially concealed by shadows as they moved among the trees.

Now hundreds of beasts stood brazenly in full view beneath the night sky. They were a varied assortment of sizes and shapes, but all of them kept their distance except for one of the green eyed fauns who strode boldly past the others heading straight toward me. I knew from Taunwee that fauns were a people much like the Twilin, created by an angel who did not wish to follow Lucifer at the time of the fall; however, since that time he and his children had bowed the knee and joined him. Which meant that this creature was a servant of the Devil.

As he came closer I could tell that this faun was not a child, or some off-spring, but was Pan himself. Unlike the other fauns, Pan wore a fine but somewhat stained, red jacket. A set of beautifully carved, wooden pipes hung from a leather cord around his neck. One of his arms held a stout, leather bag snug to his side, the straps of the bag slung over his shoulder. Though a little taller and broader in the shoulders than the others of his kind, he was still far from intimidating. His face was that of a mischievous boy of perhaps sixteen to seventeen. His horns were adorned with some golden rings and his brown hair was combed back. Surpris-ingly, his sideburns and goatee were shaved off, adding to his human appearance. His slightly crooked, smiling mouth held slightly crooked teeth. He was bare from the waist down, but he positioned the bag to hide himself from view. He held his bag in place as he bowed deeply to me.

"Good eve, daughter of Lucifer."

A collective gasp came from the women behind me.

I laughed. "Is that what he told you to get you to come here?" I laughed some more.

Pan straightened, giving me an oddly strained look. His hand stroked the flute-like instrument that lay across his chest. A nervous habit? Or did he want me to look at it and notice it? The original set of Pan pipes I presumed.

"He said that you might not be aware of your – unusual origins. Perhaps you would allow me to – err – fill in the gaps?" he said suggestively, with a wicked smile. "Would you like some wine?" He began to fumble at his leather pouch.

"Don't listen to that creature," Meridith counseled as she stepped up beside me. "He'll twist you with his words!"

"Said the crooked woman," Pan said, giving Meridith a cruel smile.

"What good could come of hearing him?" Meridith said, ignoring Pan's cruel gibe.

"Who is he?" Cricket asked. I'd all but forgotten she was in my arms.

"Pan," I said, unimpressed, as if his name were "Bob."

Another gasp from the women behind me made me smile.

"Surely there would be no harm in hearing me out." Pam gave such good in-nocent face that I laughed at the lie.

"Paa!" Meridith spat, alarmed at my delight with the creature. She reached up as high as her crooked back would allow (and I leaned down to help). She cupped my face with her long fingered hands. Her eyes were hard, determined stones that demanded my attention as she whispered urgently.

"Pan is a trickster! He is known for seducing women! He is a shameless pedophile, murderer, and abuser of women! His words are sweet lies, his wine poison, and his music can possess your soul before you know what's happening!" She ran out of steam, let go of my face and said much softer, "At least that's what all the bloody books say. Be careful, child. He might actually be as bad as my second husband, may he burn in hell." She said that last as if it were a benediction, forever attached to any mention of the man she'd married.

She grabbed Cricket by the hand and then knelt down to collect the girl at my feet, but Broken Beauty clung to my leg, refusing to let go. My tail continued to get in the old woman's way, squirming between the girl and her grasping hands. Tail liked Broken Beauty and wanted to keep her.

Meridith scowled up at me.

"Sorry, it has a mind of its own sometimes. Really!" I pleaded and gave her a face to match.

Meridith sniffed, then looked to the girl on the ground. "Stay put then, and keep your eyes closed!"

Cricket and I helped Meridith up and the old woman and her granddaughter joined the other women behind me.

Pan waited until they were gone, shaking his head with exaggerated patience. "There is nothing sweeter than youth, especially that of a young – beautiful – girl."

"Have you ever died, Pan?" I asked him out of the blue.

"Grim topic. One I'll chat about, so long as we take turns at this."

He did not speak as if he were a relic, with thees and thous. With his face and American accent (not English) he could have passed for one of the kids from my old trailer park. Actually, his face looked a little too familiar now that the thought had entered my mind. Had I seen him somewhere before?

Pan raised a hand, tapping his chin with a dirty nailed finger as he pondered. "Died? Have I ever died? Actually, dying is hard to do for something made to be undying. Immortal, you know. My kind can suffer, change shape, and even wish for death, and yet – we never find it." He made a circular flourish with his hand. "Our greatest gift and greatest curse – one in the same," he finished with a grin.

"Why have you shown yourselves to these women?" I asked. "Has Lucifer repealed the Ban?"

Pan frowned, his eyes dropping to Broken Beauty.

"Aaah, the Ban!" he sneered, obviously no fan of the injunction to have no contact with mankind. "No. Regretfully, it has not been repealed. Not altogether." He gave me a cunning smile, holding back the rest.

"Say your mouthful of crap and then tell me the rest of it."

Pan ignored my insulting reply. He considered his words for a moment, then started at a place I did not expect. "When you were nine years old, a man grabbed you at the mall. You were in the video arcade with your brother."

I blinked. I didn't remember anything like that. Playing along, I searched through those memories I shared from Rain Marie's life more carefully. I found the day, suddenly there as those memories blossomed in my head. I'd felt uncomfortable with the man leaning beside my machine. I was too young to understand that he was looking left and right, waiting for the coast to be clear. He had grabbed me as I went to walk away, a hand around my mouth as he pulled me backwards, through a door and into a room they used for birthday parties.

The heavy door slammed shut with a boom. I heard the twisting sound of the lock. It was pitch black, I couldn't see my own hands before my face, and I was so scared I couldn't think—and then suddenly, the man's hands were pulled away. There was a crash. Another crash.

"No. Please!" I heard a voice beg, down near my feet. A sound of movement – and then another crash, louder and more final, on the other side of the room.

I started to move, inching along, hands outstretched in the darkness until I found the wall and shuffled along until my hand found the light switch. In the absolute darkness of that room a voice had spoken.

"Don't turn on the light."

I, or Rain Marie, hesitated, hand on the switch.

"Why?"

"I don't want you to see what I did to that guy. This way you won't see, and you won't know, and I won't have to explain."

"What were you doing in here with the lights off?" I asked suspiciously.

"Saving little girls from bad men. Kinda creepy, isn't it?"

I laughed, the nervous flutter of air escaping my lungs as I moved past the light switch feeling along the wall for the door that had to be nearby.

"Yeah. What should I call you, other than 'creepy'?" My hand found the lock and twisted it. I hesitated with my hand on the door latch. I stood there in the dark room, waiting for an answer.

"Every girl deserves a guardian angel, yours is just a little creepy. Now scram, kid, and don't look at the blood on the floor when you leave. And don't tell anyone about this."

I'd closed my eyes as I opened the door. "Thank you, Mr. Creepy," I said as I slipped out, shutting the door behind me. I'd been nine, and I hadn't told, not right away. And a few days later when Rain Marie was finally ready to say something, she didn't because by then she was questioning herself on what had really happened. It had been dark. And she didn't want Mr. Creepy to get into trouble. If he was even real. So in the end, we never told.

Okay. Definitely strange. I determined to puzzle through what I'd just seen at some other time, in some saner place.

"Not altogether, you said?" I prodded Pan for the information on the Ban.

Pan frowned but he recovered quickly, throwing me a smile. "What of your guardian angel?" he tried to redirect.

I growled and the ground shook, thunder pealing softly overhead in a low, ominous roll. The women behind me whimpered and muttered.

Pan bowed. "The Ban," he began obediently, "has been lifted for everyone in this field. Even you." His smile was darkly wicked and more than a little threatening.

"And what will happen if I simply send them back to their homes?" I asked.

"Ah, hhm." Pan cleared his throat. "I believe it's my turn – to be fair."

"I never said I was fair."

He frowned, then started talking. "Many times, in little ways, he's been there over the years. He had no idea of how you got inside that girl or how to bring you out of her." Pan began to pace back and forth as he talked, letting his bag drop and letting his nudity be seen. The swaying pendulum motion pulled annoyingly at my eyes. "He could feel you in there from the day you were born, riding inside her like a shadow cast by her soul, but how to get you out drove him to drink!" He chuckled. "And of course, your parents had to be who they were. Quite a challenge." He chuckled some more. "As I doubt you'll let me go through all the little encounters you've had over the years with dear, old dad and his servants, let me mention the last time you saw him – face to face."

"You can tell me whatever bullshit you want, after you tell me about the Ban," I interrupted firmly. "But first, I'm a little hungry. I think I'd like to eat." I was hungry. I needed to eat.

Pan pursed his lips, a cautious and humorous expression on his face as he bent down and pawed at his bag. "A picnic then?" he said as he pulled out the bottle of wine he'd mentioned. "Shall I?"

"No! Not the wine!" called one of the women behind me. The others tittered and mumbled as well but I couldn't make out their words. They seemed to be getting quieter. A strange hunger grew within me, but it seemed the kind of hunger that could be satisfied only with flesh or sex. I stared down at Pan and watched with interest as he pulled a quilt out of his bag and began to pick up sticks and twigs and cast them away, to make the spot more comfortable.

That was nice.

The sounds around me seemed to dim and fade.

I heard Pan's muttering and felt that strange hunger as he worked, but I also heard one other sound – and feelings with that sound as well. I wondered what that sound was and these wonderful feelings that were attached to it. It wasn't coming from without, but some place within.

Voices – lots of voices – lots of—

"Grapes," Pan was saying to me.

I blinked in surprise – he was close – one hand on my stomach, the other holding a grape up to my lips.

I pushed him away and stepped back, pulling Broken with me.

Pan flew back fifteen feet, landing on his back. He picked himself up from where he'd landed, brushing dirt off himself as he watched me. He waited until I settled and met his eyes again.

"Do – you – like – grapes?" he asked slowly, as if I were simple. "Cheese? Fresh berries?" He raised bowls he'd set out on his quilt, holding a bowl in each hand filled with those items.

"No!" I snapped. "The only fruit I eat now is grapefruit, with lots of sugar. Real sugar, Pan!"

He laughed and gave me a bright, boyish smile, green eyes twinkling with mirth. "Did you think I'd use Sweet and Low?" He chucked and so did I because it was funny.

When I realized I was smiling I wiped it from my face and scowled at him. He nodded, suppressing his own smile, set his berries aside, and went back into his bag. I hoped he would find some grapefruit in there because I was so hungry.

"You're going to be wonderful," Pan muttered as he rummaged in his bag.

I heard the voices again – lots of voices, all crying out my name. What was it? It was singing, but it felt like—praying? Too curious to resist any longer I followed the sound and the warm, wonderful feelings like a trail of bread crumbs and finally, in a way I didn't even understand, my vision turned to see a place that seemed to be within myself.

Was I dreaming this?

Far below me in a field was an odd statue of a Black Lion and around it were thousands upon thousands of tiny, singing creatures.

"Twilins."

The word popped into my head as other memories began to rush back into me like a flood.

They were praising The Black Lion.

But—I'm the Black Lion! They're praising me!

And somehow I knew – this was a new song I was hearing them sing. I knew the Twilin who wrote the song. The man and his heart seemed to fill me or actually – I seemed to fill him. Kesaw Sill Shanell and his poets had rushed to prepare this song over the past two hours. A great many heartbreaking songs had been written over the millennia about "The Burning Day," but never once in all those years had one been sung that held out even a thimble full of hope for when that day came. He watched the Director of Worship lead his new song, "The Day of Deliverance." I felt the swelling of Kesaw's heart. Never in all his years had he been so proud as at this exact moment.

Tantifar Sill Lagron stood before the masses, using the skills he'd carefully honed and sharpened over thousands of years while leading the Twilins in praise to the Twilight Star. Now I felt him marvel as his own Queen sat before him as one of his charges, eagerly following his instructions. She was his chief singer in the choir he directed, offering fervent praise to the new goddess with all her heart – offering sweet praise – to me. Tantifar was amazed at her singing, but angry. He did not know Taunwee could sing in this way. He wondered why she'd held back all these years.

I knew why – she did not want to humble her people. And there was simply no need. I felt my Star's heart as she sang to me now. Taunwee no longer held herself in reserve but sang with all her heart, all her strength, and all her will because now there was someone high above her to hear her words and feel her worship. She hungered to sing louder, sweeter, truer, purer. She loved me.

They harmonized, some singing in words while others gave their voices over to rising and falling trills that sounded like beautiful, tinkling bells. I looked upon them and knew them all at once, filling my new world with my presence. As I grew to fill my inside world, my mind cleared concerning the world without.

And now I understood what was happening. Pan had tried to make me forget everything except him, but inside this small place I was simply too big for him to touch or even understand. It would be easier for him to wrap his arms around the sun, or to create it himself, than to cloud a mind that filled a hundred and thirty seven thousand, four hundred and eleven hearts.

Now that I could think clearly I realized that everything in the woods and in the clearing must have been soaked with magic and lies before I arrived. It had slowly wrapped me up, moving so delicately that I hadn't realized what was happening until the world was quiet, except for the nagging of one goat and the sound of one beautiful song stuck inside my head. It had been a cunningly devised trap. One that I'd walked into blindly and stupidly.

I had the habit of walking about, open to the world, drinking in its smells and flavors and even its magic, letting it touch me and move through me as it wanted, sometimes even letting it change me. As I'd found out once again, it was a dangerous way to live, but I didn't change myself to prevent this aspect of my nature. Not this time. Not again!

I'd learned the danger of changing myself without careful consideration. I hoped that when I looked outside myself again, Pan's magic would stay the pathetic thing that I now knew it to be. I wasn't completely sure that's what would happen, but after what I'd done to myself earlier in this same clearing I was far more afraid of myself than the goat. I wouldn't know what would happen for sure until I looked outside again. I cast a last look down at my beautiful Twilins.

If I hadn't have had this place, and the Twilins within me, Pan would have taken me. Of that I was sure. Before I left I willed a scattering of sunflowers to spring up around the field. They would be the sweetest, most wonderful sunflowers any Twilin had ever tasted or dreamed of. I didn't stay to watch the flowers grow and see their reaction to my gift but returned my gaze to the outside world and the fallen angel who wanted to rape me.

Pan was preoccupied and thankfully still keeping his distance. He was whistling happily as he lit candles. He'd been busy, placing dozens of intricately carved circular skull-like bowls all around the quilt he'd spread out, stuffing candles into each of the bowls. His confidence and arrogance astounded me. Did he think I would simply sit with him, drink his wine, eat his food, let him play me a song on his magic Pan pipes and take me right here in the middle of this field while the beasts howled and the women wept?

Pan looked up from his work, a broad grin on his face and a selfish sparkle in his green eyes. I saw inside their depths and knew (because I desired to know) that my dark imagining was *exactly* what he thought would happen. He thought he had me. A gamey, goatish smell rose around me and I saw a cloud of purple mist rise up from the ground. Pan's magic was no longer hidden because I was looking for it and I wanted to see it. My stomach growled loudly, responding to his touch. His magic no longer ruled me, it was still a speck of sand to the weight of the world within me, yet it still teased at my appetite.

Pan watched me press a hand to my complaining stomach. I played along, letting my face show confused surprise and even a little disgust as I looked at him, trying not to oversell. For the first time ever I blessed my hellish eyes. There was no way on God's green earth this speck of a creature could search their depths or know their secrets. He was an angel. I was a god—a very stupid, very childish god, but also a very angry god.

"No wine!" I barked as he was about to pour. "Food, I'm hungry, but no wine. Now tell me if these women will be left alone if I send them home?"

Pan sighed, reached across his little love nest, retrieved the cork, and pushed it back into the bottle of wine with a regretful slap of his palm. "You're the boss, no wine. The meat will arrive soon anyway." He pointed with his chin off toward the woods. I resisted the urge to look though I felt his magic pushing me to do so. "Perhaps you'll be thirsty later," he mumbled as he studied me curiously, surely wondering what was going on.

"Hey, what about some music before the food arrives?" He reached for his flute.

"No! Tell me what I want to know first."

"Oh! Co-me on already!" He sounded like a teenager expressing a fit of angst. "Surely you've heard of dinner theater. Music goes with dinner. They fit together like cold milk and Oreos."

I felt his magic again, trying to confuse me, make me forget, make me say yes. It was too small. I simply refused his will. I had my stomach growl again and let myself look confused and frustrated as he watched me. My tail thrashed about, leaving Broken unattended at my feet, but helping me express my feigned unease and my continued collapse.

Pan put his hands up in a calming gesture. "Tell you what, first, let me tell you about your last meeting with—"

"Don't go there!"

"That guy," Pan censored with a grin, "and then I'll tell you about the situation those women are in. And after that," he persisted, "we'll have some music."

"Yes," I said, then frowned, as if unsure why I'd said yes. I knew why I'd said it. I just hoped he was dumb enough to step in it.

Pan nodded. He seemed to think all was progressing well.

"You stared into a mirror a few days ago and saw a reflection there. A reflection that told you that you were all powerful. A reflection that told you to be true to yourself. That you *had to be* true to yourself." He gave me a sad smile. "Will you be true to yourself with what I've told you or lie to yourself like a child and pretend it isn't so?"

I went cold all over. Tail dropped to the ground behind me as if shot dead. I quickly filed this new horror away for "a better time and place." I was tired of playing these games.

"My turn. Now tell me what will happen if I send these women back to their homes."

Pan frowned, finally catching on to the fact that I was no longer stuck in his pantomime. His eyes cut to Broken, giving her a nasty glare as he spoke. "These women are free of the Ban, and all of The Fallen are hungry. If I could keep all of you for myself, I would. But I'm not that fast, even if I am that greedy." He gave me my answer and his magic rose up around me once again. He was trying to find some way to right things and put me back into his control. His hand itched to grab his instrument.

"Don't touch it, Pan." The ground trembled and thunder pealed deep and threatening overhead, so powerfully this time it rattled teeth and shook bone.

I heard the reassuring cry of the women behind me again along with the enthusiastic shouts of our religious convert who began to pray loudly. My tail wrapped around Broken, who was trying to sit up for some reason. Tail pulled her back down to my feet.

"He told me you could do that," Pan said, looking awed and angry at the same time.

I gave him a look. "Did he also tell you to set this trap and rape me here on your nappy quilt as your beasts raped and butchered these women and children?"

I turned my back before he could answer. I felt Pan lash out with his magic, but I refused to let it change me as I faced the women and Twilins. I felt his will behind me, like an evil, little child in a playground calling me names. If I chose to believe him, it might bother me. I ignored him and let my own will settle over the spiraling tower of tiny lights and the invisible, flightless Twilins I felt hiding in the grass, covering all of them like a warm, loving blanket.

A glittering line of lights began to stream down into my open mouth, and eventually the clearing darkened as the last of the lights vanished from this place and emerged into another. I smiled broadly and lifted my hands to my temples, thumbs hooked around my horns, fingers buried in my thick black hair as I felt the incredible surprise of both groups.

Those already within, surprised at seeing others they thought were dead, and the newcomers' surprise at being greeted by other Twilins and their Queen. I knew them all by name in an instant. All their hopes and dreams were now my own tiny hopes and dreams. They were mine.

Having finished with the Twilins, I turned in an awkward circle, stepping over and around Broken who still lay tangled at my feet. The monstrous creatures surrounding us at the edges of the clearing remained in the same place and were oddly silent. Pan stood quietly by his carefully prepared spot, wearing an evil grin, hands on hips, candles all lit and waiting. I noticed that he hadn't packed his shit but had gone ahead and finished lighting his candles. I assumed this meant he wasn't about to throw in the towel or concede defeat until he'd raped and murdered and had his way.

I stepped around Broken and turned back to the women. They seemed much more isolated and alone without the mass of glowing Twilins above them. They muttered amongst themselves and pressed even tighter together, eyeing me darkly as if I were one of the monsters. Watching me consume the peaceful, fairy lights they'd sheltered with all this time hadn't won me any brownie points.

"Meridith!" I called. She shuffled forward, approaching me with some hesitation.

"Are you through with your business here?" she asked, casting a narrow-eyed glance at Pan before turning to face me squarely.

"I need to tell you what's happened, and then I'll let you tell the others. It's not good news, and you all have hard choices to make." My voice was grave.

"And you've heard this from him have you?" she asked, wisely questioning the validity of my source.

I nodded. Shrugged helplessly. Then just to be thorough, I sighed.

Meridith smiled and even laughed grimly. "Whether he spoke the truth or not, all you can do is assume he spoke the truth." She took a step or two closer. "Out with it then. I'll tell the others and let them choose for themselves what to do or what to believe. Whatever decision they make will be on their heads and not yours."

So I told her. I offered them three options. I could return them to the city, where they might last an hour, a day, or a week. I could leave them here in this field and let them try to work out a deal with Pan—fat chance. Or they could go to Amen Hale and see if my Mother would let them stay. I also said that they could collect their families and bring them too if that was what they chose to do.

Meridith listened to all of it, asking questions only twice before walking away, her bent form swallowed into the anxious group of women.

I bent down and helped Broken stand. She moved like a Barbie doll, standing where I stood her. I brushed her off and cleaned her soiled clothes and body with my will, removing the dirt, grime, and the sickly sweat of fear, and I cleaned her urine-soaked dress and panties. I fixed her hair and grew it out another six inches to the length I liked then picked her up and held her in my arms as I waited.

After five minutes I decided to make myself a seat. Bone white roots pushed up from the ground, weaving together to form a wide, throne-like chair. Plush, white padding appeared in the cup of the seat as if sweated out by the roots themselves. I settled in and made myself comfortable with Broken.

A second, much smaller, throne-like chair made of black roots and black padding sprouted from the ground about ten feet to my left.

"Take a seat, Pan, who knows how long they'll be," I said.

He walked over, leapt up, and dropped into the chair sideways, letting his hoofed feet hang over the side.

"Thank you," he said. "And thanks for making me the third option."

"If one of the crazy women actually choose you, will you keep your promises to them?"

"For a while," he said casually. "Longer if they please me, less if they do not."

I looked down and noticed that Broken had four fingers of her hand raised just high enough to wave at Pan over the arm of my chair. She was staring at him. That was not good.

"Broken, look at me!" I ordered and she obeyed, focusing on my eyes easily. Too easily. She was broken.

"Do you remember the promise I made you?" I asked her. "You made me promise not to leave you to them. I made a promise."

"Pan." Her one word was a garbled mess but it was clear enough.

"Is it true," Pan asked as he waved coyly at Broken, "that you have never told a lie? You did promise the women that they could choose, and unless I have mis-remembered, you also promised to listen to my music after I told you about the revised limits on the Ban. Is daddy's little girl a liar?" he taunted. "Is the daughter of the Father of Lies going to be on the outside what she is on the inside?"

"I don't lie," I said. My voice was calm, but within I seethed. In order to keep my promise to Broken, if she chose Pan, I'd have to kill her, then give him her dead body, and thereby keep both promises.

"Let the girl choose, and then listen to my music." Pan chuckled darkly. His green eyes flashed in the darkness.

Thunder softly rolled across the dark sky, as if the night itself were sad. I lis-tened to it as I stroked Broken's too fine, corn silk blonde hair and prayed quietly to myself for Broken, my Twilins, the women, and myself. I hated this goat bastard. I hated the things he'd told me. I hated to think of all the horrible things he'd done through the years and what he almost did to me.

Broken kept turning to face Pan and sneaking him waves when my head was turned. The women argued loudly, going back and forth on what to do. Amen Hale or back to London.

"Liar. Liar. Liar." Pan whispered the word every minute or so from his divan chair, taunting me as he flirted with Broken. I sniffed as a fresh wave of Pan's "gamey" magic settled around me, but this time it felt oddly – misplaced.

Broken waved at Pan again, and I realized that the magic hadn't been meant for me, but for Broken. He was using his magic on her! I searched the other women with my will and found them all mired in strands of his magic. He was mak-ing them delay and talk in endless, confused circles. He couldn't touch me so he touched the others with his lies!

"So mote it be!" I growled. "I'll give the girl her choice, and I'll listen to your music, though you'll not like either."

"Sour grapes!" Pan cried with glee as he lounged in his black throne, hooves kicking out playfully. He seemed to have recaptured a measure of his old confi-dence. "I think I like the choices I see already made," he declared boldly. "Broken has chosen me, and after listening to my music, perhaps you'll stay with her – if I'm lucky."

The ephemeral mists of Pan's magic surged, encircling me and Broken like twin-ing snakes. Pan rambled on and on about how lucky he was, while at the same time he rained his magic upon us like a dog taking a piss and tried to *MAKE* his own luck. He talked about the truth and called me a liar, as he lied and lied and lied.

"*Don't you wor-ry, sweet Bro-ken girl, the tru-uth, will se-et you free!*" Pan crooned melodically. He blew Broken a kiss, toying with her, then drew a line across his neck, his green eyes on mine as he did so.

I had promised I'd kill her myself before I let them have her, but I was sure Pan's real hope was to make me stumble into another trap. The casual cruelty and utter disregard for Broken's life, already so shattered, was simply all I would endure from the wormy, little shit.

"He who claims to be my father once said to me in a mirror 'As within, So without.' He told me this, and I believed it. I took it inside me and made it a part of myself. It was a gift of his, and I think it made me a better person. I actually like that part of myself, Pan, I do."

"It certainly helped make you the devil you are today," he mocked, tapping one of his own swept back horns.

"I have a gift for you also. You use truth as a weapon, but let's see how you like it stuck in your own guts and twisted." My voice was calm and deadly as I stroked Broken's hair. "You used magic on this girl to influence her decision. Which is a lie. So I curse you."

A foul stench rose from all around the clearing as if fat dew drops had burst open and released rotten steam, but its source was Pan himself. He launched himself out of his chair, cursing in the tongue of angels, arms flailing as he fought with his own stench. Bursts of strangely aligned good cheer and well being rained down upon the beasts in the field. Laughter rose from the fauns, antler headed men dawning smiling faces while at the same time they fanned, coughed, and held their noses and fought with the stench of the magic that made them smile and laugh.

Pan's magic was still there, but the smell of it was now rotten eggs and the effect of it was the exact opposite of what he intended. From now on, to do evil, he would have to wish good. And, though I was sure he'd figure this out quickly, looking up to see down would surely drive him mad. On top of that, how much practice could this creature possibly have with well wishing?

Pan's new and improved magic swept over Broken and she began spitting over the side of the chair, as if the taste of him were in her mouth and she desperately wanted it out.

I pondered Pan's queer plight as he raged around the clearing. If he wished someone well while actually hoping for ill, would anything happen at all? Somehow, I didn't think so because he wouldn't mean a damn thing he was saying or thinking. The long and short of it was simple. Pan was fucked. But I was just getting started.

"Do you still want him, Broken?" I asked her.

Broken shook her head no, tears running from her eyes due to the stench and all the rest. Pan was shouting and stomping around the clearing, doing his best to rile up the beast men and the other creatures, urging them to attack, but he was putting out his own fires with his own magic, leaving docile and happy beasts and demons in his wake wherever he passed. After ten, fruitless minutes, he'd lost half his numbers, many of which had wandered off into the woods, chatting with one another companionably, some even singing as they left.

Meridith and the other women, now back in their right minds and flush with unexpected, good cheer gathered around Broken and me where we sat in my white root throne. Some of them patted Broken's head, checking on her and speaking to her gently while others politely asked me what on earth I'd done to Pan and what the god awful stench was, and – cautiously – why I'd eaten the "dear" little lights.

I was trying to answer that last question when Pan charged back up to me, pushing through the women violently to stand before me. "Give me the girl!" he demanded. "She chose me!" He punctuated his words with a bull-like snort and hoof stomp.

Broken still lay nested beside me in the chair. "Do you want to go with Pan?" I asked her.

A fresh wave of his magic bloomed around her, which was the last thing he should have done. I honestly think his release of magic was almost an involuntary bodily function after all these years. Whether intentional or involuntary, its effect was nasty. Broken sputtered, her eyes flying open wide as she shook her head no, turned green, and retched for all she was worth. I smiled at Pan as I held Broken's hair, my own eyes watering badly as I tried to breathe.

"Is that answer enough for you?"

"You cheated!" he snarled. "You lied!"

"No," I said. "This is the answer she would have given and the reaction she would have had if you walked up to her on the street and asked her, point blank, if of her own free will she would consent to being raped and tortured to death at your hands."

"That's not what I was going to do to her!" he bellowed and stomped his cloven foot at me.

"And as you see it, I was willingly going to lie down on your nappy quilt and let you have me?"

"Yes! You! Will!" he bellowed again, even angrier. "You promised to listen to my music. And as you said, balance is important! You *believe in it*," he said with disgust.

The women began to panic like frightened hens as he gripped his legendary set of Pan pipes with both hands. "Unless you mean to break your own word it's time for you to listen to my music and come to my bed! Though it will be far less pleasant for both of us now – thanks to you!"

He went to blow into the pipes and I willed the air to move around the openings of the reeds instead of through them. Pan blew a few more times fruitlessly before turning back to me.

"You lie!" he shouted, pointing at me, green eyes alight.

Pan shouted some verbal command instead of using his magic and the beasts which circled the field lurched into action. They snarled and growled as they charged. I willed an invisible barrier to circle around us and cover us, leaving Pan as the only beast on our side of my invisible shield. The ladies panicked, screaming, high, long and shrill, until the charging fiends crashed headlong into the invisible barrier with a sickening splat.

Pan cursed. He went over and punched the invisible wall once like an angry child, then came to stand before me.

"You said you would listen to me play," he said calmly. "You lied."

"I said I would listen to your music, but I didn't say I'd let you choose the music, and there's no way in hell I'd let you play your stupid pipes."

"So what are you saying?" He sounded defeated already.

"I'm saying I want you to sing for me."

"It's a trick," he said.

"Of course it is, you fool!" said a fat woman standing near him that he'd shoved past roughly earlier. "Work the best deal you can and get out with some dignity. And do something about that vile stench!" She pinched her nose and fanned the air.

Pan threw his head back and laughed. At one time there would have been waves of power, magic, and majesty rolling off him, but now he was just a goat dude having a mental breakdown in the middle of a bunch of women.

"If I sing your song, will you promise to remove my curse?" He actually sounded contrite.

"Will you and yours ever again hunt me and mine or these and theirs?" I challenged.

"You have my word! I swear that we will leave you and the other women be if you remove this curse from me."

"He's lying."

"Liar!"

"Lying sack of shit!"

Pan gave me a weak smile as he endured a non-stop stream of insults and small, thrown projectiles from the angry women, looking like the straight man at a comedy routine as they pinged off his head, making him blink. I laughed, a real, honest and genuine laugh, but that let too much of his rancid smell into my lungs at once and I doubled over, trying to ward off a wave of nausea.

Damn, he was foul! "Fine!" I spat out between shallow breaths. "I'll remove the curse as soon as you sing, but then get lost! I never want to see your boyishly handsome face again."

"You think I'm boyishly handsome?" Pan asked, giving me a huge grin, and then he did what came as natural as breathing to him, he tried to use his magic. Stench flooded the enclosed space of our little, people tank.

We all screamed and cursed Pan.

Broken was draped over the arm of the chair, sicking up again and Cricket was there helping her. I asked Meridith for a pen and a piece of paper and quickly jotted down three simple lines. Pan watched me, his green eyes calculating and cruel.

"What song is it that you wish me to sing then? I'm sure it's a trap, I just hope it's a bearable one." He sounded almost happy. "Will it turn me into a girl? I hear you like girls." He gave me a wink. "You sing it first and I'll join right in. I'm a huge fan of karaoke." He made light of what I was doing, but it wasn't hard to hear his worry.

I handed the scrap of paper to Pan with a straight face.

He read it and let out a goat-like snort. "I see why you didn't want to sing it." He bowed to me. "I concede defeat and release you of your obligation to hear me sing. I find your choice of music far too 'Romper Room' for my tastes." He balled up the scrap of paper and pitched it over his shoulder.

I rose from my chair and walked toward to him, my steps swaying and graceful, like a predator. Pan tensed, as if he expected a physical attack. Now that I was no longer affected by his magic, which had made him seem "more," I noticed how small he was. His head barely reached my breasts.

"I'll still remove your curse," I told him, "and you don't even have to sing for it – but if you lied to me while holding the truth to Broken's neck like a blade, you will sing my song!" The ground at Pan's feet reached up and grabbed his ankles, merging with his flesh and rooting him in place.

I leaned in and spoke with the voice of a god.

"If your words were true, then let your curse be through, if your words were lies, sing for me the horrid lines. Sing for me the song most foul, a song that never should be sung, a song most cursed upon the earth, a song that has no ending verse."

My words, filled with infinite power, consigned Pan to the fate he'd crafted for himself. By this point the women in the clearing were all terrified, watching in expectant horror. The song itself was easily recognizable for what it was to anyone who'd ever heard it before.

Pan opened his mouth and began to sing. The tempo and cadence of the horrid thing was there in all its repetitive glory:

"This is the song that doesn't end. Yes it goes on and on my friend.
Some people started singing it not knowing what it was,
and they'll continue singing it forever just because

(without pause he began again)

This is the song that doesn't end. Yes it goes on and on my friend.
Some people started singing it not knowing what it was,
and they'll continue singing it forever just because..."

The beastly faces of the creatures that surrounded us pressed closer, staring in through the invisible barrier as Pan's lone voice sang the silly song. Well over two hundred, assorted fiends remained, the ones who were hungry and doggedly determined for their chance at the women. The earth at their feet reached up, fusing with their flesh and connecting them to the earth in the circle where they stood. They threw back their heads and bellowed their fury—but then they began to sing.

What may have been comical, or even pitiable from one, broken down goat, now took on a sense of grander horror. The voices of half men, fauns, and other foul creatures did not spread into hundreds of discordant, individual voices but joined perfectly into one deep, powerful, frightening chorus, its melody ringing through the woods—again and again and again and again and again.

"This is the song that doesn't end. Yes it goes on and on my friend.
Some people started singing it not knowing what it was,
and they'll continue singing it forever just because"

The pounding sound raised goose bumps up and down my body and thrilled me to my core with its hypnotic rise and fall. I stretched out my arms as I basked in the midst of my own poured out wrath, receiving the worship of their suffering and drinking in the sweetness of their ruin like wine. Now this was wine I could drink!

When I thought of God, and how he had arranged the fate of man, I'd never truly understood how hell worked. I'd never been able to grasp its purpose or comprehend a reason for its horrible cruelty. I knew that God created all things to bring him glory, both the good and the bad, but until now, I'd never really understood hell. Perhaps I was only going mad, but I could not deny the satisfaction or the pleasure I felt as I gazed at what I'd wrought.

With my arms out, I spun in a circle like a little girl, laughing and rejoicing in my Garden of Wrath while Meridith and the other women watched me with looks that ranged from compassionate worry to outright loathing. Broken joined me. I watched madness dance in her pale blue eyes as we held hands, laughed together, and spun in circles as monsters all around us sang a silly song.

David

Soda Can

T HE WEATHER WAS good and Trafalgar Square was bursting with tourists taking pictures. The gawking, photo taking pockets of standstill tourists were a constant and never ending obstacle course for the determined Londoners, who simply wished to push through and get to their favorite pub or club or, God forbid, finally go home after a too long day at the office.

On a bare, unadorned patch of red brick wall by the street, a scene that seemed stolen from a Harry Potter movie played out as bricks came alive, shuffling and rearranging themselves to form an open doorway. People passing by on the street shouted and gathered around as women began to stagger out of this dark, mysterious opening.

Ten women stepped onto the sidewalk, bringing with them a handful of children. Cameras flashed, video phones recorded the event, preserving the expressions on the children's faces. The terrified faces of the children kept even the suicidally curious safely at bay. No one rushed for the opening in hopes of finding Narnia or Diagon Alley.

As quickly as the gate appeared, it vanished, the bricks moving again, sealing up the breach in the wall. The women began to be swamped by people asking questions about where they'd come from. Who were they? What was happening? Questions, questions, and more questions. The Bobbies arrived and started to sort things out and bring some order to the crowd.

"David!" called Paula Dent. She scanned back and forth intensely. "DAVID!" she screamed. She spied an empty can of lime flavored soda, dropped on the sidewalk off to her left.

"You all right, miss?" asked one of the policemen at her side. "Your boy wandered off? Need help looking for him?"

She dove into the crowd in that direction, as if the can were a green arrow, pushing past people like a woman possessed, clawing, scratching her way through. She broke clear of the mass of people who'd gathered around. She saw a filthy vagrant quickly pushing his newspaper lined shopping cart down the street. He turned just as she leveled a ferocious kick into the side of the cart, tipping the whole contraption onto its side.

David tumbled out along with a spray of aluminum cans and bottles that he'd been buried in. Paula dove on top of her son, holding him as she watched the hunch backed form disappear into the press of people. Paula began to work, getting at the tape. He'd been gagged and trussed up like a goose with silver masking tape.

"Don't you worry, Davie. We'll get it sorted out." She panted the words as she picked at the masking tape covering her son's mouth. David shook his head "no" as she worked. Paula stopped fiddling with the tape and met her nine-year-old son's terrified and angry eyes.

"You think we shouda stayed with the others then?"

David shook his head "yes."

Dr. Swaim

The Human Condition

"WOULD YOU LOOK at it, Levi? What a boil on the butt of humanity!" Dr. Swaim's deep, resonate voice accented his b's heavily.

"It's big." His faithful driver and attendant laughed as he navigated the massive Cadillac into the line of cars waiting for the VIP parking garage of The Atlanta Lighthouse.

The Lighthouse was a mega-church which owned all the property up and down both sides of the street for more than a city block. Swaim studied the series of connective bridges four stories above the busy street, bringing the tall structures together. Through the glass-sided walls of those aerial, pedestrian highways he watched the faithful as they journeyed to and fro without ever having to leave the blessed utopia of the belly of their monstrous beast.

An email alert drew Swaim back to his open laptop. Another interview request. Since his inspired television performance this morning, Dr. Swaim's ship had most certainly come in. He'd been busy before, but now things had gone Hollywood mad. He was being offered astronomical sums to do the same thing he'd been doing (often for free) only days ago. Swaim forwarded his newly revised set of requirements and began to review his calendar.

Levi finished talking with the parking lot attendant and hit the button to roll up the window.

"Are you sure about this, Doc? This isn't our usual cup of tea."

"True," Swaim agreed without looking up from his computer, "but this will be nationally televised, and this den of parasites has paid handsomely for my presence at their rally, and apart from an injunction on swearing, I will be free to speak my mind. That is all I have ever needed." He grunted, "At least, it was all I needed, before up became down, pigs started to fly, and the dead stared to rise—" Swaim's powerful voice started to rise as well.

"Before the chicken crossed the road!" Levi cut in happily, his tone mimicking Swaim's growing preachy crescendo.

"Before the sun rose at midnight!" Swaim continued happily. "And witches worshiped God! And cannibalism replaced lethal injection!"

"Before Burger King started serving Big Macs!" Levi joyfully threw in his new offering to the tirade and waited for Swaim to continue.

Silence.

Levi turned in his seat to find Dr. Swaim shaking his bald bull of a head, peering at him above the rim of his reading glasses.

"Burger King does not serve Big Macs. Your words must be plausible—and preferably believable—or all you'll sound like is damned fool, Levi, or a liar! Now focus on driving." Swaim pointed forward with a pudgy finger, to return his driver's attention to where he was going.

Levi frowned like a scolded child and turned to find the car in front of him gone and an attendant waving them forward. "Why didn't you complain about the chicken crossing the road?" he asked, angry.

"Do chickens cross roads?" the big man inquired conversationally.

"Yes."

"Both plausible and believable. Mmm, though somewhat lacking on relevance. It's akin to reaching for a breast and instead grasping an elbow. Both are contact, but one is confusing while the other – sensual, or at the very least, alarming." He chuckled.

"I don't want to hear it," Levi muttered. Feelings hurt. He often became sullen when something Dr. Swaim said hit a tender spot and made him feel stupid. Dr. Swaim made most people feel stupid.

"Communication is physical contact, Levi." Swaim continued his pondering, his mood growing darker as he peered out the windows of the car and watched families emerge from their vehicles and proceed toward the elevators. "These poor, gullible people come here each week to hear soul-stirring music and impassioned preaching because they crave contact. That's what this place is all about—human contact. These preachers use words that seem believable and plausible. They know just how to tease the mind, stroke the conscious, and probe the deep insecurities of the human psyche, pumping and pumping from the pulpit, thrusting again and again to bring these poor, socially isolated souls to the blessed state of religious orgasm! HALLELUJAH!" Swaim bellowed loudly, "I'm Saved!" The fat man glowered out the window at the people he scorned and began to close up his computer and gather his other necessities.

"Whatever," Levi muttered crossly, still feeling insulted and too annoyed to listen or care about his boss's sour mood.

"Don't sulk, Levi, we each have our gifts," Swaim reassured his faithful henchman. "I was blessed with a keen mind, a sharp wit, and an orator's carriage – all of it tragically confined within a prison of flesh. And though of average mental prowess, you, my boy, have your hale physical condition to your credit, and you do not have to pay for the pleasure of agreeable, female company. There are scant few on earth who would describe me as the more fortunate between us."

"Com'on, Doc! You get way hotter girls than I've ever had," Levi challenged Swaim's logic. He'd arranged things of an intimate nature for Swaim a number of times.

"That, Levi, is a matter of opinion. As you have so eloquently demonstrated, for most people to be able to enjoy an activity of the heart, that conversation or contact must be plausible, or better yet, believable, so that one might know, with certainty, that said contact is both honest and sincere. All people despise being lied to or being treated like a fool."

Swaim removed his glasses and wiped his face free of perspiration as he spoke. "I am an observant man, Levi. When I take the pleasure of a well-paid companion courageous enough to attempt a man of my – proportions – that same discordant tone always rings. Even the best liars have their tells, my boy. It could be as simple as a moment of hesitation, an extra glass of wine or two at dinner, or the dead look in her eye—it's always there. I am *loathed* by women. They endure my contact, and then run home and get into their steaming, hot showers and weep as they wish for a way to scour the inside of their mind to rid themselves of the very memory of me. They want to wake, find my money in their purse, and have no recollection from whence it came."

"Damn! That's horrible." Levi cringed, feeling pity for the big man, touched and caught up by the words.

"Does it – get to you sometimes, Doc?"

Swaim chuckled, less than average, he amended his estimation of Levi's mental prowess silently.

"Quite the contrary, my most enjoyable evenings are with the women who despise me the most and try the hardest to hide it. Which is why I am so very fond of Marsha. And now that I have her on my mind, do give her a call, Levi. Tell her three thousand—and then hang up." The big man chuckled in the back seat.

Levi gave himself a shake to rid himself the heebies. Instead of dwelling on darker thoughts, he focused on navigating the large vehicle up the narrow spirals of the garage.

Katie

Bunny Poo

KATIE WOKE WITH a ringing in her ears and the feel of her own blood pulsing at her temples and a slight, druggy haziness she hadn't felt for a very long time. They'd given her more drugs—lots more. She could feel it. She knew it.

She winced with her eyes in time to the throb of her head as she sat up, wondering as she did so if the music was still playing somewhere—they'd been dancing. She was in a very small room, and there was no music. There was a small, metal sink and toilet, right there near her bed. There was nothing else. No tables, no dresser, nothing. The entire room was eight by ten and all the walls were painted a numbing shade of weird off white that seemed to zap the life out of her. The color was bad. Wrong! Wrong! Wrong! She didn't like it. It made her feel sad.

She looked down at herself and got angry when she saw what she was wearing. It was an open backed, blue hospital gown that didn't even cover her completely. They'd taken all her clothes. She didn't even have on underwear. She wondered if the dirty, old men had done it themselves and worried what else they might have done while she was asleep.

Her arm hurt, and not from where they'd put in an IV, which was covered with a band aid, but higher up, near her biceps. She peeled back a piece of gauze and found a small incision. She touched the sore spot. She could feel something moving around, deep in her arm. They'd stuffed something in her arm—

"Hello, Katie. How are you feeling?"

The dirty, old man's voice spoke from the intercom, the noise loud and ringing in the small enclosed space. Katie grabbed her pillow and wrapped it around her head to shut out his nasty voice.

She wondered where Susan was. Did they kill her and Alfred? Where was Mr. Rabbit? No one was with her. She checked her arms and legs and stomach. Someone, the dirty, old men probably, had washed off all her drawings. Panicking, she checked the soles of her feet to be sure. Those were gone too. All her rabbits and all the other drawings were gone. She didn't have any protection from the men anymore.

The only one she had left was magic rabbit. She'd drawn two, special, magic rabbits onto paper that she and Susan swallowed, before they had to take their pills and Susan got to sing. Magic Rabbit was an inside bunny. One that lived inside and ate medicine instead of salad and pooped magic instead of bunny poo. She figured that if the bunny was making the magic for them they wouldn't have to keep making more magic pills. She hoped she still had her inside bunny.

"Rabbit, rabbit, rabbit. Chew, chew, chew. Rabbit, rabbit, rabbit. Chew, chew, chew," Katie chanted as she rocked back and forth, asking her inside bunny to eat any medicine they'd given her. She smiled as she felt some movement in her stomach. She could almost hear the chewing. As she chanted, that dreamy feel that came from the pills began to creep back into her, replacing the sluggish haziness of whatever meds they'd given her.

Katie was sitting on the side of her bed when the door opened and Sherman, one of her usual guards, stepped inside. He had a cup in one hand, a bowl of ice cream in the other, and a hopeful expression on his face. Sherman looked around the sparse room for some place to sit or set the bowl. Finally, looking shamefaced, he sat on the bed beside Katie. He offered her the cup without saying a word. Katie didn't reach for it right away, but then she felt a flutter in her stomach. She took the cup and started drinking. Sherman handed her the ice cream and she took the bowl, eating that too.

"You're not worried about us hiding drugs in the food anymore?" he asked, curious. He thought for sure she'd pour out the drink and get water from the tap and make him eat half the ice cream before she would touch it.

"Where are my clothes? Art stuff? I need my art stuff, Sherman." She took another huge bite of ice cream then held the spoon like a pen and mimed writing and drawing in the air as she swallowed. She dropped the spoon and clutched her head in pain.

"What's wrong, Katie!" Sherman asked, alarmed.

"Cold brain!" she squeaked.

"You ate it too fast," Sherman fussed as he collected the spoon from the floor.

She felt the rabbit inside her jumping up and down. "He's cold! He's trying to get warm!" Katie spoke her thoughts out loud. "Oh! My poor bunny!" she wailed, then jumped up and started doing jumping jacks.

"I froze my poor bunny!" Katie cried, as she sprang up and down, swaying unsteadily as she exerted herself.

Sherman watched Katie with an amused but sad face. The glazed look was back in her eyes. He asked her a question or two while she bounced and exercised, but she ignored him until she was sweaty – and warm.

Once she sat she asked her own questions.

"Where's Susan, Sherm?"

"In a room just like yours. She's still asleep though."

"Alfred?"

"Sleeping."

"Not dead, dead, dead sleeping?" Katie narrowed her eyes as if she thought he was lying.

Sherman shook his head no, giving her a troubled look. "I promise he's not dead. He's bruised and banged up from the fight, but he's fine. Just sleeping."

"Have they killed Benjamin yet?"

"How did you know about that?" Sherman asked, alarmed.

Katie paled, reading the answer in his face. Benjamin was dead. She stopped talking, worried by the look on Sherman's face.

She lay on her bed facing the wall, away from him. She was acting too smart. Careful! Careful! Careful! Stupid! Stupid! Stupid! She scolded herself. They would know she wasn't stupid if she wasn't more careful. She needed to be more careful. Careful! Careful! Careful!

Katie curled up around her one pillow and tried not to think about her exposed back side or the dirty, old men watching—or Sherman sitting right there on the bed. The blue thing they put on her didn't connect in the back and she didn't have any sheets to cover up with. The pillow didn't even have a pillow case. She tried to keep herself from crying.

"I hate you. You're not— You're one of—" She sniffled then finished with, "I want my parents!" loud and angry.

Sherman tried to get her to talk until two, burly nurses came in with her pills. Katie felt a little, excited leap in her stomach. She tried to look miserable and abused as she took the glass of water and drank their pills.

"I want my parents. And I want to see Susan," she said, then lay back down facing the wall.

Once they left, Katie crawled out of the bed and examined her surroundings but remembered to act sleepy and druggy when all she really felt was swimmy. She'd taken five more pills and she could hear the happy munching. She ran her hands over the door. She checked the sink and played in the water for a moment. Her face was hot and the cool water was nice but it made her need to pee. She held the pillow in her lap to hide herself form the cameras as she sat on the toilet.

Sherman opened the door just as she started to pee.

Katie screamed! and screamed! and kept screaming long after Sherman slammed the door shut, face red with embarrassment.

A new, female voice came on the intercom that sounded somewhat robotic. Katie was sure it was just the dirty, old man with a new voice. The voice said it was a woman named Vera Blanchard with child services. She knew that he enjoyed watching and being the voice and playing with the voice. Rabbit told her. She knew. She knew this female voice was just the dirty, old man. She ignored it.

She studied the evil walls with their ugly color, the high ceiling and the mirror above the sink. She was sure there was a camera behind the mirror, and maybe another one hidden in the ceiling to go with the one that was obvious, up high in the corner. Katie went to the sink and carefully began to wet sheets of toilet paper and lay them on top of the mirror like wall paper until it was useless.

She felt her inside rabbit finishing the pills. Soon he'd—do what he needed to do. Her brain was busy, busy, busy, buzzing with ideas. Ideas, ideas, and more ideas whirled through her head wanting out! Her fingers were busy – twitch, twitch, twitching – they wanted her markers, her pads, her brushes, her clay, a rock, a stick, some used chewing gum—anything!

She went back to the bed. It was made of one piece of metal, all soldered; the only screws were the ones that bolted it to the floor. She lifted the thin mattress to find that it rested on a series of metal rods instead of springy, metal coils.

Katie pulled off her blue hospital smock and stood completely naked while she worked at tucking it under the edge of the mattress so that it hung down like a screen. She was scared, naked, and angry—but most of all she was swimmy. Dreamy, swimmy, and strange. She needed to be smart right now – smart and sneaky – but she was feeling more and more swimmy, which wasn't good, she knew.

They were going to kill her soon like they did Benjamin. She needed to find some sneaky way out before they came for her. Completely naked and too swimmy to care about the dirty, old man watching, Katie went to the sink and wet the rest of the toilet paper until it was a gooey wad, but not too gooey. She gathered it up and then threw it under the bed. She ripped the cardboard roll off and soaked that too and threw it under the bed as well.

She looked up at the camera in the ceiling. "Dirty old man!" she cursed him one last time before grabbing her pillow and crawling under the bed, disappearing into the blessed privacy she'd somehow forged in a room specifically designed to offer no privacy at all.

Mr. R.

Sending Out an S.O.S.

"OH. HELLO. HELLO. Is anyone there? Is anyone there!?"

"Who is this?"

"Mr. Draper?" asked the unfamiliar, snooty voice.

"Yes. And who are you? How did you get my number? You're calling from Dyal's phone."

"Yes," replied the voice, "I have Dyal's phone, and I used it to call you. I pushed this button that said 'redial.' Is there anything else you'd like to know?"

"And you would be, Mr.?"

"R"

"Mr. R?" asked Draper.

"Yes. You may call me Mr. R."

"You have my full attention, Mr. R. Where is Dyal by the way?"

"Bathroom."

"Aaa. He left his phone unattended then. Right. Why did you call me, Mr. R.?"

"Because when you spoke to Mr. Dyal a few minutes ago he seemed quite frightened of you. I assumed you to be in some position of oversight. You must come at once and see for yourself what's happening here at this – this – detestable prison!" Mr. R's distaste for the place was evident. "The things I've observed are quite disturbing! Not proper at all! Mr. Dyal and especially Dr. Ogburn are scoundrels!"

"What seems to be the problem with Dyal and Dr. Ogburn?"

"Yes. Yes. Hmm. Problemssss plural, plural, plural. I'm afraid. Lots of issues. Not one, a whole bunch. Lots, many, plethora, scads of issues. Yes. Yes. Yes. Where to begin? Where? Where? What to say?" The snooty voice pondered dizzily over the phone then began to make his case. "The man has my Katie girl stripped completely naked and locked in a tiny cell for Dr. Ogburn to watch! Ogburn has a deviant interest in nude human activities, especially those of the young females, both the workers and your prisoners. Every bathroom in this facility has cameras! Dyal and Ogburn are not gentlemen," R reaffirmed strongly. "Their treatment of all the captives has become horrendous! I cannot imagine that this is acceptable behavior!"

"I'm losing interest, Mr. R." Draper's voice sounded unimpressed. "I'm sure they are being treated as carefully and humanely as possible. There are others there keeping watch over—"

"Keeping watch!" R challenged. "I hope you're not referring to that poor woman they work with. Ogburn just locked her in a room with one of the patients—oops! I see on camera thirty-seven that Dyal is reaching for the toilet paper. He's not very thorough, two wipes and out, regardless. From watching Dr. Ogburn's detailed study of human restroom habits, it seems that most of your kind wipe until they reach a satisfactory level of cleanliness. Ogburn and I have observed that this is not the case with Dyal. He's quite robotic about the process. Oh. And now he's flushed. I must go."

"Mr. R!" Draper called out. "Mr. R. Are you there?"

"BEEEEP. BOOP," came the sound of phone numbers being pushed.

"Dyal! Hello! Are you there? Dyal! Pick up the damn phone!" Draper called out.

The invisible Rabbit gripped the cell phone with his long, bottom feet as he aimed the pen he gripped with his mouth and guided with his shorter front legs and tried again to push the end call button.

The line went dead.

Black Rain

Hungry

I STEPPED THROUGH THE gateway that led into Vera's Worthings living room. Behind me came Broken, holding onto my tail like a black velvet lifeline. One hand kept a firm grip as she fished nuts out of the wooden bowl on the coffee table with the other. She'd been attached to me like glue over the past hour and a half and I was getting used to her being there behind me.

Vera's flat was small by American standards, but as I'd found out, it was big by the Londoner's version. Going from house to house as the women collected what loved ones they could, I'd been in some apartments so small they looked like closets. Vera's little place had a welcoming, homey feel.

On the comfortable couch in front of us sat Vera's silver-haired mother, who seemed to be struggling with what was happening. Her mouth opened and closed like a fish breathing under water.

"Are you okay, Mrs. Worthings?" I asked her kindly.

We all heard yelling coming from the bedroom down the hall where Vera was arguing with her daughter.

"Are you gonna need some help gettin um going?" Mr. Jorgensen poked his balding head through the portal I'd made in the living room. His face pinched like mine as Vera's shrill screaming reached us from the back bedroom where her daughter had holed up.

"Right then," he said, not waiting for me to answer. "C'mon, Tom," he called over his shoulder, "let's help um along." The two men, dressed in their traveling clothes and coats stepped through the portal. They stopped before the old woman on the couch.

"Good day, Miss. Sorry for – all of this." Mr. Jorgenson tipped his hat at the old woman and headed on down the hall, letting his ears guide him to where he needed to go.

"It's for the best you know," said Mr. Tippins apologetically to the old woman. He was an ordinary looking guy. Brown hair, chubby cheeks, forty something. Very "English." He looked down at the dark trail he was leaving on the near white carpet and flushed with embarrassment but didn't mention it to the senior Lady Worthings. "Don't let the horns throw you none, Mrs. Rain seems decent," Mr. Tippins vouched for me, taking in the old woman's continued fish face. "And she's doing what she can for Vera. What with the mess they've gotten themselves into. Will be—"

Something crashed in the back room. Vera started yelling at her daughter again.

"Com'on, Tom! Get in here!" called Mr. Jorgenson from down the hall.

"Pardon me," Mr. Tippins said. He tiptoed awkwardly down the hall, doing his best not to add to the other dirt trails.

I was a little surprised as the crisscrossing stains vanished and the carpet brightened to a freshly installed white. It just seemed to happen all on its own.

"You're really her—that girl from America. The Black Witch," said the old woman, her voice not nearly so frail as I'd imagined now that she'd finally found it.

I did my little curtsey. "Yes Ma'am, I was that girl once," I answered politely. "Please forgive us for coming without calling first. It was a bit of an emergency."

"Oh! Biscuits!" She looked scandalized by my concern. "It's no bother. I was just sitting here, watching my shows." She waved at the TV with a hand and smiled.

I was enjoying the silly, English way of things, watching how they reacted to me and this crisis in each of the homes I visited with these women. I'd been exceedingly polite, and they all seemed to respond so very well to it here. It made me think that the Devil himself would be treated well by these people if he knocked on the door and waited for it to be answered, and then politely asked for the home-owner's soul with a sincere apology about calling during dinner.

I laughed. Broken laughed too.

The muted TV came to life, flooding the house with music.

"Dance!" Broken said joyfully. She dropped the remote on the floor and re-leased my tail and stepped into the center of the room between the coffee table and the TV and began to dance. Mrs. Worthings had been watching some English version of American Idol.

At first I laughed, but it trailed off as I watched her, and suddenly my stomach rumbled. I was still hungry.

"I say! Where are your clothes, girl!?" the old woman declared, as if she'd just now noticed what I was wearing, though I'd been in the room for over five minutes.

Two, black strips of cloth crossed my chest, covering my breasts, and a silver chain at my waist followed the curve of my hips, from which hung a long, black loin cloth. The most intimate parts of my bare backside were more or less concealed by my tail when it wasn't swishing about. Unless someone mentioned my clothes or acted strangely I never thought of them. Or of the lack of them.

"Why on earth would ya parade around half naked like that? Quick! Fetch a coat from the closet."

I tore my eyes away from Broken and turned back to the old woman. "I'm part lion, so I don't like to wear clothes." I pointed behind me, where my happy tail was swishing about, trying to dance with Broken, matching her moves like a dance partner and copying her quite well.

"Clothes would get in the way of my tail."

"Oh!" She nodded, as if what I said somehow made perfect sense, but then she frowned. "Part lion you say?" She scratched at her chin. "Animals don't like to wear clothes, that's true enough, but lions don't have horns, dearie." She cocked her head at an angle, looking smug. "I'm old, not addled."

Broken stepped in front of me and before I knew what she was doing she shoved a cashew into my mouth.

"Hungry," she said, concern on her face. She must have heard my stomach growl.

I smiled down at her and bit into the nut, but its flavor wasn't sweet and it didn't make me want another. It wasn't what I wanted or liked anymore. I sighed sadly. Another change. I used to love cashews. I licked my lips where she'd touched my mouth and tasted the salt.

"Are you thirsty, Broken?" I asked her. "Nuts are salty. Are they making you thirsty?" She made me thirsty.

"Oh!" The old woman popped up as if stuck by a pin.

"Sit!" she ordered, waving to the couch. "Maybe I am getting addled, I've not even offered you tea!"

"Tea," Broken said, nodding.

I wanted to make some, right then and there!

"Right away! Just be a minute." The old woman hustled into the kitchen.

The tea would be out soon. I should wait. Let the old woman do it.

I took Broken's hand and led her to the couch, then drew her down into my lap instead of letting her sit beside me. I wanted to hold her. I was so large now, and I liked the way she fit in my lap. The dress she wore felt wonderful as it rubbed against me. I'd changed it dozens of times in little ways as it struck my fancy. The color was currently green and white and the material was something even softer and finer than magic fabric.

Broken seemed to really like her changing dress. She constantly scanned for new additions or alterations and modeled them for me, which I liked.

Meridith and a handful of the other women came walking through the portal and stopped before me, eyeing me with looks that ranged from concern to open distaste for how I held Broken on my lap.

"Lady Worthings's in the kitchen. Tea," I said innocently. It was like a magic spell. I pointed that way and they disappeared. I kept a tight smile and turned my head to look at Broken and giggled like a little girl, and she giggled too, as if we'd both gotten away with something naughty.

A few of the kids dashed through the portal from the forest, ignoring their mothers' angry calls to come back. The little group of mini rebels flopped down on the carpet like they owned the place and started watching the television, which they changed to cartoons, which soon brought the other, seven younger children we had with us into the room, along with their weary mothers and a few more fathers.

They left the couch to me and Broken, but the other chairs in the small living room grew occupants as weary women sank into their padded embrace. Many simply leaned against the wall or sat on the floor with their children before the TV. Now that the floodgates were open, this flat more or less became an extension of the field. Others began to pass through as they headed for the restroom where a line started to form.

Here in Vera's living room the women and children could also steal a few moments away from the singing. I'd lowered the volume of their singing. The sound was now a never ending, whispered melody in the background, which was creepy because the monsters still sang with all their might to create that small, frightening melody. I looked forward to turning the volume back up once we were done and the women were delivered to Amen Hale.

I'd turn the sound up and dance in my Garden of Wrath with Broken again. Alone this time. Just Broken, me, and the damned. We'd dance naked—

My stomach growled.

I changed her dress some more.

The room filled with people and activity, but I ignored them as I worked on Broken. There wasn't a whole lot I could do; she was already so beautiful. I redid her fingernails and erased a small freckle or two on her arms and legs, and then I noticed that two of her teeth were chipped, as if she'd fallen face first and hurt those two teeth. I leaned her back in my lap.

"Let me see your teeth, Broken." She opened her mouth for me.

My own fingernails shortened to the quick like retractable claws as I reached into her mouth and felt her chipped tooth and fixed it. I ran my finger inside her mouth, gliding along the side of her teeth, enjoying the feel of my finger inside her mouth. My skin tingled.

I growled, a low purring, rumble that vibrated the glasses on tables and made knick-knacks on shelves dance.

"What are you doing with Gretchen?"

With effort, I forced myself to be calm. Elspeth Richards, a big boned, bossy woman with flame red hair and a sour disposition was watching me from a chair in a little window seat that she'd turned about to face in toward the living room.

"I'm fixing her teeth." My voice was deep, thick with hungry need I was unable to disguise. I was so hungry.

"Did she ask you to fix her teeth?"

"No," I confessed reluctantly and let Broken sit up. She reached up and touched her teeth and nodded as she felt the repair. She approved.

"Is that ta be the way of it then?" Elspeth continued. "You just change us and fiddle about as you see fit without so much as asking?" She was calm but her voice was still challenging. Calling me out.

"I'll try not to, but I won't make promises that I can't keep. Sometimes I have accidents and change people without meaning to. A woman with a limp will have it vanish, or a man I see straining to read a newspaper, a child with a cough – you know – things like that. Often I won't even know what I've done."

"But what you're doing with this girl is on purpose," Elspeth pressed carefully. "She's no accident, and you know it."

Tail wrapped around Broken protectively, as if it were afraid she'd be stolen away. We were surrounded by these prudish women, all of them listening to us, watching me with Broken, judging me and her with their "oh so proper" English ideals!

Mrs. Debonshire, who was seated on the floor beside her children spoke up. Her voice was much less kind and more accusing than Elspeth's had been.

"That poor girl's mind is off! She's like a child. If you had any decency you'd heal her, instead of – of whatever you're playing at." She cast a worried glance over her children which she hovered over like a mother hen.

The room was quiet other than the cartoons on TV. The tension built. Men and women shifted nervously where they leaned about the room. I forced myself to study them for a moment. They looked stuck. Stuck in this situation. Stuck needing my help. Stuck watching me with Broken. I could see and practically feel them wondering how many horrors they'd see before they'd seen them all.

"You've changed her dress again and again, and each time there's less of it," said Elspeth gently. "You've done her shoes, her hair. Gretchen's not a doll to play dress up with."

I frowned. Was that what I was doing?

The tension broke as Lady Worthings and the other women came out of the kitchen, moving like soldiers distributing needed supplies to the troops as they pressed cups of hot tea into the hands of traumatized women and set saucers of cookies and glasses of milk before the children. Some of the women marched back through the gateway with cups of tea for those who hadn't crowded into Vera's living room.

They were all busy sipping tea when the men emerged from the back with Vera Worthings and one very angry, teenage girl. Mr. Tippins and Mr. Jorgenson, following behind the mother and daughter, looked miserable as they carried suitcases.

When the girl saw me in the living room, she threw her arms and legs out like a spider and searched the hallway for anchorage, not wanting to come a step closer. Vera began pushing at her from behind. The girl was opening her mouth but nothing but hoarse whispers were coming out.

"I'm not!" The girl's mouth turned on. She froze after just those two words and turned to look at me and said "going" experimentally. Both her hands flew up to her own mouth, shocked and surprised to hear her own voice.

"So much for the laryngitis," said Mr. Tippins regretfully as he and his load of bags slipped past while the angry teen was distracted. He began to navigate his way through the children crowding the floor.

"Hold up, Mr. Jorgenson," I said, then turned back to the girl. "Why don't you want to go?" I asked her from where I sat on the couch.

"I – just – don't – want to!" she said. "I'll run away! You can't make me go there!"

"How old is Max, Mrs. Worthings?" I asked the grandmother who'd taken a seat on the couch beside me and Broken.

"Seventeen. Eighteen this September. She'd be about to graduate if she'd stayed in school."

"Leave the bags, guys. Max is staying with her grandmother."

The two men looked relieved, but the women in the room looked angry. Angry at Vera.

"NO!" Vera screamed. "She's my daughter and she'll be coming with me!"

"She's staying with your Mum. Let's go, Vera," Mrs. Debonshire said as she turned off the TV and began to herd her complaining chicks toward the gateway.

None of the other women had a speck of mercy for Vera. They'd all agreed to my terms and seventeen was the agreed age of consent. Vera had told everyone that her daughter was sixteen. And it was abundantly clear that this girl did not wish to go. To force her truly would be kidnapping.

Black Rain

Keeping a Broken Promise

Vera STOOD IN her own living room on one side of the portal. I faced her from the clearing on the other side, surrounded by quietly singing monsters.

"This is all your fault!" she spat at me.

"You're the one who was in the woods, playing at being a witch, spitting into a kettle and asking the darkness for murder and favor. I've a bed for you in Amen Hale, but if you like, lie in the one you've made here for yourself."

"Screw you, you monster! One day you'll pay for this!"

I waved to her grandmother who was sitting on the couch, shaking her head. The portal snapped shut, cutting off Vera's angry words.

The women began to make a commotion, pointing off into the woods.

"Flashlights!" Cricket said as she ran up to me. "Someone's coming."

Sure enough, flashlights were bobbing through the woods in the distance. Searchers trying to locate the missing women and children or possibly policemen coming to investigate the claims of the women I'd already sent back to London. The quiet singing of the monsters wasn't loud, but it was one of those out of place sounds that carried like magic.

"What should we do?" Cricket asked.

I didn't want to lose my beautiful garden, and I couldn't leave it here for the police to find, so instead of making a gateway to Amen Hale I decided to move the land itself. First, I readied a new place to move this place into. I thought of an empty space in the middle of nowhere, outside of time, space, and everything that mattered to anything that was. I willed this space to have a circle of earth-like gravity, temperature, atmosphere, and a similar amount of dim illumination as the half moon overhead currently provided. I also gave it the ability to sustain and maintain the life within it.

Once I had my place of nurturing nothing prepared, I moved us and the land there. In the twinkling of an eye, the world became a flat disk set in an empty, black universe. The oval of earth I'd snatched from the clearing was two hundred feet wide and two hundred fifty feet long and ten feet deep. The edges of the oval were lined like a living picket fence with the singing beasts still fixed to the earth.

Five paces beyond the fence the world ended in a cliff-like edge and endless darkness. The sky and dark clouds above were gone but a dim light still filled the area, though it had no apparent source. The sound of the searchers and overhead helicopters had vanished. The few, weary men and women who'd stretched out on the ground bolted upright, feeling the change in the earth on which they lay. The place felt odd. Disconnected and removed from everything.

"Where the hell are we!? Where have ya sent us now!?" cried Elspeth Richards as she and the other women gazed in terror past the circular fence of singing beasts to the endless darkness beyond. "We had a deal! I thought you were going to help us!" she lamented.

"We are not in hell, Elspeth, and we are not in Amen Hale," I answered her.

"Then where are we!?" Meridith demanded.

I spread my arms wide. "Welcome to the place that is not a place. We are at the crossroads of nowhere and never was. This will be—hmm," I pondered and searched my brain for a name that fit. Something perfect popped into my head. "The Hell of Singing Sinners," I declared, stone faced and completely serious as I incorporated Big Trouble in Little China into my eternal theology. "It will be the first of many places inside my Garden of Wrath."

"But why have you taken us here, child?" Meridith asked, her old eyes wide with fear as she gazed about. The look did not suit her. I pointed to Pan and answered politely.

"I need a safe place for this kind of garden, Mrs. Meridith."

Elspeth sniffed and looked at me as if I were a stupid child. A god being retarded.

Meridith frowned, but nodded. "Aye, aye. I see it. It be wise, but we've had enough, child, we need to be away from here. Take us to your land of Amen Hale so we can beg the Queen for sanctuary."

Everyone except Broken was freaking out, and I stopped everything to smile as I watched her, feeling that hunger rise up in me again. She looked so beautiful. Her dress changed color from white and green to a satiny, shiny black matching the midnight world around us. The dress now reached to her ankles but had a high slit up both sides that went clear up past her hips.

She was too busy to notice the change in her dress, stretching onto her tippy toes and reaching up with one hand, as if she believed she could touch the dark sky if only she could stretch another inch. She held my tail with her other hand. Keeping close to me.

"Don't you be staring at her in that way!" growled Mrs. Debonshire. She and her husband held their children in their arms, two for each of them. The kids were all scared, weeping. "You've been far too familiar with her for hours now!" She narrowed her eyes. "Let her go!"

Five or six of the other women and a few of the husbands who'd joined the group began nodding their agreement and muttering, eyeing me as if I were a filthy pedophile. The rest of them seemed far too terrified to care if I took Broken. The two groups began to argue. The frightened ones urging the others to shut the hell up and leave me be and let me have her.

"Can you fix Gretchen? Bring her back to herself. Is it possible?" asked Meridith loudly, trying to keep the peace while at the same time taking the side of the proper ladies.

"Best not to let an improper relationship start, love," Ambrosia urged gently. "And that's what this would be. Improper." She stepped closer and took Broken's hand away from Tail, who released her hand only to wrap around Broken's middle. "Give her to me then," Ambrosia continued, ignoring Tail's interference. "I'll take care of her. It's the right thing to do. If you really love her, you need to fix her so she can think for herself as an adult, or let her go."

"But I don't want to let her go!" I said, angry, sad, and confused. My stomach hurt, the hunger in me pinched my guts. I needed to eat!

"You should heal her if you can," Meridith said. "Bring Gretchen back to herself. It be the right thing to do, child."

"You need to let her go," Ambrosia urged. "Give her to us."

"If you love her, you'll do it," Elspeth said, piling on. She shrugged. "But maybe you don't really love her after all." She sipped her tea, pinky in the air.

I glared at all of them, practically daring them to tell me to stop as I walked up behind Broken and pulled her away from Ambrosia.

Ambrosia, Meridith, Elspeth, and the others said nothing. All they did was stand there, staring at me, weighing me down with their eyes. Broken was blissfully unaware of the tension. She began reaching for the sky again as I walked up behind her. I put my hands on her hips, moving slowly up her sides and across the sheer fabric of her dress. I slid them up the length of her arms as she stretched upwards.

Tail wrapped around the two of us, tying us together. I was so tall her head fit comfortably under my chin; she fit against me like a puzzle piece and I molded myself against the back of her and reached up with my hands, up the length of her arms and past her finger tips, reaching higher, as if there truly was something up there, just out of her reach.

I wanted something to be there! Something that we both wanted, something that we both needed that was just out of her reach, but not out of mine. What the women said echoed in my head.

"If you love her, you'll do it."

"Perhaps you don't really love her at all."

I knew I needed to fix her! Let her go! But I did not want to do either!

"Please give me what I need! Give Broken what she needs! Help me! Help us!" I prayed to myself with all my heart, my words echoing out into the dark of the place that was not a place. My hand closed upon that darkness overhead. I brought my hand down and saw what I held.

A perfect, black apple.

The women and the others on our little island in the darkness of space seemed to forget their unnatural surroundings. Everyone stared at the apple. They'd all heard my words. I'd spoken out loud. They heard me pray, and here in my hand was the answer to that prayer. The apple was so black, its skin so shiny, it practically sparkled. Some of the Brits eyed it greedily (no doubt wondering what magic it contained); the rest eyed it with fear (no doubt thinking of the poisoned, black apple in Snow White).

Broken reached for it right away, but I pulled it back to stop her. My stomach grumbled, angry, loud, hungry, and I gritted my teeth in pain. I needed her! I was so hungry. My mouth was so dry. Her mouth so wet! I fought with the urge to throw the damn apple off the side of my world!

Broken frowned, seeing my anguish but not understanding its source. She pushed the apple at me. "Hungry," she said. Worried about me. So very worried about me.

I felt hot tears on my face.

"Look at me, Broken."

She stared into the depths of my hellish, red eyes with total trust and openness. I held her attention as I spoke to her, willing her to hear my words through whatever comforting blanket of fog that currently shrouded her mind. Hating what I was doing. Hating each word as I said it.

"If you eat this magic apple, you'll become Gretchen Frost again." I stopped and swallowed. "Gretchen was the girl you used to be. If you eat this apple, you will become that girl again."

Her eyes left mine and looked to the apple, and I saw the stirrings of deeper thoughts in their depths.

"If you eat this apple," I told her, "Broken Beauty will die, and Gretchen Frost will live, and I will have kept my promise."

She looked back to me and frowned but nodded.

"I – remember," she said, using two words, not one.

She was no longer greedy for it, but I pressed the apple into her hand and turned my back on her, not wanting to see her eat it. My tail released her. Tail came away reluctantly and wrapped around my own waist, holding me, comforting me, comforting itself.

I wept, already missing my Broken Beauty. I'd miss the way she could look into my eyes and not cringe. I'd miss the way she could be crazy mad with me and smile in the middle of a nightmare. I'd miss having someone who could stand in my Garden of Wrath and still be at peace. She could share this place with me. She was so perfect just the way she was. She was Broken, but that didn't matter to me. Who else could dance with me here and be unafraid? No one—only Broken—

She was all I needed. I loved her.

What was I doing! I would throw that damn apple away!

A crisp crunch sounded behind me and I cringed.

Something broke within me and I fell to my knees and vomited a flood of blood and grapes. Dozens and dozens of bright, purple grapes shone like jewels in the glowing spill of my bright, yellow blood as I retched and retched.

"Stay back, it's poison!" I managed to say to the few who came to help, then I retched again, spewing out another, massive load.

Shaking and weak, I strengthened myself. With all my will I gathered the last of the grapes inside me, along with every last scrap of the magic they held and cast it out of my body in one final, massive *heave*! Out of my open mouth came a huge spray of bloody grapes and the liquid, yellow sunshine that was my blood. I heard the sound of someone getting sick somewhere behind me as I stared down at the ground. It looked like the crime scene of a small, butchered vineyard.

I was sweating and angry. If I were human, I'd be dead from blood loss. I felt empty—and reborn. As if I'd finally woken from a long, long dream, one that could have lasted forever. Now that I was free of his magic, I knew that Pan had gotten one of his damn grapes into my mouth. I remembered it now. Once I was looking for it, Pan's magic couldn't touch me or get into me, but I hadn't been looking for something already hiding inside my own body.

I rose to my feet and turned. Somehow, I wasn't surprised to find Broken—or Gretchen—dead.

The women were holding onto her body. The entire group of sixty-eight men, women, and children were gathered together a dozen feet away, as far from me as they could go and not get too close to the wall of monsters behind them.

Lying on the grass near my feet was the black apple, missing one perfect bite. I picked it up, then reached back up, high into the darkness overhead. The apple became another part of the darkness as I opened my hand, going back to where it came from.

"I thought you were going to heal her!" shouted one of the younger women. "I thought you loved her!"

Meridith and the others shouted her down, telling her I was bespelled and that I was lucky to be alive myself.

I didn't bother defending myself. I didn't need to. But I did need to get moving, and before I did anything, or even said another word, I needed to get some goddam answers! I didn't want to fumble about anymore, and I was out of time. I hadn't spoken to or checked on Jane and Dan since I had left them outside the graveyard, and I hadn't spoken to anyone in Amen Hale since the shooting, hours and hours ago.

I wanted done with this, and then I wanted to go home to the people I loved. People who knew me. People whom I belonged to. I was tired of fighting and being strong, I wanted to go home and be the Broken Beauty myself, and let someone hold me and love me and make me forget. I wanted to be with people I could trust. That was what I wanted, but first, I had to see if there were any more lies.

I searched for lies. Tricks. Inside, outside, upside, downside, port side, or any other fucking place they might be hidden. The Father of Lies had started this fight, and I'd complicated things further by kicking my own ass because I was scared of what I was becoming. I wasn't scared anymore, and through it all, I was still me. I was still here, and now it was time for some answers.

I willed strength and power to fill me. The black apple was already gone, back where it came from, but I still needed to clean up the rest of the toxic, magic spill around me and on me. I banished the blood and grapes with a thought, sending the mess into oblivion, then walked the few dozen steps to where Pan was frozen to the earth like a popsicle stick, singing away.

His green eyes were on me, watching me as I approached. Inside his goat head were the answers I needed. As with Taunwee, I carefully avoided his memories of seeing God's face or hearing his voice. I wasn't supposed to see him. I did not belong to God. I could have chosen to be His, but I went my own way and I did not deserve to see him. It was the honor due Him, and it was one that I would give forever, or until He came to me Himself, and even then I'd look away—unless he told me to look at him, which would be scary as hell. The earth was his field, and at best, I was a guest there. I would be as respectful as I could and still be me.

With those divine memories safely sealed away, I proceeded to rip into the rest of Pan's mind, sifting through the thoughts and ideas and actions that made this creature, this fallen angel, what he was. I wanted it done, and done quickly, and so it was. What I wanted from him instantly became mine.

A monumental sense of pitiable scorn gripped me as I stared at Pan. I was amazed at how something made to be so noble had sunk so low and become such an abhorrent, disgusting thing. His entire existence after the fall seemed less than pointless and unfortunate. I'd searched Taunwee's heart thoroughly before accepting her as mine, and it was nothing like the selfish, ugly wasteland of Pan's existence.

Taunwee had her faults and even her murders, but she cared deeply for her people. She nurtured them like a mother in her own way. When she was alone where no one could see, she even wept for them. And she wept for her own sin as well. Regret. She loved God but was fallen, like me. I looked at Pan and smiled, thinking well of my Star. She was totally different from this trash that stood before me.

Lucifer's instructions to Pan had been simple and they came with two specific goals: First, he was to tell me about the key times he'd visited Rain Marie. The Devil wanted me to know how he'd influenced things in my life. He wanted me to think, or at the very least fear, that he was formational to my becoming what I was. Pan had little more knowledge than what he'd already divulged. Pan himself was certain that Lucifer had no inkling whatsoever of how I came to be.

The second goal Lucifer set for Pan was to brutalize me monstrously. He told Pan to bring me into his sway, rape me, kill the women and children in the field, and then leave me in the woods in the midst of their ruin. He hoped this would drive me into a blind rage and cause me to attack him. He expected God himself, or his angels, to step in and stop me and he wanted me mad enough to fight back.

It was the same reason he took Rain Marie. Lucifer wanted to push me into doing something that would make God move against me, or something that would endanger God's plan, like me stepping on him like a bug.

Lucifer had sent Pan, but Pan, being a deceiver himself, had his own plans. The magical grape was his magic and all his idea. It was made to hide inside me and grow slowly over time so that its changes were less noticeable. When those changes did emerge, he wanted me to see them as natural and even fight to keep them. The magic was meant to make me fall hopelessly and helplessly in love with him. He meant to have me as his own, and then challenge Satan with me as his "steed" to ride. He wanted to be God. He wanted to rule.

After overthrowing Satan, Pan intended to return to Heaven and battle God himself and take it as his own. He'd been idly pondering his name as he lit the candles around the quilt, trying to decide if he'd take God's name or keep his own.

"Pan or God. Pan has that unfortunate cooking utensil connotation, but I am fond of it."

Such were his last, happy thoughts before a small problem developed with his grand plan—the broken girl who lay at my feet. He didn't know it, but I'd already begun to fall in love with her. She was open and honest. When I first met her as she stood in the circle with the other women, she was terrified of being brutalized but not afraid of dying. She didn't run from death but embraced it as best she could. Tail and I liked her. We were excited by her. She needed me, and she'd helped me remember my own humanity. Broken had saved my life in a way.

Love was there, already growing when Pan clouded my mind and slipped me the grape. His magic worked inside me as intended, but finding a newly budding romance growing wild inside my heart, it traveled the path of least resistance and had me fall in love with Broken instead of the much more difficult path of pushing me toward a filthy goat. Pan thought he was so clever, confidently fixing up his love nest, thinking all was well. The goat was about to be God. By the time he realized that I'd fallen in love with Broken and not him, he'd changed course, trying to kill her so he could try again with a second grape.

But then the shit hit the fan and he started to stink.

And then he started to sing.

Done with Pan, I stripped his trophies and items of interest. Off to the side where he had intended to rape me, the quilt, odd skull shaped bowls, candles, and his seemingly bottomless bag still lay spread out on the ground. The loose items and the quilt rose into the air and packed themselves away into the bag. The Pan pipes that hung around his neck lifted up and away, as did the gold and ivory rings that adorned his swept back horns and his fingers. Even his old coat slipped off and went into the leather bag, leaving him bare. I sent out my will and found those items on the other singing beasts that were of the same make and gathered another small smattering of items which joined the rest, gliding into the leather bag.

Two women had apparently "appropriated" skull bowls and candles for themselves from Pan's spread. They squealed and struggled, as those items freed themselves from their bags and grasping hands and drifted through the air to join the rest. Their group watched the two women try to merge back among them as if nothing had happened. Most of them were too terrified to think or form an opinion on what they'd done, but Ambrosia and Meridith were eyeing the women with murderously grim expressions as was Mr. Tippins (who was a detective and seemed a particularly moral man).

Elspeth, however, was staring right at me.

"Elspeth! Punish them! Mr. Tippins, give her your belt," I ordered, then turned my attention back to my work, letting the red-headed woman and the cop see to the ugly business.

I wasn't sure if the two women would survive what Meridith would have done to them. That old woman was a *witch*! Still, the attempted theft gave me reason to be cautious. I reached up and gave the bag and its contents to the darkness over-head which swallowed it easily enough. I could always get it back when I was ready.

House cleaning done, I created a gateway to Amen Hale. Twin pillars of stone rose from the grassy ground and joined at the top forming a ten foot high, gothic styled arch adorned with demon faced gargoyles, beast men, screaming fauns, trolls, and gnomes. Each face was a perfect representation of those already planted in my Garden. The grotesque figures seemed to be trapped in the stone of the arch from the waist or knees down, screaming and struggling to free themselves. I knew that a similar arch had just formed inside the small walled garden, twenty feet away from Dan and Jane's old crypt.

The open space within the gateway opened to reveal the moonlit garden, and I heard the heartbroken and half crazed people who'd gone through these terrors with me begin to weep and cry for joy. I could practically feel the hope surge within them as the end of this horrifying journey drew to a close.

Intruding into the hope-filled whispers of good cheer came the swish of a belt cutting air, the crack of it hitting naked flesh, and the surprised cry as that person screamed. The joyful sounds dimmed as "Swish! Smack!" and a different scream and cries of protest. I listened to it. All the sounds seemed so appropriate here in my beautiful Garden of Wrath. If Broken were here I'd have danced with her as we listened together. I waited to hear the sound again.

"Swish! Smack!" A scream. Cursing.

"Swish! Smack!" A different scream.

"Bring Gretchen's body to me!" I ordered, reminding myself again that Broken was gone. This was Gretchen now. For Gretchen to live, Broken would have to stay dead.

"Lay her down in the exact same place where Broken fell."

They obeyed me but didn't look happy about it. The men and women dithered for a moment about the placement but soon they stood and backed away, leaving Gretchen on the ground, positioned as well as they could recollect.

"Swish! Smack!" A scream.

"Swish! Smack!" A different scream.

"Bethany, come to the Walled Garden. And have Penny bring your Blade," I said out loud, willing her to hear my voice. I knew she'd need a sacrifice as well, so I spoke again. "Lucius, please bring a prisoner to the Walled Garden for Bethany; she has work to do."

"Believer, my love, come to me! I'm in the Walled Garden by the Crypt!" I said to my husband. My God! What did he think of me!? Running off and leaving him again! He must hate me for it.

"Swish! Smack!" A scream.

"Swish! Smack!" A different scream.

Begging, whimpering, the rising noise of crying children, the whispered song of monsters.

I spoke out loud again, my voice for that place within myself, that world within my skull. I spoke to Taunwee. "I need you, my Star. Come to me," I said out loud.

"Who are you talking to – if I'm allowed to ask?" Ambrosia ventured carefully.

"May we go through the gateway now, miss?" asked Robin, Meridith's daughter as she eyed the open archway hungrily and hugged her daughter tightly.

"No," I told her. "You and Cricket need to see what's about to happen. Your daughter saw your dark ritual, and now my daughter will show you ours."

Robin met my eyes, looking guilty. She nodded.

"Swish! Smack!" A scream.

"Swish! Smack!" A different scream.

Begging, whimpering, crying children, the whispered song of monsters.

"Mrs. Debonshire," I called.

"Yes." The woman pushed her way forward, eyeing me cautiously.

"You and your husband gather the children under twelve and lead them out into the garden and wait for us there. The young ones have seen enough for one day and what's about to happen may break them."

She paled and nodded, as if what I'd said was wise beyond my years.

"Swish! Smack!" A scream.

"Swish! Smack!" A different scream.

Begging, whimpering, crying children, the whispered song of monsters, the rising sound of hopeful voices mixed with the instructions of the Debonshires.

S-C-R-E-A-M-S!

"R A I N !" Believer's voice boomed out like a blast of thunder, wind gusted around our world.

The air all around us charged with the electric touch of his power and the air pressure dropped like a rock as he stepped through the portal, filling that open space with his huge, tempest tossed body that flickered with small flashes of lightning as if a Tesla coil were hidden inside his spiraling clouds.

He stood within the gateway, his red eyes shining like raging, hot coals as he stared at me. He took a moment to look about, taking in the hell of a place in which we stood, all while the women and children cried out at the sight of my husband. All that they'd seen before was not to be compared to this new, living nightmare which made Pan seem like a child's toy. The women and children drew deep breaths and screamed as if they were plunging down the drop of a roller coaster headed straight into the bottomless pit.

I ran toward what made them scream and wet themselves and threw myself into Believer's ready arms. Those massive arms collected me, soft as clouds and powerful enough to hold me tight. He closed around me and I cried, letting my own weeping join the other sound: screams of mad terror, begging, whimpering, weeping, the sound of rumbling thunder, deep and powerful, the whisper of a mad song from the darkness, and the muffled sound of a polite, female angel speaking to me from inside my mouth.

"I mean no offense, my goddess, but—have you been sick? It smells as if you have."

Jane

Parked and Waiting

ANOTHER FBI AGENT walked away from the SUV window, disappointed at my vague answers to his questions. The FBI agents who came anywhere near me now wore special, smudgy glasses designed to obscure their vision so they didn't see us clearly. They also had ear pieces shoved into both ears, like hearing aides, which turned my words into robot speak.

The government didn't want more of their people going insane from speaking to me so they were doing what they could to cut down on my freak factor. They actually preferred to speak with Dan when they could, letting him reply back by writing notes. For the most part, I was considered too hot to handle.

Dan and I were sitting in the front seat of one of their big, fancy Suburbans, watching the news on a twelve-inch, flat screen TV built into the dash. They'd let us have the use of it (because Rain had pointed to it while she was out here and said "I need that."). No one argued. The Feds had actually been polite and accommodating, but from time to time they approached our ride with ridiculous questions, attempting to squeeze nuggets of information from us, which was pointless; we didn't have any to give.

"This must be her too," Dan said of something he'd been watching on the television about London. His voice sounded distracted inside my head, like a guy talking to his wife as he watched the ball game on TV.

"Sorry." He turned his head and met my eyes, looking very guilty. "We know she's all right, Jane, she's just busy. We're here, doing what she asked us to do, and as soon as she's done gathering up the survivors from all over the place, she'll be back." He put on a reassuring smile.

"Bullshit. Something's wrong and you know it." I leaned toward Dan and he met me halfway and we kissed.

I didn't bother telling him I was too annoyed to sit still or that I was going into the back or that I wanted to kill something to take my mind off all of it. He knew. I was glad he knew. I also knew he was trying to hide how worried he was about Rain.

She hadn't been right when she came out of that graveyard. Something was wrong with her. Those few minutes she spent with us out here had been so rushed— and strange. She'd commandeered the SUV from the Feds, then told Dan and me to stay with it, that she'd be setting up totems to send any stragglers she missed back to this spot.

"I'll be back soon. Tell them that the truck is safe, the demons can't reach them so long as they stay with the truck." That was all she had said before she vanished.

Moving carefully so I didn't accidentally step on any of the hundreds and hundreds of little people that thought they were invisible, I headed toward the back. I slipped past the second and third row of seats and eased into the small cargo area at the very back. It wasn't a huge space. It was wide like the truck, but not deep. It was large enough to hold a few suitcases and that was it.

When the magic brought the Twilins into the truck, they would appear in the middle of this open cargo area, visible to everyone for a second or two before they vanished. That second or two was a dismissible eye blink to a human. What the Twilins didn't know was that I saw all of them, all the time. Their hiding magic just didn't work on me.

I needed distraction, and I wanted away from the annoying FBI, so I lay on the floor and curled myself around the little pocket of space into which these refugees materialized and waited. The humming sound of the ones who circled overhead was comforting but the air back here seemed stagnant. It was fine for me, but I knew it had to be hot and stuffy for a living thing. There was no circulation.

"MMMM" A noise sounded from inside the back door panel as the window began to lower. Fresh air poured into the truck as Dan lowered the window.

"I bet you were hot back here." I spoke to the seemingly empty but crowded space.

I didn't expect an answer. Rain's magic brought them here but they did not speak to us. It was strange and voyeuristic in a way, watching people who thought they were invisible. Their faces were so open and unguarded. Some were angry, some looked upon me with scorn or suspicion while others were filled with hope and wonder.

I watched the most timid seeming Twilin woman stand in absolute confidence only an inch away from my face, secure in her cloak of imagined invisibility. I let my dark red pupils remain fixed straight ahead like a dead thing, though I had no problem seeing her and all the others. I lay there, utterly still, and watched the show. Thousands and thousands of Twilin, tiptoeing about.

After a long, human minute I felt the first, hesitant touches of tiny, invisible hands. Quick, fleeting touches. Like poking something with a stick to see if it's alive. No heartbeat, no breathing, still as stone—couldn't blame them. Their hands were so small that without my vampire skin and senses I'd have never been able to feel their individual, tiny fingers pressed to my flesh nor been able to discern the slight difference in the male and female hands. I even felt the tiny rings on some of the fingers.

Soon they grew bolder, lying along my arms and legs and when those less ob-trusive spots were all taken they even climbed up onto my chest and bedded down in my hair. They seemed to like the smell of me a great deal and some of them even rolled and wallowed on me, I think to try and get my scent on them.

I heard the soft whispers of their strange language that I did not understand, but the longer I listened the more the words began to make sense. I knew my own body was cool compared to the heat in the parked truck. Dan had turned off the motor when he'd seen the Twilins (through my eyes) hanging out in the AC vents. He was afraid one of them might get sucked in or hurt inside the motor.

I must be blessedly comfortable to lie on, I mused. Silky, soft skin, wonderful smell, cool to the touch. And not ugly to boot. In no time I was awash in so much activity that I was able to stop thinking about Rain and simply lose myself to the hundreds of tiny, invisible beings, coming and going and sleeping and quietly whispering. I let myself sink into a daze—not sleep, but as close to one as I could come without Rain's blood in my mouth. I drifted – and was – and watched what was unseen.

The Twilins arrived as singles but more often as groups, and occasionally a large group of fifty or more would appear. Some appeared casual and at ease, while others arrived wounded or even on fire. These were usually panting hard from running or flying and horror struck, as if they'd just escaped from hell itself. Seeing the ones who came in so hurt and frightened made me think that what Dan and I were doing was of value and important.

Hopeful and worried, I lay and watched as their numbers continued to swell and the frequency of their arrivals continued to increase. After five more minutes of steady arrivals, I told Dan to have the FBI back another two trucks up to ours so we could use it for overflow. If the demons attacked, the Twilins could cram back into this one, but until then, we had to have the space.

I lay there still as stone, only my mouth moved as I explained all the details to the open air around me so they wouldn't be surprised by the activity. The back hatch was opened and a second and third black SUV were rolled into place. Their tailgates were lowered and Dan laid down pieces of plywood between the trucks, bridging the three-foot gaps and increasing the size of our little world just as more Twilins began to arrive. The FBI were now catching fleeting glimpses of our new arrivals with their nosy cameras, but it couldn't be helped.

I had Dan bring me a box. Many were arriving with those too injured to save or those freshly dead, and the dead bodies did not vanish. They were beginning to accumulate.

"Place your dead here, and if my goddess cannot raise them up then we will carry them with us when we leave this place."

Five of the Twilin males became what they thought of as "visible" and bowed to me. Without a word they formed a burial detail. I watched them as they laid little bodies of two inch tall men and women and even tiny children onto the lid of a blue Nike shoe box. I heard the quiet voices as they mourned their dead and dying. More and more were arriving wounded or burned.

Dan brought more lids.

Black Rain

All in All

TAUNWEE, BELIEVER, AND the London refugees stood behind me as my mother, my sisters, and a group from Amen Hale entered the portal and formed up behind them. Our two groups faced off like opposing armies. Believer had come through first, barreling in all on his own and wrapping his arms around me without hesitation, but Cathryn entered cautiously. She held the others in a tightlipped, organized unit, snapping out orders like a stone-fisted general as she eyed me.

The women behind me spoke up, trying to introduce themselves.

"Be silent and be still!" my wild-eyed mother commanded without taking her eyes off me for a second.

She ignored them and Taunwee, who hovered behind me, beside Believer. All of Cathryn's attention was focused on me as if the rest of the world didn't even exist. Without a word of welcome she began to grill me with clipped, angry questions.

At first I assumed her behavior was due to the gruesome nature of our surroundings, but it soon became abundantly clear why she was so upset. My mother could tell just from looking at me that I was a new version of the "me" that she remembered. She knew that I'd died again and changed again, and she thought I'd done it on purpose after promising that I would never kill myself again.

Behind her, Mary and Emma were also grim faced, weepy, and disappointed. They were all giving me dark, suspicious looks. Cathryn was beyond upset, her distress coming out in crazy anger instead of tears. I was upset too, but the girl within me gave me tears for my mother instead of anger.

I wept as I knelt on the leaf-littered ground before Cathryn, trying to answer her accusations of suicide and oath breaking. Reese, one of the guards from Amen Hale, reached out, offering me a handkerchief to wipe my nose and tear-streaked face, and Cathryn gave him a withering glare for daring to show me compassion while she worked on me. The man shrunk away as if burned, retracting his handkerchief and his compassion at the same time. Even my own tail avoided her gaze, staying low and out of sight as it petted my back and coiled around my legs and ankles.

"But Mother!" I pleaded again. "I didn't do this on purpose! And I did not lie or break my vow! I swear by all that is and all that was and all that ever shall be that I did not break my promise! It was an *ac-ci-dent!*" I three parted the word, as if that would make her listen. "I was scared," I pleaded, "I was only trying to protect myself as I grew into my godhead. I know what I did was stupid, or *now* I know that it was stupid!" I sniffled and wiped my nose with the back of my wrist. I wanted a handkerchief now that I'd seen one and been denied it but I didn't dare make one. Mother was angry, and she clearly wanted me to suffer—so I would suffer for her. She started again, screaming and yelling.

Godhead?

Did I really just say Godhead? I had.

God head.

What a wacked out, queer little word. I don't think I'd ever heard anyone use it in real life before (outside of church), except for me – just now.

Godhead. Hmmm.

Was my use of the word correct? Was this the first time anyone had ever used it in a literal way, instead of a metaphorical one? But I think I meant it both ways, metaphorical and literal. Godhead. Hmmm. What a funny little word. It seemed—

"RAIN!" Cathryn yelled into my face.

"Sorry!" I spat out reflexively as I whiplashed back to where I knelt, blinking and looking about dazedly, wondering what I'd missed. Cathryn had no mercy at the re-emergence of my wandering spells. To her it was another clear indication that I'd changed, which meant one more reason to be angry.

She grabbed me by the horns, forcing me to stare into her angry face and her wild, frantic eyes. She began again, speaking in a tightly coiled, mockingly civil tone instead of the yelling she'd been using.

"You always have such good reasons for killing yourself, did you know that? It always sounds so logical, Rain. I wonder why more of us don't solve our problems in the same way. Dying is such a wonderful way to fix things. It's quicker than driving for hours and hours in a car or taking a plane to get home to the people who care about you and asking them for advice or help." She gave me a mockery of a smile. "If only you could come home with a wave of your hand, like magic. But really, even if you could, why bother, you're so much wiser and smarter than we are. Just kill yourself like you always do. Whatever problem you have, *that'll fix it!*" she finished acidly.

Cathryn was relentless, stabbing away again and again. She seemed intent on reducing what was left of my heart to a shredded, bloody pulp! I knew my own eyes were hopeless pits of darkness with hellish, red dots for pupils, but I willed my face to show my sorrow as I tried desperately (once again!) to explain.

"The first time WAS an accident, Mother!" I cried for the umpteenth time. "And I had to kill the second 'me'! I had to! She was a monster! A cold hearted, unfeeling, arrogant monster," this time I added, "and I wanted to live! The human part of me wanted to live!"

She sniffed in denial. "I'd like to believe you, but your actions speak loudly, Rain. You've killed yourself twice since you vanished off the porch. Twice since you promised me you wouldn't kill yourself – again – Rain."

Cathryn deliberately said my name instead of calling me child or daughter. She'd done this since she'd arrived in spite of my continually calling her "Mother" and wondering why was worse than all the yelling and screaming she could ever do.

"Tell me the truth, Rain. Who, or what, are you now?" she asked, as if I were no longer hers.

I wrapped my arms around her waist and stared up into her face, fighting to breathe and form the words I needed as my building panic squeezed my throat. It didn't seem like anything I said would ease her anger anyway. I tried and tried, but she did not want to hear words! What could I do! How could I fix it? What was happening? Why was she doing this!?

"I am your daughter!" I forced the words past the tightness in my throat. "Please – *Mom?* I love you! Don't send me away! Please! Please! Please!" I begged and prayed.

"Dammit, child!" She grabbed me by the horns and pulled me close to her face and yelled down at me, lost in her own, brokenhearted anger in a way I'd never seen from anyone before.

Looking into her eyes, I realized in that moment that my new mother was mad. It frightened me because crazy people sometimes did crazy things. But I didn't care what she did, so long as she kept me!

"Must you die every day and change every hour!?" she screamed at the top of her lungs. "With this morning's mess this makes three times in a single day that you've died, Rain! Did you even think for a minute what that means!? That's three times that a mother has had to watch her daughter die in one day! THREE!" she roared.

I cringed beneath her fury and tried to bow my head, but she yanked me up by my horns, giving me no respite nor place to hide from the pain and madness I saw in her eyes. Pain that was all my fault. Madness that I'd brought.

"Where's it going to end, Rain!?" Spittle flew as she shouted with a voice raw and ravaged. "Does it continue till I'm forced to endure your death at the top of every hour!? Each time dreading what will be left of you when you come back? You're going to ruin yourself if you keep this up if you haven't already. Or you're going to give me a heart attack, and Bethany will have to raise me for a change!"

"NO!" I screamed.

Her eyes widened as if I'd given her a brilliant idea.

"Is that what I have to do to get you to stop this madness?" She dove into this new, soft spot I'd revealed, slashing away, "Must I die for you, Rain?" She gave my head an angry shake. "Bethany's Blade is here! Must I die so you will live!? Is that what you want? Will that end it!?" she yelled. "Tell me! Is that what you want!? Is it!?"

"NO! I'm sorry, Mother!" I wailed. The last shreds of my dignity deserted me, my thoughts dissolving into uncontrolled, brokenhearted sobbing as I clung to her dress. Words I didn't even listen to spilled between tears and my desperate pleading. I cried and rambled on and on until she released my horns and let me sink to the leaf-littered ground and weep. Still she did not hold me or comfort me, which was what I so desperately wanted.

I looked around for someone else if my mother was unwilling. Alana fought to get to me, but Emma and Mary held her back. I looked behind me and saw that Believer held onto Bethany. Beyond them I saw that Meridith and Robin held tightly to Cricket. My gaze fell to my sweet Broken, who lay dead on the ground. She would have come to comfort me, but she was gone.

I turned back to my mother, thinking I'd have to weep alone, but then I felt little feet land on my shoulder and heard a beautiful voice crying with me. I looked down to find Taunwee, her face streaked with tears as she wept with me. "Nuriswe" (grief sharing) was a Twilin thing, not done lightly, and something never before done by Taunwee herself. It was a vow to share the grief, tears, and even the shame of whatever had happened as well as the punishment or the price of restitution. It was only done between mothers and daughters, first sisters, heart sworn friends, or lovers. I knew from Taunwee's own memories how important it was. She wept with me, and she wept for me—and I loved her for it.

"Enough," Cathryn said after letting us cry for a while. "Both of you," she ordered.

"Yes, Queen Cathryn." Taunwee straightened but stayed on her knees on my shoulder, head bowed.

"Yes, Mother," I said a second later, wiping at my face, sniffling and wrung out. I felt like a piece of hand washed laundry, body sore from being twisted into knots and rubbed against an old style, bumpy scrubbing board. My throat, eyes, and lungs were raw as if they'd been dunked under lye water again and again. My whole body was trembling, making Taunwee keep one hand out to balance herself on my shoulder.

Cathryn eyed us both suspiciously as she dried up the last of her own tears with Reese's handkerchief, the same one that he'd offered me earlier. I noticed the nodding heads and approving looks of the women from London. They seemed quite impressed and satisfied with the dressing down my mother had laid on me. They'd heard it all and it was obvious they agreed with my mother.

"Done is done. So mote it be." Cathryn took a deep, steadying breath and pressed ahead. "So, what's the damage this time, child? You look the same on the outside, but what's changed on the inside?" She shook her head as she stared down at me.

The fight was over but she still frowned. Mary peered around Cathryn's shoulder, giving me (and Taunwee) her own frown. She was a white-haired echo of my mother's face. Both frowning. Identical expressions. Probably identical thoughts as well.

"Are you half and half now, half god and half girl, or are you something else entirely now? What new problems or ticks have you acquired? It's obvious that your wandering spells are back, and worse, but what else has gone wrong? How bad is the damage and how badly have you been weakened by all of this?"

I noticed that Taunwee was also staring at me with concern on her face. After seeing my mother carrying on the way she did, I didn't blame her. Everyone was eyeing me with concern. I didn't answer right away because I couldn't. I was still recovering from the worst fussing I'd ever experienced in this – or any – life I'd ever lived. Everyone waited patiently until I finally regained the capacity for speech.

"I haven't been weakened, Mother." Sniffle. "I'm all that she was, and I'm all that she wasn't. I'm not less—I'm more. I'm much more than I've ever been before." I risked a trembling smile.

Mary raised her eyebrows and pursed her beautiful lips.

Cathryn didn't look convinced.

"I killed her and took all she was," I said with a little more conviction. "I'm not half and half—I'm all in all."

Cathryn listened to what I said, then seemed to shelve it. She pointed around at the circle of singing monsters.

"What is this place? And who are these creatures?"

"This is the Hell of Singing Sinners." Sniffle. "It will be the first part of my Garden of Wrath." I rose to my knees and gestured to the creatures lining the edge of the floating island of earth. "Some of these are fallen angels, half-breed Nephalim, or cursed humans. Some are even cursed animals. The Devil sent them to hurt me and these women so I damned them to this Hell. The angels are eternal of course, but this place will keep all my damned alive so they can worship me with their sufferings forever. They will hunger and thirst, but they will never die. They will sing forever down here." I kept my eyes on my mother, ignoring the others or what they might think of what I'd said. "If you like, you can build the next part of my Garden, Mother. I'm sure you have some great ideas for the next part of my Hell."

Cathryn gave me a weak, uncertain smile, as if she wasn't entirely sure I was serious, or perhaps she was still uncertain that this new version of me wasn't a monster after all.

At that moment Alana broke free from a distracted Emma and rushed to me, falling into my arms. A minute later Bethany came and latched onto Cathryn. I held onto Alana and studied Bethany. I could see on her face why she'd run to Cathryn instead of me. She had a soul deep need to make the arguing stop and make everything better. She looked from Cathryn to me, her eyes telling me whole sentences in a glance. "I'm on it! I'll fix it! I'll make her love us again!" her eyes promised. Swore! She started talking.

"We can make a room for cutting down here, Mom!" Bethany latched onto my suggestion, dark eyes alight with the idea as she chattered away. "We can do it together, Mom! Me, you, and Rain. We can make a special place down here where people won't die no matter how much we cut them or how much they bleed. We can bring the twins down here and cut them together! I'll even let you cut me if you want!" Bethany said, tearfully. "And you can cut Rain, and maybe Penny will come too. She's cut herself for me before." Bethany would have offered her anything to make her happy. Her own wrist. Mine. Her maid's. Whoever.

The Londoners had been delighted as they watched my mother lay into me. They saw Cathryn as the capable human hand that gripped the tiller of this mad ship called Amen Hale, firmly in control, directing where it went and keeping the magical creatures that called it home in check. *I* being one of those creatures. They'd clearly been comforted seeing her deal with me and knowing that she was the Queen. The Queen who would rule over them and their children. The Queen who would keep the monsters in line. They'd been so pleased with Cathryn only minutes ago, and now they stared at her in horror as they listened to Bethany offer up blood and more. The other shoe kept dropping. The Wicket Street Knitting Circle had met my mother, the Bloody Queen of Amen Hale.

Marcia

Chew, Chew, Chew

Mᴀʀᴄɪᴀ ᴘᴜʟʟᴇᴅ ᴏɴ the door and cussed for about three minutes, then ran out of energy. That was all it took to wear her out. Her arms and legs felt like overcooked spaghetti. It's wasted energy anyway, she told herself. Counterproductive even. She needed to be smart, not panic.

The video recordings would be edited until what was left made her look like a fool, or the whole recording would simply be "lost" or "misplaced." Ogburn and Dyal would deny ever locking her in here in the first place, the same way they'd deny what had happened earlier, when they'd forced her to stay in that room and get gassed along with the others. They'd deny everything and then back each other up if it ever went as far as an official investigation. They'd ruin her if she tried to fight back.

She silently promised herself that once they let her out, she wouldn't make a scene. She'd resign from the program, forget this ever happened, and never come back. She'd take whatever punishment transfer they threatened her with, Alaska, Korea, or a spider hole in Iraq if it meant she'd never have to spend another minute with Dyal and Dr. Ogburn.

Marcia sat in a chair there by the door and ran through the past few days in her head. Everything Ogburn and Dyal had done since she came here could easily be glossed over or explained away, but not this. Locking her in with any patient was psychotic, let alone a patient like Gannon (and Kim). Now that they'd crossed that line, she wondered with rapidly growing dread what would happen next.

The more she thought about the two men and how abusive they'd been, the more paranoid she became. She'd more or less ignored some of the things they did that were questionable and had given extra latitude to Dr. Ogburn's eccentricities. The oddities that could be grudgingly overlooked from your superior while on the outside of a locked door became nakedly sinister from inside the cage he controlled.

She thought it through, her frazzled mind connecting pieces that were real and inventing others that were merely possible (but now seemed probable). The more she reviewed the past few days in her head, the less she wanted the door to open. Ogburn was constantly trying to find ways to vilify these kids so he could push things to the next level and have more control with less oversight. Marcia recalled how he'd used Benjamin's attack on the female soldier to further his agenda. And why was that female soldier near Benjamin in the first place! Did he tell her to be there or was it just bad luck? Had he used her as bait? And what did that now make her if he had? Her panicked mind came to the simple conclusion.

They're going to kill me and blame Gannon and Kim.

Nothing else made sense.

All the cruel, heartless comments that she'd heard the two men make over the past few days came back to her now. She'd had her own heartless comments mixed in with theirs at the time, but in her head all she heard was theirs.

They're going to kill me.

It wasn't right. It wasn't fair. She'd gone into this line of psychology, and military work in particular, because she wanted to be the one in charge. She wanted to be the one making the rules. Saying when to get up. When to lie down. What to eat. What to say. What to do. To watch as someone else made pleasing her their one goal in the small roomed life that they led. Marcia rubbed at her arms and legs as they cramped.

It wasn't fair.

Feeling even weaker, but wanting to get away from the door more than anything, Marcia forced herself from the chair.

Gannon had retreated to the outdoor courtyard with Kim to let Marcia freak out in private. It was awkward seeing your jailor become your cell mate for no apparent reason. Fortunately for both of them, Marcia had the key to the courtyard in her pocket and not in her purse or they'd have been trapped in the same room together.

Gannon watched with growing worry as a gaunt, ashen-faced Marcia walked out into the courtyard. Gannon was seated at a little, wicker, glass top, patio table occupying one of the two seats. Kim was on the table top. Between the two of them lay their cards. All the cards had been creased down the middle, top to bottom, so they could stand on end. Gannon held his cards but Kim's were all set up on the table top and facing her in a half circle, arranged as if she had eyes and merely lacked the hands required to manipulate the cards for herself. Marcia had seen Gannon play other board games with the heart before but never cards. It was complex. The scene made Kim seem a regular person, just one without a body.

"Still no word?" Gannon asked warmly, trying not to overreact to how strung out and sickly Marcia looked.

"No."

Marcia's diminished condition brought him to his feet. Suddenly angry, he looked up at the camera mounted on the wall and shouted at the ever present voice (which had gone silent for the first time ever since Marcia's incarceration). "Hey! Jackass! You going to open the damn door or what!? Let her out already! She's not feeling good!"

"No, Gannon!" Marcia shook her head and winced in pain at the side to side motion. "Don't talk to them. Leave them alone." She leaned forward onto the table and then sagged into the open chair and dropped her head onto the table top for a split second before snapping bolt upright, eyes wide with fright, her own heart pounding as she stared down at the beating heart only inches away from where she'd just laid her head. She'd completely forgotten about it for that split second.

Gannon said nothing about her wild reaction as he reached over and picked Kim up, his brows still set in rigid, concerned lines.

"Please, Gannon, don't talk to them," Marcia whispered quietly, trying not to be heard by anyone other than Gannon.

"What's going on, Marcia?"

"Nothing. Everything's fine. It's just a misunderstanding," she said, hoping Dyal and Ogburn got the message. She didn't want to cause trouble. She'd be no trouble.

Gannon had his book of matches and his little bag of pot and papers right there on the table. Marcia had approved the dispensation of the marijuana herself.

It was a drug that he'd asked for and said helped him stay mellow. It didn't conflict with other meds easily and was nearly impossible to overdose on so she okayed it. Every pill bottle in his medicine cabinet, the Tylenol, the cold medicine, even the antacids were fake. Sugar pills and placebos, as were issued to all the patient rooms for safety purposes. Gannon's little bag of "approved" dope was the only real medicine in his entire apartment.

Her head was still pounding and her skin was crawling, but the thought of taking meds from someone like Tachi or Ogburn made Marcia cringe. Who knew what they'd give her. Her imagination wanted to go wild with that idea. She didn't want to take their pills. She knew that cannabis contained active ingredients with therapeutic potential for relieving pain, controlling nausea, and decreasing ocular pressure.

Pain relief – nausea – ocular pressure.

Her trembling hand reached toward a half smoked joint lying on the table.

Gannon had turned in his chair, whispering to Kim in a hushed conversation. Hearing the strike of a match he turned back to the table and his jaw dropped open in one of those shocked expressions reserved for rare moments of imploded innocence. The time he'd seen the nice, little, lunch lady spit in the food, he'd put on this face. That moment he walked into the living room on a day he'd skipped school and caught his mother watching raunchy porn and enjoying it, he'd put on this face. And the time he'd been stopped by a cop who shook him down for his concert tickets and his pocket cash, he'd put on this face.

"Screw you!" Marcia said roughly as she stared at "that face."

"Sorry," he said, feeling awkward and freaked out as he watched a respected authority figure bogart his weed.

Gannon set Kim on the table top again, cleaned his bloody hands with a towel, and got busy rolling a second joint without being asked. He lit it and took a toke himself before passing it to Marcia.

"I don't want to be pushy," Gannon began cautiously, "and don't take this the wrong way, but somethin's seriously fucked up here. And you're scared of something. What's wrong?" Gannon pressed, leaning in.

Marcia passed the joint and spoke as she exhaled. "It's nothing, Gannon. The intercom systems were probably damaged some when they took—" Marcia swallowed, "took care of Benjamin. You're just being paranoid." She laughed nervously. "You shouldn't smoke so much weed." She reached out and took his joint away.

Marcia's words were already beginning to echo in her own ears and her skin practically felt like it was vibrating now that the pot was kicking in. Her headache felt a little better though.

The heart twitched on the table and Gannon reached over, picked Kim up, and held her to his ear, frowning as he listened.

"Kim said that you're scared to death of something. And that you're sick," Gannon said firmly. "You need to get out of here and you need a doctor."

"I'm fine. I want to stay right here with you and Kim. I haven't spent enough time with you two lately. It's the best way to—" she searched for what to say – her mind slow to react, "to build trust. You two are just paranoid. I'm not afraid. No one wants to kill me. Why would anyone want me dead? That's just crazy talk. Like I said, you're paranoid." Marcia narrowed her eyes at the heart, as if she'd heard Kim say "bullshit" out loud.

"Leave me alone, Kim!" she told the heart crossly. "You don't know what you're talking about."

Gannon faked another drag, as he'd done the last few passes. He *was* getting paranoid and felt the need to stay at least somewhat sharp. He broke down what Marcia just let slip out as he and Kim watched her puff away.

"Marcia," Dyal's unmistakable voice spoke on the intercom. "You need to end your visit with Gannon. Please exit the courtyard and proceed to the infirmary immediately."

Marcia said nothing; she just sat there staring blankly ahead at nothing. Gannon watched her, lips pursed and brows raised, waiting to see what she'd do. When nothing happened for an entire minute he proffered the joint, hoping the action (if she took) would lead to other action. Like jump starting a stalled car. She took the joint, took another drag then handed off but made no move to get up or go anywhere.

"Marcia! Stop acting like a child! We don't have time for you to sit in there and smoke weed! You're sick and probably dying. Go to the infirmary and start decontamination immediately. Get up, Marcia, right now!"

Gannon said nothing. Marcia said nothing. Kim said nothing. They passed the joint a time or two more, ignoring Dyal's voice which grew more and more insistent and angry, going on and on about painted rabbits come to life and magical disease until guards started to enter the courtyard. Dr. Ogburn and Dr. Tachi lingered at the doorway while six guards wearing yellow hazmat suits and masks approached the table where Gannon and a very stoned Marcia sat.

"Mr. Gray, please remain seated and don't have any further contact with Marcia," Ogburn ordered from the back at the doorway. "Marcia, come with us."

"I'm fine. I need to – I want to observe Gannon tonight," Marcia said from her seat at the table. The hand holding the joint trembled horribly.

"You need to come with us now, Marcia," Dyal urged on the intercom, his voice no longer scathing and ugly but reasonable, even pleading, now that there were others around to hear what he was saying.

The hypocrisy of it made Gannon's mouth drop open. He turned his attention to the men pouring into the room and honed in on Ogburn, who lingered at the door.

"You left her in here on purpose! She screamed and shouted to get out, but you left her in here. You came in while she was sleeping and stole her purse so she couldn't get out or make a phone call! Kim told me. She saw your guys come in here!" Gannon jabbed a finger in his direction. "Or are you going to deny that you locked her in here and stole her purse?"

Dr. Ogburn took a step into the courtyard. "We took Marcia's purse because it wasn't safe to leave lying around in a patients room and because we needed to keep her secure until we were sure that others hadn't been infected with Katie's Bunnies." He turned his gaze back to Marcia. "Dyal and I didn't know you were infected until you were already in here with Gannon, and we couldn't risk coming in to remove the rabbits from your skin until we knew if it had already spread to the others. We don't know what we're dealing with or—"

"You're lying!" Marcia shouted weakly.

"Marcia, you're not feeling well," Dr. Tachi spoke up, voice calming. "This wasn't handled as it should have been. You should have never left the infirmary for a minute." He gave Ogburn a furious glare. "But there is a reason you were detained in here, and it was done on my orders, not theirs. You've been infected with a dangerous, magical, biologic organism that needs to be purged from—"

"Bullshit!" Marcia spat the word at him. Finally finding some of her outrage through all the fear she'd let build up.

"Marcia, I think they're right," Gannon tried to reason with her. "You need to listen to them. You're sick."

She stabbed a finger at Ogburn. "He wants me dead because I'm going to tell about what he's really trying to do here!"

"Marcia!" Ogburn cautioned, face angry stiff. "You're sick. And confused. *And high*," he mumbled. "I reviewed the tape in the hallway when Katie drew on your hand—"

Marcia imitated Dyal's tone and inflection, "Don't get attached to these kids, Marcia, we'll probably kill half of them, and the other half we'll need to break. It won't be pretty but it's got to be done!"

"Take her to the infirmary!" Tachi ordered the men in their protective suits. One man stepped forward with a stun gun trained on Gannon, keeping him seated and frustrated while the others closed in on Marcia.

"Keep your damn hands off me!" Marcia snarled.

"That's fine, Marcia," said one of the guards. He reached up and took off the hood so she could see his face. It was Roper, a guard she knew by name. Roper handed his mask to one of the other men and put his gloved hands up in a calming gesture. "Marcia, you really are infected with a magical biologic. No shit! Can't you tell that you've lost," he screwed his face up and guessed, "God, thirty, forty pounds or more? Katie's hand drawn Bunnies are crawling all over you!"

She blinked. The concern on the man's face seemed genuine.

"Let's go to the infirmary and see if we can wash them off before they eat you alive!" he urged passionately.

Marcia looked down at herself. She ran a hand across her stomach, becoming more concerned as she felt how thin she'd become. She reached up and felt the sunken features of her face. She had long sleeves but at the edges of her cuffs she saw a few quick flashes of ink. It looked like living tattoos crawling across her pale, sun-starved flesh.

"We've been watching on the cameras," Dr. Tachi said from the doorway. "The rabbits are intelligent! They've been hiding from you, but we've observed them on the cameras crawling across the back of your neck and ankles where you couldn't see them."

"We've got to wash them off before they eat you down to nothing!" Roper grabbed her hand and pulled up her sleeve.

Marcia and Roper and the others stared in dumb fascination at the plethora of detailed, ink creatures crawling across her forearm. The rabbits were of various sizes, some only an inch long and some as large as six inches from tip to tail. They were all colored varying shades of the same blue ink of Katie's original rabbit. Each little piece of art moved independent of the others, bouncing here and there, scratching with a long, back foot at floppy ears or rising up on hind feet to sniff and look around with eyes that held a sinister gleam of understanding. It was as if Marcia's skin were the surface of a television screen stuck playing a mad version of the bunny channel.

"Oh my God!" Marcia cried out. She reached up and started unfastening the buttons on her blouse. "Help me, Roper," she said weakly.

Marcia looked up to find Roper pulling his glove off as quickly as he could. He threw it on the ground as if it were a snake and backed away from it.

"They crawled onto the glove!" he shouted, eyes wide and breathing hard.

Roper didn't stop at the glove but kept stripping as he headed toward the door, dropping clothes in a trail as he bolted. Others followed, collecting his discarded items with what looked like tongs and dropping them in a clear glass bucket.

"Take him to the decontamination room. Don't let him touch anyone! Have him shave himself and then search him!" Dr. Tachi ordered one of his white lab coat wearing companions who took off after Roper.

Marcia was distracted, watching as Roper fled the courtyard but when he left she saw the naked terror on the faces of the others as they stared at her. They were staring at her face. She let out an unladylike snort. "There's rabbits on my face," she guessed and then burst out laughing, tripping on the weed as she watched the other men retreat from the courtyard as if she were on fire.

"Gannon! Come on!" called Ogburn. "She's infectious!"

"You're just going to leave her!?" Gannon yelled at them, outraged as he got out of his seat and came toward them.

"You need to come with us, Gannon!" Ogburn urged as he left. "She'll have to wash herself clean of the infestation! You can't touch her or they'll transfer!" his voice called from outside the doorway.

"She was right! You do want her dead!" Gannon accused angrily. "You sorry, good for nothing bastards! Why'd you wait so long to tell her to wash these damn things off!?"

"Here!" One of the guards dropped a bucket with what looked like soapy water on the ground at Gannon's feet. "If you're going to stay and help her, do it fast, kid! Wash her clean before they eat her alive! We were able to wash the Bunnies off the girls, but they weren't like these." The man's face said he told the truth better than any words could have. "I don't know if this will work, but we don't know what else to do." He sounded frustrated and resigned.

Another man handed Gannon a second bucket with scouring pads, rags, and towels and then backed away.

Dr. Tachi stood at the door of the courtyard with the other two men. "Wash the ink off and then burn your clothes and anything the rabbits spread to. If you're determined to stay, then that's what you need to do, Gannon. We can't risk this getting out," Tachi said, face set in hard determined lines.

Gannon gave him the middle finger. "Eat shit and die, you gook!"

The door shut with a slam.

Gannon turned to find Marcia already bare chested and struggling to get her pants off. He paused for a freaked out second, transfixed by the sight of both her ink crawled skin and a half naked woman. Marcia looked like a heavily tattooed biker chick, but instead of lifeless skulls or hellish demons, she was marked with a far more frightening version of living ink.

Gannon didn't hesitate; he picked up both buckets and carried them over to where Marcia struggled. He set the buckets down and then put a hand on Marcia's stomach to steady her as he helped her out of her pants. Marcia watched as the ink rabbits transferred to Gannon's arms, bouncing over with what looked like joy at having more space in which to run and make more bunnies.

"You should have let me do this myself, Gannon, now they're on you," she said sadly, covering herself with one hand as she pulled her underwear off with the other.

"Rabbits." Gannon laughed, looking at his own living ink infestation instead of Marcia. "Whose idea was it to make killer rabbits?"

"A very angry, little girl," Marcia said sadly.

"Shit!" Gannon said as he turned and came face to face with a triangle of her curly, red hair.

"This is going to be weird, Gannon, but you need to strip. The things hide under clothes and we need to wash them off. Just try not to think about it."

"Yeah. Sure," Gannon said calmly while his face said just the opposite. He was looking at her through squinted eyes that tried to center on her face.

"Just think of me as one of the guys. Now let's just get it done as quick as we can, Gannon."

Marcia grabbed a sponge from the bucket and dunked it into the soapy water. If she allowed herself to think about being naked, she knew she'd freeze up. If she froze up, the damned rabbits would eat her alive. Fear pushed modesty from her mind and the pot focused her on the task at hand. Marijuana highs went well with repetitive simple actions. In the same dull way a tattooed construction worker enjoyed his buzz while driving nail after boring nail into sheets of drywall on a job site, Marcia dunked the sponge and scrubbed. Dunked and scrubbed. Dunked and scrubbed. She ignored the cameras, Gannon's awkwardness, her own inhibitions, and focused on scrubbing ink off her skin.

The rabbits did not flee Marcia's sponge or Gannon's wash rag. The bunnies watched, raised on hind legs until the wet, scrubbing brush neared their chosen patch of flesh. When the scrubbing brush or sponge reached them, the rabbits would squat down, laying their ears flat across their backs, hunkered low on the flesh in which they lived.

Marcia and Gannon scrubbed in silence, their efforts getting more and more frantic. When the skin on one portion of flesh became so raw from scrubbing it began to chafe and bleed, the rabbits in the affected area would try to flee. After creating three bleeding and raspberried patches of flesh and only killing two rabbits and wounding a handful of others, Marcia dropped her sponge and staggered over and sat in the chair at Gannon's table.

Gannon, having come to the same conclusion with five marred and bloody patches and a miniscule death toll to show for his self-inflicted damage, sank into the other chair. Marcia picked up his book of matches and lit one of the joints lying on the table, took a long drag, and handed off.

"I can't touch you!" Gannon told the beating heart that was sitting on the table top. He'd said this a few times while scrubbing at the rabbits, somehow sensing that she had something to say; Gannon had been refusing to pick her up and hold her to his ear so he could discern her words.

The bloody heart rolled and struggled across the table top, striving to reach Gannon with her slow, flopping gait. Gannon stood up from his chair before Kim could roll off the table and into his naked lap.

For the first time, Marcia noticed his nudity, which was at eye level and only a few feet away. She turned her head. Marcia concluded with a small smile of discovery that blue was not Gannon's natural hair color.

"Kim," Gannon was saying, "I don't want you to catch these damn rabbits too."

"Don't be stupid, Gannon," Marcia said in a thin raspy voice, without looking at him. Her strength was failing, as was her will to keep fighting. "If an incinerator can't kill Kim, I doubt these stupid rabbits can. Just pick her up and tell her I'm sorry." Marcia laid her head on the table and closed her eyes. "I didn't mean to get you killed."

Gannon watched Marcia with her head down on the table top. The rabbits crawled everywhere on her skin, giving her a sense of perpetual motion and life even while she was still. As he stared at her, the certain knowledge crept into him— Marcia was going to die. Soon. And then he'd die. Dead at seventeen. That sucked.

He wondered calmly if he'd be so mellow about dying if not for the weed. He felt the familiar tingling chill from Kim, trying to get his attention again. Gannon reached for the bloody heart, but as his hand neared the organ a rabbit stampede broke out. Tiny inked creatures bounded away from the heart, running up his arm until the whole limb was free of living ink.

"Marcia!" Gannon shouted. "Look!"

She raised her head with difficulty but livened at the sight of bare, rabbit free flesh on Gannon's arm. "Well, what are you waiting for? Grab her, you idiot," Marcia said, shaking her head and smiling at him.

Gannon grinned like an idiot and picked up Kim, creating rabbit stampedes as he pressed her to his ear. The inked rabbits rushed from his face and head, down his torso and toward his lower extremities. His back became crowded, edge to edge with frightened rabbits, eyes wide, long ears high and stiff, noses twitching, feet thumping in alarm.

"Sorry!" Gannon cringed as he listened to the heart. "You're right, I was being a shit." He groaned as Kim laid into him. "Forgive me! I love you! Yell at me later, babe."

Facial expressions came and went as he listened to the bloody heart pressed to his ear. Instructions delivered, Gannon stood with Kim and backed up a step or two from the table, and then he struck. Down his right leg and up his left he drug the bloody heart, leaving a shimmering, red trail behind like the path of a gruesome snail. He went down and up again.

Gannon and Marcia, along with dozens of anxious eyes watching on the cameras, surveyed the results. Every rabbit touched by Kim was dead. The inked creatures were locked in poses of action, forever capturing their last, desperate leap or cringe as the witch's heart turned magically animated, killing ink into an inked memory of death. The rabbits now looked like real tattoos of heartlessly murdered animals. With the blood in two long stripes, it looked like a freeway scene, where some maniacal driver had crushed a swath of the creatures up and down the length of Gannon's body. The horror and emotion on the faces made the rabbits look disturbingly human.

"I guess that's it then. I'm dead," Marcia said.

Gannon's head whipped around. "What do ya mean!?" he protested almost angrily. His whole being was ablaze with hope and determination and the readiness to fight! Gannon was finally oblivious to his own nudity as well as Marcia's as he charged ahead. "Dead?" he challenged. "We're not going to be the ones dead! We got 'em whipped! Kim can save us!"

"No, Gannon. She can save you, not me." Marcia's voice was barely audible. "If you touched me with Kim long enough to kill my rabbits, I'd die." She gave him an oddly whimsical smile and laid her head back down on the table top, closing her eyes. "You may be inked up, but at least you'll live. You and Kim were always so nice to me. At least I'll die with friends."

"No fuckin way!" Gannon charged over to Marcia with Kim in his grip.

He loomed over her but hesitated. Her words of warning held him at bay. Tears of angry frustration and desperation blurred his vision as he stared down at her wizened frame. Her spine stood out, running down the middle of her back in a visible line. Bones protruded in alarming ways from her back at her shoulders and hips and rabbits still ran across her skin freely, doing their damage, intent on grinding her down to nothing.

Gannon hesitated, trapped in frustrated, heartbroken impotence until he noticed the blood. Five or so drops of Kim's blood had fallen onto Marcia's back, and the rabbits who'd been hit by the blood didn't seem to like it at all. Two actually seemed dazed or stunned, lying down and twitching or kicking at the dots of red as if it burned.

"Kim baby, are you seeing what I'm seeing?" Gannon spoke to the heart, a smile coming to his face. He held the heart up to his ear, listening for a moment. Nodding. "All right. Let's do it."

"Do what?" came Marcia's muffled voice. Her eyes were closed but she was still listening.

"Hold still, Marcia. And keep your eyes closed," Gannon said.

He would have said more in explanation, but Kim didn't give him time. She began to bleed. There was always a small amount of blood weeping from the magically animated organ, but that small amount increased to a steady dripping of red. On Marcia's back, rabbits fled in terror, running to her front or further extremities for shelter, but those who were hit squarely by the blood staggered and slowed.

Gannon carefully set Kim down on the table top, then reached down to the expanse of white flesh with its new drops and swirls of witch's blood. He pressed his own, already bloody hands onto Marcia's back and smeared the blood up and down her back as if he were painting her pale, white skin red. He grabbed Kim again and held her over Marcia, letting more blood fall onto her head, neck, and shoulders.

When her head was soaked with blood and her back drenched, he set Kim down and went back to Marcia, rubbing the blood into her hair and down to her scalp, down her too thin neck. Beneath his hands, Marcia trembled as if chilled to the bone, but she said nothing and kept her eyes closed as Gannon painted her with Kim's blood.

Marcia was dimly aware of what was happening, but she fought against the knowledge of her reality, driving her mind toward the idea that it was all a dream. She'd already died and now she was dreaming. Only dreaming. No need to worry or be alarmed. Everything from here on out was part of the last dream she'd have before the end.

She felt strong hands lift her from the chair and lay her on the ground. Chilling drops fell upon the flesh of her stomach, causing her to gasp. She still refused to open her eyes. It was all a dream; she needed to keep her eyes closed. More chilling drops fell onto her flesh. The wetness was both terribly warm and bitingly cold. How could something be both at the same time?

It' a dream, she reminded herself. Anything could happen in a dream. More fell onto her stomach, chest, and arms until her whole body was chilled and heated, trapping her oddly between both sensations. She ignored Gannon's voice and outside sounds, all of which echoed in her drug hazed hearing. She didn't want to hear anyway—she was dreaming.

Hands ran across her tingling flesh, spreading the warmth and the cold as they passed. Up her arms, down to her hands, between her fingers, into her armpits, and across her breasts. The dripping wetness fell again, onto her face and forehead this time, and then the hands came and spread it across her face, around, behind, and even into her ears. Fingers ran across her closed eyelids, down the ridge of her nose, and across her tightly shut lips.

Marcia could not taste it, but she could smell it. She knew what it was. It was blood. But that was all right—this was a dream. The dripping went lower, falling upon her lower abdomen, hips, and upper legs. Next came the hands. As his hands reached in between her legs, brushing across her opening, Marcia opened her mouth, whether to speak or simply in shocked surprise; once open, she tasted the blood on her lips. A tangy, coppery taste that was both cold and warm.

Only a little entered her mouth before she closed it again, pressing her lips tightly together. The icy burn and cold chill of the small bit of blood filled her mouth and her throat but it didn't reach her fluttering stomach and her core. She lay there as the hands moved. He rolled her over, then rolled her back and went over areas he'd covered once already.

He left her for a time.

Marcia lay there as the chill and the heat soaked down into her body, deeper and deeper, as if it meant to burst her bones like frozen winter pipes and then burn the marrow to ash. While her insides mostly froze her skin mostly burned. The warmth of the blood on her skin wrapped around her like an electric blanket left on high. She sweated and froze and wished for the end of her dream.

Though unaware of it, she begged for death. She begged Gannon to kill her. She begged Kim to let her die. She begged anyone listening to shoot her and kill her. She begged as hands forced open her mouth and poured in blood, then held her mouth shut and pinched her nose shut roughly, forcing her to swallow what was in her mouth or drown.

Again and again she was forced to swallow the blood. She stopped resisting after a while, swallowing obediently and mindlessly as her mouth filled with fire and ice. She wasn't aware of when it ended or that she continued to swallow reflexively for some time before falling asleep, covered and filled, both inside and out, in the blood of a witch's undead heart.

Rabbit Warfare

Do——or Die. Die. Die.

M R. R. MADE a second, much more threatening call to Mr. Draper using another pilfered cell phone. He hauled it into a ventilation shaft to make his call. During his conversation he mentioned going to the press with everything he'd seen. R lied, saying that he had video recordings and had copies of incriminating computer files showing the abusive practices being allowed at the facility.

Unable to placate R. himself, Draper made a three-way call to the President (which was actually one of Draper's assistants posing as the President). Connected in this manner, they quickly agreed to a change in the leadership of the facility and in the treatment of its residents, starting with Katie. Both men stalled and made empty promise after empty promise to R, stretching out the time on the call while soldiers rushed to position themselves.

They struck simultaneously. One group sealed off the area where R was located so he would be trapped within a web-work of metal shafts that ran above five rooms they'd already evacuated. At the same time toxic gas was released into the vents at both sides of R's small warren. They left one avenue free of gas where soldiers waited at the vent, ready to capture Mr. R when he emerged from his rabbit hole. Mr. R continued talking as the shaft filled with gas, unbothered by whatever it was that they piped in.

"Ahh. Soldiers." R sounded resigned and hurt. "And gas again. Gas, gas, gas. You people are fond of gas. I see that you have no true interest in speaking to me. Your intent is clear. It was all lies."

Both men shouted their hollow denials into the phone.

"My Katie girl was right, right, right," R said sadly, "She already knows you've betrayed us—oh my poor Katie! She knows—she's going – going – going," R lamented as if she'd died just that instant. "I was such a fool! I argued with her, told her you would listen to me, that help was on the way, that I had found us friends. I told her to hold out hope."

"Mr. R! Please!" Draper implored. "Just come quietly."

"We'll call off the soldiers!" cried the "President" while at the same time Mr. R could hear soldiers working away at each end of the shaft. An odd, winding sound came from the smoke filled tunnel on the left.

"You can't possibly be this obtuse. You're mocking me intentionally!" Mr. R's high pitched voice sounded offended, intellectually insulted, and heartbroken all at the same time. "Your monstrous doctors have gutted Miss Susan, plan Katie's demise, and even now your soldiers attempt to ferret me out and destroy me. So forgive me for not being more reeeasonable!" R mocked back. "Should I sit here and listen to you promise me you are not killing me while you kill me!?"

"No one has gutted Susan! That's an outright fabrication, R!" Draper challenged.

"Of all people, YOU call ME a liar!" R shouted, aghast at the accusation. "I watched them cut Susan open with my own eyes, you lout!" R squeaked in shrill, furious outrage. "Do you now intend to tell me I did not see, see, see what I saw, saw, saw!? Did I dream it, Mr. Draper? While they cut on Susan they made their plans for Katie. Are you suggesting that I can no longer trust my own hearing as well? I assure you, I have excellent hearing!"

"I don't know what you heard or saw," the man posing as the President argued, "but none of this was approved by me! None of this was done on my orders. I can assure you of that!"

R continued as though he hadn't heard, "They said that my Katie was too dangerous to let live. I heard them – discussing how they should – *do it*. As medicine did not affect her they discussed alternative methods of execution. Shooting her from a distance they said was safest but too messy and might cause questions. Breaking her neck with a quick twist they said was too ugly. Smothering her with a pillow they liked a lot, but in the end, they both settled on the idea of pumping carbon monoxide gas into her cell. Yes, you murderers like gas, gas, gas."

"I'm sure it was just idle talk!" Draper said. "Idiots running their mouths. Please, Mr. R., listen to reason."

"You were right, right, right. It's all or nothing, my Katie!" Mr. R declared boldly. "It's time, time, time – a last daring leap – cards on the table – go for broke! All or nothing. Life or death! Sink or swim! Do or die, die, die!"

Trundling down the tunnel came a winding sound and a light, piercing the mist-filled, silver shaft like a laser beam. Draper and many others watched the video feed from the robotic crawler deployed by the soldiers and sent down the shaft to flush R out. They caught the briefest stirring of the air on the screen. There was the sound of a thump as the phone hit the bottom of the vent.

When the rolling robot reached the phone, investigating the last known position of the elusive Mr. R, they discovered that he'd chosen his spot deliberately. The vents at this particular small bend hadn't matched up perfectly during construction and a crack hadn't been soldered together properly. A four inch gap had been concealed with bright strips of silver tape. The finished product looked like metal and matched the rest of the tube easily at a glance, but the chewed open hole told the reality of shoddy construction and a quick, taped over fix.

There was no sign of Mr. R.

Leftovers

The Outside Bunny

Draper relayed parts of R's ominous call to Dyal and Ogburn. A hastily assembled collection of soldiers, scientists, and guards gathered in the hall outside Katie's cell door. Dyal and Dr. Ogburn planned to enter quickly to make sure Katie wasn't up to anything disastrous in her hiding place under the bed. Then they planned to move her to a more spacious and comfortable room, clean her up, and get her dressed and presentable before their facility was overrun and others got a good look at her and her current living conditions. Both men were panicked. Draper hadn't said anything, but then, why would he?

Two men entered Katie's tiny cell dressed in specially designed clear hazmat suits. Katie hadn't responded to the intercom since retreating to her private shelter beneath the bed over an hour ago. Dr. Tachi had vented in gas before entering in hopes of keeping Katie docile. The gas was a much gentler version of what had been used to break up the dance party, but it should have been more than enough to disorient a person as small as Katie, if the gas worked on her at all.

When one of the men lifted the hanging, blue cloth that concealed the gap beneath the bed, four, small, white forms exploded into action, launching out from under the bed. Heads turned to follow the tiny, fleeing rabbits. In one second the white streaks were clear of the open cell door and out in the overcrowded hallway.

Leftovers was smaller and slower than the others, but she knew she was slower. The Dust Bunnies were made for speed, she wasn't. She left two seconds behind the others, skirting the edge of the room instead of cutting across the middle where she might be seen by the cameras. Everyone's attention was on the other rabbits, facing the opposite direction as she reached the doorway.

She quickly scanned the busy sea of feet and legs before her, then made a daring bound and landed on someone's poorly sewn pants cuff. Instead of biting a hole in the material that might be spotted she squeezed between the loose stitches and burrowed in, her little body dropping to the bottom of the cuff. Leftovers felt the back and forth motion as the man ran, swinging/jarring. Swing and crash, Swing and crash, Swing and crash.

Leftovers listened to the men as they hunted the Dust Bunnies.

"One went that way!" cried a voice.

"Get it! There's one there! In the corner!" cried another voice.

"Where?"

"Over here!"

"There!" Leftovers heard dozens of voices shouting.

Jarring, flopping, crashing—and then vicious stomping. The sound of a shoe striking the ground and a jarring impact. Again and again. Leftovers felt it, as if she, herself, were the one doing the stomping.

"Got it!" cried the voice of the man she was on victoriously. "I got one over here!"

"What the hell is it?" asked another voice nearby. He sounded out of breath. "Whoa, man! Don't touch it, are you crazy? You don't want to end up like Marcia, do ya?"

"I'm just pointing at it. Look at that. There's something inside that thing. What's that red stuff?"

"The outside looks like toilet paper, but there's darker things inside it. It looks like blood."

"Man, that's creepy."

"This is more like science fiction than fantasy, Sherman. It reminds me of Aliens."

"Aliens?"

"Yeah, you know, the movie!"

"You there!" shouted another voice. "Back away from it!"

"All right," said the man she rode. "But I got some of this thing on my shoe. I don't want to track it up and down the hall."

"You got it on your shoe!?" The voice sounded alarmed.

A defensive "yeah!" answered back. "I stomped on it. Sue me."

"I'm going to need your shoe. Here, when I take it off I'll put one of these on your foot."

"What the hell is that, a king sized condom? I'm flattered, Roy, but my dick's not that big."

Laughs from other men nearby.

"Dammit, Sherman, stop playing around."

"Can't you just clean it off or disinfect it or something. These aren't company, they're mine!" Sherman complained. "They cost me a hundred and fifty bucks!"

"I don't give a shit. You, steady him while I take his shoe and slap this sleeve on his foot."

Leftovers crawled to the top of the cuff and found a spot that was comfortable to squeeze between the stitching. She was careful to keep her ears laid flat across her back and only let her nose and eyes peek out. She stared through a strange, plastic film. The shoe was gone, already resting in a glass box, and a clear, plastic sleeve had been slipped over the man's foot, past the cuff of his pants.

It was much harder to hear clearly though the screen of plastic. She could see through it and still make out some of the muffled words. She saw the white smudge on the floor, stained with red. She wondered which of the others was down there, dead and crushed.

Shouting broke out from some distance away. The man she was on and others nearby ran toward the noise in a pounding herd.

"Bang! Bang!"

"Bang! Bang! Bang! Bang!"

"Bang! Bang!"

Gunfire! Yelling and shouting and running. The man finally stopped at a crowd of shouting people. She couldn't sort out the noise through the plastic but congratulations were being passed around by the men. Eventually Leftovers caught a glimpse of another crushed Dust Bunny, as well as another bloody shape that looked like a second, much large rabbit, now visible as blood painted his body red.

After his escape, Mr. R had made his way to this section of the building where Katie was being held captive, then chewed a hole into the spongy, drop ceiling there in the hall near her cell. As the Dust Bunnies fled, R dropped through the hole and joined in the distracting, rabbit melee. He'd grabbed the one Dust Bunny who'd gone left down his corridor, picking her up with his own invisible teeth and racing down the hall as men kicked out with big, booted heels, trying to crush the bounding, floating Dust Bunny that they could still see.

R was amazing, bounding off people, rebounding off walls yet more people swarmed around him. He made a mad spring off someone's head to get up to his hole in the ceiling as the men unleashed a hail of bullets. When their weapons emptied, they stepped back and were immediately replaced by others, waiting their turn to empty their own guns.

Investigation of the remains confirmed that all four of the Bunnies they'd seen fleeing the room had indeed been destroyed, as had the mysterious Mr. R.. After the bio scare and the fear of a magically infectious disease of flesh eating ink, there was little sympathy for the crushed, toilet paper rabbits or the other bloody bunny ruin.

Worried voices whispered Marcia's name back and forth, asking the same questions. How is she doing? Is she still alive? Does anyone else have it?

Leftovers pulled her head from between the stitching and sank down to the bottom of the cuff as if pulled down by the gravity of responsibility. She lay there in the corner of the cuff, both surprised and not surprised at all, when she felt the stirring of life inside her. An impatient movement within her middle. She lay on her back, crying quiet bunny tears for her sisters she knew so briefly as she stroked her belly with her short front paws and cooed to it.

"Not yet. Not safe. We must hide, hide, hide. Wait, wait, wait," she whispered to the precious life she carried. Leftovers cooed softly—and hoped.

They discovered Katie Lynn's body under the bed. They took photos of the strange scene she'd made of her hidden sanctuary. Odd painted circles, squiggles, and a made up gibberish language scrawled here and there in places as well as a goodbye letter to her parents written out on the back wall. All of it was written in blood.

They discovered that one of the welds beneath the bed had a metal burr sticking out which she'd used to cut herself and get her needed art supplies—red ink. She'd made herself brushes from her own hair which had also been cut on the metal burr.

Men who looked like astronauts in clear, plastic protective gear pulled her from her hideaway. They were wheeling her cloth covered, naked corpse down the hall in a space age coffin when men in black uniforms began to pour into the facility and take change of everything, including the handling of Katie Lynn's body.

A stream of steely eyed scientists swarmed over all the research already underway as well as the remains of the crushed rabbits, carrying them to labs which were being filled with new equipment. The number of guards surrounding the facility had quadrupled. The number of staff and researchers within had quintupled. The place had been a bee hive of activity before, but now it was a bee hive being invaded by less than friendly black wasps.

Black Rain

Frustrated Love

AFTER REAMING ME out, Cathryn kissed me on my forehead and told me that she loved me.

"Make me a wet rag," she bid me.

A fine damp rag appeared instantly, suspended in the air between us. It was as if she'd made it herself.

"Bethany, Alana, go to your sisters."

Alana let go of me, as did Bethany. They didn't want to, but they obeyed without a squeak or a grumble. Cathryn had scared them too. She'd scared everyone. Mary wrapped her arms around Bethany, and of course, Emma received Alana in her own way, with an embrace and a passionate kiss that made the Londoners' eyes bug out of their sockets. Those poor uptight people, I thought as I watched their scandalized reaction to the kiss. Or (more to the point) their reaction to the kiss between two girls who'd just been called "sisters."

I watched them kiss for a moment but then my gaze drifted beyond them to the body lying still on the ground. The body of my Broken Beauty. Her pale lips were parted in death. Eyes closed. I hadn't even kissed her once. I should have kissed her when I had the chance. No matter what they would have said or called me. Why hadn't I kissed her?

I forced myself to look away, then I noticed my mother. Cathryn had paused mid-motion, her hand an inch from the floating rag as she studied me. I blinked and studied her as well. I felt like a long lost daughter. We both loved each other, but we needed to reacquaint ourselves after my unwanted absence. Two lifetimes was a long time to be away from your mother.

She took the rag from the air but stopped again to consider the angel kneeling upon my shoulder. I turned my head enough to see Taunwee kneeling there with her head bowed. Everything about her posture was utterly submissive. She wasn't looking my mother in the face. Cathryn appraised her for a moment, gave a small nod of satisfaction, and then turned her attention back to me without shooing her away as she had my sisters.

She combed through my hair with her fingers, brushing the stray strands out of my face, and her gentle, compassionate touch threatened to tip me back into uncontrolled tears, which I didn't need or want. She wiped at grime and tears with her rag. I could have cleaned myself with a thought, but I wanted her to clean me. To touch me.

She wore a strange expression on her face as she worked and kept staring into my face. She wasn't looking for dirt or smudges. I wondered what it was she was searching for and—oops! Just like that, the answer was mine, whether I wanted it or not. She was looking for the face of her goddess. I'd humbled myself so completely before her that she was having a hard time believing the goddess to whom she'd been praying these past few days still lived in me. That part of me that thought of the sun as nothing but a hot grain of sand smiled at her.

Cathryn's eyes fluttered wildly and she swooned.

She would have fallen straight backward had I not reached out to steady her. She quickly regained her legs and backed away a few steps as she fought to regain her composure, while reassuring my sisters and the guards who came rushing to her side that she was well. That I hadn't harmed her.

There had been no flash of light or clap of thunder to announce a divine visitation, but somehow that brief second of a smile from the Black Lion had been enough to change her. Cathryn's face began to glow and her hair shifted color like Taunwee's changeable mane, her golden, summer blonde tresses shifting to a crisp, radiant white. As soon as I stopped staring stupidly in dumb fascination and wanted it to stop, the changes reversed themselves. Cathryn's hair color returned to golden blonde and her face returned to its natural tone.

Cathryn stared at me and wrung the towel in her hands as she considered her next move. She ordered Taunwee away then sent in the troops. First, she sent Emma to touch me and reclaim this new version of "me" with her magic. I did not resist Emma's attempt to take me as I had with Pan. I did just the opposite. I welcomed her power and pulled in all she gave. The girl I was wanted to be owned by her, and so she (the human girl) was.

Once Emma was done, Cathryn sent Mary. She carefully avoided that part of me that was the Black Lion, looking only at that part of me that was a girl named Rain, a girl she could know and comprehend. She pulled in the jumble of mixed and partial memories that was that girl and tried to make sense of it. The only thing I purposefully kept back were my human memories of Pan's grape and his magic, but the longing I still felt for Broken seemed to affect Mary as it did me. The moment she was done searching through the mess inside my head she looked toward Broken's body lying on the meadow floor not fifteen feet from where we stood with her own mix of emotions.

When she turned back to me she managed a half believable smile.

"You did the right thing, Rain," she encouraged. "Even if it sucked. Let's raise Gretchen and let her go chill with the other freaked out newbies. Don't worry, we can meet her all over again," she encouraged with a small smile.

Instead of a prisoner who looked like a rabid animal that needed to be put down for the greater good of all humanity, the guards carried in one of our horrifying, quadruple amputee captives who also happened to be an innocent faced youth. And, of course, it was too much to ask that he be foul mouthed and defiant. Noo. He was pathetic. Begging and crying like a baby.

My mother, my sisters, and a number of the others from Amen Hale cast suggestive and even pleading glances my way. They wanted me to gag and silence our cherry-cheeked sacrifice with magic as I had some of our other outspoken sacrifices. I saw their glances, but some part of me didn't want to do it. Whether it was a new part or an old part, human or divine, I had no clue, but whatever this feeling was and wherever it came from, I went with it.

Hearing his pathetic voice was painful, like a penance. Listening to the kid wail sent chills up and down my spine and made me feel soul deep dirty. With a thought I drew him into the air and held him there for Bethany. Watching a man without hands and feet getting stretched taut by invisible cords was far more disturbing than seeing the same done to a man who was whole – hands and fingers – feet and toes.

Man/boy hung there in the air making a stubby, human X. It was a shockingly ugly scene, even to me, but this was the price that had to be paid. I ran a concerned eye over our refugees as Bethany began. Some of them were getting sick, as the sights and sounds affected their heart and bodies like physical blows, hitting stomachs and soft places in their mind. I worried that the head shots might be doing permanent damage.

They'd withstood a number of horrors tonight, but this really seemed to be hitting the mark. Wives buried their faces in their husbands' chests, leaving the pinched faced, squint-eyed men to watch for both of them. I noticed Cricket, standing between Meridith and her daughter Robin. All three women looked grim and deathly pale as they held hands and watched in silence.

Before the sacrifice began, Cathryn told the refugees that Amen Hale did not sacrifice innocents, and only those who attacked Amen Hale or one of the Children of Hale would ever face this kind of fate.

"An innocent face is not an innocent heart," she said, her face and voice void of mercy despite the pleading wails of the prisoner she was forced to speak over.

I was sure Cathryn's words were the glue holding these people together as Bethany's blade arched through the air. Man/boy shrieked and shrieked as blood spilled out onto the ground and onto Bethany. The pathetic cries slowed, then finally ended. The Londoners took it all with the usual, stoic, English attitude.

Bethany dropped to the ground and wallowed in the blood of the sacrifice and rose wearing half the meadow. Dirt, twigs, and leaves covered her like a morbid, forest cloak that shone wetly in the pale light of the place. She looked suitably terrifying as she took her place above the body she intended to raise and addressed the nearby crowd of shocked Londoners.

"If you loved this girl, come add your blood to the raising." They shrank back as a group, not liking the sound of that at all.

"I beg your pardon?" Elspeth inched forward, daring to speak for the whole.

Bethany used her best "Princess" voice as she explained what she was doing and why it was needed. "If people who knew her and loved her when she was alive also give some of their own blood it helps the raising. We want her to come back to life, and life is in the blood. Blood has a memory, a flavor, and its own little spark of spirit. Blood remembers things: sins, sickness, sorrow, and especially love."

She was a tiny thing, barely fourteen, but even bloody and dirty she stood straight and proud and spoke with such grace and presence that watching her made me smile and swell with pride. Her own tail swayed behind her. My little Lion. Bethany was mine now. I knew what I was feeling was a mother's pride for her daughter.

"You don't have to be afraid. It's just a cut on the wrist and it really will help," her sweet voice encouraged. "If you know her, you should come help her."

Conversations broke out. They dithered, but after a few minutes still no one stepped out. Believer's arms tightened around me, sensing my growing tension.

"You should not do this," he grumbled. "You should stay away from her."

"But I love her!" I said. It was the truth. "And they're too damned chicken to help!" Also the truth.

He looked torn as to what to do and more than a little angry as I glanced toward the Londoners. He didn't fight me as I pulled away but his eyes were hot with worry. I ignored the whispering, chicken shit Londoners as I knelt beside Broken's body—Gretchen's body! Gretchen's body! Gretchen's body! Gretchen's body!—I repeated in my head as I stretched out my hand.

Doubts began to creep in. Should I be doing this? The girl they were raising was Gretchen, a girl I'd never met before. But my Broken was still inside this girl.

Did I even love Gretchen? Did she love me?

Bethany slid the blade across my upturned wrist before I could think to reconsider my offer. People gasped in surprise as glowing blood the color of yellow, liquid sunlight poured from my wrist and fell onto Gretchen's face and chest. It wasn't gold in color or orange like OJ; it was more yellow like some nuked up version of Sunny Delight.

Bethany laughed in delight! "Cool!" she said.

Her dark eyes glittered in excitement as she played with glowing blood on her blade, running her fingers down it and even tasting it.

I'd died twice, so my blood had changed again, and then again. It was brighter now than before and a different shade. Less gold and more yellow sunshine. I hoped Dan and Jane liked the new flavor but I wasn't too worried. It seemed that Bethany liked it just fine. She kept sneaking guilty, little handfuls to her mouth like a kitten stealing someone else's milk.

Mr. Tippins, the detective, suddenly knelt on the other side of Gretchen's body. He was already wincing in anticipation of pain as he rolled up his sleeve and extended his arm. For a moment I worried at his connection to the girl. Mr. T was a married man, and Gretchen a teenage girl.

Bethany didn't give me time to ask. Not that I would have with his wife looking on from less than ten feet away. The knife moved in a quick, sure stroke and his red, human blood mixed with my bright, yellow blood that wasn't dimming nearly so quickly as it once had. Our blood covered her face, neck, and chest, soaking into the beautiful, black dress I'd made for her.

"Gretchen's a sweet girl. A little mouthy, but that was just for show. She's watched our wild brood too many times ta count. It was a good side job for her when she needed a spot of extra cash. She was studying to be a dental hygienist..."

Mr. Tippins rambled on as we bled together companionably. My weird blood was making her body glow. My mind began to drift with the strangeness of everything. Something about kneeling on the leaf-littered ground as Mr. T droned on made me feel like we were camping, warming our hands over a glowing fire.

The air suddenly smelled of the forest and outdoors.

A light breeze began to blow across my world.

Had I wanted a breeze?

Did I make it?

Don't burn! No fire!

I looked down in alarm, not knowing what I expected or feared I'd see, but she wasn't burning. Thank God! My mental wandering and Mr. T's rambling ended when Bethany unleashed her magic. It danced upon our skin like a frigid embrace from death itself before she shouted, "Rise!"

The cuts on our wrists closed up, and beneath our hands the body twitched. I closed my eyes as Gretchen's eyes squinted tight beneath the mask of blood covering her face.

"Uugh – wha – where am I?" I listened as she spat and coughed.

I kept my eyes closed, but I could imagine her face and her disgust at finding herself covered in blood.

"Easy, Giggy, sa'll right now," Mr. Tippens soothed. "You gave us a bit of a scare there, but you're all right now."

"Mr. T. Is that you? What's all over me! Get it out of me eyes!"

"Here. Here!" Ambrosia's voice. "Take this to clean her face."

"Is this blood!? It tastes like blood, but it's glowing. Why is it glowing!?" I could practically see her fingers wiping at the mess in ever increasing horror.

"Why am I bleeding!?" she demanded.

"It's not your blood! It's Mr. T's blood and hers." I recognized Mrs. Tippens' stern, maternal voice.

"Don't forget that other poor chap," added some idiot from somewhere. "He certainly did his part."

"What the hell am I wearing!?" Gretchen shouted. "Who the hell undressed me!? Oh my God. Is this some kind of a wedding dress!? This looks like a wedding dress."

"It's not a wedding—"

"It is!" she shouted. "What kind of sick, black ritual have you evil, old hags done now! You've married me off to that Devil girl to save your own sorry hides, haven't ya!? You have! You have! I know you have, you filthy, lying hags!" She started to cry.

I couldn't take any more. I rose to my feet and swiftly walked back toward Believer and my sisters. I heard the surprised voices behind me as the blood covering Gretchen, the ground, Bethany, and the others simply vanished. Gretchen's black dress shifted and transformed into a modest, blue gown made of a thicker and plusher version of magic fabric. Something much less sheer. Something comforting and concealing. Something modest.

I hadn't taken advantage of her. I hadn't even kissed her! Upon her tender, bare feet appeared some soft, fitted slippers and around her neck appeared a silver chain on which hung a circular shaped locket the size of a silver dollar.

My sisters and mother saw the hurt on my face that I'd hidden from the girl and the others at my back. Believer positioned himself behind me, blocking off their view as I fought hurt feelings for this girl who no longer remembered me or Tail. Tail liked to dance. Who knew? I hadn't. But Broken had. Dancing with Tail wasn't crazy to her. Who would even think to dance with Tail now? With that thought, I started to cry.

My mother took charge.

"Believer, I'll need a few minutes to finish with these people," meaning the refugees. She frowned as she studied my tear streaked face. "Rain will need to go and fetch Jane and Dan as soon as I'm done with them. Go do what you can to calm her down and distract her, but don't let go of her for a second. Hold her in your arms and don't let her feet touch the ground until I send for her—and get her farther away from that girl," she growled.

My head snapped back to my mother as if I'd been caught in mischief. I hadn't even realized I'd turned back, trying to catch a glimpse of Broken. Of Gretchen.

Without so much as a "Yes, Mother," Believer reached over everyone's heads and lifted me straight up and away from the clinging arms of my sisters, quickly skulking away with my body like a thief while the girls cried out and complained. I lay in the cradle of his arms and gazed upward, staring off into the starless darkness above me as I did my best to banish the last of my tears over Broken.

Believer moved us away from the drama as far as our island would permit, which wasn't all that far. We stopped close enough to the edge that I could hear the whispered singing and the brooding melody of my damned. I listened as they worshiped me in the only way they could. The steady sound was a comfort and helped calm my mind. I sent this thought to them, not caring if that knowledge gave them comfort or pain.

Believer didn't say a word; he let me lie there in his arms and rest. He was watching me, as always. I think he could tell I was enjoying the singing, so he stayed quiet and let me listen. A hum and a flutter of troubled air preceded the gentle impact of someone very small landing on my chest and neck. I sighed happily as I felt Taunwee position herself at the hollow of my throat, lying back flat against my flesh until she was looking upward into the darkness with me while Believer cradled both of us in his arms. It felt good having her on me. I liked it.

"How are you, my lovely Star?" I asked her.

"I am well, my Goddess. While you were seeing to the raising I spent some time with your sisters."

"That's nice. Did you talk to Mary?"

"Yes," she confirmed unhappily. "She bade me to come to her, but when I lighted on her shoulder a magical fit seized her. I would have fled but her magic held me fast until she regained herself. She was still somewhat disoriented after her episode, and she said a number of troubling things."

"Hmm," I sighed. "Bad news?"

"She said that Cathryn was my mother now." She paused to gauge my reaction, then went on. "I did not deny her claim at the time because I did not know if you wished me to correct her."

I couldn't see her down there, but I felt the stillness of her body as she paused to study me again. She relaxed, apparently she'd gotten her answer from my lack of surprise or objection.

"I will submit to Cathryn as to a Queen, and a mother, for that is obviously your will, but pretending to be her daughter will be childish and vexing and obeying her commands will be quite dangerous."

That last part caught my ear. "Dangerous?" I made it a question.

"Extremely. Cathryn is mad." She laid it out there plain as day. Angel style bluntness. Not human. "I understand her heartache and some of the events that forged this scene here today, but it is dangerous and foolish for us to submit ourselves to her in all things. What if she commands us to do something that we do not wish to do, my Goddess?"

I laughed. "Of course she's going to command us to do shit we don't want to do, that's what mothers do, Taunwee. And most mothers *are* crazy. Their children make them that way." I rightly took responsibility for my mother's meltdown.

Taunwee squirmed on my neck, though she tried to pass it off as if she were merely readjusting herself and getting more comfortable. "What if she asks us to obey some command born out of her madness?" she argued. "What would you wish for me to do? And what would you do, my Goddess?"

"Taunwee," I asked, "does Cathryn feel like your mother?"

Her tiny body went rigid. "How could I possibly know?" she almost sounded angry. "Cathryn is fifty years at most. She's a child herself. She did not give me birth, so there is no reason I should feel a connection to her. But I will not lie to you, my Goddess. I will never lie to you," she said grimly. "When I look at her, I feel – something." Those last words were punctuated by a shiver. "Cathryn is my Queen. I will submit to her, for this is your will, but it will be impossible for me to think of her as my mother, so with your permission I will pretend it is so. And I will pretend with your sisters as well. The relationship will be childish, make believe, and fantasy, but I will pretend that it is real. And though I may be deceiving them, and myself, I will not be deceiving you. I would kill and murder for you, and I will do this for you as well. I will pretend that Cathryn is my mother and I will play with your sisters and call them my sisters. I will be a silly girl with them and another daughter for her. I will be anything you need me to be. *Anything.*" She swore with all her heart. "I am yours."

My own heart squeezed tight as I listened to her. Believer made a worried grumble at my unease, which I ignored. I wondered how long it would be before she realized that her pretend life was her real one. Killing and murdering for me would be easy compared to what was coming. Playing, having fun, and submitting to someone and trusting them with your heart were so alien to her.

"If pretending helps you, then pretend, my Star. Pretend. I know your heart."

"What else did Mary say that disturbed you?" Believer spoke to Taunwee himself, interrupting our tense conversation and moving things along in another direction.

"She knew about my human Roe, Benson," Taunwee said, sounding a little miffed and jealous which made me smile. "When I called him young she laughed at me as if I were a fool and said that *he* was older than *me*! She said that in Golgotha I would still be as old as the Dawn and a Queen, but in Amen Hale I would be a seventeen-year-old girl, a Princess, and a child of Cathryn and Cornelius. Does she truly know all my life and every secret I hold simply because she touched me?" She sounded horrified at the thought, but before I could respond she continued. "Mary introduced me to the Captain of your guard as Princess Taunwee Calla Hale. She knew the name that you gave me. She even spoke a few words to me in perfect Twilin, and then she called me 'beloved sister' in the tongue of Angels."

"Taunwee, after me and maybe our Mother, you'll have no greater confidant or friend than our Mary. They'll be no need to pretend anything with her," I assured her, trying to make that sound like a good thing because it was. Pretending was wearisome. "When no one else understands you or your problems, she will. Once she touches you, she knows you and loves you and cares about you in ways that are just beautiful. If you don't believe me, spend some time with her."

Taunwee's little body stiffened. Was she pissed or just freaked? Or intrigued maybe?

"You mentioned something about Golgotha. Is this some new place?" Believer asked Taunwee, changing the subject again like a conversational traffic cop waving around flashlights with orange cones stuck on the ends as he directed or redirected.

Her entire frame quivered as she answered. "Golgotha is what Princess Mary has named the world the Goddess created for the Twilins."

"What!?" I barked so loudly I bounced Taunwee into the air like a sprung trampoline. "Are you sure?" I asked as she plopped, gracelessly back onto my neck, flat on her back.

"She said that Golgotha is what you will name our world. Though she said you would often shorten it to Gotha for the sake of those she lightly referred to as 'the squeamish.'"

"Why on earth would I want to name it that!?" My own frame quivered in Believer's arms as if I'd caught Taunwee's chill. "Holy shit!" I busted out, then once again with more feeling, "HO-LY SHIT!" I lamented loudly and blasphemously.

The phrase seemed twistedly appropriate. I mean—Golgotha! Even the thought made me want to run and hide under a rock. I was floored at Mary's audacity. Sunday school, Vacation Bible camps, Bible Clubs on Wednesdays, and all those Bible conferences Rain Marie endured with her family—all of it had filled our head with an amazing array of information. Those million and one crumbled up bits seemed to keep finding odd moments to prove themselves relevant.

I knew that Golgotha was a second name for the hill outside Jerusalem that was more commonly called Calvary. It was there that the Son of God died on a cross to save fallen man from their sins. That rocky, rounded hill was also called by another name in another language, Golgotha, because that hill actually looked like a skull from a short distance away. In that language the word Golgotha actually meant "the place of a skull."

So yeah. Okay. In a purely etymological sense I could see it. But just because the world I created happened to be inside my skull didn't mean I had to name the place Golgotha—did it? And just because I accidentally killed myself as I made that place didn't mean I died to save them—even if I did—*did it*?

Believer, seeing that I was struggling and deep in thought, stepped in again. "You know that Mary sees names before they are named, but if this name troubles you then give your world some other name—if you can."

His deep voice scattered my worried thoughts like wind blown leaves. He made the "if you can" a flat out challenge. I looked up at him and laughed, drawn in by the warm wells of his smiling eyes and by the crazy complex humor of his challenging question. I knew what he was doing and I loved him all the more for it. My conversational traffic cop. An image of him in a rain coat waving those cones danced before me. Mother had told him to keep me calm and distracted and he was trying. He tried so hard to take care of me.

"What'd ya mean, if I can?" I answered playfully, finally giving him my full attention. "You don't think I can call it something else now that Mary's said I'll name it Golgotha? You think my hands are tied by destiny now? Is this some kind of test? Like asking God if He can make a rock so big He couldn't pick it up?"

Believer laughed, his red eyes drank me in as he smiled down at me. His mouth was still just a long gash across his face where a mouth would normally be, but I noticed that he'd added some finely textured shadows around the edges which made his mouth and smile more expressive. Cloud crafted brows perched in happy triangles above his glowing red eyes that looked like smoldering coals.

For a small instant I lost myself in his face. Every hour he seemed to be getting more adept at manipulating his clouds to help him communicate his emotions.

"Tempting a god is never a wise thing to do," he said in his deep, rumbling voice. "And I do not think Golgotha is a name Mary would have chosen or come up with on her own."

"Yeah, yeah, smarty pants. I know."

"You know I don't wear pants," he teased. That reminder made me look at his chest and the pulsing glow deep inside his body that most people mistakenly believed was some type of magical equivalent to a heart, beating away. Believer had shown me on our wedding night what he kept hidden down inside his clouds. It wasn't his heart, but when he put it inside me it made me feel as if my whole body became a heart for him.

It had been so long since I had floated in his clouds, surrounded entirely by him, breathing him into my lungs as he held me and touched every part of me at the same time, inside and out, as only he could. My mind drifted toward hungry thoughts but Taunwee was still keyed into what we'd been discussing.

"Can you not look into the future yourself and see if this is true? If Mary can see into the future, surely you can do the same and more."

"I don't mess with the future anymore."

"Why not?" Taunwee asked.

"I keep my thoughts on the here and now. I live in the moment. And this is a very good moment." I ran a hand across Believer's chest where pulses of white light snuck around a mass of darker, grayish clouds. I knew why he kept those darker clouds parked and swirling right there. If someone were to get a clear view of that glowing mass down inside his body it would be easy to see a rather suggestive shape.

Believer's body was androgynous on the outside. He had no sexual organs to mark him male or female because his sexual "organ" was not hung on the outside of his body like a human male, but on the inside of his body where he could keep it hidden within his clouds. And where he would use it, as he held me within those same clouds.

Taunwee stood up. I felt her anxious energy. She was still fired up. I knew she wanted to keep harping on the future "thing," but my mind was on a different "thing."

"If you can see the future," she spoke as she paced, "would it not be far safer to look ahead and know what dangers you faced instead of blindly walking into them?"

"I used to do that," I confessed. "When I was the Black Witch I could smell death coming before it arrived. I started to plan things out so death didn't take the ones I loved."

"That's wonderful," Taunwee encouraged warmly. "Would it not be wise to continue that practice and to watch the future for other dangers, like Pan and his poison grapes?"

Her tiny feet continued pacing back and forth. She meant well, trying to play teacher to her hesitant goddess, but this was something I'd already decided for myself.

"I don't want to know the future."

"Why?"

"I don't want to know! Taunwee, I want to hope!" I said with growing passion. "I want to be surprised! I want to worry over what might happen. I want to be afraid because it's human to be afraid. I want to be amazed when something freaky busts loose. Not knowing makes each moment important, but knowing would make that same moment a prescheduled appointment filled with places I must be and things I must do and disasters that I'm either causing or stopping. By living in the moment I'm just another ignorant piece of the big puzzle, bumping about with everyone else and trying to make the best of things. I love, I hurt, I laugh, I bleed. Taunwee," I gave her a big sigh, "I'm not giving up my 'shit happens' t-shirt."

"You are trying to be too human," she insisted stubbornly.

"Ignorance is bliss," was my smart-ass comeback.

"We are supposed to keep her calm," Believer interjected, windmilling his conversational caution cones.

I felt Taunwee's wings flutter in frustration. She pressed ahead boldly, ignoring Believer's gripe.

"What if you can avoid another trap? What if Lucifer is even now waiting for you to pick up your vampires before he strikes?" She stopped pacing suddenly. "Are you afraid to embrace this power because of your accident in the graveyard? You will not make the same mistake again. I am here to help guide you. It will not kill you to look toward the future!" she pleaded, emotionally now. She was letting more and more of her emotions show. She sounded so – human.

"Actually, it might kill me," I said, pulling no punches and being "angel" blunt myself, as if we'd switched places. "What if I see a horrible fate waiting for me and no way to escape? How could I live or enjoy what life I have left knowing that? To be honest, I don't know why God allows my presence here," I admitted. "But whatever the reason, I'm glad, and I try not to cause a mess or make waves, but it's getting harder every day. More and more people are wanting to follow me and sooner or later something's bound to give, even with me keeping a low profile. If I start messing with time, I think that would be the last straw. That little peek you're proposing might be the last peek I ever take."

Believer's deep voice took up my own thoughts but he made it a little more personal. "If Rain had used her power to know the future, she would not have killed your people in the graveyard and caused herself that horrible grief. Your people would have remained hidden, and therefore, you would not be here. And if she knew about this possible future a week ago she would have taken her place with Grandfather God and joined her human family in worshiping him. If she did not live in the present, I would not be here, you would not be here, she would not be here, and Amen Hale would not exist as it does today."

Believer leaned closer and shifted his gaze up, from Taunwee who stood on my neck to me. "You have chosen to live in the moment, and I have chosen to live with you, here in this moment. And every moment with you is precious to me. I have what I want and need right here in my arms. As you said, this moment, is a good moment. But perhaps I can make it even better."

I felt my face flush with surprise as he turned me in his arms and started to slip me into his cloudy body in a very provocative legs first orientation. I couldn't look up to see his face because my eyes were glued onto his chest as the swirling clouds parted, giving me a clear view of what was waiting down inside his clouds. I held my breath as he brushed that hidden part of himself along my legs and rubbed against the inside of my thighs.

My mouth went dry and my heart began to race as memories of our first and only time together began to flash through my head. I'd just about lost my mind that night! Believer's hands cupped my head and his outstretched arms supported my back as I hung, half inside his body and half out with absolutely nothing between me and him. For the first time in a long time I was incredibly aware that all I had on was a loin cloth! I reached behind my head and grabbed onto his hands as he lowered me, ever so slowly, further in while he played himself up and down the inside of my legs.

Somehow, I knew he was enjoying himself, watching me from above. Watching my face as all I was feeling flitted by. The embarrassment, the fear, the hunger, the awkwardness. He kept at it until I knew he was torturing me on purpose and drawing things out. I gritted my teeth and squirmed for him. It was maddening! Half of me wanted to scream "Just do it!" but the other half was too frightened to speak.

Taunwee bounded off her unstable perch on my chest, getting clear of what was about to happen.

"I thought we were supposed to keep her calm," Taunwee prodded from wherever she hovered nearby.

"And distracted," Believer added smugly. "Very distracted."

"You would bed her here? Now? In this place? Before everyone?" Taunwee sounded shocked and surprisingly prudish.

"Yes. Yes. Yes. And yes," his deep voice answered happily.

"Yes-ooo! Mmmm! Mm!" My own "yes" morphed into moans as Believer started to rub himself around my opening teasingly. The clouds inside his body began to draw my legs apart, spreading me open. Tail was still mostly out here with me, going wild, squeezing, frisking, and swishing about.

"Awh! NO! Grrr!" Believer grumbled loudly. I looked up and saw that he was scowling and angry!

"Oh my God! What'd I do?" I asked, baffled as to how I could have offended him. But then I heard it myself.

"Hey! Come on back, guys!" They were calling for us.

The clouds within Believer's body began releasing their hold upon my legs. "No!" I shouted, experiencing my own wild flash of frustration at being interrupted. "Just put it in for a minute!" I begged pathetically. I began to reach inside his clouds to get my hands on him but I was a moment too slow.

Believer began to laugh.

I looked up to see what his frikin' deal was only to find it written all over his face. He looked exactly like a teenage boy, smugly pleased with himself. My reaction had amused him. He quickly schooled his emotions, looking suddenly worried and almost frightened at my intense scrutiny. Worried at how I was about to react. I was a little pissed, but more that that, I was captivated by what I'd seen in his face before he gave in to worrying about me. He looked so – very – *human*. Immature, adolescent, stupid, guy – even jerk—human.

More human than me.

Goosebumps broke out on my flesh.

He lifted me out of his body and set me on my own two feet but held onto me. I think to steady me, but I didn't know. Maybe he just wanted to hold me. Who knew?

"Mom said to come back!" Bethany said as she ran up to us, then stopped suddenly, looking worried as she tried to figure out the mixed up mood of the moment.

"Sorry, my love," Believer apologized for some reason. Was he embarrassed I'd seen some of his baser human nature? He attempted a smile. "You did say that you liked surprises," he offered, rather sheepishly.

Bethany leapt skyward in a powerful, cat-like bound, and Believer collected her easily with one arm as she climbed up and snuggled into him. Again, I watched his face as he smiled at Bethany. Our daughter. I saw it again. So very, very human. It gave me the chills as I thought again that I'd almost had to live without that "human" part of myself.

"You guys aren't fighting are you?" She frowned as she eyed the two of us. "What surprise did he give you?"

"Not the one she was expecting," Taunwee answered Bethany's question from where she hovered in the air beside me. I think she was trying not to laugh. "You should go, my goddess. You don't want do disobey your mother." She landed on my shoulder, smiling up at me as she rubbed it in. So very human. She sounded like a teenage girl.

"Our mother," I reminded her, then headed obediently in that direction. Because she was right. I didn't want to disobey.

Dining Hall Discourse

MERIDITH AND AMBROSIA kept a watchful eye on Gretchen who sat on the bench, sandwiched between them. Robin and Cricket sat on the other side of the table facing them. Sharply dressed servants rushed about, striving to seat and serve the unexpected crowd in the high ceilinged Dining Hall.

"We're so glad you're here," said the man filling Cricket's glass with American style "cold" iced tea. "And from what I'm told, you're all witches. That's wonderful!" He beamed at them. "You'll adapt to the household far better than some of the others."

"And what, exactly, do you mean by that?" Ambrosia asked with a sour expression. "Hmm?"

"Oh, nothing – just making friendly conversation," the server answered vaguely then quickly moved on down the table, filling other glasses with the pitchers he carried.

A man with a black, leather duster coat, shiny, red shirt, and short, spiky, black hair stopped beside their table next to Gretchen. "Hello, Gretchen. My name is Lucius." He put a hand out to shake hers. His left hand. "I hear you died today," he said with an easy smile.

Gretchen nodded, looking troubled by the subject of conversation and the man himself. He was an impressive and imposing figure. Both handsome and mysterious. Gretchen said nothing; she simply stared at him with wide, frightened eyes. He leaned closer as if to share a confidence. With a hand held close between their two faces he pointed up to the High Table where a number of the Lords and Ladies of Amen Hale were seated with the King and Queen.

"See that woman with the crown of fire on her head?" He pointed, though she'd be hard to miss.

"Yes."

"That is Lady Dana. She died today for the second time and was raised again. She's been through it twice now." He pointed to others. "So did Princess Alana; she's died twice too." He pointed again, all the others at the table now following the conversation, looking where he pointed. "King Cornelius was raised days ago; he was the first to be raised. Oh, and Izzy, that one there. Princess Emma, she died too. And Penny, that little black girl there, she died today, and so did I." He stuck his pointing finger through a hole punched into the front of his shiny, red shirt. "The bullet went in right there."

"You died today?" Gretchen asked, surprised.

"Sure did."

"What on earth is going on around here!?" Ambrosia demanded with an indignant scowl for Lucius. "Does this type of carnage happen every day in Amen Hale?" she puffed. "Should we be issued flak jackets and helmets?!"

Lucius regarded Ambrosia's imperious expression with a dark smile of his own. "Today has been a little worse than usual," he admitted. "It seems we had some people casting curses at us and praying for us to die all day long. You wouldn't happen to know anything about that, would you?"

He turned away from Ambrosia's surprised, puckered mouth and back to Gretchen. "If you need to talk to someone, I'd say go to Lady Dana," he suggested, then grinned. "But be ready to have your ears heat up if you do. She cusses like a sailor." Frightening encouragement delivered, the man walked away.

The women were quiet, all sharing the same, sick expressions as they took in Lucius's words. They considered the deaths and looked again at the High Table, at all the faces. All those people—dead, dead, dead, dead, dead.

"We deserve to be here," Gretchen said, sounding miserable and looking sickened at herself. Accepting of judgment.

Cricket, Robin, and even Meridith nodded in somber agreement. Ambrosia on the other hand did not. She sniffed. She hadn't spat in the damned cauldron and she wasn't pleased to be stuck in this damnable situation. She'd never really given much thought to her privileged status before, she'd simply always had it. The other women were working class, but Ambrosia had been born to money, married it (twice), and outlived both her husbands. The only work she'd ever engaged in was finding new and interesting ways to give her own money away. She was accustomed to a lifestyle of wealth and luxury and now it seemed that she was fated to be nothing but a common laborer. A servant. The thought disgusted her more than she'd like to admit.

"Everyone's so friendly," Robin said. "The people seem glad to have us here."

Everyone had gone out of their way to welcome them, the doormen, the servers, the cooks, the men working out on the patio when they had first entered the building (cleaning up what looked like blood). Even Lucius's odd attempt at counseling with Gretchen was obviously well intentioned. The other citizens of Amen Hale they'd seen who didn't seem currently engaged in some task or other also seemed happy to have them there. Despite the situation behind their need for refuge, no one shot them dark looks or sinister scowls. All in all, they felt very— wanted.

Ambrosia fanned herself and pouted. Lucius's dour revelations were more salt in a wound she felt she didn't deserve. She'd gone along with the others and given her oath of lifelong service to Queen Cathryn, but she'd done it in that horrible place, surrounded by beasts and hideous creatures. The words had come easily from her lips with the echoes of the dying man they'd sacrificed still ringing in her ears and her vision stained with imagined or remembered flashes of crimson. Time had lessened her shock. That queer, dreamlike moment had faded and bitterness had set in.

"I don't see how anyone could eat after all we've seen today," Ambrosia complained, then reached for her empty glass. She sniffed again. Louder. It was the third time she'd reached for it to find it still in the "empty" condition. "The service seems a wee bit slack," she complained tartly then noticed that the other women had ceased their conversations and were staring at her. She stiffened defensively. "What?! Don't get prickly with me!" she challenged. "I'm not eating, not after what I've seen today, but I like having my cup full. Since when is that a crime!?"

Robin looked around the room. There were over a hundred men and women seated in the dining hall, plus the dozen or so who were currently seated at the High Table with the King and Queen of Amen Hale. The servers did look stretched thin, rushing about as they tried to see to their own people and this unexpected crowd of new faces who'd just walked in from the garden unexpectedly.

She stood up.

"Are you all right, girl?" her mother asked.

"I'm fine Meri – Mum." Robin smiled at her mother. She was still getting accustomed to calling her mother "mum" instead of "Meridith." "Really, Mum, I'm fine." She kissed Cricket on the head and walked away, passing through the doors that led toward the kitchens for some reason.

"What's gotten into her?" Ambrosia said, concerned by the odd behavior.

"Should I go get her, Ganna?" Cricket asked.

"No, child. Leave her be," Meridith told her, though she was curious herself as to what her daughter was about.

Five minutes later the servants started to bring out the salads and fruit bowls, and Robin was there with them. She was dressed in a black and white uniform like the rest, hair already slicked back and pinned up. She was smiling and seemed happy as she helped deliver food to tables, but they could see tears on her face as she served.

Gretchen got up and walked off toward the kitchen without saying a word to anyone. Cricket stood up as well, obviously meaning to follow.

"Sit back down, young lady!" Ambrosia snapped at her. "You're too young to be serving. You're just a child for goodness sake!"

Cricket glared at her in embarrassment and anger.

Meridith was silent, watching the tension between the two but not interfering.

"But today was my naming day, Aunty Am," she said, as if that mattered.

"Yes. I'm very proud of you." Ambrosia didn't sound proud.

Cricket's faced hardened. "I spat in a black cauldron and called a killing curse today, Aunty Am," she argued quietly, but her voice rose steadily as she continued. "I faced monsters and nightmares and went to a place that was not a place! I saw a man sacrificed and a girl raised from the dead!"

Ambrosia waved her hands and urged her to be quiet and sit, but Cricket's voice grew even louder, drawing more attention to herself.

"I took my oaths of service with the adults! Not the children! I am a witch!" she shouted. Cricket stilled as she noticed the quiet.

She looked up.

No one was moving. All eyes were now on her. She turned in a slow circle, letting her defiant gaze rake the hall before looking back at the table and seeing the hurt and heartbroken expression on Ambrosia's face. Cricket didn't break down into tears at the sight. And she didn't run to Ambrosia and fall on her neck. And she did not ask to be forgiven for yelling. Cricket held onto her anger, letting it warm her.

Without a backward glance she turned and walked toward the kitchen. Half the room didn't notice that the double kitchen doors swung open for her on their own as if they were automatic doors at a department store. But half the room did notice.

Five other, new arrivals rose to their feet and followed Cricket's example. They paused at the doors as if they expected them to open, but after an embarrassing delay they ended up opening the doors themselves and walking through.

The two, old women now sat alone at their end of the table. They stared at each other silently.

Ambrosia sulked and nursed her hurt feelings.

Meridith pretended not to notice.

"I suppose you want us to go join them," Ambrosia said, sick of the silence.

"Am, my back's too bent and your ass is too fat," Meridith said wearily. She studied her veined and weathered hands on the table in front of her and added, "We're too damned old. Let the girls see to things."

Ambrosia sniffed. "I suppose you're right."

After a few more minutes Robin reached their table with their salads. Very nice looking salads. Ambrosia took one (she didn't want to be rude). And then a smiling Cricket arrived at the table in her new, black and white uniform with a chilled bottle of white wine already opened and breathing for her aunt and a cup of hot, Earl Gray for her grandmother.

Leftovers

A Safe Place

Hours had passed. Sherman and many of the others were questioned. Then searched. Leftovers was sure the strange, plastic sleeve over Sherman's foot saved her when they brought in dogs. They sniffed and sniffed at the plastic bag but then went away. It was late when they finally let him go.

He was upset and angry. Angry that Katie had died. They'd spent the last half hour actually trying to reassure and calm him down. Leftovers thought that it was strange for him to be mad since he was one of the people who was trying to kill her.

Finally, they let him go home.

Sherman walked into the men's restroom of the Kangaroo Mart and stood in front of a urinal. Leftovers squeezed out of the gap in his pant cuff stitching and dropped to the floor. Overhead she heard the reassuring sound of Sherman's piss striking the urinal. She dashed away in the opposite direction from the wall he was facing, to the cover afforded by a stall on the opposite side of the restroom. Leftovers huddled down by the white porcelain of the bowl, letting its color make her own white body all but disappear.

She waited.

Sherman zipped. Washed. Left.

Leftovers rubbed her stomach and cooed to it softy. She waited, and the precious, little life inside waited too. That life she held trusted her now. They waited together. She watched those who came in, looking for someone safe. A big man with big feet came in, talking on his phone.

"Charlotte and Michael are at it again?" He had a big voice that echoed in the bathroom. "That's the third time this week, Kibble, what are we gonna do with them?" ... "Sure." ... "All right."

As he talked he positioned himself in front of the urinal, tilting his head to the side and trapping the phone between his ear and shoulder as he unzipped, then peed while he talked. He had nice, tan dress shoes, each with a pair of dangly tassels.

Leftovers made her move. She shot across the floor of the bathroom, bounded onto the huge shoe and snuggled down between the two tassels. She used her teeth to bite down on the leather between the two tassels to fix herself securely to her new ride.

"Yeah, well I'm at the Kangaroo, not the Winn Dixie, Kib. It'll cost a fortune."... "All right! All right! I'll get some."

He put the phone away, zipped up, and walked from the bathroom and out into the store. Up and down the aisles. Bags of potato chips and other candies on the bottom shelves whizzed by as her new human walked the store with brisk strides.

"Good Lord! Six bucks for a box of Corn Flakes!" Still grumbling, he grabbed the box and a few other items and carried them to the counter. He paid, then left the store and climbed into a gray sports car. Up and down, up and down. Leftovers rode the bouncing shoe as he worked the clutch. Ten minutes later the man parked, exited the vehicle and entered what had to be his house.

"Daddy! Daddy! Daddy!" Happy squeals and the sound of running, little–feet rushing, coming closer!

"Good Lord! Why are you shrimps still awake!?"

"It's Saturday and Mom said we could stay up till you got home!" answered one of the children.

The man went into the kitchen to meet his wife as the children swarmed around him. Frightened she might be stepped on, Leftovers bounded upwards, up his sock and under his pant cuff. Sharp, rabbit teeth bit into the fabric of the sock. She dangled there like a wash cycle lint ball as the pounding of little feet danced about.

The man, who had only been called "Daddy" so far, handed his groceries off then herded the children up a flight of stairs. Up the sock as she was, Leftovers couldn't see anything, which wasn't safe. The children were wild and the smaller ones had grabbed onto the man's legs more than once already. She needed to move.

As soon as she felt his steps level off at the top of the stairs she dropped down to the shoe top, scanned about quickly, then bounded toward the light peeking from the bottom of a closed door there in the hall. She landed and squeezed underneath in a flash.

Huge, brown eyes regarded Leftovers from the toilet on the other side of the narrow hall bath.

"Eew, a rat." The girl pulled her feet up from the floor, arms wrapping around her legs.

Out in the hallway the squealing and back and forth stomping mayhem intensified. Leftovers didn't know which direction to run.

"Mouse," the girl reappraised.

What to do? What to do? She'd already been seen. Surely a bunny was less frightening than a rat or a mouse. Leftovers stood up on her hind legs and looked at the girl from across the distance of the bathroom. She raised her long ears and twitched her tiny nose.

The girl squinted. Shoulder length, brown hair framed her confused face with large, wet ringlets. She was older than the other children, about thirteen or fourteen. She was naked and wet, like she'd just gotten out of the shower and hadn't bothered toweling dry before sitting down.

"Rabbit?" she guessed.

Leftovers nodded.

"Did you just nod?"

Leftovers nodded.

"A talking rabbit?"

More nodding. Her stomach twinged. Leftovers lowered herself. She rubbed her belly with her front paws and cooed to the life she carried.

"Ooohhh." The girl cooed along with her, leaning forward on her seat. "A pregnant, talking rabbit," she whispered. Leftovers looked up, taking in the expression on the girl's face.

She nodded.

Mr. Draper

Cleaning House

"I'M SORRY SIR, but it had to be done." Draper spoke into his phone, his shoes making no sound on the tiles as he walked down the hall toward the observation room.

All he was was a voice on a phone. No body. No soul. A voice. A gravely, scratchy voice.

"This girl makes THREE that have died there!" the President shouted. "The media's going to say we're exterminating them one by one! You know how it's going to play out!"

"It had to be done," Draper insisted calmly, "and with the surgery to remove the rabbit from Susan's stomach, the opportunity was there to end things cleanly, so I took it. The story is simple, sir. One, sick teen killed another with her magic 'bunny' parasites. With one of our agents already lost to the disease it should be obvious that this wasn't malicious." Even if it was. he said to himself. "We don't kill our own agents." He sounded sincere as he said this.

"Draper, you keep saying 'It had to be done.' Now tell me why it had to be done. Be vague and feed lies to everyone else if you need to, but I don't get the run around or the bullshit. Now I want to know *why* you did this." The President's voice was intense and nakedly suspicious. "Explain it to me, Draper. And it better be the truth, and it better be good."

"When she woke, she would have been more than angry. Susan had a very wild temper, and she'd already attempted a mass overthrow of the facility a few hours earlier. If her powers had grown exponentially, as some of the others had, who knows what might have happened if she regained consciousness. My fear was that she'd start to control those around her with nothing but her mind and skip the need for singing or verbal commands altogether."

"Hmm."

Draper smiled as he listened to the thoughtful sound and the breathing on the other end.

"No one else dies unless I approve it!" The voice was still firm, but no longer accusatory or suspicious.

Draper pushed for some space to work with. "Even if they are killing our men or about to escape? That's very limiting."

"I don't care." The President's voice was firm. "My approval before any lethal action is taken against another one of these kids in our *care*." He stressed the word "care."

"Very well, sir." Draper agreed. "I shall see that your orders are firmly established before I leave the facility to its new handlers."

The President of the United States hung up without another word. Another simple but firm way of expressing his displeasure in Draper's call to terminate Susan Palamino.

He rarely second guessed himself, but in hindsight, the head of the NSA found himself wishing he'd had the girl quietly lobotomized instead of having her killed. He did have a career to consider. And the agent infected with the magical flesh eating rabbits wasn't one of the teens, so the prohibition didn't count. He'd already told the President that she'd died, so now all they needed to do was collect her and make sure that was correct.

Draper put his phone away and stepped into the observation room. Instantly a chair was cleared for him. The only people in the room were members of his team that he trusted to control the flow of information and be completely on board with his wishes.

"Someone give me an update," he said as he dropped into the plush, leather seat. "Tell me what I'm looking at."

He knew something had to be wrong from the tension in the room. On the biggest screen a heated argument was going on. Gannon, still naked and covered in blood, was holding the heart in his hand, shouting at men in hazmat suits who were inside his courtyard enclosure brandishing stun weapons and keeping him separated from Marcia, who was being loaded into a tube-shaped gurney that looked like a space age coffin. Another group of men were wearing thick, orange gloves that turned their hands into crab-like pincers instead of five digit tools.

Sloakam, one of Draper's nerdish techs monitoring the cameras, took up the task of turning the on screen visuals into words. "What's left of our team is taking the infected agent out to the hall to do the deed, then she's off to the sealed lab for testing. The staff has a new room ready for Gannon and Kim, *the undead heart,*" he leaned on the words, "and there's a second team standing by to torch the room and scrub and decontaminate Gannon as well, but as you can see, he's not cooperating."

"Agent Sloakam, what happened to the rest of our team?" Draper asked.

"Oh, yeah, sorry, I—"

"Don't apologize, William, just tell me."

"The girl's entire body is cold now, like the witch's heart. When our guys touched her they got zapped right through the suits. They're in the infirmary now. They can't feel their hands up to their elbows, which is why they've double gloved." Sloakam pointed to the screen. "They had those gloves made for handling the undead heart, and it's working for this dead girl too."

"And is she dead?" Draper asked.

Sloakam and the others shifted around nervously. "Not yet, sir," answered another member of his team. "We were waiting till we had the girl out in the hall and away from Gannon before we injected her."

Draper nodded. "That would be best," he agreed, then contented himself to watching the action.

The girl was loaded and the coffin-like gurney was sealed. His team pushed the infected agent out into the hall. As soon as the door was shut and they were away from Gannon's shouts and angry watchful eyes, they opened the door of her coffin/gurney to inject the stricken agent with a lethal dose of poison. They watched as her feeble attempts to push the hands holding the needle away were thwarted. The needle went into her arm. The plunger shoved down.

The woman's struggling arm dropped.

They shut and resealed the lid then carried her toward the infirmary as if nothing had happened.

"Damn shame," Sloakam groaned, shaking his head.

"In what way?" Draper asked.

The nerdish man answered somewhat sheepishly, "Well, we reviewed the video some and saw what happened. She went through so much horrible shit to survive those rabbits, and—"

"And now we've killed her?" Draper finished. "Is that it?"

"Well, yeah."

"I doubt you'd feel the same if the rabbits were eating you alive, William," Draper chuckled. "Now clean everything. Go through the—"

"Hey!" They all jumped as one of the men shouted, pointing at the screen. "She's back! The heart must have magicked her back into the room."

Standing in the enclosure beside an enraged Gannon was Marcia. Wild eyed and angry, she hesitated only a moment before stepping into Gannon's waiting arms. The two began speaking quickly as together they eyed the space suit wearing invaders in the enclosure with naked hate.

Marcia had been completely covered with caked on blood when they'd loaded her into the bio-hazard containment coffin and wheeled her out, but now she was completely free of blood and absolutely clean, even her blood hardened hair was clean. She was still naked, and her rabbit marked skin was both stunningly beautiful and alarming now that it was visible from head to toe.

"Turn up the volume. What's she saying to the boy?" Draper ordered.

"... tried to murder me!" she was saying. "They stuck me with a needle, Gannon! I told you they would!" She turned and glared up at the camera almost as if she could feel them watching. The timing was too perfect. Hairs raised on the back of the necks and arms of most of the men in the observation room who still had a soul.

"You tried to kill me!" she shouted and raised a finger and pointed at the camera. "You fucking bastards!"

Without warning, she attacked. She reached out and grabbed the arm of the nearest man. The protective suit provided no defense from whatever power now ran through her body. The man howled in pain and dropped, clutching his arm where she had touched him. Using Kim like a hand held weapon, Gannon joined the fight, but these men were ready for trouble and they didn't hold back. Gannon fell to the floor as the stun gun hit him and Marcia dropped a second later. The badly overpowered weapons left them twitching on the floor and nearly unconscious. Draper used a hand set to speak privately to the earbud of his lead man in the room.

"Martin, put her back in the carrier. Get the boy to his room then put two in her heart, *quietly*, and roll her to the infirmary."

Martin looked up at the camera and nodded. The team got to work. Two men with orange gloves loaded a dazed Marcia back onto the gurney while another man with gloves scooped the heart into a box while two others grabbed Gannon and hauled him to the new enclosure next door and dumped him and the heart into the shower, turned on the cold water, and left him there, still twitching and recovering from being hit with the stun guns.

After a minute a naked and gasping Marcia appeared in the shower with them.

"Shit! Shit! Shit!" Marcia's hands leapt to her bare chest, frantically feeling at where the bullets had torn through her flesh and heart only moments ago. She inhaled deep gasping breaths, eyes wild, nude body trembling in the frigid water. The memory of it was still so fresh; though the pain of what happened was gone the memory and shock were still there. The trauma of dying, of feeling her heart's desperate fight to carry on and finally failing, the warmth of the blood as is spilled from her body one damaged pulse after another. Her fear and frustrated rage as she stared up at the cruel smile on the man's face and watched as he put his weapon away. His eyes watching her die.

She finally took stock of her surroundings. She was in a shower. Ice, cold water falling down.

"Shit!" she shouted for Gannon's sake when she looked down and found him lying there with her, crumbled up on the tile floor. "What'd they do to you!?"

She sat him upright. With nothing else to do, and since they couldn't stop the stun gun bastards even if they wanted to, Marcia didn't jump out and try to hold the door shut. She just stayed in the shower and started to wash the blood off Gannon. Occasionally she picked up the heart and spoke to Kim. They both began to worry, and then to panic over Gannon's worsening condition; he still hadn't woken up. When Marcia found that he'd stopped breathing, and the heart (Kim) had stopped beating, she began to do CPR on Gannon and scream for help.

When help came, they didn't try to revive Gannon or see to Kim like she hoped; they shot her again. In the head this time. They watched until her dead body vanished from the shower floor. The agents looked all around, waiting for her to reappear, but she didn't. This time she was just gone. They checked all the monitors. She was nowhere in the facility. Agent Marcia Castillo, carrier of the magical, flesh eating, rabbit plague, had vanished.

Draper paced back and forth in the hall as he made the call.

"Draper."

"We have a problem, sir."

"Oh. I agree," he answered. "I'm actually in a meeting right now discussing the problem. We just got through watching the live video feed Mr. Sloakam's been sending over, and I agree, Mr. Draper, we have a serious problem."

"Sloakam?" Draper's mind whirled but the conversation went on without him.

"Now you've killed Gannon, which brought the kill count up to four teens, and you also managed to kill the undead heart of Kim Ainsley, which would make it five teenagers. And of course," the President's voice wasn't gloating, just tired and angry as he added, "we don't kill our own agents, do we, Mr. Draper. How many times *did* you kill Ms. Castillo?"

Draper noticed two agents he didn't recognize take up positions in the hall behind him and two more down the hall in front.

"But, sir," Draper licked suddenly dry lips, "Mr. President, sir. Please let me explain." His voice was desperate. His scratchy voice unnerved and fearful for the first time in years and years and years. "There were reasons for my actions! I can—"

"Draper!" The President cut in soundly. "You've left me no choice, it just has to be done."

What Comes Around, Goes Around

A NEEDLE-LIKE SHAFT OF stone pierced the surface of the blacktop. People scrambled to their positions as the stone structure rose through the suddenly porous asphalt without making a sound. In less than a minute, a ten by ten gothic arch peaked by a six foot high finial stood in the center of the two-laned, mountain highway. Its arrival wasn't unexpected. The arch even surfaced in an area they'd already taped off and set aside for it or something like it to appear.

A mirage like shimmer, and the everyday view through the stone framed opening changed like a switched channel on a mammoth flat screen. The new program was more scifi or possibly horror judging by the view alone. A shadowy mist filled landscape. A gust of warmer air poured through the open portal kissing the skin of those chilled by the frigid mountain air and further distressing those who didn't wish to believe their eyes just yet.

Lucius stepped out of the portal with sure, confident strides and headed toward the nearby tent where the American delegation waited. Black boots clacked on the highway in the crisp quiet of held breaths. His black, leather duster billowed around him from the warm, venting wind at his back. His one, blackened hand and the red, glowing eyes set into his skull head buckle made him even more of a spectacle.

The fantasy imagery would have been laughable if not for the simple fact that this was all real. The wind. The Archway. The changed man. All real. And unlike Utopia, Narnia, Oz, Atlantis or all the other magical lands of fiction, the land of Amen Hale had an address in reality. It occupied a portion of land in North Florida where a historic plantation house sat on the banks of the St. Johns River nestled among cypress trees and ancient oaks. Amen Hale was a real place, with real people, and real power.

The delegation received Lucius gladly. Seeing him by himself, without minders, guards, or other members of Amen Hale's self-styled nobility they felt at liberty to press for this and that and even hint that he should, in fact, work to promote their agendas.

Lucius endured a few minutes of this shoulder rubbing gamesmanship then delivered Amen Hale's demands if there were to be an official meeting of any kind between Amen Hale and America. Only twelve soldiers and twelve government officials were to be within a mile of the meet. Of course those seeking to enter Amen Hale would be here as well but everyone else would have to leave the area immediately.

Those in charge quickly agreed, though they did petition for only four soldiers and twenty government officials. Same number of bodies, just more with suits and mouths instead of uniforms and guns. Even at twenty, a large number of very self-important people were going to be upset.

Lucius agreed, then left, leaving through the portal which closed behind him, the channel switching back to its original, mountain side program.

Orders were given and the arguing among the VIPs began in earnest. Among the military, things moved more smoothly, but there was a great deal more to move. Sergeants yelled, soldiers marched. Military vehicles headed toward the two checkpoints loaded down with men clinging to the sides or on any vehicular surface they could find purchase, while others marched down the sides of the road in long columns weighed down with all their gear for the two mile hike north or the three mile hike to the south.

The group of scientists and anthropologists who'd been studying the Twilins had to be physically restrained and hauled away by soldiers. The ugly scene blended in with all the bedlam of soldiers breaking camp. Weeping scientists were forced into waiting Hummers already crowded with emotional and uncooperative government aides who'd had their heart set on seeing things they'd only dreamed of seeing. To be asked to leave at the last possible moment had made rational grown men and women bawl and argue like emotional five year olds who insisted again and again that this *wasn't fair!* They wanted to go to the party and pet the pretty ponies and watch the magic show. Heartbreaks galore.

Black Rain

Twilins in My Mind

W HAT TAUNWEE HAD said about this being a trap made me cautious. Before we stepped through the gateway I cursed, jinxed, hexed, and shielded the place we were about to walk into, protecting us from every threat I could possibly think of and carefully capping the whole magical mess so that it would vanish like an unplugged drain once we left.

    I'd been doing better since the Londoners were sent on to Amen Hale, but even without my odd fidgets over Gretchen, Cathryn and the others were still treating me like a broken vase held together with super glue. Delicate in mind and bruised in spirit. They didn't want outsiders to have access to me or even to see me if possible. Cathryn didn't even want me to walk the short distance down the road to the three black SUVs where the Twilins were congregating. She told Believer to carry me there inside his clouds.

He picked me up and held me against his chest, and I slipped down into the swirling mix of clouds trapped within the contours of his body. All sights and sounds of the outside world vanished, as did the weight of my own body as I floated inside the warm, embryonic world of his clouds. Living clouds surrounded me, filled my lungs, and touched every part of me, holding me tight and secure.

I didn't try for sex and Believer (wisely) kept that part of himself out of my sight. I relaxed and let him hold me in his wonderful embrace as the gentle, swaying motion of his movements lulled my body almost instantly toward a half sleep. My mind still crawled along slowly, like a determined, poky turtle, safe inside its magic shell as it thought easy, unhurried thoughts. I don't know when my eyes closed.

Cool, soothing hands gently shook me awake and I opened my eyes to find Jane, right there with me, floating weightless inside Believer's clouds.

"Hi." I gave her a warm, sleepy smile that seemed to surprise her.

I watched her as she carefully searched my face in that vampire way that she and Dan had, her fears lessening as she inspected me and handled me. She sniffed at my hair. She was too close not to reach out and hold. She kept her hands on my face as I pulled her to me, looking and reading me with her intense and serious eyes. I didn't care. She could read all she wanted in my face. I'd been so worried about her and Dan, it felt wonderful to have her safe in my arms at last.

"I missed you," I told her.

"I can see that. Us too," she said back as she continued her inspection from a few inches away. "You died again." It wasn't a question. "You died in the garden first, and whatever you you that was that came out of the graveyard and spoke to me and Dan and left us here died somehow—and now you're here."

I nodded. "Yeah. That's about it."

"So you were out there, fighting demons and devils while Dan and I were here, taking care of Twilins?" She didn't even sound pissed.

"Of course I'm not pissed," she said, reading my face as if I'd spoken out loud. "I get it. Really," she said. "You're not the one who left us here, that other you did. Who were you two fighting out there?"

"Devils, demons, and gods," I answered her question as if I'd said Tom, Dick, and Harry. "All of the above."

Jane scowled. "She was out there kickin ass and taking names without us. That bitch. I'm not surprised though. She was cold." Jane brushed back my cloud damp hair, liking what she was seeing in my face more by the moment from the looks of her. There was a little smile at the corner of her mouth and compassion and hope in her eyes as she spoke to me. "I can see that you've been through a lot,

Rain, so please don't take this the wrong way, but I'm glad that other you is dead. Something about her was off—way, way off." She nodded to herself. "I like this you a lot more. Major upgrade."

The air we were breathing vibrated with Believer's gentle rumble of a laugh. He could hear what we were saying.

Jane was still focused entirely on me. She arched a lovely eyebrow. "I hope you still taste good."

"Jane," Believer's voice rumbled in warning, the sound coming from all around us as if the clouds themselves spoke.

Jane sulked a little. I could feel her tension as she fought her temper and tried not to growl.

"I'll let you taste me before Believer takes me to bed," I promised gently. Their venom was distant, two lifetimes removed, but I could still feel her hunger and her worry about what my blood would be like now.

"Who killed your evil twin anyway? She didn't seem like she'd be easy to take out." She grimaced darkly, remembering that version of me and the cold emotionless way she'd gone about her business. "Did the Devil kill her," she asked, "or was it some sniper or some human shit again?" She shook her head in confusion. "She was intense. I can't imagine what could have killed that 'Black You' short of God himself. I mean, she was really, REALLY—" Jane widened her beautiful violet and lilac eyes and made a grim face that finished the thought better than any words could have.

I smiled at her a little darkly myself, and whatever she saw in me at that moment seemed to frighten her too.

"You were right. She was off, Jane. She looked like me but she wasn't. She wasn't like any of the other me's who've gone before. She ripped out her human soul. All she had was a spirit. She thought it would be safer to live like that. Angels and Twilins do it, but as I found out, a human isn't right in the head without a soul."

"That's for damn sure!" Jane agreed soundly.

"Jane," Believer's voice urged us along.

She frowned, unsatisfied. "You've got some explaining to do when we get home. And I still want to know who killed her."

"I killed her myself," I told her quickly.

Now Jane looked confused, angry, and more than a little frightened. "What do you mean?" she said softly. It wasn't often that Jane looked so befuddled like she did right now.

I hated that I was the one she was scared of, but the vulnerable look on her face made me want to hold her tighter and keep her safe forever. I leaned closer and whispered, "Have a little faith, Jane. I, human Rain, killed that bitch and took all she had, just like a vampire. Now kiss me, and let's get Dan and our Twilins and go home."

Believer let us kiss for a while before rushing us along to collect my Twilins.

The area around the vans dimmed as the tiny, spiraling constellation above the SUVs funneled into the black hole of my open mouth. Twenty eight thousand three hundred and seven glowing balls of Twilin life vanished from beneath the star dotted sky, that endless firmament created to declare the glory of God to all who cared to look up and wonder at who made it all.

Like so much blackened ash, the singed and burnt refugees he no longer wanted in his creation spewed out of the mouth of the great Black Lion statue inside the world I'd made for them. They landed in the field before the statue. The winged and the flightless shifting back to their Twilin forms and staring about in wide eyed, open mouthed wonder at what would be their new world. Their heaven. The grass in the field where they stood was soft, green, and lush, but unlike the grass of earth. It was alien.

Everything was new and strange. Soil and smells, the wind, even the feel of the world beneath their feet. In the darkened sky hung a lesser light high overhead that looked like a full moon, its constant glow lighting the field with a silvery radiance equal to that of a full moon of Earth. Out beyond the moon that was not a moon, in the distant canopy of the night sky, keen Twilin eyes could just barely perceive the network of lines, cracks, and fissures spidered across the dome of the heavens. The inside of my skull.

They breathed me in and out of their lungs, they drank me in from the streams, and they ate the fruit of the land, which was my flesh. I filled their bodies with life. I warmed them. I held them safe within me. Every Dam and Roe and bit. I knew their thoughts and dreams and hurts and heartaches. Their collective lives were all there like a pulse beat to my land. That part of me that was a god had no difficulty filling the space in each spirit and holding all things together by the power of my word and will. It was a simple thing.

The part of me that was all girl watched them from above or focused on individuals in the crowd that caught our heart and eye.

Some lucky few reunited with loved ones while others rejoiced with others of their kind they'd never seen before, while others were too broken by the horror of the Burning Day to do more than sit on the ground and weep. This remnant had been saved as brands snatched out of the fire, and many wore the burns from their narrow escapes. I could have healed them all instantly, but I let them tend to their own wounded and bear their marks. It gave them purpose and something to do and reminded them of what had happened and what they'd been saved from.

Weary hands lifted and helped others and stopped thinking about their own loss and pain as they labored. Life's pain wouldn't be removed altogether in my new world. I would not be an invisible God, uninvolved and removed, but neither would I fix every hurt or right every injustice. I didn't know myself how this was going to work, but I did know that this was better than oblivion. Better than the Burning. Better than simply ending, like a candle snuffed out in a dark room. Life would continue, and we'd have to face it together and do the best we could.

These people had been born into a hopeless, unfair situation. They had no life without Taunwee. The spark of spirit that gave them life was borrowed from a fallen angel. God had no place for them in his world other than to suffer his judgment and bring him glory in that way one, final time.

And once again, I'd stolen from the White Lion. I'd gathered this remnant, a small pinch of ash from the pyre, kept back, just for myself. *He* cast them out, but I wanted them. I wanted them very much. *He* was through with them, and I hoped he would not be angry that I took the crumbs from his table, crumbs that he'd tossed into the trash, and then dropped into the incinerator.

These ashes had been His, but now they were mine. For better or worse, I would be their God, and they would be mine.

So mote it be.

The Devil's Day

I T WAS SATURDAY, August the sixth, 2016.

Angry with man, and wroth with His own church, who'd chosen to follow the lead of witches, idolaters, and greedy men, God gave fallen man what they'd prayed and fasted for. He gave all Amen Hale and all those that were connected by blood to the Kingdom into the hands of the Devil to do with as he wished.

One Day of Judgment.

Lucifer's first plan had been to take advantage of the girl's human emotions and her weak control. He tried to drive Rain into a rage by killing off those she loved most and having his demons ready to quickly take their souls to hell where she could not save them without provoking God.

His one success, the murder and capture of the soul of Marie, had been ruined by Taunwee, who managed to talk Rain out of attempting a rescue of Marie's soul. And she didn't even attempt to seek vengeance on Cain. Which would have put her face to face with God. A trap within a trap, and none of it worked!

Next, Satan attempted to beguile Rain's mind and make her into his instrument in that way. He sent Pan, his most cunning servant, but Pan failed. And to add insult to injury, Pan and many of the Fallen creatures with him had been taken to some place beyond his reach and left in a "hell" created by the girl herself.

Lucifer felt mocked.

Enraged by his failures and unwilling to let his day pass without taking the girl or provoking her into folly, he determined to have his army attack her directly when she came to collect the last of the Twilins and the two vampires from the mountain graveyard. Those few with physical forms waited in the woods safely out of sight, while millions upon millions of fleshless minions lingered in the earth beneath the road, waiting in anticipation like hell's hungry worms, all of them safely out of sight of the red gaze of the vampires that could see both angel and demon alike.

No more mistakes! No one shouting warnings or whispering prayers! No more dumb luck or quirky oversights. This was his day! God had foolishly given it to him. He had free reign, and Satan planned to take every Child of Amen Hale who presented themselves, including Rain herself should she step on this side of the portal. He would kill her quickly and drag her soul to hell along with the others if he could.

The world of men went about its business, blissfully ignorant. The mountain air was still and brisk. Hell's armies were paused. Ready. Hungry.

The eyes of the closest demons hidden in the woods saw her on the other side of the portal where she paced back and forth nervously wringing her hands. Just before she stepped through she stopped, then spoke. Her words and will passed through the opening and out into the air where the unseen legions waited. Suddenly, a force like an invisible wind pushed the demons and the Fallen back. It pushed and pushed and pushed, and drove spirit beings and the physical creatures like wind driven chaff until they were miles away.

Their vast numbers had been flung back by her word alone. Nervous, unsure words at that.

The armies of darkness were stunned.

More than stunned.

Lucifer stood in shoe deep, leaf litter on a shadowed mountainside and pushed against the unseen barrier.

It didn't give.

"*Yyyeaah*. We tried that," Azreal dared to mock.

"What shall we do now?" asked another of the Princes who stood at his back.

"She will take what she came for and retreat behind her walls." Lucifer's voice was thick with scorn and frustrated rage. "She thinks she's safe inside her Kingdom but she is nothing but a stupid child!" His feet kicked through fallen leaves, plowing a groove as he paced back and forth before the unseen barrier. "She has gathered her favorites into her keep, but she has left her fields, the cattle, and the servants for the spoil."

He turned to the Captains of his Host. "Use the last hours of our freedom to pour out my wrath upon those that share blood with Amen Hale!" he bellowed in his human voice. The much louder answering cry from the masses of demonic throats sent the creatures in the surrounding woods scampering in all directions.

"Rend! Rape! Destroy!" Lucifer commanded darkly. "Give her horrors too dark to go unanswered. Too disturbing to be set aside. Defile all that she loves! Drive her mad with *rage*! Let her eyes look upon it! Now go!" he commanded.

There was a rush of movement. Some creatures left by wing, others by foot, most simply vanished to go about the task in the two hours that remained before dawn.

Lucifer resumed his pacing. She'd taken his people into her "Garden of Wrath."
So be it, he thought.

"All that you love and all that love you shall be my Garden, and I will plant the seeds of my wrath inside their ruined flesh and let it grow. Gather my bloody grapes, little girl, and then bring them back to me." He laughed, the sound human and not nakedly sinister as he pressed his open palm to the invisible wall. His gaze fixed on the splayed fingers held at bay by nothing he could see or discern, yet still, it was there.

A paradox.

An impossibility.

Like the girl herself.

I WILL BE GOD!

Lucifer swore to himself and gritted his teeth, working through the possible paths in his head and how best to meet what was to come. How to gain what he sought.

"Come and get me, Goddess," he growled darkly. "Come take your revenge. Come pour out your wrath upon me. Come."

www.ingramcontent.com/pod-product-compliance
Lightning Source LLC
Chambersburg PA
CBHW080742250626

47162CB00010B/2993